A NOTE ON THE AUTHOR

KATIE HICKMAN is the author of seven previous books, including two bestselling history titles: *Courtesans* and *Daughters of Britannia*. She has written two travel books, one of which, *Travels with a Mexican Circus*, was shortlisted for the Thomas Cook Travel Book Award. She was shortlisted for the *Sunday Times* Young British Writer of the Year Award for her novel *The Quetzal Summer*, and her novels *The Aviary Gate* and *The Pindar Diamond* have been translated into nineteen languages. Katie Hickman lives in London.

katiehickman.com

@PindarDiamond

HOUSE *at* BISHOPSGATE

KATIE HICKMAN

BLOOMSBURY PUBLISHING

LONDON · OXFORD · NEW YORK · NEW DELHI · SYDNEY

BLOOMSBURY PUBLISHING
Bloomsbury Publishing Plc
50 Bedford Square, London, WC1B 3DP, UK

BLOOMSBURY, BLOOMSBURY PUBLISHING and the Diana logo are
trademarks of Bloomsbury Publishing Plc

First published in Great Britain 2017
This edition published 2018

A catalogue record for this book is available from the British Library

ISBN:	HB:	978-1-4088-2114-5
	TPB:	978-1-4088-8221-4
	EBOOK:	978-1-4088-3413-8
	PB:	978-1-4088-4333-8

2 4 6 8 10 9 7 5 3 1

Typeset by Integra Software Services Pvt. Ltd.
Printed and bound in Great Britain by CPI Group (UK) Ltd, Croydon CR0 4YY

To find out more about our authors and books visit www.bloomsbury.com
and sign up for our newsletters.

For Alexandra Pringle
beloved editor, beloved friend

PROLOGUE

*Oxford, 1643. The King's Temporary Court during the
English Civil War.*

THE OLD MAN SAT alone in a darkening room.
Some way from the vestibule in which he was
sitting, at the far end of a long gallery, two courtiers, secretaries to His Majesty, were conferring together over a pile
of papers.

The first was at a table making careful entries in a ledger.
In one column he had written a list of names, and then
beside them a sum of money, either given or pledged; in
a third column he would occasionally add some observation. The second and younger of the two stood beside him,
marking off names on a list. He shuffled uneasily, waiting
for instructions. The table between them was scattered
with papers.

Although it was not yet dusk on a late autumn afternoon, it was already so dark that the candles had been lit.
Until recently, when it was commandeered by the Court
for the purposes of war, the gallery had been a dining hall
for scholars. It was panelled in black wood, and its high
windows did not admit much light at the best of times.
Outside a wind was blowing, a sighing, keening sound that
echoed through the rafters, rattling the leads in the windows.

From somewhere in the distance came a muttering of
thunder.

'Dirty weather we've been having.' The younger of the two courtiers looked up uneasily. Unlike his companion, who was soberly dressed in a plain leather jerkin, he wore a collar of falling lace, and a pair of voluminous sleeves, deeply slashed, as the new fashion now was at Court. Every so often, when he thought his companion was not looking, he plucked at them, pulling the shirt-stuff through, arranging it to better effect.

The older man glanced up, but did not reply immediately. He settled a pair of spectacles more firmly on the bridge of his nose; and his pen made a soft scratching sound against the paper.

'And so...' he said eventually, rubbing his eyes and pushing back his chair, '...and so, Robert, who do we have next?'

'That's all for today, Lord Rivers. There is no one else. Unless of course you count him.' He gave a nod down the gallery to where the solitary figure of the old man could just be seen, very upright in the little vestibule at the far end of the long gallery.

On a sconce on the panelled wall behind them a single candle guttered. From a distance came another faint rumble of thunder, a sound like a kettledrum.

'What, the old fellow from this morning?' Lord Rivers peered over the top of his spectacles. 'You mean to say he's still here?'

The young courtier followed the older man's gaze reluctantly. 'I don't think it's worth troubling yourself about him, my Lord.' Then he added, with an air of bravado, 'Old fellow doesn't look as though he has a pot to piss in.'

'How many times must I tell you, we must see everyone who brings something in the name of the King's cause,' said the elder, resuming his writing. 'Pissing pot or no,' he added drily.

In a small minstrels' balcony just above them, a door was thrown open briefly. It let in the cheerful sound of voices, some of them women's, calling to one another; the scrape of knives on plates, and then, in the far distance, the musical notes of a viol tuning up. But then, just as suddenly, the door shut, leaving the gallery entombed in gloomy silence.

The young courtier looked up at the balcony with longing, and then down the gallery to where the old man was still sitting in the shadows. He turned back to Lord Rivers.

'Will you go to the revel later, my Lord?' he asked. His hands were at his throat now, nervously fiddling with the falling bands of his collar.

'Revel?' Lord Rivers dipped his pen into the inkhorn beside him. 'How can you think of a revel at a time like this? Don't you know we are at war?' He shook his head. 'I shall go to my bed. If no one else has got into it before me, that is. I'm told there are no longer any lodgings to be had for love nor money in this beleaguered city, not even a scholar's cot, God help me.' He ground the point of his pen into the paper irritably, and as he did so a fine stream of ink sprayed out, leaving an ugly blot in the observations column. 'Damnation... now look! That's all I need. This pen is hardly fit for purpose.' He picked up a knife and began to sharpen the end of it, but he went at it too quickly and the quill snapped. 'Damnations!' He flung the pen away from him in disgust and leant back in his chair.

'It is late, my Lord, and you must be... you must be... so very tired.' The young man's gaze strayed again to the door in the minstrels' balcony, from the other side of which, albeit very faintly, now came the sound of music, and of feet stamping in time.

'If only you knew how true that was. I swear I cannot write another word today, not for all the silver plate in

3

Oxford.' Rivers rubbed his eyes again. 'If the gentleman has anything to give to the cause, he can come again on the morrow.'

'What shall I tell him?'

The old man was standing now, taking a turn to stretch his legs. He was a small, lean figure, dressed from head to foot in dusty black, in a style that might once have passed for fashionable in another, happier age. Robert took in the stiff, old-fashioned ruff, the narrow doublet, and his hand strayed to the lace of his own collar tumbling fashionably around his shoulders. The old man's legs were slightly bowed, as though he were standing on the deck of a ship, but despite this there was something refined, almost scholarly, in his bearing.

'What shall I tell him?' he asked again. The sight of the old man, waiting so patiently in the draughty vestibule, made him feel doubtful suddenly.

'Tell him. . . oh, how should I know?' A tired shrug. 'Tell him what you will: that the King is weary and desires to retire.' Rivers sprinkled sand on the last entry to blot the ink. 'Tell him that we are *all* weary and desire to retire. He must come again tomorrow.' He blew the sand away, and banged the heavy ledger shut.

'He's been waiting here all day.'

'I can't help that,' said Rivers impatiently. 'Tell the gentleman to come again on the morrow and we will attend to him then. But it is as you say, Robert, the old fellow does not look as though he has two sticks to rub together.'

'As you wish.'

With a twitch of his sleeves, the young man made his way down the gallery, his top boots echoing on the bare swept floor. He conversed briefly with the old man.

'He says that it is impossible,' he said when he came back. 'He says that he cannot come on the morrow, for he must away to London again. He says his business there is urgent.'

'Urgent business?' Lord Rivers's lips grew thin. 'Is the King's cause not urgent business enough for him?'

'There is more.'

'Well?'

'He says that His Majesty would be very sorry indeed not to take possession of the gift he has brought.'

'Is that so? Well, tell him from me that if he has anything of value, it will be quite safe to give it to one of us, and we will appraise His Majesty of it as soon as it is convenient.' He began to gather up the papers on the table in front of him, shuffling them together until they formed a single bundle. 'And let that be an end to it.' He banged the papers together on the desk. 'Well, get on, get on.'

For the second time the young man marched down the gallery.

He was back again a few moments later.

'He says that what he has must be given directly into His Majesty's hand, or he will not give it at all.'

'What, does he think the King sees every last person who brings a few shillings to the cause. . .'

'He is quite insistent on the matter.'

'God in his mercy. . .' Rivers muttered to himself, passing a weary hand over his face. All he could think of was clean sheets, fresh linen and a hot shave. 'And what, pray, is this great gift that we cannot be trusted with?' He peered at the young man over his spectacles. 'Has he some great chest of treasure with him? Bars of silver? Bags of gold?'

'No, my Lord. He brings nothing with him that I can discern. He is – he seems – quite alone.'

'Not that you can discern?' An impatient click of the tongue. 'Come, Robert, surely you have asked him?'

'He will not tell me, my Lord.'

'What, is he so old that he has lost his power of speech?'

'He speaks, my Lord,' Robert said rather desperately, 'but it is in riddles.'

'Riddles?' The older courtier raised one eyebrow.

'He says. . .' The young man looked abashed, '. . .he says that he brings His Majesty his heart's desire.' He frowned. 'At least I think that's what he said.'

'Then his wits are as addled as his years are advanced.' Rivers took his spectacles off his nose and polished them on his sleeve. He put them on once more, and through the deepening shadows scrutinised the solitary figure a little more carefully this time.

'You are right, the old fellow does not look as though he has a pot to piss in,' he began, 'and oh, what a simply delightful phrase that is—' But then, as if suddenly struck by some forceful observation, his voice tailed off. For a few moments he sat in silence peering down through the deepening shadows. The old man was only just visible now, an inky cutout beneath the single guttering sconce.

He turned to Robert again and said, a little more thoughtfully this time, 'What did you say the old fellow's name was?'

The young man shrugged. 'He says he is a merchant. A merchant of the Levant Company. Or was one once. I didn't quite catch his name. I suppose his shillings are no different from anybody else's shillings these days. . .' he said, with a melancholy look up at the minstrels' balcony again, the fingers of one hand stroking the silken velvet nap of his sleeve. 'I suppose I can go back and ask him,' he added, his expression sulky now, 'if you so desire.'

'Yes, I do desire it. But wait. . .' Rivers was gazing more intently now at the old man standing in the vestibule, '. . .his name. It isn't Pindar, is it, by any chance?'

'Yes, I do believe it is something like that.'

'Well, I'll be damned.'

'You are acquainted with him?'

'Pindar? Paul Pindar? But of course I am. Everybody is. Or was. God's blood, I thought he was dead.' With a look of great discomfiture, Rivers half rose from his chair. 'God's blood,' he muttered to himself again.

'Shall I fetch him?'

'Yes, and quickly!' Then, thinking better of it, he caught Robert by the sleeve. 'Wait, no.' He sat down again, making the leather chair creak. 'I must think for a moment. You say he's been waiting here *all day*?'

'I . . . I fear so, my Lord. Forgive me, but I had no idea—'

Rivers groaned. 'Never mind, never mind,' he waved his hand impatiently. 'I must think, that's all; think what to do.'

At that moment a door behind them opened and a third man entered the gallery. He carried a linen napkin in his hand. In the room behind him candlelight blazed, and the faint but encouraging aroma of good claret and roasted meat wafted towards them.

'There you are, Robert, we've all been looking for you.' Like the younger courtier, the third man also wore a lace collar that covered his shoulders and sleeves. 'Why in heaven's name are you standing here in the dark? Why, you look as newfangled as an ape.' He dabbed at his mouth with the napkin. And then, seeing Lord Rivers, 'My Lord Rivers,' he said, giving the secretary-courtier a precise and elegant bow. 'Forgive me, I didn't see you. Are you hiding here from the revels?' His eyes, which were intelligent and brown, crinkled at the edges. 'I've come to beg for the release of young Robert here,' and then added, with a wink at Robert, 'I am sent by *a lady*, so you see you cannot refuse.'

'Fanshawe! Just the man,' Rivers said. 'Come here a moment, will you.' He indicated the old man. 'Body of God, tell me I am not dreaming. Is that who I think it is?'

He leaned over and whispered into the third courtier's ear.

'No. You are not dreaming.'

'It is he, is it not?'

'It is, as I live.'

'I thought he was dead.'

'I am not surprised.' Fanshawe dabbed thoughtfully at his mouth with the napkin. 'We all thought he was dead.'

'He must be four-score if he is a day.'

'Four-score and ten, at the very least,' Fanshawe said. 'A very Methuselah.'

'Dear God, Fanshawe.' Lord Rivers wiped his brow on his sleeve. 'What do you think he's doing here?'

Fanshawe looked amused. 'The same as everybody else, I shouldn't wonder. Come to give us his last silver shoe buckle.'

'But he has already given so much to the cause. Why, only last year he sent the Queen a great quantity of gold. Do you suppose he brings more?'

'Have you not asked him?'

'Robert here says he speaks only in riddles. Whatever it is, he will only give it if he can do so directly into His Majesty's hand.'

'His jewels, then?'

'Think you?'

'*The* jewel perhaps.'

The two men exchanged glances.

They saw the young courtier looking at them both quizzically.

'Robert here is too young to know. Too young to have heard the stories.'

'Stories? Is that what you call them? Scandal, more like.'

'A scandal?' The young man's smile was polite, disbelieving. 'The old fellow in black?'

Fanshawe and Rivers exchanged glances once more.

'That old fellow in black, my boy.' Lord Rivers put a hand on young Robert's shoulder, 'that old man without a pot to piss in is Sir Paul Pindar, merchant of the Honourable Levant Company, a famed scholar and collector, and for many years His Majesty's, the old King's, ambassador to Constantinople...' he enumerated in a low voice, '...and the possessor of one of the greatest fortunes that was ever seen in the City of London.'

'And a collection of gemstones that must have made the Duke of Buckingham weep.'

'Jewels?' For the first time there was a flicker of interest in the young courtier's eyes.

'Pindar's jewels were part of his legend. When he came home from the East they said that the greater part of his wealth was tied up in a collection of gemstones. Kept them under the floorboards in the great house in Bishopsgate. Everyone talked of it.' Still whispering, Fanshawe turned to Rivers. 'Surely you recall?'

'I do indeed.' Rivers frowned. 'But if my memory serves me, he sold most of them, or gave them as gifts. To the old King, to his present Majesty, and we all know what that means. Most of them will be in the hands of moneylenders by now, pawned for the Cause, in Antwerp or Amsterdam, just like everything else. They say the Duke of Buckingham carried off the rest—'

'But you remember the stories, surely?'

'What stories?'

'The stories about the great stone. It was always said that there was one jewel he would never be parted from.

9

One great stone. A diamond. No one – not the King, not even Buckingham – could ever persuade him to part with it, although I've no doubt they tried.'

'And the old man was involved in some kind of scandal you say?' A polite smile was still playing around the young man's mouth.

'The scandal was part of his fame. What *was* it all about? D'you remember, Fanshawe? Damned if I can recall the details now. It must be thirty years ago at least.'

Fanshawe thought for a moment. 'There was a mystery, was there not?' he said slowly. 'Some kind of a mystery about his wife.'

There was a short, thoughtful silence while the three of them peered down the gallery to the old man standing in near darkness now.

'Was she not she some kind of curtezan?' Rivers's brow wrinkled with the effort of remembering.

'A curtezan? No!' Fanshawe turned to the younger man. 'Here, Robert, you will enjoy this. They used to say that Pindar's wife was a princess of some kind. A slave woman – or a concubine – to the Great Turk, I don't remember which. They said that he brought her back with him when he came home from the East.' He pulled at the young man's sleeve, drawing him in a little closer so that he could whisper in his ear. 'They say he built that great house at Bishopsgate Without, just so that he could keep her hidden. Kept her there, as though he were some kind of pasha. As though she were a curiosity in his cabinet.'

'But that was not the scandal, surely?' Rivers was leaning in towards them too. 'That's it, I have it now. The scandal was about his brothers.'

'Brothers? He had only ever one brother that I recall. I remember *him* quite well. Ralph. Ralph Pindar, of the

Muscovy Company. Unpleasant fellow. A *libertine*. Rich as Croesus like his brother.'

'I am sure you are mistaken,' Fanshawe shook his head. 'The scandal was about the great stone. Or his wife.'

Around them the afternoon light was fading fast. The courtiers were in familiar territory now: the whispering behind doors and in draughty corridors; the rumours, the gossip, the surmise. They fell to it as though they were in the Palace of Whitehall again, and not in the draughty and discommoding lodgings of an Oxford scholars' hall.

'Wasn't there a rumour that his wife was bewitched?'

'No, no, they used to say that it was the stone that was bewitched.'

'No, it was the wife. She was burnt as a witch, I am sure of it,' Fanshawe said. 'Ten guineas says I'm right.'

The three courtiers stood together looking down the gallery. If the old man in black could hear their murmurings, he gave no sign.

'I met them both once, you know, at a Court Masque,' Rivers said. 'Pindar and his wife. But that must be thirty years ago, when I was still a boy. I played a fay in the *Masque of Oberon*.'

'No, not *Oberon*, surely, it was *Love Freed from Ignorance and Folly*—'

'You are mistaken, it was most definitely *Oberon*, for it was old Queen Anne's masque at Twelfth Night. I remember it as if it were yesterday. Now, ten guineas says *I'm* right—'

They smile together. Memory is a fickle thing. In the dark present, the old stories soothe and comfort them. The old man is soon forgotten, means no more to them than faded gilt on an old shoe buckle.

But for Paul Pindar, waiting so patiently in the draughty vestibule, they are the gatekeepers of this moment; standing guard, did they but know it, at a door between two worlds. There is no one else now with whom he can share his memories.

John Carew. Celia. Annetta.

Even his brother Ralph.

All gone.

He is the last. He is the only one left who could tell the tale of what happened that long-ago winter.

Who would believe it, if it were not true?

In his hand, hidden inside his pocket, he holds the great stone. With his finger he traces over the inscription.

A'az ma yutlab. My heart's desire.

From somewhere on the other side of the vestibule an unseen door opens and then bangs shut. And each time a draught comes whipping in. He feels the dried leaves, like whispers from the past, skittering at his feet. They blow past him, and up the gallery, across the bare swept floor.

ONE

Celia

January, 1611. Aleppo.

E VEN ON THEIR VERY last evening, when every crate had been packed, and every strongbox sealed, Celia had gone, as was her daily custom, to watch the sun set over the roofs and hazy mountain tops of Aleppo.

For some seven years now she had followed the same ritual: climbing the narrow stairs to their rooftop garden to drink sweet mint tea and enjoy the breezes of evening. Now, as she settled herself on the cushions beneath the shade of the jasmine arbour, it was with a bittersweet feeling that already had in it the seeds of loss, as though her body were still there but her mind were already somewhere else.

From all around her, the women from the neighbouring households were now starting to appear, settling themselves, like Celia, to enjoy the cool of the evening far away from the streets and the eyes of men. It was a familiar scene: the little groups of women, their babies, and their children, many of whom she had seen grow from their earliest infancy. When they saw Celia, they called out to her.

'Farewell,' they called. 'Farewell, lady. May God go with you on your voyage.'

'*Inshallah*,' she answered them. 'If God wills it. Thank you, my friends. May God go with you too.'

Turning towards the sinking sun, she shut her eyes, committing to memory the familiar sounds of the evening. In the distance she could hear the sound of the muezzin calling the faithful to their sunset prayers; the cries of the children laughing and quarrelling; and from just behind her, in their cage, the soft, throaty sounds of the pigeons her husband Paul Pindar, Levant Company consul in Aleppo, kept to carry messages to his fellow merchants living far away on the coast and in Damascus. There was a smell of spices being cooked and a faint hint of rose-water.

All of life was played out on the rooftops of Aleppo. Sometimes there were wedding parties, when the female relatives of a particular household would gather to sing and dance and to henna the hands of the bride. At other times there came fortunetellers, or the blind eunuch storyteller brought from the bazaar. But it was the children Celia had always loved to watch the most, observing them with that piercing hunger that only another childless woman could ever understand. Once, a woman had actually given birth only yards away from Celia's own rooftop garden, her labour coming on so suddenly that the midwives attending her been obliged to bring the birthing stool to her right there. They had put a screen around her to shield her from view, but Celia would always consider that she had borne witness to the birth all the same, she had heard the sounds of a woman in labour, not so much cries of pain as a strange primitive noise, more animal than human, coming from somewhere deep within.

Was this how her own labour had sounded, all those years ago? Perhaps, after all, it had been better to forget. Celia's child, the result of a great violence done against her before she married Paul, had lived no more than a month, and afterwards benign Nature had thrown such a dark veil over her memory that Celia was able to recall almost nothing of those long-ago events. But that day the sound of the labouring woman on the rooftop had awakened a sleeping part of her mind. And now, if she thought about it hard enough, she could sometimes catch glimpses of her baby's little face, hear its mewling cry, watch its tiny finger curling like a fern over her own.

There had been, so far, no other children.

A movement behind her interrupted these musings.

'So here you are. I wondered where you had been hiding.'

Celia turned and saw her husband emerging on to the rooftop behind her.

In 1611, on the eve of his journey back to England, Paul Pindar was a man in his middling years. His long years abroad in the service of the Honourable Levant Company – first in Venice, where he had been sent when little more than a boy as factor to the London merchant, Parvish; then, as a merchant in his own right to Constantinople; and latterly as the Company's consul in Aleppo – had not so much aged as honed him. He was a little greyer now at the temples, and his beard, which he still wore cut unfashionably close, had become flecked with grey, but he was still a youthful man. Neither riches nor age had altered his figure. His leg was still good, his waist slender. If anything he seemed stronger, leaner than before: with age had come a certain *gravitas*. The only difference was that instead of his customary black merchant's attire, in Aleppo he had taken, like his wife, to wearing loose robes of oriental silk.

'Ah, but what are you doing here! You know you should not—'

Celia pulled Paul down out of the women's sight behind the balustrade that circled the rooftop.

'I thought on our very last night in Aleppo I should be afforded just a glimpse of the place where you have been hiding away from me these many years,' he whispered.

'Oh, what a story – I never hide from you!'

'Ah, so you say, my lady—'

'Oh, but I do say – and, hush, for pity's sake, they will hear you,' Celia put her finger to his lips. 'You know as well as I that men never come to the rooftops, unless they be gelded. In all these years I have never seen one venture here. The rooftops belong to the women, you know. They are *haram*. You will frighten them away if they see you.'

Unperturbed, Paul settled himself beside her, stretching himself out easily upon the cushions that had been laid out, Ottoman style, upon the floor.

'I stand corrected, but I couldn't resist just one little look.' He leant across to peer through the jasmine that grew thickly around the latticing. 'What do these ladies all *do* up here? I've always wondered.'

'They gossip together, tend to their infants, play with their children.' Celia gave him a quick sideways glance. 'Grumble about the importunities of their husbands, I shouldn't wonder.'

'The preserve of married ladies everywhere—'

'Hush, I tell you,' she said again, but he could see that she was pleased that he had sought her out.

Encouraged by this, he leant over to her.

'In England it will be different,' he whispered, his lips so close to her that she could feel his beard tickling her ear, 'no more hiding from me or from anyone.'

In England. . . in England. The words had been such a constant refrain for so many months that it had become a joke between them.

'I know, I know. In *England* men and women are used to being in society together, and not separated into their different quarters as they are in the Orient. In *England* I must sit upon chairs and not upon the floor, which would be considered most improper.' Celia ticked each well-rehearsed point off on her fingers. 'In *England*, when in company, I must submit to having my bodice tight-laced, for what is being able to breathe besides the necessity of being in fashion? I must learn to wear high shoes, not slippers, ditto, and have my sleeves and petticoats and I know not what fastened together with any number of inconvenient pins.' She looked up at her husband with a smile. 'And I do declare that in England I must straight away find myself a lady's maid, for if I left it to my unlucky husband to lace and dress me, I fear I shall never get out at all.'

'I confess I have made you a very poor lady's maid, it is true.'

'And I a very poor pincushion.'

After more than ten years living among the Mohammedans, adopting their ways and dress and manners, there were many things to which Celia was now quite unaccustomed. Paul had been solicitous in his attempts to prepare her for their new life together.

Together they had practised sitting on chairs, eating at a table, and the rudiments of English etiquette. But when it came to learning how to dress as an Englishwoman, in clothes that would befit the wife of a wealthy and well-respected merchant, Paul had proved so clumsy, and had pricked her so often with the offending pins, that eventually she had begged him to give up the attempt. Worse still were his attempts to remind her of English manners, for the sight of her husband Paul Pindar, the renowned Levant Company merchant, bending his knee to her and sinking to the ground in an English lady's courtesy had made Celia laugh so much she could hardly stand.

'Ah, but *in England*, your English wives would not dare to mock their husbands so,' Paul had said, but privately he had been struck by how very well his wife looked when she laughed.

And later that night, and on many subsequent nights, when lying alone and sleepless as was his too frequent custom, Paul had returned in his mind again and again to that moment, reflecting on quite why it was that his marriage to Celia, thus far, had given neither of them much cause for laughter.

When Paul had first met Celia Lamprey, he had observed an arresting young woman; with her reddish-gold hair, and her pale skin of extraordinary fineness, some might even have called her a beauty. It was only on their second acquaintance he had been struck by her other qualities.

Perhaps it had been her unusual upbringing that, in his mind, had set her apart. When Paul had first come to know her, Celia had sailed to Venice and back with her father, the sea captain Tom Lamprey, more times than Paul himself. She spoke the Venetian tongue perfectly, knew the difference between a capstan and a clew-line, and could identify the stars in the night sky. Very soon Paul came to think of Celia Lamprey as being quite unlike any young woman he had ever met.

Brought up by her father, she was more used to the company of men than of other young women (and given the subsequent calamities that followed, it was an irony that was not lost on him). Unlike most women he had come across, there was nothing coy in her manner when she spoke to him, but neither had she been roughened or made vulgar by her experience at sea. Nor had she learnt to ape the studied *ennui* of so many of the merchants' wives of his acquaintance, young women – for the most part married to much older men – too rich, too fashion-able, too bored.

He could not exactly say that she was learned, but she was curious, eager for knowledge, open to the world. When he showed her the compendium he had just bought from Henry Cole's new shop on Cheapside, or his prized kid-bound copy of Gerard's new herbal, she did not look at him with incomprehension, nor turn away with an ill-concealed yawn.

More than anything, though, there had been a peculiar lightness in her manner. As a serious and ambitious young merchant, subject himself to occasional fits of melancholy, no one but Celia Lamprey had ever been able to laugh and tease him out of himself. And her gentle exterior belied an inner fortitude quite as strong as that of any man. She was, in short, perfection.

Lying alone in the darkness, Paul had often wondered which of the many twists in his fortunes, that the Almighty had seen fit to visit on him, had been the most cruel: to have had Celia taken from him, or to have won her back again – so strange, so silent, so marked by the calamities that had befallen her in the intervening years that there were times when he thought she would never recover.

It had been on the very eve of their marriage, as she sailed to meet him in Constantinople, that Celia, together with her friend Annetta, had been captured by Ottoman corsairs off the Adriatic coast, and sold as slaves into the Great Turk's House of Felicity. That much of her story was quite clear. But of the rest – how Celia had eventually escaped from the Old Palace, washing up, like a broken reed, more than a year later in the Venetian lagoon – that would only ever be conjecture.

Although Celia's almost total loss of memory about these travails meant that Paul had had to resign himself to never knowing the full story, the physical injuries she had sustained during them were another matter.

In Venice he took her to see the best physicians. They were all agreed that Celia had been cut by a blade, perhaps even a sword, across the backs of her legs. But, God be praised, the cuts were flesh wounds and had missed the vital tendons, and although Celia, even now, occasionally walked with a stick, these cuts were almost healed. Of her other injuries he was much less sanguine. There had been a child – it died – that much he had always known, but when they had lain together as husband and wife for the first time, he had found out something that he could not have known until then. Celia's body – her woman's parts – were quite closed against him. No old spinster's virgin membranes could have been so tough, so unyielding. In vain had they tried – with unguents, with oils, with the help of numerous useless physics and implements – but none of these, nor the advice of all the physicians and barber-surgeons in Venice, had been able to help them consummate their marriage.

A few months later, Paul had been appointed by Honourable Levant Company as their consul in Aleppo, and Celia had travelled there with him. Both of them had quite despaired of their situation when they were recommended the services of an old midwife, the consort of a eunuch of Egypt, who was compatriot of one of their own household servants.

Neither of them would ever forget the day Bint Gulay came to them. It was during the heat of midday, at the very height of summer, when she arrived to examine Celia, and the shutters had been drawn to keep in the cool. She had been shown in to see them in the half-darkness: a tiny bird-like creature, black as soot, in a blue and white cotton robe, and a white cotton headdress, shuffling into Celia's bedchamber in her threadworn slippers.

Without so much as a by-your-leave, Bint Gulay had pulled open the shutters to let in the light and set to, examining Celia immediately and intimately, communicating with her in a strange wordless sing-song. With a series of hums and sighs and clicks of the tongue, she pulled and pushed her into position, parting Celia's legs and examining her carefully. At one point she spread her hands, so they could see a single long nail on the index finger of her right hand.

'Dear God, she's just like Cariye Lala!' Celia said, with what was either a sob or a laugh, but before he could ask her what she meant by this, Bint Gulay began to speak. Since she spoke no tongue that either Paul or Celia could understand, their servant, the midwife's kinsman, standing behind a screen which had been put up for this purpose, translated for her.

'She says that your wife has been very badly torn in her labour, and her parts have healed, but poorly. Tissue has grown where the opening should be.'

Bint Gulay then said something emphatically.

'She says she has seen some cases like this before, where the woman has been sewn up deliberately after giving birth, as is sometimes the custom. But this is not the case here.'

Bint Gulay's voice became quite shrill.

'She believes it must be evidence of an evil eye at work. She asks: has your wife enemies? Have you enemies?'

'Never mind that,' Paul said impatiently. 'All we want to know is whether there is anything to be done? Can she help us?'

'Yes. . .' There was a pause. 'But only if your wife will agree to be cut again. She has performed similar procedures many times. But afterwards your wife must be sure to protect herself at all times.'

'Protect herself?'

'From witchery, of course.'

So, at Celia's insistence, he had allowed Bint Gulay to do her worst. He had given his sharpest blade into the midwife's hands. He had stood by as Bint Gulay sliced, like a butcher, with quick and dexterous movements into his wife's body. He remembered holding the basin that she had put into his hands, and the metallic sound of the blade falling into it when she had finished, and then the fall of blood, black as tar, that gushed from between his wife's thighs. He remembered the stained and blood-ied sheets, and it took many of them before they could staunch the flow of blood, but most of all he remembered Celia's screams.

After the cutting, Celia had fallen into a fever. For many days afterwards she had hovered delirious between life and death; on two occasions Paul was quite sure that he would lose her altogether. Bint Gulay had not only hung Celia around with amulets to keep off the evil eye, but she had also made fresh poultices and dressings every day, and, unusually for a midwife, she had kept everything around Celia scrupulously clean. And so eventually, mirac-ulously, after many weeks, Celia had not only recovered, but her woman's parts had healed, just as Bint Gulay had said they would.

Although the intervening years had not been espe-cially happy ones, he was aware that now, on the eve of their journey back to England, something was differ-ent between them, something had changed. As they sat together on the rooftop garden, Paul was aware that he was seeing his wife, if not exactly like the old Celia, then someone very like. The thought of their return home, and their preparations for the voyage, seemed to have brought them together again in a way that at the beginning of their marriage he had not thought possible.

It had been the smallest changes that Paul had noticed at first. Celia talked more, even laughed sometimes, and had become less prone to long days of solitary melancholy. When he talked to her of the great house in Bishopsgate that he had begun building for her on their betrothal, she began, slowly, to take an interest in the outside world. Paul had sketched out plans to show her how the house was laid out: where her bedchamber was to be, and where his; he drew pictures for her of the great first-floor gallery with its fine stucco ceiling, its massy fireplaces, its carved window casements made from solid oak.

As her interest in the world returned, together they chose Turkey carpets; hangings of finest Ottoman velvet for the walls; pale pink silks from Venice for the bed curtains in her chamber; a magnificent set of blue and white plates and tureens, the very latest and most expensive imports from Cathay; dressers and chests set with *pietra dura* and mother-of-pearl made by the finest craftsmen in Damascus; rare bulbs and tubers from as far away as Shiraz and Isfahan to be planted in their garden.

Gradually, Paul had begun to tutor her in the ways and manners of the English merchant class to which they would be returning, and under his renewed attentions Celia began to shine again. Glimpses of the person she had once been became more frequent. Perhaps, Paul thought, perhaps in England it really would be different. . .

Now, in the gathering dusk on the rooftop, the little charcoal fires were being lit, glowing like fireflies, and the air became blue and hazy with the smoke. The air was warm and soft against their skin.

'Do you remember how it was when we first came to Aleppo? When you could not walk, and we had to pull you up here in a basket?'

Celia smiled up into the darkening sky. 'Yes, I remember.'

From a far rooftop there came the faint sound of women singing and clapping together, the smell of spices being cooked and a faint perfume of orange blossom.

'We leave at dawn tomorrow. Are you prepared?'

'As prepared as I'll ever be.' She reached out and took his hand, noticing with a stab of pleasure that for once he did not pull away from her touch.

'And you?'

'Never more so.'

Lying side by side on the cushions, they looked up at the sky in which the first stars had begun to shine.

'Look, there is the dog star.'

'And there's Venus.'

'And Aldebaran.'

'Will we still see them in London?'

'Yes, but in a different part of the sky.'

They lay together for a while, in silence, looking up at the night.

'You are not afraid, then?' Paul ventured at last. 'It would be quite natural you know.'

'Afraid?'

'Of the voyage.'

She shook her head. 'No, I am not afraid. Have you forgotten? I was all but raised on the high seas; after my mother died my father took me everywhere with him.' She moved slightly, so that her head came to rest against Paul's shoulder, and still he did not pull away. She sighed, breathed in the warm smell of his skin, thought that never in seven years had she felt this happy.

'When I was a child, I used to bribe one of the cabin boys with sweetmeats so he would lend me his clothes, and then I would climb the rigging with them; the sailors used to call me their little monkey, I was so quick and agile. Sometimes I used to race them up the mainsail and could climb up to the crow's nest quicker than any of them. Ah, it was rare up there, you can't imagine, with the wind whipping through your hair – and the seabirds swooping all around you—'

'Until your father caught you—'

'—and threatened to whip me if he caught me again. But I paid him no heed. And after that he was obliged to pretend not to see me, for he was too fond a father ever to raise a hand to me. And I believe that secretly he was proud of my fearlessness.'

'Tom Lamprey! I remember him as though it were yesterday. As honest a man as ever lived – for all that he sent me away with a flea in my ear the first two times I made him an offer for your hand—'

'If by honest you mean plain-spoken, that he certainly was. My father always spoke his mind.'

'He thought I would take you away with me and that he would never see you again. So who could blame him? Not I.' Paul gave a sigh. 'I am happy to see that you can speak of him now without pain. But Celia, England will feel strange to you at first, now that your family are all gone.'

'But I do have a family, your family is my family now,' she said simply. 'Is that not so?'

The truth was that Celia had no very great recollection of England. Of her mother, who had died giving birth to a stillborn child when she was very young, she had almost no memory at all, nor of her other sibling, an infant

25

named Grace, two years younger than she, who had died soon after their mother. She had two memories. One was of a tree in an autumn garden, its leaves dropped on to the ground beneath, shining like a lake of gold in sunlight. Another was of a woman sitting at her sewing in the casement of a window, a little child at her knee. She was wearing a blue dress, and her hair hung loose around her shoulders, the same fine red-gold as Celia's own. Perhaps it had been just before her mother's third confinement, which would account for her undressed hair, or perhaps it had been merely a dream, or some distant recollection of a painting of a Madonna and child in a Venetian church, and not a true memory at all; she would never know.

All Celia knew for certain was that she and her father had become all in all to one another, which is perhaps why he had been so opposed to her marrying the ambitious young merchant, Paul Pindar, then the Venice factor to one of the most successful merchants in the City of London, Giacomo Parvish. At first, Celia's father had been adamant. The Lampreys, her father argued, were of a different estate from the Pindars entirely. The Pindars were an old Wiltshire family of landed gentry; they would never agree to such an alliance. And Tom Lamprey did not approve of it either. A love match? Who had ever heard of such a nonsensical thing? Neither family could countenance it. Love alone could not be the basis of any marriage: love did not last, what lasted were wider family ties, cargoes of wool and cinnamon, bricks and mortar. Besides, her father had fretted, he could not give her a dowry of anything like the size Paul's family would expect. What if they should reproach her for it after? Celia would be storing up nothing but unhappiness for herself.

In the end, it was the lovers who prevailed, although Tom Lamprey did not live long enough to see their union, and in the intervening years fate had kept Celia from England entirely, and from the scrutiny of her new family.

Now, on the eve of their departure, Celia had become increasingly curious, and not a little apprehensive, at the thought of meeting them at last.

Of Paul's father it seemed that there would be no difficulty.

'He will love you as his own daughter,' Paul said to her, 'of that I am quite certain. Look, see here,' he would say, showing her his father's latest letter, 'he desires that I should take you down to the old place as soon as is convenient.'

So of Paul's father Celia was reassured, but when it came to Paul's brother, that was a different matter.

'And your brother Ralph, what kind of a man is he?' she would ask.

But whenever Celia mentioned Ralph, Paul became vague, and said that he had not seen his brother for so many years now that he really could not say what manner of man he had become.

Over the years there had been a number of letters from Ralph, but for the most part these were short, business-like missives keeping Paul abreast of news from the Pindar estate in Wiltshire, Priors Leaze. They contained information about crops and buildings needing repair; news of their father and his various old man's ailments; servants who had been dismissed or hired; and an on-going discussion about who would take on the running of the estate after their father was gone. Paul had some-times read out parts of them to her, but they contained nothing of any real interest to Celia. Ralph had sometimes included polite but dutiful salutations to his new sister, but apart from that there was nothing especially brotherly in the letters that she could detect. Celia had never been able to form any great impression of Ralph, either for good or for bad.

But what Paul knew, and Celia so far did not, was that there was plenty that was brotherly in the letters, but not of the kind that he felt inclined to trouble her with just yet.

'*They tell me you married the Lamprey girl, in Venice,*' Ralph had written to him. '*I suppose I must wish you joy. It is known everywhere that the family of Captain Lamprey was ruined when his ship sank and he was drowned off the coast of Dalmatia. You must have become rich indeed, brother Paul, to have joined our house, and your fortunes, to so winged a bird.*'

Instead, Paul would guide their talk to a happier subject, to 'the old place', as he called it. Priors Leaze, in the country of Wiltshire, was Paul's childhood home, the house where he had grown up with his brother Ralph and John Carew, their childhood companion. Paul had often described the little manor house to her, with its orchards of medlars and quince trees, its golden fields and its old-fashioned moat, its woods and its hills where sheep grazed; a land traced with ancient mounds and walkways that no one now understood, a place so remote and isolated from the world that it was like a little kingdom all to itself.

And Paul would describe how as boys, he and Ralph and John Carew would sit in the fire-hall and listen to their nurse tell stories about the ancient burial grounds at the top of the hill, and the spirit folk who lived beneath them.

It was these stories that Celia loved to hear the most. And Paul found, somewhat to his surprise, that it gave him special pleasure to recount them: stories about the fairy huntsmen on milk-white horses, who on moonlit nights would chase their phantom prey across the brow of the hill.

'And if you listened carefully, they said, you could hear the tiny *hulloah* of their phantom horns winding down the holloway they call the Drover's Path; and the lonely cry of their hounds, and the beat of ghostly hooves. God's blood, how it did make the very hairs stand up on the back of our necks. It makes me shiver even now to think on it.'

'And tell me about Pitton,' Celia would say.

'Ah, well, Old Pitton. Old Pitton, the blind man, was the gransire of our present steward. They say that he was the last man who is known to have walked the length of the Drover's Path. When we were boys, we were told that Old Pitton had seen the midnight huntsmen once with his own eyes, on some long-ago winter's night, and came back bewitched to tell his tale, and he told of how, with a great crack, the ground had opened up and in that very instant all the fairy huntsmen were swallowed up inside it, the sight of which was the cause of him going blind—' Paul broke off with a laugh. 'Great God, Celia, how many years is it since I thought of these tales? I had quite forgotten them until now.'

'And do you believe them?'

'No! They are but village stories, of course.' Smiling, he pulled a lock of Celia's hair. 'And you are not to believe them either. But I will tell you one thing. . .'

'What's that?'

'When we were boys, I used to dare Ralph and John Carew to follow Old Pitton down the lane. Ralph was always too afraid, but Carew and I would follow that poor old fellow across the fields, and to the water-meadows, and then throw stones to make him turn so we could see the two holes, red and rheumy where the jellies of his eyes had once been, and then run like the wind for home before the bewitchment could turn in upon us.'

'I wish I could have known you all as boys.'

'You'd better thank the stars that you did not.'

'But is it not strange,' she had often said to him, 'that the only one of your family known to me is John Carew, who is not your relative at all?'

Something more than a servant, and yet not quite family either, John Carew had always occupied a vivid but ambiguous space in Paul's household. A servant who did not serve, and a cook who did not cook, Paul's continued patronage of him despite his misdemeanours was a mystery most outsiders found impossible to fathom. Celia had first met him with Paul in Venice, and she knew his story well. A village boy who had been orphaned at a very young age, he had been taken into the Pindar household by Paul's father. At first he had worked for them as a kitchen boy, but later had accompanied Paul for many years on his travels, somewhere between a licenced fool and general factotum. As Merchant Pindar's fortunes rose in the world, Carew's quick wits and his absolute loyalty had made him the most trusted member of Paul's ever expanding household.

And Celia had always loved him. John Carew: scowling, maverick, his long hair falling into his eyes, with his kitchen knives at his belt, as likely to be drawn in a brawl as used for any culinary purposes, a permanent lord of misrule. Carew had a genius for attracting trouble, and an equal genius for extracting himself from it. Over the years he and Paul had quarrelled and fought, and protected one another, and there was more of a kind of rough affection between them than anything indicated by Ralph's dry correspondence. No one had been more sorry than Celia when, after the last breach between them on the eve of their departure from Venice to Aleppo, Carew had just simply disappeared one day, and they had never heard from him again.

As for Paul, although he spoke of Carew less often these days, Celia knew that he still felt his absence painfully. Over the years he had come to rely on his counsel in a way that he was often too proud to admit. It had been Carew who always knew if a servant were stealing from him or if one of his cooks were taking more than his *sou*; it was Carew who could usefully be relied upon to glean small snippets of intelligence from the whorehouses and taverns where Paul could not go. It was Carew who had once spent a whole night hidden inside a cupboard in the Doge's Palace kitchens... Paul had never discovered why. It had been Carew, too, who looked after Paul when he fell into one of his habitual bouts of melancholy, when he gambled too much, or drank. It had been Carew – who else? – who had looked through a grille in the wall in the Sultan's palace in Constantinople and discovered Celia, still miraculously alive, two years after she was thought to have been shipwrecked and drowned. 'Things happen to me, you know how it is,' he used to say. *Stronzo*! Paul shook his head. But it was only too true: Carew had been at Paul's side on every one of their adventures and misadventures during the long years away from England; his one and only precious link with family, and home.

On the Aleppo rooftop the air was becoming chill, and it was time to withdraw. Celia made a move as if to stand, but Paul, pushing his thoughts about Carew to one side, knew that this was the moment to raise another, harder, subject between them.

'But there is something else of which I should warn you,' he said. 'You will be returning to London as a married woman with a large household of her own. The wives of my fellow merchants will be eager to visit you on your return. A most unprofitable and tiresome custom, in my opinion, to have so many strangers clattering in and out of one's house day and night and disturbing our tranquillity, but it is a custom that must be borne, for it is one that our English matrons are most determined not to give up. And these ladies, my Celia, can be very direct. If they ask you why you have no children, you must not mind it. After seven years of marriage most women will expect to have half a dozen or so, and they may be curious to know why you do not, and I fear they will not be shy of asking.'

Half expecting her to pull away, Paul drew her still closer to him, but Celia replied with an equanimity that surprised him. 'Fear not, I can manage your English busybodies.'

'Then bravo, my brave Celia, if you can manage them, I have no more fears for you.'

But he could tell there was something on her mind, and after a few more moments, she ventured, 'Your English matrons, what will they make of me, do you suppose? Will they know my story?'

There was only the slightest hesitation in Paul's reply.

'They will know that you have lived for many years among the Turks. First in Constantinople, and then here with me in Aleppo,' he said, choosing his words with care. 'There is no need for them to know more – unless you yourself should choose to tell them. I leave that to your own good sense. Should you make an intimate friend, I see no reason why you should not tell her your story.'

'But you forget, I already have an intimate friend. I have Annetta. For she is coming to us, is she not? To our house in Bishopsgate, and when she comes I will have all the friends I could ever want. And with her there will be no need to tell my story, for she already knows – she was there, after all.' Celia squeezed his hand with sudden anxiety. 'But are you sure – quite sure – she will come?'

'Your friend Annetta has braved shipwrecks, corsairs, and I know not what else. I am sure one short sea voyage will be no very great impediment to her. Besides, I have the letter from the Mother Superior right here, that and the papers ordering her release – I believe I have shown you both quite one dozen times already,' he teased. 'But this Annetta – you have spoken of her so often and so warmly of late that I begin to grow quite uneasy. Will I have a rival for my affections?' He pulled a lock of her hair gently. 'Tell me, my Celia, what is she like, this little nun who is so precious to you?'

'Annetta?' Celia smiled. 'Annetta is... how can I describe her to you? She is... small, and... cross... and has quite the best heart of anyone I have ever met. And I do believe there is no one on this earth less suited to the life of a religious—' She saw the look on Paul's face. 'But it is not what you are thinking. She always said that she cared not one *piastre* for the company of men, until she met John Carew.'

'Small and cross?' Paul could only laugh. 'Then she and Carew are most perfectly matched – but if the only reason she comes to us in London is to find him, then I very much fear she will be disappointed.'

Over the years Paul had made many attempts to find Carew, making frequent enquiries about him through his extensive network of Levant Company merchants and factors. There had been occasional rumours; and once or twice news had reached them that there had been an actual sighting of him, but never any news from Carew himself.

'If I know John he is most likely dead in a ditch somewhere by now,' Paul had said in exasperation on more than one occasion, 'I have never known anyone more likely than Carew to end up that way.'

Paul's words sounded harsh, but Celia knew how much he would grieve to hear of Carew's demise, and she always countered this theory with one of her own.

'Impossible,' she had always replied. 'Carew can't be dead. He is like a cat: he has at least nine lives. Besides, Annetta would never forgive him.'

'Carew will come home,' she said to him now. 'We will find him at home in England, you'll see.'

To this Paul did not reply. Instead, he put his hand into his pocket and drew out a parcel: a small round object wrapped in a little Ottoman pouch of embroidered velvet.

'Now we are on the subject of your friend Annetta, I have something to show you.'

He opened the pouch and shook out the contents carefully. A diamond the size of a baby's fist rolled out into the palm of his hand. Even in the dusky evening light, the stone glittered with its strange pale fire.

Celia looked at it for a moment without speaking.

'The Sultan's Blue,' she said at last. 'Where have you kept it?'

'In my strongbox. Where else?'

Paul handed her the diamond and Celia took it from him. She held it up briefly between her fingers so that they could both see the extraordinary skill with which the stone had been faceted. 'It is a marvel, is it not?' she said, turning it. 'I had quite forgot.'

Along one side was an inscription engraved in the tiniest hand imaginable. '*A'az ma yutlab*,' she read out, 'my heart's desire.' When she drew her finger along it, it was as though her skin seemed to tingle slightly at the touch.

'And now?'

'And now we take it to London with us.'

She saw Paul looking at her steadily. 'So you are quite decided then?'

'Quite decided. I had an offer for it only last week. A factor working for the Mughal king—'

'Ah, Paul!' she chided him gently. 'The Sultan's Blue should never be sold, only passed on, that much we both know. After all, it's how it came to us. Or who knows what *malas fortuna* will come our way,' she added, only half in jest. 'Like Old Pitton on the Drover's Path.'

'You are quite right. It is part of the legend of the stone and I, for one, have no regrets about that.'

Celia watched as he put the diamond back in the pouch.

'Are you sure?'

It would be no small thing, they both knew, to give away a king's ransom.

'Quite sure.'

'Here, then.' He turned to her. 'I have something else for you. It is but a trifle; a small thing I found when I was on the road to Damascus last. I have been so distracted of late with our preparations and farewells that I keep forgetting to give it to you.'

Celia looked down and saw that he had placed a small brown pebble in the palm of her hand.

'Oh! how very curious – a stone in the exact shape of a heart.'

'You see, this is what comes of giving up a king's ransom,' he teased her. 'It is but a small thing – and no exchange at all for the Sultan's Blue – but I thought it might please you all the same.'

'Oh, but it pleases me very much.' Celia gazed at it. 'You cannot imagine... no jewel could please me more.'

'Then why the sad look?'

'Sad? How can I be sad at a moment like this?'

But he knew her too well.

'You have always had my heart, Celia, you know that, do you not?' he said to her gently. 'Ever since you were a

35

maid, a young girl of nineteen, you have always had my heart.'

Then why? she wanted to cry out. *Why, now that I am healed, are you still so afraid to touch me? It is not I who am afraid, it is* you*!*

But she did not. She had promised herself she would not. With an effort, she forced the words back down. She was here, in his arms, was she not? And she would not now, not for all the world, break the loving ease that had grown up between them, on the eve of their journey home, on their journey back to a new life.

In England. . . in England. In England all things would be different.

In England, Annetta would come. And so would John Carew.

In England, diamond or no diamond, she would make Paul love her again.

Celia had quite made up her mind.

The Feast Day of St Matthew

21st day of September, 1611

To my loving and most esteemed brother, Paul Pindar, etc.

I am informed by my fellow merchants at the Honourable Muscovy Company that you and your household are shortly to arrive back on our shores; and I write to you now to express how very much I regret that I shall not be in town to trumpet your return among us after so long a sojourn. I have some business to take care of in Salisbury – the affairs of a young friend Lord Nicholas, having become somewhat entangled of late – which will take me from London for a sennight or more. On my way back I hope to stop at the old place to see how our father fares.

I am imagining your face as you read this, brother! As I live, it is as fine a jest as I ever thought on, is it not? For, yes, I am penning you these words of greeting from your very own house! As you read these words, you can imagine me sitting at your very own desk and holding what I believe must be your very own pen! Are you laughing as hard as I? There has been so much talk at the Exchange about the opening up of your great mansion at Bishopsgate Without after all this time, that I felt I must come and see it for myself. To persuade the watchman to let me in was a thing of the moment, and I have spent a most pleasant few hours here walking around the house and grounds. How long has it lain empty? Ten years at least, by my reckoning. They tell me that it is that old gossip Merchant Parvish, who has overseen the work here in your absence. And it grieves me to say that the result is very fine. A most handsome mansion, brother, most handsome. The first-floor gallery is the very last word in refinement. The moulding on the ceiling is exquisite, the finest I have ever seen. The fireplace seems to me to be of Mamara marble, no less. It must have cost a small fortune. The carved oak front is like nothing I have ever seen in this town. I see you are to have a grotto in your garden, as well as an orchard. God's blood, you will be the very height of fashion.

I do most heartily congratulate you. As you know, I am planning to rebuild the old place after our father's demise, and you have set the bar high indeed.

But there, you will have seen all this for yourself by the time you read this. I shall leave this letter, together with some other correspondence that I was able to pick up for you at the Exchange (you see, I think of nothing but your convenience) where – ah yes, inside one of these very fine ebony cabinets I see before me. I am still laughing to think of your face as you read this!

But one last word before I set my seal. There were those I can tell you who crowed to hear of your losses some years back, but not I. No one rejoices more than I in the knowledge that your fortunes are restored. It is as though he has robbed a Spanish fleet, my friends are saying; to which I reply, indeed, perhaps he has robbed a Spanish fleet. I would never be surprised by anything my brother Paul might do (I jest again, of course).

I believe I shall come and call on you at Bishopsgate on my return from Wiltshire. We are brothers after all, are we not? And brothers should be friends. Besides, they tell me that the great diamond you are bringing back with you from the Orient is on its own worth the visit. I have a great fancy to see it. (It is said that you will not sell, but knowing you as I do, I surmise that this that cannot be but rumour.)

A diamond fit for a king, brother. Or a Prince. Need I say more?

Your loving and obedient brother etc.

Ralph Pindar

TWO

Celia

Autumn, 1611. Bishopsgate.

F OR ALL THE TRIUMPHANT fanfares predicted by
Ralph, it was not altogether an auspicious return.

Much later, as is the way of these things, Celia could
never quite remember exactly how she had imagined the
house. She would remember only that she had always
pictured it in summer, with trees in full bloom, and apple
blossom in the orchard, a green sward soft beneath their
feet, the sun shining kindly. Sidney's *Arcadia* could not
have presented a more perfect scene.

But of course it had not been a summer's morning, but
a chill early autumn day, somewhere towards the middle
of the afternoon, with a bitter wind blowing from the east
and the light already fading from a colourless sky, when
their carriage finally passed through the city walls. What
Celia first saw, as she craned to look out of the carriage
window, was not the green and pleasant place that Paul
had so often described to her, but a muddy thoroughfare lined with houses, and choked and churned by more
carriages and carts than she had ever seen in her life. She
sat back quickly, trying to hide her dismay.

Shortly after their betrothal, Paul had bought a plot
of land just outside the city walls at Bishopsgate, a

thoroughfare that was at that time little more than a country lane, the buildings lining it almost entirely surrounded by fields. There had been three small cottages on the land, and a garden house, all left derelict after an outbreak of plague in the parish of St Botolph's, which he had soon pulled down to make way for the construction of his own much larger mansion. But that had been back in the last days of the old Queen. In the decade that had passed since they had lived away from London, a great deal of building had taken place besides their own.

Where were the country fields Paul had described to her, on which the laundresses laid out their washing? Where were the wild cherry trees and the running brooks; the fields where horses and their foals grazed? Had Paul known how changed it might be? She glanced at him quickly, but her husband, looking out as keenly as Celia for their first sight of the house, was turned away from her, and she could not read his expression.

Then, with a sudden jolt, the carriage drew to a halt.

They had arrived.

Paul was the first to climb down from the carriage. He stood alone for a few moments in silence. A thin fine drizzle of the kind that in Venice they call angel's tears had begun to fall, but he hardly noticed it. As he looked up at his house there was a constriction in his chest. Here it was at last: the house that he had dreamed of and planned for; the house into which, over the years that he had been gone from England, he had plunged so much of his time and energy, his love and his grief. Towering over all the other houses in the street, was an immense four-storeyed pier-fronted mansion. The middle two storeys were embellished with a magnificently carved oak façade (it had taken the wood from six oak trees and was still quite the finest, so Parvish had assured him, in all London).

What did it matter that there had been so many changes to Bishopsgate since he had last been here that he could barely recognise it. Looking down the street he could see that there were houses now all the way from the city walls to the Priory of St Mary Spital, and even beyond that as far as the once open space of Shoreditch. With its gatehouses, its gardens, and its newly planted orchards rolling out towards Moor Field, for sheer size and magnificence, there was nothing to compare with his own.

Heralded by the arrival of their baggage train earlier that day, news that the great house, left empty and deserted for so many years that for the working people in the parish it carried more than a whiff of ill omen, was to be opened up again had already reached the streets. Rain was falling heavily now on that cheerless afternoon, but despite it a crowd of onlookers had lined the muddy streets, waiting for the Pindars' arrival. It was not every day that an entourage of this size came to Bishopsgate. Sensing the holiday atmosphere, hawkers were plying their wares among the crowd. Paul saw a boy selling meat pies, another with a tray of hot codlings, from which rose the comforting smell of baked apples. There was even a man with a dancing bear. Looking round with amusement at the scene, he tossed the boy with the tray of codlings a coin; and when he bit into the pie the comforting taste and aroma of baked apples – the memory of his childhood – almost unmanned him. *Christos*! When was the last time he had tasted baked apples?

When he looked more closely at the waiting entourage, however, he no longer felt quite so amused. The baggage carts, which had preceded them from the docks earlier that day, were banked up the street towards St Mary's in a long line and were still loaded with their luggage. His household, comprising a dozen or more servants whom he had employed at Tilbury docks, where their boat had arrived some few days previously, were standing around idly, picking their teeth, and shivering in the chill afternoon. Clearly, there was no one here to instruct them. Paul looked around for his steward, a man named Cartwright, whom he had hired with the express purpose of overseeing their luggage, the new servants, and the provisioning of the house for their arrival, but he was nowhere to be seen.

Paul took out an inventory of their household goods from his pocket.

Besides his own coach, a total of five and twenty baggage carts had set off from the docks that morning containing the following items: two trunks full of plate; nine boxes full of copper and pewter vessels; twenty-five boxes containing pictures, mirrors, tapestries, fine linen, cloths for his servants liveries, and other *objets de virtu* which they had brought with them from Aleppo; two dozen chairs and armchairs; ten large chests full of provisions; two large and two small cabinets; half a dozen trunks full of his own and Celia's apparel; and some twenty further boxes, bales, valises and portmanteaux containing miscellaneous household items.

Looking up at the sky, Paul could see that the light was fading rapidly. God in heaven, it was going to be a job of work for them to get all the baggage into the house before nightfall, and in the rain too.

Behind him Celia was now descending slowly from the carriage. After her came a female companion, one Lady Sydenham, the widow of a recently deceased English merchant, whom they had agreed to escort from Antwerp back to London and who was to stay with them a few days before returning to her own people. At the sight of Celia, a fine lady in velvets and a fur-lined cloak, a hush descended on the crowd, followed by a ripple of excitement. The companion, a woman who Paul guessed to be only a little older than Celia, was now helping his wife to pick her way through the churned-up thoroughfare on to a less muddy walkway. As he watched she darted back to the carriage, retrieving a shawl from inside, which she folded deftly over Celia's shoulders. He saw her bend toward's Celia, and whisper something in her ear.

At once Celia looked up at the house, and then around at the muddy thoroughfare doubtfully. Then she came towards Paul alone, walking stiffly in her unaccustomed new clothes.

'Well.' She put her arm through his. 'Here we are.'

'Like a band of strolling players.' Paul looked around at the staring crowd, and then back at the house. 'What think you?'

For a moment, they stood together, the two of them, on the threshold, looking up at the house.

'Well?'

'It is fine... so very, *very* fine.' If there were uncertainty in Celia's voice, he did not catch it. 'Indeed, I never imagined that it would be... this fine.'

'*In England*... Remember what we always used to say?'

And for a moment his excitement caught at her. 'How could I forget.'

They looked at one another, smiling.

'Are you ready then?' He was about to step over the threshold, when he paused, looking back over his shoulder, to where their travelling companion was still standing.

'Wait,' he said. 'Would it not be a courtesy to have Lady Sydenham with us as we go in, do you not think? Shall I ask her to come?'

'The lady is so very solicitous of our happiness that she desires us to go ahead of her.' Celia smiled up at him. 'She has divined, although I hardly know how, that you will

43

want to show me the new house privily, the first time we go in.' Leaning towards him, she added in a whisper, 'I do believe the lady is quite a marvel.'

'Very well.' But all the same he found himself looking back to where the woman stood, a solitary figure, wrapping her cloak around herself against the raw autumn rain. Seeing his hesitation, she called out to him, 'Please, do not trouble yourself about me, sir. I will find Chance and Quirkus, and follow you directly. Go to, go to, you will catch your death.' And she turned away directly, so that they would not press her.

When Celia first walked through the door, she knew that Paul's eyes would be fixed upon her, trying to gauge her first impressions. But the truth was that her very first thought had been that the house was like a skin that would never quite fit.

In the hard grey October afternoon, the light was not kind. It was dark inside the hall. Dark and cold. The floor was lined with small black-and-white tiles. Against the far wall stood an immense chimneybreast, in the grate of which a fire had been laid but not lit. Ahead of her was a great oak staircase, spiralling up into the darkness above.

Her second thought, coming swiftly upon the first, was, 'What will Annetta think?'

The thought of Annetta steadied her a little. Celia stood for a few moments trying to compose herself, aware of Paul's eyes upon her, willing herself to look as pleased as she knew he wanted her to be. She took a few paces into the hall and looked around. For a moment it was as though the house yielded to her; then, in the next instant, she knew that it had not. For all its grandeur, it was quite one of the most cheerless places she had ever seen. *This is not my home*, was all she could think. *My home is a place of bitter orange and lemon trees, of clear water running through courtyards. It is a place of sunlight and air that is always soft against my skin.* And she felt a wave of loss come over her, like a sickness, for the home she had left behind.

As she stood there Celia felt crushed suddenly; tired, uncomfortable, overwhelmed. Her new clothes seemed to constrict her in a way she could not have believed possible. She could hardly breathe. She wanted to cry, but she was determined not to let Paul see her distress. To stop herself Celia squeezed her eyes shut and thought of Annetta again: Annetta, who was soon coming to live with them at Bishopsgate, was at this moment still in Venice – and Celia thought she knew exactly what Annetta would say.

Santa Madonna! What's this, the Doge's Palace? She imagined Annetta standing beside her, one hand upon her hip. Celia could see the beautiful beak of her nose, the mole, like a beauty spot, on her upper lip. *Why, Goose, will you not lose one another altogether in a house this big?*

And then suddenly, like a wave breaking behind her, the house was full of people. Maids, footmen, kitchen boys, grooms, carters – they seemed to swarm around her like ants on a sugar bowl. A few were familiar faces but most were entirely new to her. There were servants carrying chests and strongboxes from the carts; kitchen boys fetching victuals and bundles of firewood. Two men carrying a metal-studded chest came up to her; the veins on their necks were bulging with the exertion.

'Where's this to go, mistress?'

Beads of sweat stood out on the speaker's forehead. Celia looked round for Paul, but he seemed to be in some kind of altercation with one of the carters.

'Cartwright?' She heard him say sharply. The man mumbled something in reply that she could not catch. 'The Crossed Keys? You mean the inn at Gracechurch Street? *Christos!*'

The men with the chest were still standing there, waiting for her instructions.

'Put it there,' she said, pointing to the stairwell.

'Yes, mistress, but there's four more where this one came from.'

'Put them all there for now,' she said, 'and mind how you go—' But the admonition came too late, and the edge of the chest clipped the banister as the two men deposited it, none too gently, on the floor.

On their heels there now appeared a very small dog, Lady Sydenham's spaniel, Chance. Excited by all the commotion, and by its newfound freedom after long confinement in a cage on top of one of the baggage carts, the dog began barking shrilly, making little darts to nip at the men's ankles. Behind him came a silky-haired monkey with a black face. The monkey Quirkus bounded up on to the chimneypiece, and hung there, chattering.

Paul came up to her, holding the paper inventory in one hand.

'It seems that we've lost our steward to the alehouse. I should have known better than to give him some wages in advance.' He looked up at the chattering monkey, and down at the yapping dog. 'Dear God, what is this, a menagerie?' he said, by now thoroughly vexed. 'Have we not confusion enough?'

'Oh, hush,' Celia said, putting her hand on his arm. 'They are Lady Sydenham's creatures, and will quite soon be gone—' But before she could say more a quiet voice interrupted them.

'If it please you. . .' They turned to see the widow standing on the threshold behind them. 'If it please you,' she said in her pleasant, low voice, 'perhaps I could be of some service here?'

Lady Sydenham's quick gaze took in the scene of confusion in an instant, not only the yapping dog and the chattering monkey, but Celia, dishevelled and tired from the journey, with mud on the hem of her dress, and pins falling from her unaccustomed new clothes.

'If you would be good enough, madam, to start by controlling your creatures—' Paul answered her almost rudely, but she appeared not to hear him.

'If all these chests were put in one place – as I am quite certain is your plan – in, say, this little antechamber here,' she went on, pointing to a small room just off the hall, 'to be sorted through later in a, shall we say, a calmer moment,' she addressed Paul with quiet self-assurance, 'then, why not let me direct them? Then you can be free to take your wife and show her the rest of her house in peace, and away from the importunities of every last carter and kitchen maid.'

Before he could say anything she had taken the inventory from his unprotesting hand and run her eye down it, stopping only to glance up at Celia.

'Fear not,' she murmured to her, 'I will be up later to see about those pins! Go, quickly!'

She managed all this with such mild-mannered good humour that it did not occur to either of them to refuse.

It was only now, roaming the corridors and galleries, the attics and pantries, of her new home with Paul, that Celia felt her spirits lift. Although they had only two candles between them, and there were more stairs on the house's two staircases than she had ever seen in her life, with Paul there to help her, she hardly noticed the ache in her legs. Instead, a holiday mood seem to take them over. At Paul's direction, his old friend Merchant Parvish had overseen the opening up of the house, and some of their furniture was already in place. On the first-floor gallery there were two ebony and ivory cabinets, which Paul had bought in Antwerp; a desk inlaid with *pietra dura* work, and two high-backed chairs. In the room that would be Celia's bedchamber immediately above it, now stood a vast four-poster bed hung with pink Venetian silk.

She heard Annetta's voice again immediately.

Dio buono*! This bedchamber of yours! It's bigger than the Valide's!* Even after all the years they had been apart Celia could remember exactly Annetta's manner of speaking: sharp, often critical, plain-speaking to a fault, belied always by that merriest of merry faces. *And that bed! Why you could sail to sea in a bed that size! Does it really have to be quite so big?* Annetta said, casting her a sly sideways look. *You will lose one another altogether, Goose, in a bed that big...*

Impatiently, Celia pushed the uncomfortable thought away.

It had been Celia who had spotted Ralph's letter.

After their inspection of the house, they had repaired to the first-floor gallery. While Paul went to call a servant to start the fire and bring them some lamps, Celia walked its length again. Unlike the hall, which she found dark and oppressive, the gallery had a fresh, clean smell of paint and new wood. Even in the failing light there was much to admire: the elaborate mouldings in the ceiling; the marble chimneybreast, carved with the figures of two Titans, each holding an amphora of water; and beneath it, flanking the fire-dogs, two female sentinels with fishtails.

Parvish had positioned the two ebony cabinets they had had made for them in Antwerp, setting them upon stands on either side of the bay window. She went over to one and examined it. The doors were divided into panels, on each of which was a hunting scene, the figures – huntsmen, dogs, deer, even a bear, all exquisitely inlaid in ivory. In the soft light of her candle the carved wood gleamed. The key was in the lock. Celia turned it carefully and opened cabinet doors. Inside she found a series of tiny drawers, with a mirrored aperture at the centre. She was running her hand along them, admiring the inlay work, when she saw the letters.

There were half a dozen of them in all, neatly stacked in a pile in the mirrored niche. Next to them was an ink stone across which a quill pen had been carefully balanced, and a stick of wax.

Paul was just then returning with a servant and a supply of candles.

'Look,' she called to him, 'I found these, just here inside the cabinet.'

He recognised his brother's seal on the top letter immediately. He broke the wax and read it through quickly. Ralph! Sweet Jesu, he had not been in England ten minutes before his brother was poking his nose into his business.

He did not know what was more unsettling: that Ralph should have been wandering unasked and uninvited around the house, or that he should somehow have found out about the Sultan's Blue. What was he after? As if Paul couldn't guess. Whatever he had, Ralph immediately had to have it too; it had been like that since they were boys. He went and stood by the window, staring down on the muddy thoroughfare.

Sensing the change in him, Celia came and stood beside him.

'Is there something wrong?'

He handed her Ralph's letter.

They tell me that the great diamond you are bringing back with you from the Orient is on its own worth the visit ...

A diamond fit for a king, brother. Or a Prince. . .' She looked at Paul with surprise. 'So he knows about the diamond?'

'Seems so.'

'But how?'

'I have no idea,' he added, seeing her expression. 'But one thing is for sure: if my brother knows it then half of London does too. Do you have it safe?'

'Of course.' Celia put her hand to the pomander pocket hanging from her waist. 'It is here, where no one would ever think to look – they would have to steal me away first,' she added in an attempt at levity.

But Paul was no longer in a laughing mood. 'Give it to me – we must put it away quickly before anyone comes.'

Celia took the little velvet pouch from the pocket at her waist and handed it to him.

'Shut the door, but first make sure no one is outside.'

While she did so, Paul went over to the second of the two cabinets and opened the ebony doors. Like the first, this also divided into two halves with a mirrored middle section. Each side contained several rows of tiny drawers exquisitely inlaid with flowers and leaves in coloured stone. One day soon when the house was in order each drawer would contain a treasure or a curiosity that he had brought back with him from the East – a shell, a coin, or a gemstone; in the larger drawers below, there were sections for Paul's burgeoning collection of Mughal miniatures, drawings and prints. Along the top of the cabinet they would display the finest of their blue and white porcelain from Cathay. But for the moment the cabinets were empty. Paul felt carefully around the central section, but he could not seem to find what he was looking for.

'Here, let me.' Taking over from him, Celia felt along the joins of the mirrored niche until her more subtle fingers found what they were looking for. A hidden catch sounded, freeing the middle section, which she was now able to ease carefully from its aperture. Paul took it from her and turned it round, revealing a row of secret drawers on the back. Swiftly he opened one, and placed the diamond in its pouch gently inside. Then he slid the piece back until the catch clicked again.

'Remember, you must never tell anyone of this hiding place,' Paul said. 'No one at all – not even your most trusted friend. Not even Annetta. Understood?'

Celia nodded. 'Yes, I understand.'

Although the diamond was now safe in its hiding place, the feeling of unease caused by Ralph's letter continued to trouble Paul. He went over to stand by the window again. The crowd outside had thinned out a little, but some of the onlookers were still milling around, watching the last of their baggage carts being unloaded.

'When I first bought this land, all you could see from here were open fields, and now look,' he said, gesturing to the plot of land on the other side of the road where the foundations of another mansion, similar in size to the Pindars', were being laid out. In the gloaming, a man was holding a lamp, while another, with a piece of paper in one hand, was pacing out the distance, pegging it down with pieces of string.

'Has it changed so very much?'

'There were two fine mulberries there, most beautiful to be looked on, but it seems that they are long gone.' He pointed to the sad stumps of two tree trunks in the builder's yard opposite. 'And in this weather, look at it, the whole place has become a mire...'

'But the summer will come again—'

'—and in the summer it will be worse, mark my words. Imagine the dust. We will be breathing their dust for months—'

'Who are your other letters from?' Seeking to distract him, Celia handed him the pile of unopened letters left by Ralph. 'Perhaps there might be news of John?'

Paul broke the various seals, and read the other letters through quickly.

'This is from our factor in Chios. This from John Sanderson in Patras; and this third from Thomas Glover – but you remember Thomas, of course...' Paul held the letters up one by one. 'I am almost ashamed,' he said. 'Our company's factors – the last of them no less a personage than our ambassador in Constantinople – have better things to do than to be running around looking for John Carew and yet, to oblige me, they have done so, for they are the only ones, alas, who are likely to know when a cozening Englishman washes up on their shores—'

'And?' Celia looked at him hopefully. 'Is there any news?'

'Yes... and no.'

'Must you speak in riddles? Has he been seen or not?'

'It seems that Carew has been seen everywhere,' Paul said with a weary sigh, 'but is nowhere to be found.'

'Oh.' Celia sat down in the window seat. 'My poor Annetta. I was so very sure...'

'The most likely intelligence comes from Thomas.' Paul looked down at the letter again. 'If you remember, he knew Carew when he was with me in Constantinople, but he writes here that, last heard of, the captain of the *Hector* had given him a safe passage back to England, but...'

'But?'

'But I heard it on good authority when we were docked at Tilbury that the *Hector* arrived two weeks ago.'

'And?'

'And as you can see for yourself, Celia, Carew is not here.'

Looking out of the gallery windows, Celia tried to collect her thoughts. From here she could see over the garden wall of the house opposite them to the promised fields. In one of them were three horses, like black paper cutouts in the falling dusk. They were standing quite motionless, their heads were bent, as they tried to shelter themselves against the driving rain; there was mud up to their hocks. It was a melancholy scene. Celia thought she knew how they felt. There was a good six inches of mud on the hem of her own dress... but it would not do to think of such things now.

'If Carew was on the *Hector*, and he did arrive two weeks ago, but is not here...' she said, 'could it not be that there is somewhere else he might have gone?'

'Such as?'

'To the old place, of course, to Priors Leaze. Your father is an old man now – forgive me for saying it, but he cannot be much longer for this world. After all these years, would John not want to see him?'

'Perhaps...'

'Well, you know what to do then.'

'I do?'

'Write to your brother.' Celia went over to the fire, and stood there, warming her cold hands. 'He tells you in his letter that he is going to Priors Leaze on his way home from Salisbury. It is simple enough, surely? Your father can tell him straight away if John Carew has been there or not – and who knows, perhaps he is there still.'

'Trust me, my brother would need no encouragement to seek John Carew out, but if he were to find him, as I live, it would not end well.'

'You are speaking in riddles again.'

'There is bad blood between them – always has been – since they were boys.'

'But they are not boys now, they are grown men!'

'You don't know Ralph.' Paul folded the letter in half.

'You told me yourself you had no idea what manner of man he had become,' Celia reasoned with him.

'There is nothing for it, I must go to Priors Leaze myself.'

'And so you shall – and I shall come with you, and receive your good father's blessing just as we planned. But we cannot go today – or even for a few days' hence, not until this house is at least in some kind of order. Besides,' she added, 'you told me in Antwerp that the elders of the Honourable Levant Company have desired you to attend their next high council meeting; after so long an absence from London would it be quite politic to refuse? It is only a sennight from now, nothing much can change in that time. So in the meantime, my sweet love, I beg you, write to Ralph.'

If Paul heard her he did not immediately reply, for in the muddy thoroughfare below he had caught sight of Lady Sydenham, come out to talk to the last of the carters. She had pulled the hood of her cloak over her head – its shadow making a mystery of her upper face; she did not look up, but he could sense that she had seen him watching her. And Paul found himself thinking what a very curious creature it was who had wished herself upon them.

As Celia had said earlier, the lady was a marvel indeed. For anyone less like a grieving widow than Frances Sydenham it would be hard to find.

THREE

Celia

Bishopsgate.

D ESPITE HIS MISGIVINGS, PAUL followed Celia's
advice and wrote to Ralph the very next day asking
him to find out what he could about Carew's where-
abouts. As it turned out, it was a blessing that he did, for
very soon after he was laid low by an attack of bilious
fever, which for some time made even the short ride to
the Exchange impossible, let alone a long journey along
the uncertain roads to the old place in Wiltshire.

As for Celia, the house continued to elude her.

For all old Parvish's best efforts – the fresh paintwork,
the teams of carpenters and glaziers and masons that
he had employed at Paul's direction – it felt to Celia as
if the house had quite simply lain empty for too long.
Doors slammed shut for no reason and then refused to
open again; cupboards jammed; a dead cat was discovered
beneath the floorboards in one of the attics. The upper
corridors and chambers still smelt of damp. And as for the
stairs, there were so many of them it made her legs ache
just to think about them.

With Paul laid low so soon after their arrival, and the
house still in a chaos of unopened sea chests and trunks
and strongboxes and all the paraphernalia of a long sea

voyage, not to mention a dog and a monkey and a dozen or more as yet untried servants all needing direction, the situation would have been enough to try the temper of even the most practised housewife. Celia, with little or no experience, was all but overwhelmed.

In Aleppo no one had been more assiduous than Paul at acquiring fine objects with which to fit out their new house, and for a man of such ascetic personal appearance her husband's tastes were princely. When the last of their sea chests were finally unpacked the great house at Bishopsgate would be the last word in Asiatic luxury. The dressers would be crammed with silver plate; the great gallery on the first floor and the other withdrawing rooms hung with Turkey carpets and embroidered arrases; the antechambers showcasing Paul's collection of coins and medals and fine porcelain. But her husband, she knew, had never had the practical touch.

A subsequent and more thoughtful inspection of their servants' quarters had straight away revealed that the kitchens, the laundry, and the several pantries and sculleries were almost entirely empty of equipment. Apart from a few sorry iron pots and a spit jack there was hardly a copper pan, skillet, or even a knife to be found. When, with some effort, Celia managed to climb unaided up to the attics on the third floor where most of their household was to reside, it was to find them as empty as they had been when she had first seen them. There was barely a stick of furniture, let alone any bedrolls or bolsters for their servants' use. The linen presses at the top of the servants' staircase may have been crammed with embroidered cotton, with linen sheets trimmed with the most sumptuous Venetian lace, but were quite devoid any ordinary supplies. The most exquisite blue and white porcelain dishes from Cathay adorned the new dressers in the upstairs gallery, but where were the plates, the knives, the cups for their everyday use?

Where was Carew when you wanted him? Or Annetta? How Celia longed for someone to help and advise her.

While chaffing at his unexpected confinement, Paul was for several weeks too ill and weak to be of any help to her. The physician Celia eventually managed to find for him – a thoroughly unwholesome-looking fellow with stained yellow fingernails and a robe smelling of stale sweat – pronounced that a surfeit of apple coddlings had brought on the sickness, but despite this dubious diagnosis (Paul, who had a thorough mistrust of all English physicians, whom he claimed were out and out barbarians when compared to the Persians and the Ottomans, insisted he had only eaten two, his own and later Celia's when she said she did not care for baked apples) had nonetheless bled him most efficiently, and prescribed nothing more violent than daily purges and rest.

'I can manage, you will see,' she had said to him; but she spoke with a confidence she did not altogether feel.

That night Celia had retreated with her household books to her own chamber, but the numbers and figures swam before her tired eyes, and eventually she gave up the unequal task. She would ask Paul to show her again on the morrow.

In England it would be different, how often had she said those words? And so it had proved; but she had not thought that it would be quite so different. Marooned in her silk-curtained bed, Celia looked around her chamber uncertainly. The detritus of their long sea voyage – boxes and half-emptied chests – were still stacked along the walls, spilling their crumpled contents on to the floor. For all its newness, the room smelt musty, with a faint trace of salt, like the inside of a ship's cabin.

At the very centre of the room, and still the only piece of furniture in it, was the heavily curtained four-poster.

The bed was so large that when Celia had first climbed into it, she had the notion that it was almost as big as the ship's cabin she had just left. Once inside she had imagined herself back at sea; for a moment she could almost feel the familiar, vertiginous swell of the waves rising and falling in her belly. She did not mind it; in fact, sometimes she even thought back with regret to those peaceful days in their ship's tiny cabin.

Lying back, she closed her eyes, listening to the sounds of the night. How different they were from the sounds that she had been used to: instead of the muezzin's familiar cry in the distance, she could hear the thin coppery sound of a church bell – St Botolph's perhaps, or even St Mary Spital's – from a little closer to hand came the barking of a dog. Both seemed to Celia as she lay there listening, to be solitary, melancholy sounds. She wondered what was happening on the rooftops of Aleppo right now. What she would give to spirit herself back there, just briefly, to hear the cheerful gossip of the women, the happy shriek of children; to smell orange blossom and jasmine wafting on the evening breeze... As she thought this she felt another wave of loss for the home she had left behind.

Just then she heard the sound of someone knocking softly at her door. It was Frances Sydenham.

'I saw the lamplight and I wondered...' She took one look at Celia's face. 'Oh my poor child, why whatever is the matter?'

Celia tried to wipe away her tears, but it was no good, she could not dissemble.

Frances went over and sat down next to her on the bed. 'My poor child, you can tell me...' she said, taking Celia by the hand, 'tell me *everything*...'

When Celia first met Frances Sydenham in Antwerp, she had been presented as a newly widowed young Englishwoman, all alone in the world. Celia's understanding had been that she was in need of their protection, and she and Paul were soon agreed that it would be an act of charity to escort the grieving widow as far as London from where, it was given to them to understand, she would join her family, and take up the reins of her own life again.

At first Frances had appeared to be a quiet, unassuming merchant's wife, modest in her manners and demeanour. She kept herself to herself, and was hardly ever without a book in her hand. In the early days of their acquaintance, both in Antwerp and on the voyage, she appeared to read a great deal and speak very little, and almost never about herself. She was not beautiful, but with her high cheekbones and her curious slanting eyes, she always seemed to Celia more foreign than English. (There had been a slave girl from Tartary in the House of Felicity, she remembered, who had similar looks.) From the beginning she had been an object of curiosity, even of fascination, for Celia.

Later, on the voyage itself, when Celia and Paul would take a turn on the deck together, they would come across her standing on her own on the deck, her cloak wrapped around her, looking out to sea. She seemed so alone, and so private in her grief, that Celia's heart had gone out to her. After so many years of her own ill health and melancholy, it was almost a pleasure – no, most decidedly a pleasure – to have the power to be of use to someone else.

Once she was installed with them at Bishopsgate, however, Frances Sydenham had seemed in no very great hurry to leave.

In Antwerp there had been a vague mention of a cousin living at Winchester, and of some of her deceased husband's family in Norfolk, but as the days and then the weeks went by, and neither relatives nor friends had made any attempt to contact her, the talk dwindled, and finally they heard no more about it. It would have been unkind in the extreme, Celia reasoned at the time, after Frances's so recent bereavement, to press for her departure.

The truth was Celia had reasons of her own for wishing Frances to remain with them. In those early days, with Paul still recovering from his fever, and her worries about the house pressing in upon her, Frances Sydenham had seemed heaven sent. After that first afternoon, when she had overseen the unloading of their luggage, a very natural delicacy at the thought of interfering in another woman's household arrangements had prevented the lady from offering her services again so soon. But after their talk in Celia's bedchamber everything changed.

Before the next day was out, Frances had undertaken to order in the wood for the fires, to source the best supply of candles (both tallow and wax) and oil for the lamps. It was under Frances's direction that a team of carpenters had arrived to fix the warps in the window casements, the squeaking stair treads, the leaks in the attic roofs.

So essential did she prove, that before long she was in possession of copies of all the keys to their household. She carried an old-fashioned wax tablet on which she scratched quick little notes to herself, keeping a careful score of their kitchen supplies in bundles of five. When three of the maids hired by Paul proved both lazy and incompetent, she helped to supervise the hiring of three more. It was even Frances who proposed that they should fit up the garden gallery overlooking the orchards at the back of the house, as Celia's very own private chamber.

When Celia protested, half-laughing at her industry – saying that she had only asked for advice, and not for Lady

Sydenham to become their unpaid steward – Frances would reply, with touching earnestness, 'My dear madam, after all your kindness to me it is the least I can do.'

If Celia thought the sudden change in Frances was in any way strange – from melancholy widow, bookish to the point of unseemliness, to domestic whirlwind – she was too relieved to have found someone to help her to think about it overmuch. A convalescing Paul, trying in vain to keep pace with his Levant Company paperwork from his sickbed, distracted, vague, often irritable with fatigue, could only approve. Getting the house in order was women's work, his attitude implied.

Slowly Celia began to fear that he was slipping away from her again.

It was Frances, once more, who came to Celia's rescue.

In the evenings, she took to seeking Celia out in her chamber. The pretext usually was to look over the household accounts, or some other such business, but as often as not it seemed that she simply desired Celia's company.

Lady Sydenham did not care to talk about herself very much, but she proved to be the most excellent listener. In fact, she had what amounted almost to a genius for it. She never pried, very rarely asked direct questions, but would listen to Celia so intently, with an expression of such sympathy, that anyone would have been beguiled. An understanding look, a soft consoling hand upon her shoulder, a low murmur of *Oh, my dear Mrs Pindar...*, and Celia found herself telling Frances a great deal more about herself than she might otherwise have done.

To be heard, to be listened to, with a woman's warmth and a woman's understanding, was intoxicating. Soon it was no longer Lady Sydenham and Mrs Pindar, but

Frances and Celia. And before the week was out, Celia had told her almost everything. She told her about her baby that had died, even about the injuries to her woman's parts.

When she heard this even the unfailingly good-humoured Lady Sydenham had given a gasp of horror. 'Oh my dear. . .!' She put her handkerchief to her lips.

Celia was touched. 'Do not distress yourself, by God's will I am quite healed now.'

'God be praised!' She seemed genuinely moved by what Celia had told her. 'I cannot imagine. . . no, really I cannot,' she said, putting her hand on her heart. 'Ah, you must forgive me. . . but no,' she checked herself, 'not for all the world – no, not for all the *world* would I ask you such a question – it would be most indelicate. . .'

'Between two married women there is no indelicacy,' Celia said. 'There was a midwife, in Aleppo, who visited me, a wise woman. In her own country she was quite used to performing such procedures. She said I would not heal until I was cut again—'

'She *cut* you?' Frances seemed scarcely to believe what Celia was telling her. 'She cut your woman's parts – again?'

'Cut me and then sewed me up. Among her own people I believe it is not unusual.'

For a moment Frances had said nothing. When she spoke again her look was very grave.

'Dear madam, I do believe you are the bravest woman I have ever met. I can only wonder at how anyone could have borne that ordeal. No wonder your husband loves you so.'

It was a curious thing to have said.

'Oh, you really think so?'

What wife would not have been pleased by such an observation?

'Most assuredly, he loves you to distraction.' Frances leant forward and kissed her lightly on the cheek. 'Despite—' She seemed about to say something when she stopped herself, turning her face away from Celia suddenly. 'Well, you know...' Her voice trailed away.

'Despite?'

Lady Sydenham looked confused. 'No, no, you must excuse me. I fear I have said too much.'

But Celia insisted. 'Despite what?'

'Ah no, forgive me. I would not for all the world offend you so...' But the questioning look she gave Celia belied her words. She waved a hand vaguely around the room. 'Separate bedchambers?'

For a moment there was silence. Dear God, how did she manage it? Frances seemed to divine what was in her thoughts almost before she had even thought them. The desire to tell her one remaining secret pressed down on Celia as though it were weighted with lead. She struggled with herself. But no. This was Paul's business as well as hers, she had already said too much.

Frances, wisely, did not press her.

'Do not worry, my sweet, I won't tell anyone,' she said, with one of her good-humoured laughs. 'And there's no need to gaze at me like a frightened doe.'

But later, lying alone in her chamber, Celia did worry. Had she told Frances too much? Even if she herself did not think so, Lady Sydenham clearly did, for after that her evening her discretion was such that her visits became fewer and fewer.

During the daytime, however, she became more industrious than ever. The smaller of the two galleries in the house, the one overlooking the gardens that was to be Celia's special room, occupied her particular attention.

Celia had described her rooms in Aleppo, and Frances, who had a genius for these things, soon had it fitted up in full Ottoman style, with bitter orange and lemon trees in pots and several little braziers and cushions covered in the finest embroidered cut velvets on the floor.

Paul could not but admire it. 'The lady is, as you say, quite a marvel,' was his immediate observation.

But not everyone approved.

Madonna! She is worse than the Valide. Is it quite wise to let her govern you so? Annetta, the voice of conscience, whispered in Celia's ear.

Oh, don't you worry, sweet child!' she said, twiddling a bunch of imaginary keys beneath Celia's nose. *I am quite used to running a large household and am so much better at it than you!* Annetta, that wicked mimic, delighted in imitating Frances's smooth tones. *And besides, I have full use of my legs and do not lie around all day like an invalid!*

She gave Celia a long hard stare. *And have you ever thought what else she might be better at?*

But Celia, who now found that there was at least one place in the house apart from her own bedchamber where she could sit at her ease, was in no mood to listen.

What nonsense! Frances is kindness herself. And besides I do not know how I could have managed the house without her, really I do not.

If you say so, you frightened little doe! Annetta's tone was sarcastic.

If I am a frightened doe, then you are a cross old hen.

Frightened doe!

Cross old hen!

Doe!

Hen!

Doe!

Hen!

Celia smiled up into the pink silk pleats of the canopy. What heaven it was going to be to have Annetta with her at last.

But Annetta had not finished. *And so how is the scheme coming along?*

What scheme?

There's only one that I know of – the scheme to get your husband to lie with you again. And don't ask me what John Carew likes because I have not had a chance to find out, more's the pity.

Well, what do you suggest?

Oh, use your imagination. Get him to unlace you, wear your jewels... Annetta rolled her eyes. *How should I know? I'm a nun!*

Celia took out a looking glass; and for a long moment held it up to her face. She shook out her hair, watched it fall, reddish-gold, around her shoulders. She pulled her nightgown down off her shoulders, admired the whiteness of her own skin.

What did Paul see when he looked at her? There was still barely a line on her face or a fleck of grey in her hair. But what of her mind, her soul? Who was she now? Where was the fearless young woman who had sailed the seas more often than Paul himself, who climbed the rigging of her father's ship right to the crow's nest quicker than any man. Where was the Celia who knew the names of all the stars, and who had once astonished him by her knowledge of the workings of his very first astrolabe? If only she could show him that it was not only her body that was healed, but also her mind—

But the sorry truth was that now that he was recovered from his sickness, Paul was so busy with his affairs that she hardly saw him from one end of the day to the other. He spent more time at his desk, or closeted with Merchant Parvish, than talking with her. How unlike the time on their voyage home when they would spend whole hours together on the deck of the boat watching the dolphins play on the bow waves.

There was one sea chest still unopened in her room. In it Celia found her writing box, and the journal she had started to keep in Aleppo. Soon a detritus of materials – paper and pens and an ink stone – was strewn across the bedcovers.

She sharpened her pen and pondered a moment what she must write. Somehow she must marshal her thoughts and write them down – write down everything that had happened. Celia dipped her pen in the ink, and her pen scratched softly across the page.

She looked up suddenly. The dog that had been barking had stopped, but there was the church bell again. Celia cocked her ear. It rang three times, a thin coppery sound piercing the silence of the night. A thought occurred to her.

She could guess what Annetta would make of Frances, but what would Frances make of Annetta?

For there was now no doubt in anyone's mind that Frances would still be here when Annetta arrived.

But she could not think about that now. Instead, she bent her head again to her task. If only it could have stayed as it was, when they were at sea, she and Paul, just the two of them, back in their cabin. When it had been just the two of them, she had been quite sure that she could bring him back to her. But now, it was all so different. But not at all in the way that Celia had expected.

At sea she was not required to sit on chairs, or stand, or talk, or be looked at; to be someone that she was not. At sea she was not puzzled by the rules of engagement that she did not understand.

At sea there were no visits.

FOUR

Celia

Bishopsgate.

S HE HAD BEEN SITTING by herself in the private
gallery overlooking the garden when the first of the
visits occurred.

My Lady Peters and My Lady Ormiston.

How could she ever forget them?

At first Celia had thought that they must be the
wives of some of the late Sir Aubrey Sydenham's fellow
merchants come to pay their respects to his widow, but
from the moment they walked in they had looked like no
merchants' wives of whom she had ever heard tell.

With their loud voices and their jingling jewellery, my
Lady Ormiston and my Lady Peters had come clattering
up the stairs to her garden room as though they owned it.
Two servants bearing folding chairs followed close behind
them, into which furniture, without so much as a by-your-
leave, they settled themselves.

At first Celia was so surprised she could only stare.
Who were these women who had burst in upon them
so rudely? Her next thought was that they could not
possibly be Frances's acquaintance. They were dressed so
outlandishly and stared at her so insolently that for one
wild moment she thought that Frances must be mistaken

and that these must be players from the theatre dressed as women, or even – God forgive her – common women who had somehow unaccountably strayed into her house, although quite how Frances had come by them the Lord alone knew.

But she very soon saw that she was mistaken. Not only did Frances welcome them, but from the deference she showed – standing with her hands clasped in front of her, just a little behind their chairs – Celia came to the unwilling conclusion that these must after all be Frances's friends.

Both ladies, matrons of a certain age, had grey hair unbecomingly frizzed and powdered at the temples. They wore skirts that were hooped so wide that it was a miracle they had been able to squeeze themselves up the stairs at all. The ruffs at their necks – so unlike the crisp, snowy-white folds that she had grown accustomed to see among the well-to-do burger women of Antwerp – were dyed a hideous, liverish yellow. A red substance, in the shape of two roughly circular discs, was smeared on to the apples of their cheeks. Celia stared. The sight of these two strangers, planting themselves squarely on their chairs, in the middle of her gallery, was as strange to her as if two wild animals from the Sultan's menagerie had blundered their way into her home.

It was only later that she came to realise that this was her first encounter with ladies of fashion.

The two *miladies* took some time to settle themselves to their satisfaction. Not only were their gowns puffed out by hoops of outlandish size, but they had a number of fans and pockets and shawls about their persons that needed attention. Footstools were required. Then there was something wrong with the chairs, and others were sent for. A small brown-and-white lapdog with silky ears, borne aloft on a special taffeta cushion all of his own, was carried in behind them by a footman. But when the two *miladies* saw him, there was some objection – Celia did not quite gather what, for no one in all this time had troubled to address a word to her – and the dog was taken out again on his silken palanquin to wait out the visit in the carriage. Servants – both her own and the *miladies'* – scurried back and forth fetching mislaid items from the carriage outside. She heard their feet, full of importance, crunching along the garden paths. They filled the room with bustle and confusion. They brought mud in on their shoes.

While they waited for their servants to finish arranging things, the two *miladies* conversed together in loud voices, looking around at the surroundings with apparent satisfaction. Although the Pindars' mansion was unusually large, the garden gallery, her private room situated towards the back of the house, was nothing out of the ordinary, an almost old-fashioned feature in the large, airy modern building: a first-storey wooden structure running along an entire length of the property, such as any town mansion might have, from which the garden could be viewed. What was unusual about it was the way it had been decorated, a fact that the two *miladies* seemed to appreciate very much.

They noticed everything: the Turkey carpets; the silk drapes from Aleppo; the little braziers in each corner, which had been lit to counter the November draughts; the bitter orange and lemon trees in pots ranged along the back wall. There were no chairs here, other than those the servants brought in, only long low cushions to sit on, arranged on the floor in the Ottoman style.

Seeing Celia still standing, one of the women turned to her, and made an imperious sign that she should sit. Celia, whose legs ached if she stood for too long, was only too glad to obey. She sunk down on to the cushions on the divan. Presently the servants were dismissed and the room fell silent. The *miladies* were now gazing at her with the expectant air of two people at the theatre, as though they were waiting for something to begin.

Had Frances known that her friends were coming? And if she had, why had she not given Celia some warning? It was not that she minded – not exactly – but she thought that Frances had understood that this was to be her own private space; it was all the more puzzling in light of the fact that it had been Frances's idea in the first place. Celia would have preferred, if Frances had thought to ask her, not to receive visitors here at all. It was curious, she thought, and not a little awkward, that she should be reclining on her cushions at floor level, Ottoman style, while her visitors, in their rolls of padded silk, their bodices of bone and horsehair, towered over her. It was a little awkward too that she was not dressed for a visit but wearing the loose Ottoman trousers and robe that she preferred in private, and not the stiff, terrifying garments that took hours and hours and hours to pin together, threatening to become unravelled at the smallest provocation, which was what she was required to wear when in company.

But it was this Ottoman clothing that seemed a particular source of fascination to the *miladies*. They did not so much stare at her as devour her with their eyes. They put their heads together, whispering to one another behind their fans.

'Breeches!'

'Like a man.'

Their voices – shocked, delighted – were strange and high-pitched, like the squeak of bats.

Celia was at a loss. Clearly something was expected of her, but she did not know what. Paul had told her to expect visits, but not what to do when she had one. She looked to Frances for some indication of what she should do. Send for refreshments? Cakes? Wine? Perhaps she should stand up again and offer to show them the view of the garden? She looked to Frances to give her some clue, but Frances had just at that moment turned away and she could not catch her eye.

And presently the older of the two women was speaking something at her. Celia struggled to understand, but she – Lady Peters – was speaking in accents that were barely intelligible to her. Her companion, Lady Ormiston, kept silent throughout. It was her eyes that did the speaking. Small and black as raisins-of-the-sun, they darted here and there, never coming to rest in any one place for too long. Celia could not shake off the impression that she was half-afraid of what might be about to happen, as though someone, Celia perhaps, might bite her.

When Celia did not answer, Lady Peters tried again so loudly that she almost shouted the words. Finally, she turned to Frances.

'Can she nae spek English?' She sounded indignant. 'Lady Sydenham, I thought ye said she could spek English?'

'Yes, Lady Peters, naturally she speaks English.' Frances turned to the visitor with a dazzling smile. 'She *is* English.'

Her gaze met Celia's – at last! – over the top of their grizzled heads. Frances gave an almost imperceptible shrug and rolled her eyes to the ceiling as if to say: *Can you believe this? No, neither can I. What a pickle!* There was a gleam of amusement in her eyes. *What a pair of gobbling old turkeycocks,* her smile seemed to say. *How we shall laugh about them when they are gone!*

Catching her look, Celia was reassured. She thanked God for Frances. Frances could always make things right. What was the English phrase? *All at sea.* She would have been all at sea still, Celia believed, without her. So, when the visitors finally stood to go, and Lady Sydenham made a signal that she should show them a courtesy, Celia obeyed with good grace. She stood up, and without thinking dropped to one knee, bowed her head, touched her hand to her forehead, her breast. Something like a sigh escaped the two women. Although it was a bitter day in November, the woman who was Lady Ormiston reached for her fan and fluttered it violently in front of her face. They bent their heads together.

'*So charming. . .*'

'*The puur wee creature.*'

It was only later that Celia realised that, in her distraction, she had given the kind of courtesy that she would give a high-ranking Ottoman lady, nothing like the English courtesy that Paul had taught her.

My Lady Peters and my Lady Ormiston. They did not stay long. It had turned cold, with a sharp wind that tasted of snow, so only Frances went with them to their carriage. She strode out beside them, quick and energetic as always. It occurred to Celia, her small pale face staring down at them from the great gallery at the front of the house, that at least one of them was dressed for visitors. That day Frances had worn a striking dress of pale grey silk, with an over-mantle of black-and-white stripes. Quirkus, the monkey, was with her. He followed like a reluctant child, hunched and miserable against the cold. Although she had been walking holding him by the hand, Celia saw that Frances had slipped on his chain, which ran from his neck to a strap around her own wrist. Celia, who had no especially friendly feelings towards Quirkus, felt a stab of pity for the creature.

The afternoon had dwindled to a violet dusk. A footman in livery made himself busy tucking rugs around the ladies' legs. With the padded hoops beneath their skirts it was quite a business. New coals had to be brought for the foot-warmers; fans and shawls and pockets restored to their rightful owners. But once they were safely installed in their carriage, the ladies showed no great hurry to leave. Although Frances was wearing no more than a thin shawl, she stood talking to them for a long time at the carriage door.

She came in again like a whirlwind.

'Come and sit by the fire, you must be cold,' said Celia.

They were back in the garden room again. Celia had put fresh charcoal on to the braziers. But Frances was in no mood for sitting down.

'Not me, I never feel the cold.' There were two warm pink spots at the top of her narrow cheekbones. 'You were wonderful!' She strode up and down the gallery, every so often breaking off to embrace Celia, kissing her on both cheeks. Despite having stood outside in the cold November dusk, her skin was warm to the touch. She seemed exhilarated. 'Truly you were...' She stopped in mid-sentence. 'I never would have thought...' She held Celia out at arm's length and there was an expression in her eyes that Celia could not quite read. 'But never mind that – they *loved* you.'

Apparently Celia was supposed to rejoice in this news. The two women had some mysterious currency for Frances, but whatever it was Celia had yet to fathom it.

'Loved me?' Celia repeated, frowning, 'but why?'

What her connection could be with them, or they with hers, she was at a loss to know, but Frances, spinning round in her silk dress seemed not to hear.

'*The puur wee creature... the puur bonnie wee lass.*' She began to imitate the two ladies, but somehow the sting of mockery was no longer there. 'Oh, the *puur wee lass*,' she was laughing now, teasing Celia as she chanted the words, 'you *puur wee bonnie lass*.'

Celia tried to laugh with her, but at the same time she was aware of a faint discordant note, like a tiny distant bell. She had the impression that Frances would not call them gobbling turkeycocks now.

But the feeling of faint unease was over almost before she had registered it. Frances was in such gay spirits that Celia felt suddenly light-hearted again herself, although she hardly knew why. Lady Sydenham had a knack of pulling you into whatever mood – light or dark – she happened to be in. And Celia wanted to get there; more than anything she wanted to put all dark things behind her, to move into Frances's light.

'Come now, madam! Don't look so coy. Do it again. Go to, go to.'

'Do what? Do what again?'

'You know very well, you cunning creature. The courtesy, of course, the special courtesy.'

Frances dropped to one knee and tried to imitate Celia's gesture. But although normally so quick and decided, she looked awkward, impeded by her full skirts. When she touched her hand to her forehead, it became a wooden parody of Celia's graceful gesture.

Unbidden, the shade of Annetta was at Celia's side.

Madonna! What does she think she looks like, all the grace of a sack of millet, if you ask me.

Oh go away, not now! Celia pushed the thought of waspish Annetta to one side.

'No, not like that. Look, watch me.' Patiently, Celia repeated her action, only more slowly this time. 'Like this.'

She watched as Frances sank to the floor again, her skirts pooling around her in silken ripples.

Still looks like a sack of millet if you ask me. Annetta, even more sniffy than before, was not to be so easily

74

dismissed. *And who are those women, anyway? And what do they want with you?*

'My Lady Ormiston and my Lady Peters. . .' Celia ventured, 'have they been your acquaintance a long time?'

But Frances seemed not to hear her, more interested in mastering Celia's Ottoman courtesy than answering her question.

'How did you ever think of doing this, you sly thing?' She sank to her knees again. 'Lady Peters wanted to know if this is what you did in the presence of the Great Turk?'

Celia stared at her for a moment, unblinking. This was the first time that Frances had made such a bald reference to Celia's experience in the past, and for a moment she did not know what to say. But then, in the general mood of exhilaration, she was surprised into giving a direct answer.

'Why, yes it is, but it was not my intention. . .' she began, but Frances was so elated that Celia felt she could hardly explain that it had been a mistake.

'Well, then, we must be sure to tell them next time.' Lady Sydenham, who had subsided on to the floor once more, gave her one of her dazzling smiles. 'You must give them some satisfaction you know.' She looked up, her head to one side. 'My sweet Celia, these are ladies of *rank*. It won't do to keep silent *all* the time.'

Ladies of rank! At this, despite Celia's best efforts to keep all thoughts of Annetta away, her shade came bursting in again, a little more shrill this time. *Ladies of rank! Santissima Madonna, she cannot be serious, can she?* Celia had never heard Annetta so scathing. *Not only do they have no manners. . . but. . . but. . . they are as unwashed as peasant women! Didn't you see? There was dirt beneath their fingernails! Mud on the hems of their dresses. . . And as for the smell. . .!* Santa Madonna, *they stink like polecats! I almost fainted dead away.*

75

And it was true. Celia had tried, and failed, not to notice the dark stains on the silk beneath the *miladies'* armpits. In the room a faint but pervasive odour of stale sweat lingered in their wake.

But Frances, when quizzed again, was quite sure. From the conversation that followed Celia gathered that the two *miladies*, while not themselves attached to the Court in any official capacity, had important connections there. Connections, apparently, were the thing. Connections would advance her husband in the world. And, most especially, connections at Court. Lady Peters had a cousin who was a Gentleman of the Bedchamber. Lady Ormiston's sister was a lady-in-waiting to the Queen herself.

Che stronza! Annetta said rudely. And Celia, listening to this information as gravely as she could, hoped that her face did not betray her inner smile. It was quite literally incredible to her that these two women should be in any way connected to the Court.

Where we come from. . . Where we come from such a thing would never have been allowed.

And it was true. In the House of Felicity, where personal cleanliness was an almost religious duty, even the lowest-ranking of the *kislar*, the sweeping women *cariye* Tata and *cariye* Tusa, would have behaved with more grace. They most certainly would have been cleaner.

The thought, unbidden, jumped into Celia's mind: what would the *Valide* say?

Annetta snapped back the inevitable answer. *We both know* exactly *what the Valide would say.*

It was only with an effort that Celia pushed these thoughts away. She knew she was not supposed to think these things. She was supposed to have left all of that behind her. She had been told she must forget. But how could she?

Over the years, since she and Paul had been reunited, it had been so much easier not to speak at all than to forget. Which is why, for such long stretches, even now, so many years later, she had kept silent.

To be silent was to be safe. For she knew that if she spoke, she might give life to the thoughts than ran inside her head; thoughts and memories that on no account must ever be thought or remembered, but that must be kept safe and secret, locked away inside her head, where no one but she – Celia Lamprey – could ever find them.

To mask these unsuitable feelings she jumped up and went to open a window. She wanted all traces of the two *miladies* out. The smell of them, like two feral cats, was beginning to make her feel quite ill. She opened the casement, leant her head against the wooden window frame, and breathed in the bitter November air.

FIVE

Paul

Bishopsgate.

T HAT EVENING, THE FIRST when he had felt well enough to rise from his sickbed, he went upstairs to bid goodnight to Celia. He met Frances Sydenham at his wife's door.

'Have your visitors gone?'

All day he had been aware of an unaccustomed excitement in the house: of carriages arriving, and the sound of footsteps and women's voices on the stairs.

'Yes, I thank you.'

'I did not know you had such a wide acquaintance.'

'Well, sir, you know how English ladies are,' she said, whispering.

'Do I? I fear you have the advantage on that question,' he whispered back

'Ah, your English ladies, they love to visit. It is quite a vice with them.'

'I can think of worse.'

'But I fear that they may have tired your wife, sir.' Frances looked concerned. 'I fear that *I* have tired her with these visits...' Her voice trailed away. 'So if you would rather that she did not receive?'

He took her meaning immediately.

'Celia has no acquaintance. At least, not here. It may do her good...' He searched for the words '...to have society. She is not used to it – society of the English kind, that is. I have tried to prepare her as best I could, but such guidance as you can give her...'

Frances Sydenham looked at him gravely.

'I understand completely,' she said, her hand still resting on the latch of the door, 'but you have nothing to fear. Celia has such a way about her, she is so fresh, so natural – everyone who meets her thinks it.'

'Is that really so?' Paul said, pleased. 'Then I am glad of it.'

'Trust me.' She smiled up at him, 'I will take care of everything.'

'There seems to be no limit to your talents,' he said. 'I cannot thank you enough. With the house, and with Celia. You have been more than kind, Lady Sydenham. My wife tells me she does not know what she would have done without you.'

He made as if to pass her now, to go into Celia's bedchamber, but Frances was still standing in the doorway.

'Ah, you husbands... Come, sir, your wife is tired. Let her rest for a while.' There was the tiniest suggestion of a raised eyebrow. 'And you are just risen from your sickbed.'

When Paul looked at Frances he saw the way one strand of hair had fallen forward, and was curling behind her ear. From the pierced lobe of her ear there hung a tiny diamond-studded star. He thought, on balance, it would be best to ignore her implication.

'And you? Are you not tired too?' he asked.

'You should know me better by now, I am never tired.'

'No, madam,' he replied, 'I don't believe you are.'

There was a pause as their eyes met. Frances's hand was still on the latch of the door.

'I fear she may be asleep by now—'

'Nonetheless...'

Paul waited courteously, and eventually she moved silently away.

The first time Paul had set eyes on Frances Sydenham she had been standing by a window, in the flat Antwerp light, holding a book in her hand.

The room was in the apartment where he and Celia had lodged for a month on their voyage back from Aleppo, while Paul looked after his business affairs. One day, shortly before their departure, a Levant Company elder had drawn Paul aside and explained how one of their number, Sir Aubrey Sydenham, had died unexpectedly there of a short illness, leaving his young widow all alone. Would he and his wife take care of this defenceless woman and escort her safely back to London? Widowhood and obscurity, it was given to Paul to understand, awaited her. The elder's gaze had shifted uncertainly. In the name of the Honourable Company, and of the Christian God, surely it was only right that they should look after their own?

That day, in the few moments before she became aware of his presence, Paul had observed a dark-haired young woman perhaps five or so years older than Celia, wearing a dress of tawny-and-white striped silk, a pointed hood of black-and-white fur down her back. The book she was holding was one of a number in his own collection that he had been cataloguing. She had looked up, met Paul's gaze with an expression that seemed to suggest that she was almost annoyed by the interruption, and he remembered thinking the odd thought that perhaps no one had yet told her that her husband was now deceased, for anyone less like a widow it would have been hard to imagine.

'*Opus astronomicus quaeorum prima de sphaera planetarium,*' she read the Latin from the title page fluently. 'Are all these yours?'

Not so much as a good morrow. Well, two could play at that game.

'You can read Latin?'

'I asked first.' Her gaze was steady; almost, but not quite, discourteous in its directness.

So: she had not come to him in the role of supplicant then. Strangely, this fact amused him.

'A fair point,' he conceded. 'They belonged to a friend of mine in Constantinople.'

The room, on the first floor of their lodgings, over-looked the harbour. Outside the windows the sky and the water were the exact same colour: a flat pearly-grey light, extraordinary in its clarity.

'Ah!' She seemed gratified by this response, as if it were a clue to some question she had been asking herself. 'So that's what this is, the language of the Ottomans.'

The page she had open in her hands had elegant-looking script, in a neat hand, in both red and black ink.

'No, not Ottoman. Arabic in red, Syriac in black.'

'And you can read these?'

'You sound surprised, madam.'

'Ah, no, sir!' Perhaps aware that she had struck a discord-ant note, she turned to him with a brilliant smile. 'Your reputation precedes you.'

'My reputation?'

'Everyone knows that Merchant Pindar is a great scholar.'

He was aware that she was trying to charm him and found himself not in the slightest averse.

She sank down into a courtesy of such silken extrav-agance that for a moment he half-suspected she was laughing at him.

'Then you have been sadly misinformed,' he said, return-ing the courtesy. 'I am no scholar. But in answer to your question I can read Arabic, and some Syriac. Since I have been living in Aleppo these last seven years, it would be surprising if I could not. The books are a present to a friend, Sir Thomas Bodley – perhaps you know him? They belonged to another friend who is – who was – an astronomer.'

'Your friend is deceased?'

'Alas, yes; my friend Jamal al-Andalus is dead.'

'I am sorry to hear it, he must have been a man of great learning.'

She was still holding the book in her hand. 'There is a water mark on this one, have you seen?' She picked up another of the volumes on the table. 'One of your travelling chests must leak.'

He saw that she handled the book lovingly, stroking the vellum pages with her fingers. 'You should take better care of them. What will your friend do with them? Is he a scholar?'

'He wishes to start a library at Oxford.'

She lifted the book to her face, and gave a small, cautious sniff. A fragment of pinkish-brown paper, fell from the open page. Not paper, but a petal.

'Look, someone has pressed a flower in these pages.'

First one petal, then another, spun slowly to the floor.

'How can I help you, Lady Sydenham?' Paul took the book from her hands and placed it with the others on the table. 'They tell me that you are looking for a passage home?'

'I would be most grateful.' She reached down and picked up the rose petals from the floor, crushing them between her fingers. They gave off a faint desiccated perfume, at once dusty and sweet. She looked up at him, with that same cool gaze. 'It seems as though I find myself alone again in the world.'

It was the first of many conversations with Lady Sydenham about which he did not tell his wife.

Salisbury.

The Feast Day of St Daniel

10th day of October, 1611

Esteemed brother,

I thank you for your recent letter. As it happens my intention was always to stop by at the old place on my way back to town from Salisbury on All Hallows or thereabouts (a small business matter that I need not trouble you with), and I will make enquiries from there as you request.

One of my acquaintance, either Lord Nicholas, or most likely a French gentleman, Salomon de Caus, will I am sure undertake to bear this letter to you. Your intelligence will have informed you – and, if not, I have no doubt that that old gossip Merchant Parvish will have obliged – that de Caus is employed as ingenieur *to Prince Henry at his palace at Richmond, where he not only instructs him in perspective, but also brings with him all the latest ideas from France and Italy on gardens. The Queen herself, they say, is much taken with him. It is no longer enough to have lavender beds and a bit of orchard and a bowling green, but it must be fountains and waterfalls, summer houses and galleries, statues that move and spout water and I know not what other fancies.*

De Caus tells me that at the Prince's new gardens at Richmond he is constructing a speaking giant; an automaton three times as large as the statue in the gardens at Pratolino, with whole rooms inside the body, a dovecote in the head, grottoes in the base and I know not what else. And I have managed to convince him to come with me to Priors Leaze as we pass by there on our way back to town, to advise me on hydraulics for a grotto that I intend to build there when the old man is gone.

As we travelled all the way from town in the coach he spoke of nothing but mechanics and hydraulics, of Hero of Alexandria, and Ctesibus, and Philo of Byzantium, until my head ached like a girl's and it was all I could do not to box his French ears. The man is a lamentable bore for all they say he is a genius.

I said to him – you must meet my brother Paul, the other Merchant Pindar, they tell me he is fond of books. But as to me, I told him, I am but a simple merchant. If it is newfangled and expensive then that is good enough for me, and I intend to have it. I do not give two straws for the provenance. I will have waterworks in my garden and a prospect from my window, even if I have to tear down the old place to get it.

I remain your dutiful brother,

Ralph

Postscript
I trust you have by now given some further consideration to the sale of the great diamond? They say Prince Henry has spent seven thousand pounds on gemstones in the last year alone. His Majesty the King has bestowed knighthoods for less. Think on it well. It would bring our family great favour. Make up for the stain of mésalliance you have brought upon us. . . But there, what's done is done. I hope I remain so loving and dutiful a brother as not to rub salt into the wound.

SIX

Celia

Bishopsgate.

R ALPH MIGHT HAVE BEEN of the opinion that
Paul's marriage to Celia was a *mésalliance*, but it was
not everyone's view.

Clearly, my Lady Peters and my Lady Ormiston were
more than satisfied by the entertainment afforded them
at Merchant Pindar's new mansion at Bishopsgate. Their
curiosity to see the Great Turk's former concubine so
far outweighed any ordinary notions they might have of
propriety or rank that a few days after their first visit not
only did they call again, but this time they brought two
friends. And the following day two more.

'Lady Rich and the Countess of Somerset!' Frances
was overjoyed. 'Lady Rich is of course no longer received
at Court after her divorce,' she added pensively, 'but my
Lady Somerset! Now that really is a feather in your cap.'
Frances was highly gratified. 'She played the part of the
Queen of the Night in the last Court Masque. And one
of her children was an attendant, I believe.'

It was amazing to Celia that Frances should know these
things.

'Why, what a simpleton you are,' Frances teased. Her
attitude seemed to suggest that this was quite as ordinary

as knowing the price of bread. 'Everyone knows about the Court masques.'

But by what mysterious process she had gathered this information was hard to tell. Apart from the occasional excursions to her haberdashers, or to the mercer on Cheapside, Frances rarely left the house. She was not addicted to pamphlets, nor did she appear either to write or receive any letters, or not so far as Celia was aware. Her intelligence seemed plucked out of thin air.

When Celia asked her how she came by it all, Frances merely gave one of her sphinx-like smiles.

'Gossip, my sweet,' she had laughingly said, 'just good old-fashioned gossip. You are a success, that's all that matters, the talk of the town.' She slipped her arm through Celia's. 'Who would have thought it? Did you know there's a rumour that your husband has you wear his great diamond every day like a diadem on your forehead? Or is it hung between your naked breasts? I never can remember which.' She laughed as though this were the most enchanting thing she had ever heard. 'Is it not too absurd? You'll be invited to the masque yourself next, you mark my words. There'll be one this winter, or at Twelfth Night, and then you'll see.'

When they had first arrived at the new house, Celia had been able to share in Frances's energy, but as the weeks went by – and she had been with them nearly a month now – it began to have quite the opposite effect. Far from being studious and demure, as she had first presented herself in those early days at Bishopsgate, Frances Sydenham had showed herself to be energetic to the point of frenzy. At first she had deferred to Celia, but before long there was a hint – the merest hint – of impatience when Celia tried to intervene. There were times, if Celia were completely honest, when she felt sapped by her, as though there were only so much air in a room, and Frances took it all.

And as for the visits, they became more and more irksome. And far from abating, as Celia's fame grew, so did the curiosity to see her. Her private gallery, hung with silks and Turkey carpets, warmed with braziers, and scented with bitter orange and lemon blossoms, was beginning to seem quite crowded. But even the tiniest hint of *ennui* on Celia's part was soon dealt with by Frances, who was only too quick to jump upon even the tiniest hint of dissatisfaction.

'I don't think you realise the honour they do you in coming all this way.'

'Honour?'

'Why, to be sure.' At these moments, Frances was never less than reasonable. 'They are ladies of *rank*, my dear,' she explained. 'We must do what we can to show them our respect. And you know how much it pleases your husband. He never stops telling me so.'

Could that really be true? Celia bowed her head over her embroidery. The idea of Frances and her husband discussing her gave her a sudden disagreeable twinge of unease.

There was worse to come.

'And so tell me,' Frances said, busy with one of her wax tablets, 'have you asked him about the great diamond yet?'

Celia, frowning over a dropped stitch, did not immediately answer.

'You mean the Sultan's Blue?'

'Ah, so that's what you call it?'

There was something in the tone Frances's voice that made Celia glance up.

'Yes, do you not remember?' she said lightly, still examining her tablets. 'You were going to ask him if you might wear it when the ladies come visiting.'

Celia could only smile at this misapprehension. 'I fear you are mistaken. I am quite sure I did not.'

'What, do you not recall? I remember thinking how clever you were to think of it. It would impress them all *very* much you know. Merchant Pindar's Great Diamond is the talk of London. I can imagine how vexed their husbands would be to think of their wives being the first to see it.'

'You are mistaken, madam,' Celia could only repeat, 'very much mistaken. I am quite sure I would never have said such a thing.'

'But you did, I most distinctly remember it.'

'Then I am afraid your memory serves you ill. We must have been taxing it too greatly of late,' Celia said. 'I am *entirely* certain I never could have said such a thing.'

Frances seemed quite put out by Celia's firmness. 'Do not distress yourself, it was but a small thing.' A warm flush suffused her neck, crept slowly up to her cheeks. 'Please. Forget I ever mentioned it.'

'I am not distressed, madam.' Celia put down her embroidery. 'Merely certain.'

Lady Sydenham seemed so discomfited that for a moment it was on the tip of Celia's tongue to explain about the diamond and its mysterious properties. A second's reflection made her think better of it. She and Paul had been quite agreed that she would say nothing to anyone, and she would not go against that.

Frances, of course, knew better than to press her point, but her displeasure was clear.

'It was but a small thing,' she repeated. 'I thought you might do it to please me – but no, no, I can see you are distressed.' There was but the tiniest hint of coolness in her voice. 'Please forget I ever mentioned it.'

And there was no more talk of the diamond, for a few days at least.

Paul, preoccupied with his own affairs, did not interfere with the comings and goings in his new home. With Frances Sydenham as her companion, Celia seemed more settled that he could have hoped in the house. And if Lady Sydenham desired to bring her acquaintance to visit Celia – so long as he did not have to meet them himself – well, it was a plan which he found unobjectionable. Any scheme which might help his wife settle into English life was one of which he could only approve. Lady Sydenham managed it all with admirable tact.

But as the stream of visitors increased, even Paul began to be perplexed. Hardly a day went by when he did not see My Lady Somebody's carriage at the gatehouse, or hear the trip of unfamiliar feet on his stairs, or in the garden, or in his wife's gallery.

When Paul asked Celia about her visitors, most of the time she could not remember their names.

'One was a countess,' she said vaguely. 'Frances knows who they are.'

'A countess?' Paul tried not to sound too surprised. Frances might call herself Lady Sydenham, but she was only a merchant's wife, after all, and hardly a member of the aristocracy. He leant down to examine the buckle on one of his shoes. 'Frances has a friend who is a countess?'

'An acquaintance,' Celia corrected him. The truth was she could not imagine the ladies who had so recently been sitting in her chamber, peering at her from behind their fans, to be anyone's friends. Not even each other's. 'I suppose.'

'Well, well,' Paul frowned down at the buckle which had come loose from the leather. 'I had no idea she was so well acquainted. What did you talk about?'

'Oh. . . this and that.'

'But you did. . . talk?'

'Oh indeed.'

'Well. . . that's excellent.' Paul sounded delighted.

'Oh, yes.' Seeing how pleased he was, Celia agreed, 'It is indeed. Most excellent.'

But later that day, when she had retired for the night, Celia found herself wrestling again with the same thoughts. At first it was Frances's unsettling mention of the Sultan's Blue that was uppermost in her mind. Her insistence that Celia should wear the diamond had struck her as strange – more than strange – but thinking about it now, of what could she really complain? That Frances had been angling for a look at the Sultan's Blue? Well, that was hardly surprising. And besides, she had surely meant it as more of a joke than anything else – when Celia imagined telling Paul about it, she felt sure that was how he would see it. She was too suspicious, Celia decided, there was no need to involve him after all. But on the subject of the visits in general: that was another matter. The truth was that her visitors were beginning to exhaust her. They came at all hours, and she never felt safe from their intrusions. Frances might insist that they brought honour and influence, but Paul himself had never said anything to her about it. She had been wrong to hesitate: she must speak to him about it after all.

It was the next day when she and Paul, in a rare moment alone, were taking a turn in the orchard that she found her chance.

The Pindars' garden had been meticulously planned on the same grandiose scale as the house: it was large, commodious and above all, modern. In the watery morning sun it had the tilled, raw look of a field in winter, a place where gardeners had only recently tramped and dug, but the bones were there. The pleached pear and plum trees along the south-facing wall, the raised beds, the fashionable grotto – already the piles of Welsh flints were in place – all of it the very height of fashion. The Pindars' garden would one day rival Lord Zouche's in Hackney for the range and rarity of its plants.

After days of wind and rain it was set to be a fair day. The sky was a wash of pale blue; from somewhere a mistle thrush called.

Paul, stopping to admire a bed of autumn tulips, heard it first.

'Listen,' he said, 'is that not a beautiful sound? Sweeter than a nightingale. I didn't realise how much I have missed the sound of our English birds.' He saw Celia looking at him. 'Why the look?'

'Can a wife not look at a husband?' she said, delighting in his pleasure. 'I can't get used to seeing you always in English clothes, and all in black moreover.'

'And—?'

'And I find it suits you very well.'

'You don't think it makes me look old?'

'No, not old at all,' she laughed. 'And vanity is a deadly sin, you know.'

She put her hands against the black velvet of his doublet, rubbing one finger backwards and forwards on a little patch of the stuff.

'There is something—' she began, when Paul also spoke.

'I just want—' he said. 'But did you want to tell me something?'

'Yes, but you first.'

'Very well,' he said, taking her hand. 'I just want to tell you how proud I am.'

'Proud of me?'

'Don't look at me with such surprise. Do you know what a pleasure – nay, what a joy – it is to me, Celia, to see you as mistress of this house at last? And I find that you have managed it all so well, and with no help from me at all.'

'Well, I did have some help—'

'Your Lady Sydenham has made herself most useful, I can see that, but you are the true mistress here, Celia, are you not?'

Celia could not but agree to this.

'After everything you have suffered – I don't think there is another woman in England who could have borne it all as you have. I know I have been distracted of late. Can you be patient with me a while longer? I have a hundred things pressing on my mind – it is the greatest possible help to me, to know that I do not have to worry about you. These visits – you are quite sure about them?' he asked. 'For if you don't like them, Celia. . .'

'The visits are but a small thing—' she began, choosing her words carefully, but Paul did not wait to hear her out.

'I am relieved beyond measure to hear you say so,' he said, squeezing her hand. 'There have been times when I have thought there might be too many for your absolute comfort, Celia, but if you ask me they seem to be doing you nothing but good.' He put his arm through hers and together they continued on their walk. 'How I remember how you chided me in our first week here, when you said we must be kind to poor Frances, did you not? And do not imagine for one moment, my Celia, that I don't know what a great kindness it is on your part to oblige her.'

What could she say? What could she possibly say now? In her mind's eye Celia saw herself climbing to the crow's nest on the topmast of her father's ship, her hair flowing behind her in the snapping wind. . .

When they stopped again, for Paul to speak to one of the gardeners, Celia turned and looked back at the house. Why was it that she had never quite got over her first impression that the house was like a skin that would never quite fit? The windows that gave out on to the garden appeared dark in the bright sunshine, and Celia was struck by a curious fancy that they were like so many eyes peering down at her. She gave a small shiver. But wait, there *was* someone looking out; in one of the top windows she clearly caught sight of a woman's face.

Someone, she could not from this distance see who, had been watching them all this time, her face a pale smudge against the blackness.

And so the visits continued unchecked.

At the beginning, Frances had encouraged Celia to talk – to show their visitors the Ottoman courtesy, and explain its variations and its uses – but now there was an unspoken expectation that she would remain silent. Having heard Celia explain it so many times, Frances now knew exactly what to say in reply to their questions, so it was Frances, naturally, who did most of the talking.

But the plain fact was that these ladies for whom she had such an inexplicable regard; these *miladies* with their insolence and their loud voices, some with a hint of last night's malmsey still on their breath; these ladies with their outlandish clothes, their skirts padded and hooped and stitched with jewels and sequins, so hard and shiny that they seem to Celia like the carapaces of insects, did not seem to want much from her, other than to look. Mostly they talked to one another, whispering she knew not what behind their fans.

Even so, however much she wanted to, it seemed impossible now to admit to Paul that their presence in the house had the very opposite effect from the one he imagined. Far from bringing her out of herself, they made her want to shrink right back into her shell. Far from dreaming that she could ever be their friend, Celia had never felt more keenly that she was nothing but a sea captain's daughter.

Their effect on her was to make her feel not so much inferior as insubstantial, as though she were not really there at all: a ghost in her own house. Celia put her hand out to one of the bedposts as though to hold herself down. Sometimes she had the odd notion that the merest puff of wind might blow her back out to sea. She imagined what it would be like to glide down the Thames, skimming and dipping the tip of her wings into the grey waters, past the Isle of Dogs, and the Queen's palace at Greenwich, the grey swamps and reeds all the way to Tilbury docks and beyond...

And she longed, more than ever, for Annetta.

What are you thinking, don't be such a simpleton! What does this Lady Whatsherface get from all of this, have you ever asked yourself that? And must she really call you 'sweet child' all the time. Che stronza! The shade of Annetta wrinkled her nose in disgust. *There's no one in this world, Goose, who does something for nothing.*

When Frances goes, Celia assured herself, they will no longer come.

But even Celia had to admit that Frances still showed no sign whatsoever of going.

The White Hart Inn,
Marlborough,
Wiltshire

Feast Day of St Theresa

15th day of October, 1611

Esteemed brother,

I bring you news from the old place as you requested, although in truth there is not much to tell. I am stopped for a few days at Marlborough on my journey back to town, and I took the opportunity to have my aforementioned travelling companion, the Frenchman de Caus, come with me there to view the grounds. He was not best pleased by the diversion, so the visit was necessarily brief, but my pleasure prevailed in the end.

In answer to your query: I am assured by our people – by Pitton and the two maidservants – that there have been no visits from strangers in these parts. I hope you are satisfied.

As for the other matters, what can I tell you?

It has been a wet autumn. Although the weather is fine now, it has barely stopped raining since Michaelmas, and the roads are so infernally bad in these wild parts that I would not trouble myself to visit the old place at all were it not to carry out your enquiries (you see how obliging I have become!). The old man is what he always was, peevish and wearisome. He sends you his blessings, and asks that you come to visit him as soon as you may.

There is one other matter I should mention. Now that I am at Marlborough, and to lie here some days (Lord Nicholas's lady, being big with child, is somewhat indisposed), I have sent for our father's lawyer, Wilkes, to see if we might draw up papers in preparation for the break-up of the old estate. I know what your arguments will be: that it would be usual to wait until the old man is gone and his will proved, but I can see no reason to delay. Our father ails, and it cannot be long now. You always were more womanish than I in these matters, but since there are just the two of us now, I trust that you are still in agreement? I want the land, which you do not, for which I shall recompense you handsomely, so there should be no difficulty.

John Carew is dead, brother, six foot under in a foreign land; he will never return, and it is God's will that you and my father should accept it. And even if he were, by some happenstance, still living somewhere, the good Wilkes assures me that after seven years he is as good as dead in so far as our father's will is concerned. So let that be an end to it.

Your dutiful brother,

Ralph Pindar

SEVEN

Paul

Bishopsgate.

I T WAS SEVERAL WEEKS before Paul was well enough to visit the Exchange for the first time. He was just leaving the house when he received Ralph's third letter, which was delivered by a snot-nosed, barefoot street urchin who ran off with Paul's tossed coin before he could question him. He broke the wax, and read it quickly, twice through.

John Carew is dead, brother, six foot under in a foreign land...It is God's will that you and my father should accept it.

He read the words with dismay. Until now, Paul had not realised how much he had allowed himself to hope that there would be good news from Priors Leaze. Carew could not be dead! Impossible, he would never forgive him! He was like a cat with nine lives – the sorry scoundrel must have at least one of them left. While he had been waiting for Ralph's letter to arrive, he had even allowed himself to imagine him returned home safely, sitting there, large as life, by his father's chair in the old parlour, scowling at him over the lip of a glass of malmsey.

Well, what did you expect? You don't get rid of me that easy, Pindar. He could almost see the familiar glint in Carew's eye. *And have I got some tales to tell you...*

What had possessed him to involve Ralph? The only thing he seemed to have done was to unleash troubling talk about lawyers, and wills, and the break-up of the estate. He should never have written to Ralph; should have gone straight to Priors Leaze himself. High council meeting or no high council meeting, he must not delay any longer.

Paul put the letter in his pocket and, dismissing his horse and servant, he set off on foot to the Exchange, hoping that the walk might clear his head. Making his way down the thoroughfare of Bishopsgate he soon reached the city walls, but there, instead of passing through the gates and carrying on south towards the river, he struck off to his right towards Moorgate. This way, which he had been used to take during his apprentice days, would take him west along the old city walls, then south to St Paul's before doubling back along Cheapside and Lombard Street, to the Exchange.

On Paul's last return to London in 1600, the old Queen, cantankerous and penny-pinching in equal measure with her blackened gums and her wrinkled dugs, her face half-rotted with lead, lay not-quite-dying on her throne at Whitehall. In those days the Court was all but moribund, starved of funds, the city decimated by plague. But it had been apparent this time to Paul from the moment he stepped off the barge that had brought him and Celia from the Tilbury docks, that under the auspices of the new Scots king and his Danish queen the city was transformed. There was peace with Spain. There were new buildings everywhere. The very air was alive with energy and ideas.

Already he had plans to view Secretary Cecil's New Exchange in the Strand; and to take Celia to see the Queen's gardens at Somerset House and the great works on Prince Henry's palace at Richmond. But this way, along the old walls, took him through a city that was still much as he remembered it: the backstreet London of his apprenticeship days.

As he walked he passed a barefooted boy herding a flock of geese; a cart piled high with firewood; a woman with a churn of butter on her hip. A child, naked from the waist down, its face smeared with soot, came tumbling out from a makeshift shelter, and stood staring at him open-mouthed.

Paul tossed the child a coin, and walked on, hugging his cloak more closely to him. To his left were large houses and grounds of the well-to-do, much as he remembered them, chief among them the long walled garden and towers of the old Augustinian Friary, now a rich man's residence; but on the other side of the thoroughfare, pushed up against the walls were many more makeshift shacks, some no more than a few planks of wood tacked over with pieces of cloth. These he did not remember. Whole families up from the country with their old and their young, some shared their makeshift shelters with livestock. The air was foul with the stench of human ordure.

He found the old hiding place easily: the little secret staircase concealed behind the old midden at All Hallows-in-the-Wall. Even after all these years, the hole in the masonry was still there, the fall of stones that gave a good foothold if you knew your way around them, and then the staircase that led to a viewpoint on top of the wall itself. The climb was tighter than he remembered, but the stench was the same, acrid with pigeon and bat droppings. Brushing masonry dust from his shoulders, he emerged on top of the wall just as the sun was rising.

To one side of him, looking south, the whole of the great city of London lay before him. It had rained in the night and the air was clean and cold. As the sun rose a faint vapour came streaming from the city roofs, mingling with the wood smoke, which rose from chimneys in thin blue spires. The steeples of the churches, the flattened tower of St Paul's, and the gilded grasshoppers on the top of the Great Exchange all gleamed in the early morning sun.

But below him on the other side of the city walls, what a difference. The old Moor Field that he had known as a young man – the common ground where the city's washerwomen came to lay out their linen and the young men to set up their butts for archery practice – was no more. What had once been rolling green sward with a few scattered houses and orchards was almost entirely covered over with new buildings; the green fields crowded out by rows of upstart houses and gardens. Cows still grazed by the edge of the ditches, but whereas once there would have been nothing to break the pale golden furze of the autumn branches in orchards and gardens, there was now hardly a break in the rows of houses, until the white windmill sails of Finsbury Field on the distant horizon to the north.

Although it was still early, already he could feel the great city stirring; could hear the distant church bells tolling the hour, the rumble of carriage and cartwheels, the cries of the market sellers, the rip and flow of the muddy grey tide waters of the Thames, and the strange high-pitched call of its wherrymen; and at its very heart, the Exchange itself, Thomas Gresham's great bourse, humming and pulsing like the blood through his own veins.

The old apprentice hiding-hole at All Hallows-in-the-Wall was one of the places Paul had come looking the first time John Carew had gone missing. His father had written to him from the old place to say that the boy had run away, had left Priors Leaze in the dead of winter. He had been in some kind of fight; knives had been involved. The snow drifts on the hills and in the fields were three feet deep that year, the roads impassable. The most likely thing was that the boy was already dead, frozen solid in a ditch somewhere with half his face hanging off. Food for the crows. And they never did find him. But then, when almost a year had gone past, someone saw him, or thought they had, working the wherries on the river. And then again, some weeks later, at the playhouse in Southwark. His father had written to Paul a second time begging him to keep looking, although why all this trouble for a kitchen boy was anybody's guess.

Paul had found Carew eventually, not here, in the apprentices' hiding-hole, but south across the river, in some Southwark stew, wouldn't you know it, waiting tables and washing dishes for the landlady at the sign of the Blind Bear.

A bitter day in December.

Paul had taken in the dismal surroundings with one glance: the beaten earth floor, bare of either rushes or sawdust, the wormwood-eaten stools, the smell of stale beer and piss.

Through the centre of the room a small ditch ran with evil-looking effluence. A few old bottles, black and sticky with age, were lined up on a shelf behind the counter. Out of the corner of his eye he saw the edge of a woman's dress, a flash of scarlet, as a figure ran past the back door and up the stairs behind the counter. It was hard to imagine anyone could be so desperate for home comforts – for a drink or a fuck – that they would find their way in here. Apparently he was mistaken.

Although it was some years since he had seen Carew, Paul had recognised him at once – something about the dishevelled hair, the angle of the hip – standing at one of the tables with his back to him.

'Well, well, what d'you know.' Without preamble Paul had gone up behind him and seized him by the ears. 'If it isn't Dick Whittington himself.'

When the boy's feet were almost swinging off the ground, Paul let go of him so suddenly, and with a kind of shove, so that he fell forward and went sprawling into a table, cracking his head against the wall.

'They'll be making me Lord Mayor next year, hadn't you heard?' John Carew lay on the ground, rubbing his head, and then his ears, looking up without apparent resentment, or even surprise. 'Good day to you and all, Mr Paul.'

In the dreary light of the windowless room the boy seemed, if possible, even smaller and scrawnier than Paul remembered. A scar from a recent knife wound – the tissue pink and raw-looking as a newborn thing – ran from his cheekbone to the corner of his mouth.

'And what in God's name do you think are you doing here?'

'Aren't I the one who should be asking you that, Mr Paul?' The boy, unrepentant, looked up at him with a grin. 'But on second thoughts perhaps I won't.'

'Come here, you little bastard. . .' Paul aimed his boot at Carew, but the boy, who had always had an uncanny ability to avoid the blows and cuffs that so frequently came his way, ducked nimbly away out of his reach. 'Still got a lip on you I see.'

'Some lip!' The proprietress of the Blind Bear, vast and greasy-skinned, had been sitting behind the counter, sucking on a pipe. She had been watching this exchange silently, but now she let out a low wheezing laugh. 'Too right, sir, ee's got a lip on him a-right,' she observed. And then, jerking her chin in the boy's direction, 'Ee belong to you, do ee, the backhouse boy?'

'I wouldn't say that exactly.' Paul had answered her without looking round. 'But I'll be taking him with me, if it's all the same to you, madam.'

'Ee stolen something or what?' the landlady enquired with interest.

Paul, who had no intention of entering into conversation with such a person, did not reply. Instead, he gave Carew a stony look.

'Do you know how much trouble you've put me to? How many weeks I've spent. . . Oh, what's the use. Just get your things,' he said to him, stabbing his finger in the direction of the door out back. 'I'll wait for you here.'

Through the thin ceiling Paul could hear the sound of low laughter, and then a man's heavy tread on the dipping floorboards. The landlady followed his glance.

'You in the mood to keep company, sir? While you wait, I mean. You'll find nothing but prime Winchester Geese on my premises. I believe my Salley's waiting out back. She's ever such a quick worker, if you'll take my meaning.'

'Thank you kindly, madam, but I'd rather get the pox some other way.' Paul was in no mood for pleasantries.

'Suit yourself.' She took one of the bottles down from the shelf behind her. There was a hollow sound as the stopper was pulled from its neck. 'A little drink then, to take your mind off your troubles? This here's the very best porter,' she waved the bottle at him, 'keeps out the winter cold.'

'I'd rather drink wormwood.'

There was a pause while the landlady slopped a generous dram into a cup, drank it back.

'I can't pay no wages if he don't work out the week,' she said, smacking her lips thoughtfully.

'As you wish.'

Another pause.

'Are you the one what slashed 'im?'

'No.'

To this the woman said nothing. Instead, she made a little gesture, a quick jerk of her chin, signifying either disdain, or disbelief. Possibly both. It made the lappets of her several chins tremble like a turkeycock's. Paul turned away: the smell of her made his stomach turn.

'Nasty business, if you don't mind my saying so.'

Paul, who did mind her saying so, did not reply.

'Had to get the apothecary in the end,' she went on in her imperturbable way. 'No end of expense. Pus everywhere. Said he'd stitched it up his-self first time round, with a needle and thread, can you credit it?' Her hands hovered over the bottle. 'I took him in, though, didn't I?' There was a heavy pause. 'Like I said, sir, no end of expense.'

Paul, who finally understood her meaning, took out a coin and threw it on to the counter. 'Here, take that for your trouble.'

The woman picked up the coin with an expression of the utmost contempt, bit into it to test its metal, and then put it into her pocket. Her look was long-suffering. 'Must have been a good-looking lad before that.'

To Paul's silence, she poured herself another drink. The skin of her face – mottled purple and red – was stretched so tightly over her bones it resembled cat-skin on a drum.

'It's just. . . he may be trouble and all, but he's a good worker that one and. . .' There was a pause. 'And my girls. . .' She hesitated, the drink had made her loquacious, and now, he sensed with foreboding, was on the brink of being confidential. He hoped to God she would keep Carew's business to herself. Whatever he may have done, or not done – and who with – he really did not want to know. But whatever she was going to say she thought better of it.

'He's sharp, that one,' was all she said. 'Sharp as a box of knives.'

'Sharp? I'll give him sharp. For once I agree with you, madam. So sharp he'll cut himself one day.'

There was a pensive pause. 'Looks like ee's already gone and done that.'

When John Carew returned he was empty-handed.

'Where's your parcel?'

'Parcel?'

'Your things.'

John Carew looked faintly puzzled for a moment, then he grinned. 'I don't have no parcel, Mr Paul.'

'What, nothing at all?'

'No.'

'Then get your cloak.' Paul sighed with irritation. 'Get on with you, I haven't got all day.'

'Cloak?'

He might as well have asked him if he had the Crown jewels.

'That's what I said.' Paul twitched his own cloak, heavily lined with beaver fur, over one shoulder. 'And do you have to keep repeating everything I say?'

'Don't have no cloak, Mr Paul.'

Paul knew he must have had one once. Every year at Twelfth Night all the servants at the manor were given one as part of their livery. In the last few years he had been charged with buying the cloth himself, the best worsted. The boy must have sold it; well, that was his own lookout.

'So. . . you bought nothing at all from Priors Leaze?' It was taking him a while to process the fact that the boy had found his way all the way to London in the dead of winter, with only the shirt and doublet on his back.

John Carew, mistaking the stare, gave Paul a sheepish look.

'Well, there was just one thing.' He opened his jerkin to show a gleaming kitchen blade hanging on his belt. 'I reckoned I'd be a-right if I had a knife. It weren't stealing, I only borrowed it...' An anxious look passed over his face. 'You won't tell the old man, will you?'

'No, I won't tell the old man.' Wrapping his own cloak around him against the cold, Paul turned on his heels. 'So if you weren't collecting your parcel,' he said over his shoulder, 'what in God's own name took you so long?'

'Oh, you know.' The boy looked at him, and then grinned so widely he almost split his face in two, 'Just keeping company, sir.'

Outside the Blind Bear, the winter air was crisp, the sky piercingly blue. A light dusting of frost lay on the thatched roofs; glittering icicles hung from the gutters of the houses. Even the gargoyles on the Bishop of Winchester's palace were bearded with ice. The Southwark streets, normally ankle-deep in mud, were frozen solid. Carew ran ahead, stamping on the frozen puddles until the ice cracked and shattered. He jumped up to break icicles off the eaves. He moved constantly, restlessly, as though his limbs hardly belonged to him, as though it were an effort to keep still. Perhaps, Paul thought now, he had simply been trying to keep warm. At the time it had been like being buzzed by a bluebottle. What was it about Carew that always made you want to swat him like a fly?

'Where to now, Mr Paul?' John Carew did not seem unduly perturbed by the idea, just mildly curious. 'You sending me back to the manor?'

'That depends.'

'Depends on what?'

Paul thought for a moment.

'Depends on what you are good at,' he began, and then, taking one look at the boy's face, put his hand up quickly. 'No, forget I said that. I don't want to know.'

The truth was that Paul had no idea what he was going to do with him. It was only now that he had found him at last that Paul realised that his father had not sent instructions about what to do with him next. It looked as though he was stuck with him, or that they were stuck with each other, for the time being anyhow.

'How old are you now, John?'

'Couldn't rightly say, sir. Old enough.' Another grin.

Paul did some quick calculations. The boy must have been about six, or thereabouts, when his father had first brought him to live with them at Priors Leaze, and that had been in the year when Paul had first come to London to be apprenticed. Now, five years later, Paul's apprentice-ship was complete and he was working for the Venetian Merchant Parvish as a factor in his own right. So that, including the year that John'd been missing, would make him about twelve, although his small, malnourished body made him look more like a feral child of nine or ten.

'Can you cook?'

The boy shrugged. 'I can use a knife.'

'What happened to your cheek?'

'What, this?' He put his hand up, fingered the scar as though surprised to find it was still there.

'Did my brother Ralph have anything to do with it?'

Paul had not meant to say anything about Ralph, but somehow he found that the words were out anyway. The boy, leaping and bounding on ahead of him, did not turn around.

'Couldn't rightly say, sir.' The boy's breath condensed in the freezing air. The sky above them was as blue as a blackbird's egg.

They had come to the top of an alleyway at the far end of which Paul could just see the distant glitter of the river. The way here was so narrow that two people could hardly pass along it. The tops of the houses almost touched one another. He guessed this to be a short cut to the bridge.

'Is that so?' Paul had turned to walk down it, and began picking his way over the uneven ground. 'And what else couldn't you rightly say?'

The boy made no reply to this. Instead, Paul found himself taken gently by the elbow.

'Not that way, Mr Paul. That's where they throw out the slops. You'll get yourself all dirty, all that fur and fine velvet and all.' The boy's hand on Paul's quilted sleeve was red and raw with cold. 'Put your foot here... and there... that's it. Quite the gentleman now, ain't yer?'

Paul gave him a sharp look, but one glance at Carew's face told him that there was no mischief intended by the remark. If anything there was something like pride in his voice.

'We'll go by the Bearhouse. Road's better. And there's someone there I'd like to say goodbye to, if it's all the same to you.'

'That woman, the one at the Blind Bear—'

'Old Ma? Ma Kettle?'

'That's the one. She said she had to send for the apothecary to stitch you up.'

'Ma Kettle? Send for an apothecary?'

'Why? Is that such a merry idea?'

'Oh no, sir, not at all.' The boy looked at him without expression. 'Good thing I came back when I did though,' he said, wiping his eye with the corner of a filthy sleeve. 'Mind you, a shrewd gentleman such as yourself would never fall for one of Old Ma's tricks. Anyone else and she'd have had them pressing a grateful shilling on her before you could say Whittington's Dick.'

In the end Paul never did send John Carew back to Priors Leaze. Even with the boy's unusual powers of survival, so long as Ralph was still there he might not be so lucky the next time. So instead he stayed with Paul, on and off, for the next twenty years.

Paul read the letter from Priors Leaze through one last time. Once again he asked himself, what had possessed him to write to Ralph. When he put the letter down, another memory came to him unbidden, a memory that had lain undisturbed for many years.

He had been in Constantinople with John Carew, on the wall of the ambassador's house looking down over the Golden Horn. The ambassador, Sir Henry Lello, had expressly forbidden anyone to sit on the wall but Carew, naturally, was sitting there anyway. Lounging. Hair unkempt. Scowling. The person, Paul realised, that after Celia and his father he had come to love best in the world.

He had been cracking nuts, Paul remembered, those salty green nuts the Ottomans were so fond of, which they called *pistach*. As usual he was in trouble: there had been some *contretemps* with the ambassador's own cook, some kitchen brawl – yet another – he had forgotten the details. With Carew there was always trouble of some kind.

'If the ambassador sees you here, Carew, after he expressly—'

'Lello can go hang.'

'You'll hang first, my friend,' he had replied, 'I've always said so.'

And now, more than ten years later, to his own amazement, Paul put his head in his hands and wept.

EIGHT

Paul

Bishopsgate.

I T WAS NOON BEFORE Paul finally reached the Exchange, Gresham's great bourse at the top of Lombard Street. On the steps he spied Parvish immediately, deep in conversation with a group of fellow merchants. He ran lightly up the steps to join them.

'What news?'

The merchants looked up when they saw him approach. There was a brief uncomfortable hush. And then:

'Well, by the saints, if it isn't Merchant Pindar,' said one jovially.

He did not actually say 'speak of the Devil' but the words hovered in the air.

'We were just quizzing Mr Parvish about you, and he was telling us what he could.'

'We hear you are just back from Aleppo.'

'And home safely, Pindar, God be praised. We are most glad to have you back among us.'

This last merchant, a man from the Muscovy Company, had small eyes, round and black as abacus beads, and a swift, calculating gaze that swept over Paul, measuring him out like a bolt of worsted. Paul could almost hear the beads clicking.

'And looking so prosperous.' He inclined his head in Paul's direction, 'God be praised.'

'God be praised,' the others murmured their assent.

'He is indeed, God be praised.' Paul felt Parvish's gaze on him too. 'Home safe after ten long years.'

Breaking ranks, the group of merchants crowded round. Some of the younger ones jostled at the back. With their hairless chins, their faces as round and fresh as schoolboys, to Paul they seemed hardly more than boys.

'A spring in your step this morning, Merchant Pindar.'

'What news from Antwerp, sir?'

'Or, should we say, what *curiosities*?'

Stifled laughter came from the back.

'And when can we see your great diamond, Pindar? Is it true His Majesty wants to buy it?'

'But that you won't sell?'

'Is it true that it is cursed?'

'They say that you have determined to give it to your brother.'

'That he is determined to have it at any price—'

'And if you won't sell that he will take it from you.'

The older merchants turned around and tried to hush them. They pulled their beards and looked grave.

'We hear you have opened up your great mansion in Bishopsgate—'

'And that your family is much visited there—'

'We hear your wife is quite the fashion—' a third, more strident than the other two, chimed in from the back.

Paul answered them as best he could, but was not sorry when Parvish, putting his hand between Paul's shoulders, swept him deftly past the little group and into the Exchange. As they stepped inside, the noise, that could be heard only as a curious and steady hum from the steps, erupted into a cacophony of voices.

Three hundred or more merchants were crammed together beneath its roof. Some stood in groups discussing the business of the day on the trading floor; others were sitting at their counting tables, long trestles arranged in rows around the sides of the room among piles of teetering ledgers. Secretaries stood behind them, sharpening quills, grinding ink stones, making careful piles of trading slips and promissory notes. Apprentices ran in and out bringing midday sustenance: flat breads and roasted capons, hot drinks from the alehouse. Stray dogs wandered in and out, quarrelling over the bones. There was the sound of *getons* scraping across the wood, the furious clack of abacus beads. Every so often a shout went up. The merchants wheeled and turned together on the trading floor; they waved their arms, their black sleeves and mantles flapping like a murmuration of starlings.

Together Parvish and Paul made a round of the colonnades. It was less noisy away from the traders, but not greatly so. All manner of tradesmen were selling their wares. There were booksellers, purveyors of clocks and watches and navigational instruments. Their progress was stately. Parvish, who no longer came to the Exchange with any great frequency, nonetheless had a large acquaintance, and it was his pleasure to greet them all.

In among them Paul found many of his own acquaintance, too. Some were old friends, colleagues from the Levant Company and the former Venice Company; others he recognised only vaguely, faces he recalled from twenty years ago, once shivering young apprentices like himself with holes in their boots, now grown stout, red-faced and velvet-coated with prosperity.

With each group they stood and talked for a while. With one they discussed the price of wool and the falling value of cinnamon and cloves; with another, the expected arrival of a consignment of cotton cloth from India; with a third, a shipwreck in the Azores.

Gossip about the new court was on everyone's lips. His Majesty had spent more than £1,000 at the goldsmiths and gem dealers in the last fortnight, while his son, Prince Henry, for all his youth, was making a court around him so magnificent that the King's nose was out of joint. It was widely believed that there was no love lost between them.

In the days of the old Queen, young men had flocked to court, flattering and flirting their way to preferment, and it seemed that not much had changed under the auspices of the new. King James, they said, looked coldly upon women, even pretty ones, and preferred fresh-faced young men. Robert Carr – Viscount Rochester as he now was – was the King's special friend, his favourite. There was no scandal attached to his friendship with Carr. Or not yet.

There was a rumour that he was to be created a Knight of the Garter, when he was only made a viscount five minutes ago; and much speculation as to the fate of Secretary Cecil who, the whisper went, had now leveraged himself so deeply with the city merchants it could only end in ruin.

'Alas for Cecil, what will become of him?'

'The hunchback? Don't waste your time.'

'They say he owes more money than he can ever repay.'

'Some say he's sickening—'

'Shrivelling up, and like to die—'

'Everything except his hunch, that is.'

'The hunch gets bigger every day.'

'Someone should pickle him,' said the Muscovy merchant with a sly look towards Paul and Parvish. 'Put him in Merchant Parvish's cabinet.'

There was a shout of general laughter

Paul moved away, the sound of their merriment still in his ears. He stopped at a stall belonging to a silk merchant, John of Morocco. Sample bolts of brilliant coloured tissue were piled to the ceiling. Paul spoke to the Moor in Ottoman, but found himself slipping into Arabic, the tongue that he found easier after seven years in Aleppo. And Parvish also, greeting two Venetian traders, lapsed into his native tongue. Two women in masks hurried past. A couple of stray curs quarrelled over a bone.

At the far end of the colonnades they stopped again at a bookseller's where Parvish had a commission. Paul settled in to wait for him. Parvish, he knew from long experience, had an oriental disregard for time when it came to his library or his cabinet. He would have liked to look at the books himself but today his heart was not in it; his mind was still full of Ralph's letter.

Paul picked the books up idly from the table, turning them over in his hands and running his fingers expertly over them, opening them to test the quality of their bindings, allowing himself to be soothed by the grain of their leather, the glimmer of tooled gold. He found a second-hand copy of Gerard's *Herball, or Generall Historie of Plantes*, annotated by the previous owner in spidery brown ink; Abraham Ortelius's *Theatrum Orbis Terrarum*; an edition of Coryate's *Crudities* in sleek calfskin.

As he perused the bookseller's tray Paul became aware of two young men walking past. He had half an idea that these were the same fellows whom he had seen sauntering back and forth past him several times already. He looked up from the books, and as he did so they raised their hats to him, but the gesture, it struck him, was exaggerated, devoid of courtesy.

Fancy a game of primero, *Pindar?*

Paul looked up again, more sharply this time. Could they really have said that, or was he imagining it? The two were looking back over their shoulders at him, as though to see if the barb had struck home. Scrutinising them more carefully he saw that they were not merchants; their dress announced them as men of independent means, young aristocrats perhaps, young men of fashion. They wore high-crowned hats and doublets of tawny chamois stamped with gillyflowers in gold leaf; their short velvet cloaks were lined with crimson silk; and there were roses of outlandish size on their shoes.

Fancy a game of primero, *Pindar?* The first young man's voice was low, no more than a whisper. *I hear they play it at the Mermaid's Head.*

At your wife's head, Pindar, the second had whispered at him. *But I'll wager she was no maid when you married her.*

He felt a hand on his shoulder. 'A word in your ear, Pindar.'

He looked around to see the Muscovy merchant with the calculating eyes at his side. He leant towards Paul ingratiatingly.

'They say His Majesty is much interested to see the great diamond,' he said in a low voice, 'but I am charged to tell you that His Highness, Prince Henry, would pay more.'

'The stone is not for sale,' Paul said, annoyed by the man's manner. 'I thought that much was well known?'

'Everyone has their price.'

Paul looked at him coldly. 'But the stone does not. Good day to you, sir.'

NINE

Paul

Lime Street.

L ATER, PAUL WALKED PARVISH down Cheapside
to his house on Lime Street.

'Something is troubling you, my boy.' The old merchant's
stick tapped on the ground. 'I know you too well.'

Paul explained briefly about his attempts to find Carew.

'Carew? No longer with you?'

'I did tell you, sir, but you have forgot,' Paul said to
the old man gently. 'I wrote to you to say that he did not
come to Aleppo with us, do you not recall? I left him
in Venice. Or he left us. I can never quite remember
which.'

'So you quarrelled, *hn*? Not again.'

'Not this time. Not exactly. There was a girl.'

'There was always a girl.'

'This one was different. Or so he would have us believe.'

'Is that so?'

'It gets better. She was a nun. He wanted to marry her.'

'A nun of Venice?' The old man gave a snort of laughter.
'Ah, this is why I always liked John Carew. He is better
than your comedy at the playhouse.'

'The nun caught the plague.'

'*Ah*. A tragedy then.'

'But then she recovered, or so we are told. But by the time this became known to us, Carew had disappeared. A comedy of errors, if ever there was one. For a long time we thought he must be dead. But of course it turns out that he was not after all so obliging.'

'*Dio buono*. I don't know what you would call this?'

'A tragi-comedy, perhaps. The nun herself is on her way here to find him. It seems she never took full orders.'

'But you'll take him back again, of course. You must. You always do.'

'I've had a letter from my brother Ralph, from Priors Leaze. He says he has not been seen there. After all these years he thinks Carew must be dead.'

'Nonsense! That *scapestrato* is like a cat, he has at least nine lives.'

'I have to go to the old place myself, Parvish. I have delayed too long already. My father is very frail now, and I have to see for myself that Carew is not there. Maybe he went there and has now left again. The people will talk to me, as they might not to my brother. There might be things I can find out that he has not troubled about. The fact is I don't trust Ralph – there is too much bad blood between them.'

'All in good time, my boy, all in good time.'

'You don't understand, I don't think this matter can wait—'

'But wait it must,' Parvish answered him serenely. 'You must attend the next high council meeting.'

'I am very much afraid the elders will have to wait a while longer. I *must* go—'

'I do most strongly advise against it, my boy, most *strongly*.' Parvish's walking stick tapped a little faster against the cobbles. 'As their former consul in Aleppo so recently returned, they will expect you to be there, and it will give grave offence if you are not – and on what they will think of as so slight a pretext. There is something I should mention to you, but I tell it you in the strictest confidence, *hn*? Your name has mentioned among us as the next ambassador to the Sublime Porte—'

'Have pity, I have not yet been home a month.'

'Not immediately, but in the future. It is not an honour to be thrown away lightly. Come, the meeting is only a matter of weeks away, surely there is nothing so urgent that it can't wait until then?'

They were now approaching Lime Street. At the sight of the old merchant returning home, a group of urchins, playing at knuckles on the street corner, shouted to one another, scattering out of his path like sparrows. Some pebbles flew through the air; one glanced off Parvish's back, and then another from his cap.

A small boy was sitting on a doorstep nearby, chewing on a piece of grimy bread. As Parvish reached up to put his key in the lock, his mother, covering her face with a shawl, darted from the doorway opposite and snatched him up. Above them, a window slammed shut.

'What's this, Parvish?' Paul was astonished. 'Your neighbours throw stones at you?'

'*Ach*, pay no attention.' Parvish shrugged, but Paul felt the old man's fingers grip his arm more tightly.

'On the contrary, let me find them and give them a good whipping.'

'Leave them be. *Sonno le ragazzi*, they are just boys.'

'*Ragazzi* who should be taught a good lesson.' Paul looked up, trying to find the source of the flying pebbles. 'They don't favour strangers here?'

'This is Lime Street,' Parvish said flatly. 'We are all strangers here.'

At Parvish's house the old courtesies were still observed. A woman servant greeted them with a basin and a ewer of rose-water, which she poured over their fingers. As she helped Parvish with his fur-collared greatcoat, Paul looked around. He took in the tooled-leather wall coverings, a little scratched now, the low ceilings and the narrow twisting staircase which led to Parvish's cabinet on the first floor. There were bowls of potpourri in the window enclaves, and a pervasive smell of dried rose petals, a little dusty now, laced with spices, cinnamon and cloves. The smell of the past. Parvish sent his servant for wine, and together he and Paul made their way upstairs.

Parvish's cabinet was exactly as Paul remembered it. A long low room on the first floor of the house in Lime Street, every inch of which was crammed with objects. On shelves along the walls there were densely packed boxes of shells and corals and crustaceans, arranged according to size and colour; compartments full of coloured stones, and yet others of dried plants, seeds, tree bark, and strange-shaped pods. Paul read the labels, familiar to him from his apprenticeship days: *Ligna, Radices, Conchiliata, Animalum Partes, Mariana, Lapides, Mineralia, Salia, Fructus, Metallica.*

Against the wall at the far end of the room was a display case containing a collection of coins and medallions and lucky charms; facing it, at the other end of the room, stood its companion piece in which were arranged birds' heads, beaks, feathers, a shimmering display of iridescent insect carapaces, another of animal teeth and jaws. The ceiling too was hung with objects, shields made from sharkskin, feathers, tooled leather, and tortoise and armadillo shells. There were garments too: some made entirely of fur, others decorated extravagantly with feathers, or stitched over with intricate patterns of pearls and seeds.

'I see that our honourable merchants weren't jesting.' Paul took the glass of wine that Parvish offered him.

'How so?'

'The only thing missing from your cabinet is the Secretary Cecil's hunchback.'

'Think you?' Parvish sat down heavily in his chair.

'And they enjoy their almanac-discourse every bit as much as they did when I was last at home,' Paul added, taking a mouthful of wine. 'A most excellent malmsey, if I may say so.'

The old merchant did not answer immediately, but sat silently for a few moments, his eyes on the ground, his wine untasted.

'But do they really have to let every last apprentice on to the steps these days?'

'*Hn!* Those boys are no longer apprentices, just behave like them.'

'And the others?'

'Well, what did you expect? There is more gossip among our honourable merchants than your washerwomen at the village well.'

Paul remembered the casual insolence of the two young men at the Exchange – *Fancy a game of* primero, *Pindar? I hear they play it at the Mermaid's Head. At your wife's head, Pindar. But I'll wager she was no maid when you married her* – wondered briefly whether to tell Parvish, and decided against it. He swirled the wine in his glass. Well, what had he expected? The old courtesies perhaps. Not to have his private business flapped in his face like so much dirty linen every time he stepped outside his own door. Something like that.

'I gather I am quite the fashion,' he said instead, hoping to turn the conversation. He held the glass to his lips and took a sip of wine, felt the liquid burn in his throat.

'Oh?' Parvish, putting his fingertips together, regarded Paul gravely.

'*Oh*? Is that all you can say?'

'What they mean is. . .' Parvish searched for the right words, 'that your wife – that Celia – is much visited.'

Paul took a second small sip of wine. He held the beaker up to the light for a moment.

'She is much visited, it's true,' he said, observing how the glass was marvellously blown with delicate spirals: they circled, milky white, against the clear glass. He had not seen any workmanship so fine as this since he left Venice and he wondered vaguely where Parvish procured them. 'I am told that your married women enjoy that kind of thing.'

Parvish's expression was inscrutable. He wondered whether Paul was aware of the scandal surrounding his household; decided that he was not. 'I believe it is your wife who is the fashion.'

'Celia?' Paul's look of surprise gave way to a laugh. 'Celia has become the fashion?'

Parvish raised his glass slowly to his lips; for a few moments allowed Paul's question to hang unanswered in the air between them. How blind we are to those things that are closest to us; how oblivious to that which is happening beneath our very noses.

'Ladies of fashion visit her. Ladies of the court. They say she is to be invited there. That the Queen herself wishes to see her. Will soon send for her. Is that what you want?'

But Paul seemed not to hear him.

Celia the *fashion*? The very idea of it was an absurdity. In the old Queen's time they did not have such things as *fashions*. . . Paul caught himself, almost smiled. *Christos*, what was happening to him? He was beginning to sound like Parvish.

'Not quite.'

Parvish was sitting back in his chair; he must speak now, he knew he must.

'I can see that you have been gone from us too long.' He eyed Paul thoughtfully. 'At the Exchange there is a. . .' He waved his hand in the air, spread his fingers, searching for the right words, '. . .a perception – that if Celia is the fashion it is the much married widow – the Widow Sydenham – who has made her that way.'

To this, Paul at first said nothing.

'Frances believes it is good for her to have visits,' he said carefully after a while.

'Frances?'

'That is indeed her name.'

'I do not need to know her *name*!' Parvish almost shuddered. To a man of his generation the use of the Widow Sydenham's Christian name was almost obscene in its familiarity. 'I did not know you had taken the lady so far into your confidence.'

'She – we – think that it will bring Celia out of her—' For a moment Paul was going to say *bring her out of her shell*, but at the last minute he managed to shy away from such a marine allusion. 'Bring her out of herself.'

'I see.' Parvish nodded, more pensively this time.

At the Exchange, he was thinking, they believe something else altogether. At the Exchange there was even a rumour – exaggerated he had no doubt – that Lady Sydenham was actually charging for the entrée. If the truth be told, Celia was not so much the fashion as a curiosity. A figure in a raree-show, like a giraffe or a two-headed baby, put on display in Lady Sydenham's closet.

But for the moment he said none of these things. Instead, he put cold fingertips to his eyes. Points of light dazzled and danced in the darkness. For Parvish, whose own cabinet of curiosities was one of the wonders of London, there were so many ironies to this twist in Celia's fortunes that it made his head hurt just to think about them.

For a while the two men – the old merchant and his former apprentice – sat together in silence.

Well, Parvish was thinking now, *I have done what I can. I am absolved. Perhaps, indeed, it will all be to their benefit in the end, to come to the attention of their Majesties.* Perhaps Paul had known all along what he was about. Experience had taught him that he usually did. It occurred to Parvish, not for the first time, that perhaps preferment at Court was what Paul was playing for, and that his eyes had been open all along to this new twist in his fortunes. It seemed more like the kind of game his brother Ralph might play – not really Paul's style at all, but who was he to judge? And if that were the case then he, Parvish, should keep his peace, and not interfere further. Although, then again, if even half of what he had heard was true, it seemed so... unnecessary.

Parvish sighed. Really, he was getting old for this kind of thing. *Come, come, these are women's matters. Enough.* They should be discussing the real business of the day. Parvish opened his mouth to ask about the latest news from Antwerp, whether Paul had shown his new stones to the London gem dealer, Cornelius Lull; anything, in fact, to change the subject. Instead he heard himself say, 'Talk to me, Paul. You have never talked about it. It has been seven years since Celia was found. Talk to me.'

'I—' Paul opened his mouth, but he found suddenly that he could not go on. 'She—'

Suddenly he had no words – sometimes he thought that there were no words – to describe what had happened. For a moment he feared memory would unman him. He leant forward; put his face in his hands.

He remembered the day they found Celia. It had been on the lagoon front in Venice. He could see it now: the gondola coming towards him through the mist. How often had he repeated it in his mind's eye? The sight of it was seared into his brain. There were two people sitting in the gondola, which came floating slowly towards him.

The *primero* game was over. He had won the Sultan's Blue, the diamond that ransomed Celia, and then lost it again at the flip of a coin, but somehow it had found its way back to him. The black gondola had emerged like a ghost ship. Sitting in the rain, in the deserted *piazza* beside the lagoon, he held the stone in his hand: the diamond on which he had gambled his entire fortune. He had not slept for two nights and three days. He hardly knew who he was any more, could barely speak his own name. He was but a shadow of what he had once been. And yet somehow, in his madness, as he sat soaked through to the skin on the lagoon side, he saw the gondola approaching. And at some point he had become aware that the man standing on the prow of the boat was not just any boatman, but his own John Carew. And the woman... at first he had not seen who the woman was. She was sitting at his feet, wrapped in a cloak. The mist eddied and swirled about her, obscuring her face, but somehow he knew, in the very deepest part of himself, who she was. He would have known her anywhere. It was a ghost. It was Celia.

It can't be – he heard his own voice. *Please God...*
But it was.
And she was calling to him. Calling out his name.
And he was falling to his knees in the rain.

⫷⫸

When Paul took his hands away from his face, his eyes were dry. What did the Greeks call love? A kind of madness. Perhaps it was true.

Be careful what you wish for.

He looked up and saw that Parvish was still contemplating him over his fingertips.

'Seven years, Paul. Tell me what happened.'

Paul did not answer him. Instead he stood up with a decided air. 'Show them to me, Parvish. I want to see them.'

The old man looked up at him, but made no move.

'Show me your cabinet, Parvish.'

'You have seen my cabinet, Paul, many times.'

Their conversation was slow, like a dream.

'No, not lately.'

Paul held out his hand to the old man, but Parvish did not take it. Indeed, he seemed to shrink from him, sink still further into the folds of his fur collar.

'I'd like to see the cabinet.'

'You are looking at it.' Parvish gestured to the shelves that lined the room. 'You see it all around you. My coins, my birds' beaks, my strange and curious animals. A crocodile from Egypt. The elephant's tail. Oh, and did I tell you about my unicorn horn? Let me show it you –'

'You know my meaning,' Paul interrupted him. 'Children do not run from you in the street because of your coins and crocodiles, Parvish. They do not throw stones at your shadow, or snatch their infants out of your path because of your shells and birds' beaks. I mean your other cabinet. The secret cabinet.'

'Would that be wise—?' Parvish began, but Paul was not in the mood to be deflected.

'I want to see them, Parvish; I *need* to see them.'

When he saw that Paul was determined, the old merchant rose stiffly to his feet. He put a hand on Paul's shoulder.

'My boy. . .' he said sadly, slipping into the speech of long ago. 'If you are sure? If you are really sure?'

'Quite sure.'

Parvish inclined his head. 'Then so be it.'

He went to a recess in one of the walls, put his hand up to find the catch. When he pushed against it, there was a small click, and one of the panels in the wall swung silently ajar.

TEN

Paul

Lime Street.

A T FIRST ALL PAUL could make out of the room
beyond was a darkened space.

Although he could not see very clearly, he could feel it
at once. The air in the room had a different quality from
the one in which they had been sitting. It was denser,
somehow, and damper, like an underground place, a cellar,
or a tomb. A curious smell emanated from the interior,
reminding him of something he could not quite put his
finger on: an alchemist's laboratory, perhaps? But no, that
was not it. And then it came to him: the smell was like that
of an anatomist's workshop he had once visited in Padua.

Parvish was standing in the doorway. Behind him, Paul
could now see the hidden room, a space no bigger than
the smallest closet, dark and lined with shelves: Parvish's
secret cabinet.

The shelves were stacked with jars: glass amphora,
such as you might find in an apothecary shop. Inside the
jars there were objects that might, or might not, be piles
of bones. For a moment he thought that Parvish was
going to stop him from entering, but he did not. Instead,
he went in ahead of Paul, walked to the window, and
opened the shutters.

The late-afternoon sun came streaming in, piercing the glass jars and sprinkling them with silvery light, so that their contents were suddenly illuminated. Only then was Paul able to make out what the jars contained.

At first he thought they must be asleep, so peaceful did they appear. Some had their arms still wrapped around each other, their heads pressed together. Others lay head to tail, fitting snugly together like pieces in a children's puzzle. One was turned slightly inward as though he were whispering to his brother; another had a hand half raised to his mouth, as though sucking his thumb. Their tiny faces, nearly human, stared out at him sightlessly; half-formed hands, delicate as ferns, pressed up against the glass.

Paul put his hand up to the glass as though to touch one of the little hands, to trace the line of a face. His hand shook. One body, two heads. One head, two faces. A skull monstrously swollen to twice the size of a body. A tiny baby, with his even tinier twin, growing like an incubus from its chest. In the silvery light they seem to float in space and time, creatures from some other world.

For a moment they stood in silence.

'Where did you get them?' Paul said eventually.

'From midwives, mostly. They know of my. . . interest.'

'And they bring them to you?'

'Yes, they bring them here.'

Paul turned back to the jars. His mouth felt dry. He peered up against the glass. 'But you have someone who preserves them first?'

'I work with an apothecary. He is highly skilled.'

'Then I congratulate him. They look. . .' He searched for the words, '. . . as though they do but sleep.'

Parvish gave a small bow of acknowledgement.

'What does he use?'

'Bitumen. Pitch. A mixture of different minerals, there are so many more available now than there were.' Parvish shrugged, 'But it is an inexact science. To tell the truth, it doesn't always work.'

'Nonetheless the results are... remarkable.'

There was another silence.

'What became of the mothers?'

'Dead.' Parvish tucked his hands into his sleeves. 'At least I believe that most of them are.'

'And the families... do they not want to bury these little ones? Do our priests not claim them?'

'Your priests?' Parvish looked as though he had tasted something sour. 'Your priests say that these creatures are against nature. They do not allow that these children should ever have been born, far less baptised. There is no consecrated ground for them.'

'They are in limbo then?'

'Limbo? *Hn*! Even that is not allowed them. Your priests say there is no place at all for creatures such as these.'

'What, have they no souls?' Paul said, his expression stricken.

'They are lost souls,' Parvish said gently. 'They do not belong here. At least, that is what your priests would have us believe.'

'And you, Parvish. What do you believe?'

Parvish thought for a long moment before he replied.

'I believe that it is very natural to be afraid of what we do not understand, but I also believe that not understanding is the beginning of knowledge. Confusion is the beginning of wisdom: is that not what the ancients tell us? We should not look away from these creatures; rather, we should look at them more closely, try to understand why they are as they are,' he hesitated, 'at least, that is what I have come to believe.'

Paul was still contemplating the creatures inside the jars. 'They look as though they are dreaming.'

He put his hand to the glass of one of the jars again, traced it across the child's face. Its tiny hand was perfect, like an unfurled bud, and for one moment he had the idea that the infant was reaching out to him, to close its little fist around his finger. He imagined that gossamer touch against him, lighter than a butterfly wing.

Parvish was watching him sadly. 'There is nothing to be afraid of, my boy—' he began.

'Afraid? No! You misunderstand me.' In the half-light, Paul looked old suddenly. 'It is not *these* I am afraid of—'

He went to the window and looked down over the garden below. When he had first come to Parvish's house as a green apprentice of seventeen, the place had seemed so large. Now, more than twenty-five years later, everything appeared to him almost absurdly small and old-fashioned. The ceilings were too low, the staircases rickety. The capacious garden of his memory was a mere pocket handkerchief of green, crammed awkwardly between high walls. Like the house, it seemed not to have changed at all since he had first come here as a boy. There were the same lavender hedges, the same raised beds of coloured earth. There was even an old bowling green, now covered in moss, although it must be twenty years at least since anyone played there. Walls of red brick were covered with espaliered fruit trees, their trunks speckled with lichen. Come the summer he knew exactly what flowers would be growing here: sweet william, marigolds, pinks.

There had been rain, and the sweet, innocent smell of the garden triggered a sudden memory: it was in this garden that he had met Celia for the first time, Tom Lamprey's girl, the daughter of a sea captain. His memory reached out to her: a slender young woman, her reddish-gold hair shining like tarnished sunlight, eyes the colour of the sea. He could see her now – could see them both – but only faintly, as figures in a distant landscape.

Resting his forehead against the window casement, Paul put his hand up, covering his eyes for a moment.

'Celia wants a child, but I can't give it to her.'The words were out before he could stop them.

'But she is your wife,' Parvish said, puzzled. 'That she wants another child is as it should be. And besides,' he almost smiled, 'how can you prevent it?'

'Celia is my wife. . .' Paul struggled with the words, '. . .and yet she is not my wife.'

To this, for a long moment, the old man said nothing. The air in the room between them seemed heavy with what he did not say, with the questions that he did not ask. Paul felt as though there was something pressing down on his chest, a weight so heavy he could hardly breathe.

'But you. . .? Surely?' Parvish began hesitantly. 'At least sometimes?'

'No.'

There was a pause.

'No?'

'No, I have never known her.'

'In seven years?'

'In seven years.'

Again, Parvish said nothing.

Paul looked out on to the garden again, and this time it was a long while before he spoke, but when he did so at last the words came rapidly.

'When Celia made her escape from Constantinople, a terrible violence was done to her. She was violated by one of the men – by several of them in all likelihood – men whom until then she had believed to be her saviours. She does not remember it clearly, thank the Lord. The result was damage – a great deal of damage – to her woman's parts. But she is healed of that now. I have always told her that this was the reason... that I feared to hurt her. But the truth is... the truth, Parvish, is a far darker thing.

'You say "don't be afraid", but the truth is, I am afraid, Parvish. I am afraid that she will give birth to another one of these...' He pointed to the creatures sleeping in their jars.

'The result of that violence was a child. But you know all this, all of London knows it. My wife gave birth to a monster. A child with a human body and a fish's tail. A mermaid baby.

'When they found her, in some godforsaken place, they thought that neither she nor... it... was likely to live, but it did. It lived just long enough for every collector to be running after it. Including yours, Parvish,' Paul said bitterly. 'Ambrose Jones! Whatever happened to Ambrose?'

'Ambrose is dead.' Parvish made a movement with his hand, as though pushing the thought aside. 'And besides how was he to know? How were any of us to know?' Then he carried on quickly, 'The priests say that these creatures are monsters, but I do not believe it is so. We call contrary to nature what happens contrary to custom, but nothing can be *anything* but according to nature; how could it be otherwise?' He put his hand on Paul's shoulder. 'Whatever, or whoever, it may be.'

Paul turned again to the window. Outside in the garden the afternoon light was fading. Somewhere, hidden among the apple trees, a blackbird cried out its brief, piercing evening call. And the sound of the blackbird, and the red-brick garden walls, and the lavender beds, and fallen apples, and the memories of Celia and his own seventeen-year-old apprentice self, became merged, and for one utterly intense, pure, moment he experienced what it was to be home, to be connected to this place, to England, the land of his birth. For that same moment he became again the person that he had once been – a young man in love, sitting in a garden – and not the stranger that he had become, a person he did not recognise.

He tried to turn his thoughts to Celia again, but somehow he could not hold her there. Each time he tried, she seemed to slip away from him, and all he could see was Frances Sydenham, her naked body stretched out beside him.

ELEVEN

The Feast Day of St Eustace, 12th day of October, 1611.
Events occurring near the Priors Leaze Manor in
the country of Wiltshire.

I T WAS DUSK WHEN he came to the crest of the hill.
Although it was a dark day and the light was fading
fast, he saw at once that it was the place he had been
looking for. Ahead of him the pathway forked. Dropping
away on one side was the Drover's Path they had told him
about, a walkway disappearing into the nape of the hill,
so ancient that it had been ground down deep into the
hill. The entrance was so overhung with branches and
vines that it appeared more like a tunnel than any ordinary pass. On the other side, to his right, rose the lip of a
small escarpment. Scrambling up its bank, the man pulled
himself to the top and looked over.

Beneath him through a clearing in the trees the valley
was spread out like a map; he could see a distant patch-
work of small fields and pastures, yellowish brown, fading
to dark. The small squat tower of a little church. Orchards
and a tithe barn. Lights, very faint, glinted from the
windows of a small manor house, reflected off black water
from what might be a either a moat or a small lake, but at
this distance it was hard to tell which.

He had arrived there just in time. It was dusk now – owl light – and white limewash in between the half-timbered walls gleamed as though with a faint iridescence, like sea spume.

'This it, then?' Moocher, who had been standing behind him all this while, called up.

The man did not answer, and so Moocher, with much jangling, heaved himself up behind him on to the escarpment edge. A big man was old Moocher, in his queer rat-skin coat, and cumbersome too. Pots and pans, and a jumble of strange implements, cages and traps made from carefully sprung willow, hung from him like mummers' props on an assortment of leather buckles and pieces of threadbare string.

'This it, then?' he repeated, his voice wheezy from the exertion. 'This the place you bin looking for?'

But still his companion said nothing.

'Don't say much, do ye?' Moocher said, half to himself. He turned and spat reflectively over his shoulder. ''Bout time, if you axe me.' He sniffed the air with something of the knowledgeable air of a dog or a wild beast. 'Frost tonight.'

For a few moments the two stood together looking down over the darkening valley, and the little moated manor house beneath them.

The air was cold as a stone.

The shadows in the valley grew longer, but still the man seemed reluctant to move. On the horizon, the pale disc of a hunter's moon had begun to rise.

'What's this place called, then?' Moocher pulled his coat more closely round him.

'Priors Leaze. Priors Leaze Manor.' The man spoke without turning.

'You bin here before, then?'

'I didn't say that.'

There was another silence. Moocher, who was beginning to feel the chill in the air, shifted heavily from one foot to the other. His boots creaked. Already his toes were numb. The sight of the manor house, with its twinkling windows, made him think of a warm hearth and something hot in his belly; hunger gnawed and rumbled at his innards like a rat in a trap. On the hilltop the dew was already beginning to fall.

He decided to try again.

'D'ye know this place, then?' he asked, jerking his chin in the direction of the manor house. And then, trying not to sound too hopeful, 'They like to favour strangers?'

For the first time the man turned to look at his companion. Beneath the hood of his travelling cloak his face looked pinched, although whether it was with cold or with hunger Moocher could not say.

'Strangers?' he repeated.

'Travellers, then.' Moocher shrugged, trying not to sound too hopeful.

'A pair of vagabonds, more like.' His companion turned away abruptly, stood staring as before down over the valley. 'Manor belongs to a family called Pindar,' he said, after a while. 'There was an old man, but he's most likely dead by now. He had two sons. Paul and Ralph. They'll have you in the lock-up before you can croak Our Father – at least there's one of them that would.'

'We could sleep in the barn.' Moocher jerked his head in the direction of the tithe barn. 'Like I said, frost tonight. It'll be perishing out here. If we could only just—'

The man turned to him. 'What part of "no" don't you understand?'

Moocher opened his mouth to protest, but one look at his companion's face made him think better of it.

It was almost dark. The man made his way into the shelter of the woods. Moocher limped heavily behind him, his boots creaking. From the way they moved – one to collect firewood, the other to clear a piece of ground of flints and brambles – it was clear that both were well used to the wayfaring life.

It was their good fortune that a full moon was rising. The night when it came was clear and still. From one of the capacious pockets inside his rat-skin coat, Moocher pulled out his tinderbox, from another a handful of dry grass. He unhooked the belt from his waist, bent to tend to the fire, breathing on it, coaxing it into life within the shelter of his gnarled hands. Then, from another pocket, he drew out a handful of something soft and dark and mossy-looking, from which he extracted a large spherical object, and two smaller white ones, holding them up like a conjurer.

'Eggs!' He held them up with a sly look of triumph. 'Goose or bantam? What's your fancy?'

'I'm not particular.' Pulling his cloak to him, trying not to shiver in the cold night air, the man was watching him with a face like a famished hawk. 'What else you got in those pockets of yours?'

Moocher put his hand into a second pocket and brought out two more packages. He sniffed at them delicately.

'We got brambles,' he said, holding up the first one. 'And we got cobs.'

'*Stronzo!*'

In the darkness he felt rather than saw the man's sudden smile.

'Fruit and nuts! You'll be handing out sweetmeats next.'

'I don't know nothing about no sweetmeats.' Moocher gave the man a sly sideways look. 'But how's about a bit o' gammon to go with them eggs?'

'Gammon?'

Moocher rummaged around in his pockets and brought out something long and soft-looking that hung limply in his hand. 'Well, not *pig* gammon.' Moocher regarded the object in his hand thoughtfully. 'Not ex-*actly*—'

'For the love of God!' The man hung his head between his knees. 'What then? Just so long as it's not one of your rats,' he said faintly. 'I think I could eat anything, anything at all, but please God, don't let it be rat.'

'Rat?' The old man drew back with an affronted look. 'Lord love you, good sir, of course it's not *rat*.' He proffered the dead animal in the man's direction. 'Whatever do you take me for? This here's as fine a piece o' skreel as ever I saw.'

'Skreel?' The man regarded the object hanging limply from Moocher's hand. 'Ah.' He hung his head between his knees again. '*Fanculo*,' he said faintly.

'That's what I said. Din'cher never eat no skreel before?'

'Squirrel? No.'

'Ah, well then, good sir. Nothing like a nice bit o' roasted skreel to go with yer egg.'

'If you say so.'

'And so I do, sir, so I do.' Nodding to himself Moocher took out a knife from his knapsack and prepared to skin the animal.

The man watched Moocher's efforts with the knife for a few moments with the same hooded look, but although Moocher was surprisingly nimble for one of his size, his knife was too large, and his eyesight, in the failing light, too poor. His companion suddenly leant over and took it from him.

'Here, let me do that.'

'But—'

'I'll see to it.'

He took a knife of his own from a row on the belt at his waist. In his hands it seemed to fly; the blade glinted briefly in the moonlight and then fell down hard with three or four quick blows, severing the creature's head and tail. Then, he took out a second knife, smaller and sharper than the first, and with the delicacy of a seamstress he made an small incision along the belly of the dead creature, pulling the pelt back deftly. Then the squirrel was skinned, gutted and spatchcocked. The whole procedure was over in a matter of minutes.

'A sharp blade is all it takes,' he said. 'There's no sharpness in yours, you should get it ground.'

Moocher looked down at the skinned squirrel in his hand, regarding it thoughtfully for a few moments.

'You done that before,' he said eventually.

When the man made no reply, he began to hum to himself again, busying himself with the squirrel and the fire; carefully pulling out the eggs, which he had placed to roast in the embers. The man ate the roasted eggs, together with some old bread that he produced from his knapsack, and after he had eaten he seemed to relax. For the first time since their chance encounter earlier that day on the lonely hilltop pathway, he regarded his travelling companion with something like interest.

'You make that coat yourself?'

'That I did,' Moocher turned, squaring his shoulders, showing off an expanse of crudely sewn animal pelts. 'I can catch anything with my traps. Rats. Rabbits. Moles.'

'Not to mention skreels.'

'Them too.' He pushed at a log with one of his boots, making the sparks fly. 'Rat-catcher. Soldier. I were a player once, and all. When I were a lad, that is. At St Paul's.'

'A rat-catcher, eh?' A quick grimace that might almost have been a smile flitted across the man's face.

'You find that amusing, sir?'

'Not really.' He moved a little closer to the fire. 'Only that someone I once knew used to call me a rat-catcher,' he ventured unexpectedly.

For a moment Moocher thought he might be about to say more, but he lapsed into moody silence again.

'You come back from the wars then?' Moocher said, a little while later.

'Why do you ask?'

'Foreign. You speak foreign.'

There was a pause while the man considered this statement.

'I've been away, it's true. Venice. Constantinople.'

'Ah.' Moocher nodded his head sagely, as though this explained everything. 'How long you been gone?'

'Five years. Ten. I weren't counting.' His companion shrugged as if it were a matter of the greatest indifference to him. 'Reckon the walk home's taken two or three.'

Moocher threw another log on the fire, his expression imperturbable. 'Long walk.'

'You could say that.'

As the flames rose the man pushed the hood from his face. A shock of unkempt, curly dark hair fell to his shoulders. He stared moodily into the fire. A long, thin scar, silvered over now with age, ran down one side of his face, from his cheekbone to his lip. And his hands, when he held them out to the warmth of the fire, were criss-crossed with old cuts and burns. If Moocher saw these he gave no sign.

'I were in the war,' Moocher added companionably as the fire began to crackle.

'That so. And what war would that be?' The man did not look up from his contemplation of the fire.

'There's always a war somewhere,' Moocher grinned. 'The Earl's war.'

'Oh?'

'In Ireland.'

'I heard.'

'Bad business.'

'I wouldn't know.'

'Lost two toes – see there?' Moocher removed one of his boots, two blackened stubs where the toes should have been.

'Careless of you.'

'No, not careless,' Moocher said, 'the frost, sir, the frost.'

'That so.'

'That's so, sir, that's so.'

For a while all that could be heard was the crackling of the fire. Moocher hummed to himself under his breath.

'Don't say much, do yer?'

'I didn't come all this way to have pretty conversations.'

'So what did you come for then?'

'I've come to settle an old score.' The man turned to him with what was almost a snarl, 'that good enough for you? To settle a score. And you'll stay well out of my business if you've got any sense.'

'A-right, a-right.' Moocher put his hand up appeasingly. 'I were only axing.'

They fell to staring into the fire again. But then, after a few moments, Moocher glanced up at him again curiously. 'Well, if you don't mind my saying, you look as though you've come back from a war somewheres.' He gave the fire a poke with a stick. 'That where you lost yer ear?'

'My ear?' The man put his hand up to one side of his face, from which the lobe had been crudely sliced.

'That frost, too, sir? Or maybes you bin brawling? You looks like a brawler, if you don't mind my saying so.'

The man regarded him steadily for a while; he seemed about to say something, but then thought better of it.

He pulled his travelling cloak more tightly around him against the cold night air.

'You ask a lot of questions, old man.'

'Name's Moocher, now yer axing.'

'I didn't ask.'

'Name's still Moocher,' he said, picking between his teeth with his knife. 'And may I have the honour of knowing yours?'

There was a pause as though the man were going to refuse, but suddenly he seemed to change his mind.

'Name's Carew. John Carew. And my master's business is trade, not war.'

'A merchant, then.' The old man nodded with satisfaction. 'That's good. Must be rich.'

'You think so?' John Carew gave a small laugh. He did not seem to think all that much of the idea.

'Why, sir, all merchants are rich.'

'If you say so, old man.'

'Indeed I do, good sir, indeed I do.' Moocher nodded his grizzled head several times. 'That much is well known.'

For some reason John Carew seemed to find this thought amusing.

He reached into his shirt and took out small, faded velvet pouch. 'I'll tell you about riches, old man,' he said in a low voice. 'See this?' He held up the pouch, swung it on its strings this way and that, so that the silver embroidery glinted in the firelight. 'All my master's riches were held in this pocket once.'

'What, in that poor rag?' Moocher looked at the faded old pouch with disbelief.

'The very one.' John Carew continued to hold out the pouch for Moocher's inspection. He was watching closely for his companion's response. 'This pocket, this very pocket is where he kept his diamond. A diamond as big as one of your eggs, old Moocher,' he added mischievously. 'A diamond big as a goose egg.'

'Never heard tell of a diamond that big.' Moocher shifted uncertainly and his leather boots creaked. 'Sounds like a trickster's tale to me.'

'Gospel. Saw it with my own eyes.' John Carew stuffed the little pouch away, not into his shirt this time, but into his knapsack. 'Not asking you to believe me if you don't want to.'

He lay down, exhausted now, wrapping himself in his cloak and a thin blanket, readying himself for sleep, and putting an end to their conversation.

Only old Moocher was left, staring at him over the dying embers of the fire. His expression was no longer simply curious. If Carew had been watching, he would have seen that the old man's eyes had become narrowed, sly.

'Where did it come from then, this diamond?'

'It belonged to a lady.'

'A lady?'

'A lady I once knew.'

'Where is she now?'

There was a pause. Such a long pause that Moocher thought he had fallen asleep.

'She's dead. Died of the plague,' Carew answered him eventually. 'Like I said, old man, you ask a lot of questions.' John Carew, wrapping himself more closely in his cloak, would say no more.

'Can't an old man be curious?'

'Curiosity killed the cat, old man, you'd do well to remember that.'

'I were only axing.' Moocher, giving the sleeping Carew a sly sideways look, fed some more pieces of kindling into the fire. 'Can't be no harm in axing.'

Later, he was never sure how much later, Moocher woke from a deep sleep to find his face and beard wet with dew.

He was cold to the bone; the fire no more than a heap of glowing embers. At first he thought that it must be near morning, but the position of the moon – which was shining on to his face through the canopy of the trees – showed that it was still the dead of night. He sat up, rubbed his aching frostbitten foot though his boot. Although the trees protected them from the worst of the dew, his rat-skin coat was wet through.

It was few moments before he realised that John Carew was nowhere to be seen.

Moocher got to his feet, and went over to where his companion had lain. There was his threadbare blanket; his knife belt with all the knives still attached to it; his knapsack. The talk of the diamond had whetted Moocher's curiosity. As quickly as his old bones would allow, he got to his knees, and with a practised hand searched swiftly through John Carew's small parcel of belongings. His fingers soon found what he was looking for: the little velvet pouch. Greedily, he emptied the contents into the palm of one hand, inspected them by the light of the moon, but all that he could find were a handful of Venetian coins, and a piece of paper folded up very tight. Nothing else. He pocketed the coins with disappointment, and put the paper back, before heaving himself up again clumsily.

It was only then that he became aware that a little way off, in a small clearing beneath him in the little copse, something white was shining through the trees. Still half-asleep, Moocher stumbled towards the milky brightness. When he reached the clearing he saw that the grass was covered in a thick layer of frost. The full light of the moon was streaming down into the clearing, making the white rime sparkle. He stood for a moment, rubbing his eyes and blinking at the wonderful sight.

The horses were standing beneath the trees.

They were standing so still that Moocher almost missed them at first. They stood as though they were made of stone; their heads up, forelegs bent slightly forward, ears pricked as though they were listening for something. Were they listening for him, the intruder in their woods? He could not tell. In a trick of the moonlight, their pale coats seemed to glow bluish-white against the black trees. As Moocher watched, he saw that beneath the trees where the air was warmer a fine mist had begun to rise from the forest floor. It hovered, like smoke, just a few inches from the ground, twisting around the horses' feet and legs so that for a few moments it seemed to Moocher's dazzled eyes as though they were floating on clouds.

He must have been mistaken about Carew, for when he returned to their camp he found him there, sound asleep as before.

TWELVE

Carew

The Feast Day of St Edward the Confessor, 13th day of October, 1611. Events occurring near the Priors Leaze Manor in the country of Wiltshire.

T HE NEXT DAY AND the next, at John Carew's insistence, they hid out in the woods at the neck of the Drover's Path.

Carew took up the same position on the top of the little escarpment from where he had watched the manor house the night before, and showed no signs of wanting to move. What, or whom, he was watching for, Moocher could not tell, and by now he knew better than to ask.

The weather, unexpectedly, had turned fine, bringing them the last shining days of autumn. Moocher roamed the hedgerows ablaze with bright orange hips and haws, foraging for glistening brambles and the last of the wild damsons. He came back to their camp with his pockets full. He had set his traps and caught a pair of coneys, which John Carew skinned with the same skill as before, and then baked in an underground oven of his own devising with an onion and wild herbs.

If John Carew had been uncommunicative the night before, during the day he became utterly silent, intent on some private business that Moocher could not fathom.

The only time he spoke was when Moocher made as if to set out on one of his hedgerow forays down the Drover's Path itself, in the direction of the valley.

'I wouldn't go down there if I were you, old man.'

Moocher turned. Put his hand up to shade his eyes. 'What's that you say?'

From where he was standing, Carew's face, just above him on the grassy escarpment was cast in shadow. 'Like I said, best not go down there.'

'Why's that then?'

'It's one of the old ways. Treacherous. So they say.'

Moocher looked back to where the path fell away beneath him. After the dazzling sunlight at the top of the hill, the path was dark, the branches of the trees so thickly knotted overhead that it was more like a tunnel than a shepherd's pathway. The air there was cool, almost cold, against his skin. But there were more brambles there. He could see them glistening, and some hazels in which he would be sure to find the last of the nuts.

'Looks a-right to me,' he said, and made as if to walk that way, but John Carew called after him, more insistently this time.

'Didn't you hear me, old man? I said: it's one of the old ways.'

Moocher looked towards the path, and then back again.

'Don't understand you, John Carew,' he said, stubborn now, 'I'll be a-right.'

'Suit yourself.' Carew shrugged. 'But remember what I said, old man, curiosity killed the cat.'

In the end John Carew's words made him think better of it. Sitting down on a grassy spot at the top of the escarpment that was sheltered from the wind, Moocher took off his shirt and coat, sat sunning his chest, luxuriating in the unexpected midday heat. All around him the last of the autumn leaves glowed like gold and silver doubloons. If it had not been for a faint curl of wood smoke from the manor house, it would have seemed that there was no human habitation in the valley below them at all. The smoke hung on the air, mingling with the smell of autumn leaves.

Eventually Carew's patience was rewarded. Occasionally during the day the figure of a woman had come out of the house, carrying a basket of laundry that she proceeded to spread out on a smooth stretch of grass; and sometimes she was followed by a second, much smaller figure, the toddling form of a child. Occasionally a dog barked, but apart from that the place was as lonely and wild as anywhere he had ever been.

But now, on the third day of watching, Moocher saw his companion give a start. A carriage had come into view, and was making its way slowly towards the manor house along the rutted dirt road.

Whether this was the sign that John Carew had been waiting for, Moocher could not tell: Carew seemed to tense at the sight of the carriage, but still he made no move and no sound. From his vantage point he watched as two men got out; they went inside and almost straight away emerged again from another door, making their way slowly to the back of the garden where there was a small orchard. One, the smaller and thinner of the two, was dressed in black, the other in a travelling suit of green. Even from a distance it was possible to see the glint of jewels on his fingers and pinned to the crown of his hat. The man in green walked about for a good while, strutting and pointing to this and that; his general demeanour was displeased. He held a piece of paper in his hand, and from time to time the two would stop to look at it together, until he handed it back to his companion with a contemptuous wave over one shoulder.

Presently they went back into the house again and were gone from view. Carew sat back, let out a long breath, almost a sob. Even now he did not move away from the spot, but stayed sitting there for the best part of the day, his eyes fixed to the place.

While Carew kept his lonely vigil, Moocher kept himself busy. With fingers stained with berry juice, he took his knife and began carefully scraping the remaining flesh and sinews from the squirrel and rabbit pelts, laying them out to dry in the sun, mending his traps, but something – perhaps it was the restless nights on the cold and stony ground – had made him sleepy.

Moocher rubbed his eyes. He put down the trap he was mending and gazed down into the valley below. On the far side, he could just make out the white dots of a flock of sheep grazing on the brow of the distant hills. He pressed his knuckles into his temples and blinked. His lids felt heavy, as though they were weighted with coins. What was wrong with him? He could hardly keep his eyes open. A mid-afternoon stillness had descended on the valley. There was not a breath of wind to shake the last remaining leaves, not a rustle of a vole or mouse in the hedgerows, not a bird to pierce the silence.

It was a windless afternoon. The sun had heat enough in it for Moocher to remove first his boots, then his shirt and his rat-tail coat, and sit sunning his naked back and chest. The sun was so warm on his skin, and the tussocky grass so soft beneath his back, that after a few moments gazing up into the dazzling blueness overhead, he closed his eyes.

After a few moments the knife fell from his fingers. Moocher slept.

He must have slept for a long while, because when he woke it was to find that the sun was already beginning to dip behind the hill and the valley beneath him was filled with shadow. Judging by the white dots of the sheep on the distant hills, which had now reached the middle fields, he had been asleep for many hours.

Already there was a chill in the air. He was about to reach behind him for his shirt and coat when he felt it for the first time, a trembling in the ground beneath him.

Then he heard it. It seemed to come at him through the silence, slowly gathering in volume and pace, until it became a great wave of sound: the drumming of horses galloping towards him, their great hooves thudding against the ground. Moocher had only heard a sound like that once before, it was unmistakable: the sound of a hunt in full chase.

He started to raise his head above the edge of the little escarpment behind which he had been sheltering, so that he could see from what direction they were coming, but he was too late; he could tell from the trembling of the earth beneath him that the horses, streaming down from the hilltop above, were almost upon him. Instinctively he crouched down, throwing his arms up over his head to protect himself. The sound was deafening now; he could feel it hammering in his chest and rattling against his sternum.

Cradling his head in his hands, Moocher screwed himself into as tight a ball as he could, squeezing his eyes shut. And then, just when he thought he would surely be crushed to death beneath the horses' hooves, there came a sudden break in the thundering. He felt rather than saw the heavy bodies soaring above him, the lather from their steaming necks flying; heard the grunt and rush of breath as they hit the ground again, nostrils flaring with exertion. And then, as though of one mind, the herd swerved all together down to the left, crashing and thundering towards the Drover's Path, which opened up and swallowed them.

Instantly, all was silent again.

When he opened his eyes there was nothing and no one to be seen. Moocher, his ears ringing, was alone again, his hilltop camp as lonely and silent as before.

John Carew was gone – blanket, knapsack and all – leaving not so much as a trace behind him.

THIRTEEN

Paul

Bishopsgate.

ALTHOUGH IT WAS LATE, she was not yet quite asleep, the curtains of her bed still open as though she had been waiting for him. A detritus of writing materials was over her bed. Stepping into her room he was aware of small flurry of movement among the bedclothes.

'Oh,' she said when she saw him, 'it's you.'

'Why, were you hoping for someone else?' he teased. He leant towards her and kissed her on the forehead. 'And what are you hiding from me, wife? You must not hide anything from me, you know.'

When he moved the curtains aside, the papers pinned to the inside lining rustled. And fastened to the inside lining of the bed curtains were scores of pieces of paper covered in her fine, sloping hand: bits of poetry that she had copied out from their library, her own verses and snatches of songs, odd lists, and receipts, everything, in short, that she had written down. When they were drawn close, the curtains seemed to whisper at her, making a curious susurration, like a faint breeze through autumn leaves.

'Oh, you know I would never hide anything from *you.*' From beneath one of her pillows Celia drew out a sheaf of papers. 'Annetta's letters, that's all,' she said, holding them out to him. 'I thought it was Nan coming in to unlace me, and I know she reads them.'

'Nan can read?'

Paul sat down and began to pull off his shoes. He lay down beside Celia and laced his fingers into hers, and they lay like that for a while, side by side, looking up at the silk canopy, like two marble figures on a sarcophagus.

'She learnt in the last house she worked in. Her mistress taught all her servants.'

'Then I'll get you a new maid.' Paul rolled on to his side, put his hand out to pull at a strand of her hair, 'One who can't read.'

'I don't want a new maid.' A small shadow flitted across Celia's face. 'And besides,' she added, 'I thought you liked it if women had some learning.'

Paul hesitated, as though contemplating a reply to this, but in the end he only said quite mildly, 'Well, not among my servants. And besides, I hardly think Nan qualifies as learned. Let me talk to her.'

'You don't have to; Frances says she will.'

'Ah.' Paul rolled over, gazed up at the canopy above him, to where there was a slight water mark in the dusty pink silk. He wondered vaguely how it had got there. '*Frances!*' The name came out with an emphasis that he did not fully intend.

'Why do you say her name that way?'

'And what way would that be?'

'*Frances!*' she echoed him, with the same decided air. 'I thought you cared quite as much for her company as I do.'

'I don't understand you.'

'You understand me perfectly.' Celia rolled over so that she too was lying on her side.

'I do not think that Parvish cared for her,' Paul mused, still examining the water mark in the pink silk, 'but then Parvish is an old man now and does not care for anyone much. He is as full of affection for you as he ever was, though.'

But Celia was not to be deflected. 'Poor Frances, you must be kind to her. She is all alone in the world.'

Poor Frances. The incongruous words hung in the air between them. Paul seemed about to say something, but then thought better of it.

'But I am kind, surely you know that.' He caught at his wife's hand and held it between his own. 'Am I not kind?'

'You are kindness itself.'

'Oh, my Celia.' Still looking at the canopy Paul raised her hand to his lips and kissed it.

They lay for a moment in a silence that was still companionable. On the windowsill behind the bed was a small earthenware jar in which someone had put a bunch of gillyflowers. Candlelight caught at them, so that the petals glowed briefly, tiny splinters of jewelled glass.

As he stroked her hand, he became aware that she had moved still closer towards him, was pressing her body against him, as though feeling for his warmth.

'You are cold? It is cold in here. Why has no one been in to light the fire? I'll call them to light the fires.' Solicitous for her, Paul made as if to get up, but she pulled him back.

'No, don't go, not yet. You come here so seldom.'

'Why, what is it, sweetheart?'

'Frances says—'

'What?' He turned to her, half-impatient. 'What does Frances say now?'

Hearing his tone, Celia decided to try another tack.

'Unlace me...' She pressed against him, whispering into his ear. 'They say that it is not good for a husband... nay, nor even for a wife... not to... never to... you know...

Don't you remember what we used to say to one another in Aleppo. . .?' She trailed off, sensing a sudden stillness in him.

Paul let go of her hand. 'You speak about such things with Lady Sydenham?'

'No, but why do you ask? Is it wrong?'

'No, but I would have thought the lady had more sense than to put such ideas into your head.'

Paul made to stand up, but Celia held on to him, and he felt her guide his hand to her breast.

'Husband.' Her voice was barely a whisper, 'why do you not love me?' The pain in her voice was palpable.

'Celia. . .' Paul's hand rested against his wife's body for a moment. Beneath the stiffened silk of her bodice he could feel the shape of her breast, small and high and perfectly round – everything a woman's breast should be, like a line from a poem, he found himself thinking – before he began gently to pull his hand away.

'No, Celia.' He closed his fingers over hers, held her hand in his. 'I love you, of course I love you,' he said with a heavy heart. 'Come, let us not have this conversation again. It is a dark place it takes us to, you know that as well as I—'

But Celia held her ground. 'No – no, I do not know. Tell me why.'

'Must we rehearse this again?'

But, for once, she would not let him go so easily. 'But I am quite well now. I am healed.' He felt her grip on his hand tighten. 'And *you* are well now too, please—'

'No, Celia—'

'But why? Why? Do I not make you happy?'

'Of course. You are my wife. Of course you make me happy.'

'You do not answer my question. Do I make you happy. . .' Wretchedly she searched for the right words, '. . .as a wife should make her husband happy?'

When he did not immediately reply she put out her hand, feeling between his legs, pressing him there. He felt her small hand. He could feel her whole body tremble even as she touched him, and he knew that she was amazed at her own daring, as though this were something she had been thinking about a long time, and his heart turned over for her.

Did he love his wife? What a question. All the time she had been gone from him, he had loved Celia to the point of madness. Or so he thought. All the years he had thought her dead, he had mourned her; when he found that she was alive, he had given everything he had to bring her back to him.

But now? Did he love her now?

Wordlessly he took her hand away again, and as he did so he felt the ease between them begin to ebb slowly away, like sea foam vanishing into sand.

'I thought I would find you in a happy mood for once,' he said, trying to change the subject. 'Your friend Annetta will be with us very soon now. I have had a letter from the Mother Superior to say that they have at last received the necessary dispensation to allow her to leave the convent.' He tried to keep the tone of their conversation light. 'It has cost me more than a quinquereme of spices to secure it, but it will be worth it to see you happy.'

But if anything his change of subject seemed to make her more anxious than before.

'Do not speak to me of these things now. I ask if I make you happy and you do not reply,' she said, her voice full of sorrow. 'Ah, but I do not. I do not, I do not, I do not, I do—' Celia closed her eyes, and her voice began to rise. 'You said it would be different here. You promised!'

'For pity's sake!' He gripped her arm, gave it a little shake. 'You know you must not excite yourself with these fantasies.' His tone was sharp, but more with fear than anger. When he saw her chastened face, he added, more gently this time, 'That is not it, Celia. You know why it is; you know the danger. There must not be another child.'

'Who says not? Why not? A child might make us happy. You are my husband. You should not. . . no, husband, you cannot deny me.'

'Who has put those words into your mouth? I am beginning to think that your Lady Sydenham has over-reached herself this time.'

'Do you think I am so simple I cannot think any of these things for myself?' Celia was sitting up now, strands of her reddish-gold hair falling around her shoulders. 'What about me? Do you think I cannot *feel*? Do you think I have no desire?'

In the dim light of the candles Celia's skin looked so smooth and pale it was almost translucent. She looked for a moment like a beautiful statue he had once seen in a garden in Venice. And for a moment Paul was struck into silence.

'Why do you look at me so strangely?'

'I'm not. . . it's nothing. . .' He passed a hand before his face as though waving the thought away.

But now, before he could get up, she had begun to kiss the side of his face. He could feel her breath on his eyelids and against his cheeks, shallow and quick, like the flutter-ing of a moth; smell her unexpected heat. 'Celia. . . no. . .'

But when he turned his head towards her, his lips brushed briefly – unexpectedly – against her neck. Her skin was – how could he have forgotten? – somehow creamily thick, and of a thread count that was extraordin-ary in its fineness. Had she been planning this moment? He thought perhaps she had, because she had put some perfume there, on the pulse just beneath her ear, some-thing that smelt dark, sandalwood, perhaps, or the resin the Arabs call *oud* – which mingled with her own female smell, which was musky and clean. Although he knew he must pull away, he found himself instead bending towards her, kissing her neck again, heard her sharp intake of breath at his sudden touch, then an answering sound that must have been his own.

He turned over, raising himself up on one arm so that he was looking down at her, and took her small head between his hands. He felt her hand slip into the opening of his shirt, run her fingers across his chest, her touch warm against his skin; her other hand, palm facing upwards, fingers curled, lay over her head, a position of surrender. He kissed her, and as he did so felt her shiver, felt the tilt of her hips, lifting up towards his.

He bent towards her, but as he did so he heard something that made him pause.

'Wait.' He lifted his head. 'What's that?'

He listened. A small scuffling, or scratching noise, at the door.

'There it is again.'

'What?' Celia's hand was on his arm. 'I can't hear anything,' she whispered. 'It's probably just a mouse.'

'No, that's not a mouse. There it is again. Can't you hear it?'

'The house has been empty so long, the wainscoting creaks.'

'No, wait – listen—'

'It's nothing, don't mind it,' she said, trying to keep him with her, but already Paul was pulling away.

'That's no mouse that I ever heard.' In three strides he was across the room. He flung the door open. A young woman, a servant dressed in his own livery, stumbled forwards, almost knocking him over, as though she had been crouching down and leaning against the door.

'What are you doing?'

'Nothing, sir.'

There was a pause.

'Nothing?'

The girl met his gaze levelly. 'If you please, sir, I was coming to help my mistress undress. The lady sent me.'

'Then why were you kneeling down?'

'I dropped something, sir.'

She bent down again, fumbled as though she were searching for something, which she now picked up and concealed behind her back.

'Is that what you dropped? Show it me.'

The girl held out a handkerchief, a small balled square of cotton. Was that what she had retrieved from the floor? He could not be sure, had not been looking closely enough.

Paul looked at her. The girl had a pretty enough face. Blonde hair tucked into a lace cap. Eyes like a cat. He did not remember having seen her before, but then that could apply to almost half the new household, but something about her, something about the way she met his eye too steadily, made him quite certain that she was lying.

'What's your name?'

'Anne.' She was still staring at him, 'but they call me Nan.'

'Well, then, Nan,' he said in a low voice, 'you are not needed now. Go.' He made a curt motion with his chin. 'I'll send for you when your mistress needs you.'

Without another word she turned and walked away. Paul watched her go. She did not scurry in the way most maidservants might if they had been caught peeping through their mistress's keyhole, but walked away slowly, as though perfectly aware of his gaze, and with her head held high.

Oh, the insolence of English servants. *Christos*! Paul had forgotten about it in his long years away. He could almost wish that Carew were still with him. Carew would have dealt with a chit like that in a trice, Paul would only have had to give the word. But Carew was not here any more, more's the pity.

John Carew is dead, brother, six foot under in a foreign land; he will never return, and it is God's will that you and my father should accept it – Ralph's words came back to him.

The letter, Ralph's last letter, he remembered now that that is what he had come to talk to Celia about. He put his hand to his pocket but it was not there, he went downstairs to his own room to fetch it.

When he opened the door to Celia's room, he felt the change – something heightened, a quickening of the air, a fluttering along the pulse – before he saw it.

'Well, looks as though you were right about that Nan, after all—' he began.

She was kneeling on the bed, facing him. Her shoulders and breasts were uncovered. Every inch of her body was glittering with gemstones. There were diamonds hanging from her ears and strung around her neck. The diadem of seed pearls that he had bought in Aleppo from a Sephardic Jew glittered in her hair. There were rings on all her fingers; delicate chains hung around her ankles.

But what drew his gaze beyond all else was the enormous jewel that hung between her breasts, suspended on a thin gold chain: a diamond the size of a baby's fist. The Sultan's Blue. The great stone seemed to pulse in the candlelight, blue fire and blue ice together.

At first, the strangeness of this scene was almost beyond his comprehension. It was as if he had fallen into a dream, but it was not a dream. Who had put this idea into her head? His wife – Celia – decked out in gemstones like a Venetian whore.

For a moment neither of them spoke. When at last Paul took a step towards her, he could see that her breathing was both rapid and shallow, and her skin – the beautiful pale skin that had been so prized by the Ottomans – had on it the sheen of perspiration. He had seen her perspire like this only a few times during the very hottest months in Aleppo, when even the thickest walls with the cool blue tiles, the green and watery breezes from the fountains, and the lemon and bitter orange trees in their courtyard, gave no relief from the heat.

He himself felt suddenly cold. He knew then that it was not desire that she felt, but fear. And with that realisation the spell was broken. Paul blinked, and somehow – like snuffing out a candle – the moment had passed. It was Celia again, his wife, her hair dishevelled, looking at him anxiously from among the crumpled linen of the bed.

'Where did you get it?' When Paul spoke at last he did so gently. 'Did you take it from the cabinet?'

'Of course, where else? From the secret drawer where you hid it—'

'Did anyone see you, Celia?'

'No!'

'Are you quite, quite sure?'

'Of course I am sure.'

'And the rest?'

'From there—' She pointed to the polished steel casket.

But the casket had a key. His hand went to his belt, where the key always hung, but it was no longer there.

'And the key? How did you get the key? Did you take it from my belt?'

'No, I swear it.' He saw her retreat, at once, as she always did if he used a harsh tone to her, shrinking back into the safety of the curtained bed as though his very words had the power to bruise her. 'The key was already in the lock.' Celia pointed again. And there, sure enough, was the key with its tassel of blue and red Venetian silk, still sitting in the lock.

Celia began to take off the jewels, but the diamond was still hanging around her neck. *In the name of God take that off, it makes you look like a whore.* Did he actually say the words, no, thank God: less harsh words, he knew from bitter experience, would make her spiral into a silent melancholy for days on end.

He went and sat down next to her on the bed, and tried to take her hand. At first Celia shook her head, withdrew still further back into the rustling darkness.

He looked at her sadly. 'Do you shrink from me?' he said. 'No, do not shrink from me, Celia. I can bear anything, but not that.'

There was a small pause. Reluctantly, with her face still turned away from him, she put her hand in his.

'Look at me.' He took her fingers gently in his own.

She shook her head.

'Look at me, I say—'

'I cannot.' Her gaze fluttered briefly towards him and then away. 'You are angry with me, I can bear anything, but I cannot bear that.'

'No, not angry. Look at me,' he urged. 'Not any more. I know you meant no harm.'

Celia had taken the diamond from round her neck, and now she held it out to him on the palm of her hand.

'Here it is, the Sultan's Blue. I'm sorry I took it. I wanted only. . . I wanted only to please you,' she said simply, 'but it seems that whatever I do, I cannot.'

FOURTEEN

Paul

Bishopsgate.

L ATER THAT SAME NIGHT, Paul Pindar sat alone
in the great first-floor gallery, holding the Sultan's
Blue in the palm of his hand.

It occurred to him that in all the years they had been
in Aleppo, when the great stone had lain hidden in his
strongbox, he could not recall one single instance – apart
from their very last night – when he had taken it out to
look at it. Now as he sat holding it was as though he were
seeing it for the first time: a diamond more beautifully and
skilfully faceted than any stone he had ever seen. Who
would not be dazzled by its beauty? He remembered the
day when he had first seen it at Zuanne Memmo's ridotto
in Venice, remembered the pricking on the back on his
neck, in his fingers when he picked it up. And his feelings
of – what?

Exhilaration. Desire. A lust for possession.

I have to have it, no matter what the cost.

He held the diamond for a long moment, turning it in
his fingers, studying its shape and form, the feel of it cold
and hard against his skin. The weight of it alone thrilled
him. When he held it up to the firelight, he saw to his
amazement how the light refracted in it; every shade of
blue, from the palest moonshine to the blackest sapphire.

Sometimes he even had a fancy that light was coming from inside the stone itself, as though it had, by some magical means, become trapped there. Three hundred carats of pure starlight, last seen hanging from his unhappy wife's neck.

Celia, decked out in her jewels like a Venetian whore. Celia, giving herself to him. And he had wanted her, too. He could not get the thought of her out of his head. So why had he pulled away? He had allowed her to believe that they could start again in England, but he had failed her. . .

Paul put the stone down, pressed his fingers against his closed eyelids until spots of light danced and spiralled through the darkness inside his head. Did she make him happy as *a wife should make her husband happy?* Its answering question, its pigeon pair, more troubling still than the first, nagged at him. Did he make her happy, as a husband should a wife?

He loved Celia, had felt a sharp desire for her that evening. So why? Could it be that she was not the only one who needed to heal? He had told Parvish that he feared to have another child, but was that the real reason? When Paul thought of embracing her, all he could see was the midwife in Aleppo. The knife. The blood. Her screams.

Although the lamps were all lit, and he had kept the fire well banked up, it was still cold in the room. Beneath the table at which he sat was a brazier of the kind the Ottomans use. From time to time he fed it abstractedly with little lumps of charcoal from a brass scuttle at his side.

Paul shivered. In front of him was the polished steel casket that he had brought down from Celia's room. He opened it, took out his wife's jewels: the pearl in the shape of a ship, the intaglio ring with the head of the goddess Isis, the little parrot cut from an emerald, a carnelian squirrel, the quartz cat's eye monkey – trinkets that he bought to amuse her during their years in Aleppo. But it was the diamond to which he always returned.

He picked it up again, and carefully drew his thumb over the largest of the facets, searching for the inscription – and there it was: the Arabic script so perfect, so tiny, it seemed to him that it must have been carved out by djinns.

A'az ma yutlab.

My heart's desire.

That the diamond was magical was never in any doubt. But who among them really knew what the stone's powers were? Had the stone brought him his heart's desire? There were some who might think so. He had everything, did he not? Paul ran his hand over his eyes again. In the seven years that the diamond had been in his possession, his fortunes had been restored; he had the wife he had longed for and thought he had lost; he had the biggest mansion in Bishopsgate. And so why was it that in his mouth was the taste of ashes?

He wondered now, and not for the first time, whether some malign influence was at play. It was as though he could hear the whisper of desert djinns in his ear: *Be careful what you wish for*. Paul pressed the tips of his fingers against his eyes. These were night thoughts; his demons come to haunt him again.

A noise behind him made him turn, and as he did so became aware of a figure standing in the shadows at the door. Instinctively pushing the diamond out of sight, Paul half-rose from his chair.

'Celia?'

It was not Celia, but Frances Sydenham standing in the doorway.

'I'm sorry, I didn't mean to disturb you.' She had her hand to her throat, as though she too had been startled.

'You are not disturbing me; I thought everyone was asleep.'

He wondered how long she had been standing there.

'It's after midnight. I saw the lamps still lit, and I wondered. . . I thought everyone was in bed.'

She turned as if to go, but then, half out of the doorway, he saw her hesitate.

'Actually. . .' She looked at him over her shoulder, 'actually, I was looking for Quirkus.' He saw her quick gaze scan the room, the great carved breast of the chimney-piece, the two cabinets, one on either side of the window. What else had she seen? The jewel casket was open in full view at the foot of his chair. He had been able to drop the Sultan's Blue back into its little velvet pouch, but Celia's jewels, and the diamonds and other gemstones in his collection were spread, like a dragon's hoard, all over the table. With anyone else, his instinct would have been to sweep them all quickly behind a pile of papers, to get them out of sight, but with Frances Sydenham, something – a sense of old-fashioned courtesy, perhaps – held him back.

'You haven't seen him, have you?' she was saying. 'You know how he likes to hide, the troublesome creature.' Her gaze came to rest on table, skimming over it, and then quickly away. 'I'm afraid he may have gone up one of the chimneys.'

'Alas, I'm afraid I have not.'

There was a small pause.

She hovered in the doorway, as though expecting that he would say something more, but when he did not offer anything further, she turned as if to go. On a whim, he called out to her, in a low voice, 'Quirkus? Is that why you couldn't sleep?'

Despite the boxes ranged around the sides of the room, the room still had an echoing and empty feel to it; his voice seemed to bounce off the walls, unnaturally loud. They had not talked together alone like this since the evening he had come across her outside Celia's room. Perhaps because of the lateness of the hour, he was aware that the ease that was usually between them had turned to something else. In its place was – what? Something at once harder, more tensile. A feeling that he could not yet quite articulate. He remembered how at Parvish's house he had imagined her naked body, stretched out for him, covered in jewels—

'I couldn't sleep – I don't sleep – not much. . .' She gave him one of her quick, confiding smiles. He saw that while she had not yet prepared for bed – she was still wearing the same dress that he had seen her in earlier in the day – she had removed her shoes and stockings. Her dark hair hung loose around her shoulders. She seemed smaller, more vulnerable than she ever did during the day. He saw that her feet were bare beneath the hem of her dress.

'Your room here, it's quite comfortable?' he said, cursing himself for sounding so stiff, so formal, 'I hope?'

'Oh yes, I thank you.' Once again, she seemed on the point of turning away from him.

'Please, there's no need to thank me – us—' Paul corrected himself. 'No need to thank us at all. I am rather beginning to wonder how we ever did without you.'

She turned again, and he could see the curve of her neck and the fall of her hair in the candlelight.

'Well, then, goodnight.' She put her hand on the door, as if to close it behind her. 'It's been a long day.'

'Very long.'

173

She did not quite linger, but clearly had not made up her mind to go either. Paul began to think that she must have something else on her mind, but whatever it was she did not say it.

'Ah, well, goodnight then, Mr Pindar.' She turned away from him, holding up her candle towards the staircase, and this time he did not stop her; her form disappeared into the darkness, a dwindling mass of shadows.

And for a long time afterwards, Paul sat staring into the fire. It was no longer Celia he saw, but Frances Sydenham, barbarously bedecked in his wife's jewels. And in his reverie, in the deepest and most secret part of himself, she is waiting for him. Her face and neck are heavily veiled, but her feet and ankles, her slender calves, are naked beneath silk skirts. His vision shifts. She is looking at him now and willing him to come to her, although at the same time he knows that if he does, she will fight him off; will pit her woman's poor strength, uselessly, against his own, willing her own surrender. He finds the thought of it – of handling her roughly, of tearing at her clothes, of forcing her to submit to him – almost unbearable, as though, by some erotic alchemy, she has found the key to his darkest self.

In his mind's eye he sees her very clearly now. She wants him to watch her, and he does so; watches as she pulls her skirts slowly up to her thighs, so that the merest ribbon of naked flesh is visible where her stockings meet skin. Her lips are slightly parted; the tips of her fingers rest against the flesh of her inner thighs—

A log fell in the grate – the vision was gone.

FIFTEEN

Carew

Events occurring in and around Priors Leaze Manor in the country of Wiltshire.

T HE FIRST THING THAT struck Carew as strange was that the dogs did not bark at his approach.

In the old days they would have started their hulloahing long before any stranger reached the gateway, but on this night all was silent as the grave. The dew was falling and already a rime of white had formed on the grass at his feet, but so intent was he on his approach to the manor that he neither felt nor heard it crunch beneath his feet. Nor did he feel the night air, cold as a stone, against his flesh. As he crept towards the manor, Carew was but the most fleeting of moonlit shadows upon the grass.

Over the last few days from his hilltop camp near the Drover's Path, he had had the chance to scrutinise the old place in a way that he had never done before. When he was a boy, the manor had seemed to him like a castle; but now, after all the years of travelling among the shining cities of Europe and the Levant, he saw it through new eyes, saw it for what it had been all along, had he but known it: a dusty little manor house in a rural backwater of England.

It was all so much smaller than he recalled. The manor had been old even in the time of the old Queen, and very likely long before. The lake, with its pair of swans, its fishing herons, and its fearsome pike – so monstrous, according to local lore, that it would gobble up a small boy in one gulp – was, he now saw, a stretch of water no bigger than a village pond, a curve of shining water that must once have been a part of a moat surrounding the house when it was first built.

Carew took in the old-fashioned mullioned windows; the black-and-white timbered walls; the farmyard and orchards unashamedly abutting the house, where in the daytime geese and chickens roamed at will on what remained of the old bowling alley, churning it to farm-yard mud. He noticed the way the whole house seemed to list slightly to one side, growing up out of the fields and the nape of the hills that surrounded it as though it were made somehow not of bricks and mortar, but of vegetable matter.

He had almost reached the house now, treading carefully and keeping to the shadows. And again he wondered, where were the dogs? In the old days they would have barked themselves hoarse by now at the presence of a stranger after nightfall. At the window he paused and looked in. Although there was a fire lit in the hall, the room was empty, except for the dogs by the hearth.

There were three of them altogether. Two lurchers with shaggy grey pelts, he had never seen before; the third, lying on her own a little apart from the others, was a little black-and-white cur. He moved in closer, and as he did so the dog, perhaps sensing a presence there, pricked up her ears briefly but, lulled by the warmth of the fire, soon put her head down and went back to sleep again.

At the sight of her, something sharp shifted in his breast. Robin, his dog! Carew breathed in sharply through his nose, and then slowly out again.

Carefully, Carew breathed against the pane of glass, rubbing it with his sleeve. Next to the fire there was a chair and a footstool, upon which lay the remains of a recently eaten supper: some chicken bones, a bottle. A knife had been stuck, blade down, into a wooden trencher. So he was still here, after all. Ralph! That primping green popinjay! With the old man dead, and the other brother, Paul, still living in the Levant, Ralph was the only one who could be using this room. He would not have left the fire stoked if he had retired for the night, so he must have stepped out to go to the privy. . .

Carew drew back from the window. After all these years he reckoned he could wait a moment longer while the gentleman took his piss.

Even now it was not too late to change his mind. Even now he could turn away from this enterprise, could take his dog, and be gone before anyone was the wiser. But now that he was here, now that he had looked inside the old place, seen the dogs, the parlour, the very chair where the old man used to sit, he was seized with a such a longing to see it again he could barely breathe. The feeling came to him like a sickness, so powerful he had to lean back against the wall for a few moments to steady himself.

Carew made his way round to the back of the manor, to the old yard where the dairies were, and the entrance to the kitchens. At the kitchen door he paused, his hand on the latch. He pulled the door open, and through long habit slid one foot over the stone lintel, just as he always used to, remembering its familiar smoothness, the dip in the middle. Even now, after all these years, he could have made his way around the old place blindfolded.

At first, Carew moved cautiously around the dreaming household. For all he knew there was another kitchen boy here now, sleeping as he once had all those years ago in the crook of the old fireplace. It would be a mistake to wake him – the last thing he wanted was the whole household in an uproar – but he need not have worried. When he reached the fireplace it was empty of a kitchen boy. Instead he found embers that were still warm. From old habit he spread them out with the toe of his boot, kicked at the charred and still smoking remains of a log. The old double spit was still there; the gridiron, pot-hangers and pippins; the copper pans hanging from hooks high on the ceiling. Probably still the same cobwebs in the rafters, he thought, glancing up.

It was the bones that first alerted him that something was awry. They were just old chicken bones, gnawed by the dogs but lying scattered heedlessly on the floor and in the hearth. Next he found the half-chewed remains of a bread trencher, then, vegetable peelings. This would never have happened in Mr Bull's day. But Mr Bull – the old cook at Priors Leaze – like so much else at the manor, was long gone.

He went on a little way. Through the darkness he could just make out the old door to the distillery, another to the dairy, then two little steps down and one step up, and he was in the second, smaller kitchen with its pantries and storerooms. Even he was amazed by the ease with which he was able to find his way. Carew's feet seemed to glide over the smooth flagstones as though he were floating.

He opened the door to the first of the pantries. The hinge still squeaked, just as it always used to. On the far wall was a window through which moonlight came streaming, so bright after the inky blackness of the big kitchen that at first it hurt his eyes. Carew looked around him, expecting to see the gleaming rows of bottles and preserving jars, the bunches of dried herbs, the rows of pickles and preserved fruit, the bottles of plums in a dozen different shades of pink, the violets and cowslip balls crystallised in sugar, the quince cheeses and sacks of raisins-of-the-sun, and it was several moments before he registered that the room was empty. The pantry had a mouldering feel to it, as though no one had set foot inside it for many moons. He drew one hand along the shelves and felt rather than saw the marks his fingers left in the dust. A few blackened bottles of some indeterminate liquid stood together on the end of a shelf near the window. Beneath them lay a tray of wrinkled apples. By the smell of them he knew they had seen better days.

Still moving softly, Carew crept out of the kitchens and made his way past the back stairs and into the old fire-hall. The door into the parlour, where he had seen the sleeping dogs, stood ajar. Was Ralph back yet? He listened, but there was no sound. He stood for a moment in the moonlit hall, surprised yet again that the dogs had not yet been disturbed – they must be older and deafer than he thought. Well, that at least had played into his hand. He listened again, but there was still no sound coming from the room. All he could make out was the faint glow of firelight in the crack beneath the door.

He looked towards the carved oak staircase to the upper chambers of the house. And then back towards the parlour door.

Well, in for a penny. . .

As though in a dream, Carew made his way slowly up the stairs. In fact, at one point he began to believe that he *was* actually dreaming. The only reason he knew he was not was the fact that he was shivering, not from cold – for, strangely, he was not cold at all – but from excitement, like a dog.

At the top of the stairs he paused, and then turned to find himself walking down the long gallery, its wainscoted walls hung with dusty portraits. Slowly he made his way through the interconnected upper chambers. There were no drapes on any of the windows, and each room was flooded with moonlight. It was a part of the house that, even when he lived here, Carew had visited very seldom, but still he found his way with ease, as though his feet remembered every last creaking floorboard, each little step up and step down. They never made a mistake.

As he roamed the moonlit rooms, Carew looked around him with a sense of growing dismay. It was not only the kitchens that were neglected. In every room, even in the upper reaches of the manor, the air of decay and neglect was palpable. There was cracked glass in the windowpanes, patches of damp in the ceiling. In one room he found mould sprouting from the old Turkey rugs. He shook his head in wonder. How anyone could have allowed this to happen was beyond his reckoning.

In one room he found a pair of small portraits hanging on the wall. They showed two merchants, prosperous in their black velvet caps and lace collars, and their carefully trimmed beards. Paul and Ralph: the old man's sons. Carew stared at them, fascinated.

Paul was the older and darker of the two. His face looked pinched, his forehead was too high, giving him a somewhat scholarly air, but otherwise it was a good likeness. And then there was Ralph. The fat boy Carew remembered from his childhood had become a thickset man: small eyes, broad shoulders, handsome in a florid, bullying sort of way. Even now, after all these years, the sight of him made Carew's flesh crawl. But for some reason he could not stop looking at him. Whereas Paul wore only his customary merchant's black, there was a lustre to Ralph. His cape was lined with fur, his buttons were covered with gold brocade – no sumptuary laws for him – there were gold rings on his fingers, the glint of a jewel in his cap. You could see he had money – Carew, the former street urchin, looked him over with an appraising eye – you could almost *smell* the moneybags. Ralph stared straight back at him: *Lay one finger on me, kitchen boy, and I will crush you like a worm.*

Presently Carew came to the door of the largest bedchamber. He hesitated for a moment, his hand on the latch. Once, when he had lived here, this had been the old man's chamber, but who lay here now?

Gently he pushed the door open and looked in. Where there had been a bed and walls hung with tapestries and painted cloths, there was nothing now but an empty space. The oak boards had no coverings: no old-fashioned rushes, not even straw on the floor for comfort or cleanliness. From the corner of his eye Carew saw a flash of something moving: a mouse darting for the safety of the wainscoting.

He made his way through the empty chamber to the next one, and the next. The second room was as bare as the first, but in the third and last chamber there was a bed: a huge, ungainly construction, country-made, its oak posts thicker than a man's leg.

Carew crept up softly and pulled the curtain open a crack. Inside, curled up together, were the woman and the child he had seen from the Drover's Path. He recognised them as such, but even close to he did not know them. They had not lived at the manor in his time, of that he was sure; but belonged instead to this new and troubling dispensation.

He stood there for a moment or two watching them. The child's face was pink with sleep. A curl peeped from beneath its cap, small fists thrown up above its head. As he watched, he became aware that, in that disconcerting way of sleeping children, the child's eyes were half open. The whites caught the moonlight, glinting at him, making him start. For a moment he thought: Dio buono, *the child is dead,* and a chill descended on his heart; but almost as soon as the thought occurred to him, the infant gave a small sigh, and turned, murmuring something in its sleep.

And, suddenly, Carew was a child again himself.

He is five or six years old perhaps – Carew has never known his exact age – and just come to the manor. He is lying in this very bed. The old man – Paul's father, Ralph's father – has brought him here. He is not sure how he got here, but, like the sleeping child he contemplates, he is lying safely in the crook of his protector's arm. The old man has a comforting smell: a faint, clean odour of harness leather and soap, and his hand, which is clasped gently but firmly over Carew's shoulder, is warm and dry.

In the old man's arms he knows he is safe. It is a singular feeling. He has not felt safe for a long time, perhaps ever, in his short life. The bed has several mattresses, the top one is stuffed with goose down. After the stone-cold hardness of the kitchen floor where he has been used to stay at night, it is like lying on a cloud. He can feel his eyelashes fluttering on his cheeks as he slips into a dreamless sleep.

And then suddenly he is being sucked, with unkind force, back into the waking world. It is light. Bright sunlight streams in through the window. He has the impression that the curtains around the bed have been pulled violently open and that this is what has woken him.

'*Ho*, you there, kitchen boy—' Ralph's face, the face of an angry nine-year-old, is peering down at him. 'What are you doing here, kitchen boy?'

Still half asleep, Carew rubs grubby fists into his eyes. 'I – I don't know, Master Ralph.'

He can hear himself clearly, in the piping voice of a child.

'Don't you know this is my father's bed, you snivelling little toad. Who said you could come in here?'

'I – I couldn't rightly say.' The young Carew regards the older boy with terror, and begins to scramble hastily out from beneath the coverlets.

'You've still got your boots on!' Ralph says in tones of outrage.

'Beg pardon, Master Ralph.' Carew, clumsy with sleep, begins to stumble towards the wall. But since he can't remember how he came in here, he has no geography of the place. He staggers round the room, but no matter how hard he tries he can't seem to find a way out. Eventually he gives up. He falls in a corner, where he crouches over, covering his head in his hands, waiting for the blows.

And then, like a miracle, Ralph drops his arm. The old man is there. Carew can hear his voice speaking from the doorway.

'What are you doing, Ralph?'

'Nothing, Father.'

'I think you were about to do something.'

When he is displeased, old man Pindar has a way of speaking which is both soft and hard at the same time.

'No, Father—'

'I think you were going to strike the boy.'

A statement, not a question.

'He was in your bed, Father,' the boy speaks out accusingly. 'He had his boots on.'

'He has night terrors.'

'But he is the kitchen boy!' Ralph's tone is incredulous. 'He was in your bed!'

'He's just a child, Ralph. He is a-feared.' The old man's voice is gentle. 'He has not slept for many nights. You should pity him.'

'A-feared... of what?'

There is a pause.

'Of the dark,' the old man says at last, 'he is a-feared of the dark, Ralph.'

'I don't like him.' Carew can hear that Ralph is about to start snivelling. 'Why can't he go home?'

There is another small pause. When he speaks again the old man's tone is not quite so gentle.

'He has no home, Ralph. You know that. Not now.'

'But—'

'This is his home. We are his home.' There is a warning edge to the old man's voice. A wiser child, a child on its mettle, as Carew is, would have detected it and stopped. But Ralph is not, and never will be, a subtle creature, or perhaps he does not want to stop himself.

'Then what about his mother? I've heard them talk about his mother. Why can't he go away with her?'

'His mother?' There is another very faint pause. Then: 'He is like you, Ralph,' the father says, quite slowly this time, 'the boy has no mother.' Then he adds: 'He deserves your pity.'

'But, I thought—'

'It is not for you to question what I do.' His voice is harsh now, dismissive. 'The boy is here now. This is his home. Let that be an end of it.'

The old man turns and walks from the room. He does not look back because he knows that in this family – his servants and his sons, the cottagers on his land – his rule is law. At Priors Leaze he is obeyed unquestioningly. Or at least he was once, Carew thinks, in those old times.

In his mind's eye Carew can see him now: a small, wiry man (his sons, Ralph and Paul, will outgrow him sooner than anyone imagines) but as strong as tempered steel. Even in his middle years, he carries not one ounce of spare flesh. A man of plain habits and plain words; doughty, God-fearing, in the old way. He wears, as he always does, the same stained country doublet and hose. Later, the excesses of his merchant sons, with their vast new-minted wealth – especially of Ralph, aping the aristocracy with his love of fripperies and baubles and cloth of gold – will be something that he will never understand, and will therefore abominate. He will think it the work of the devil.

Outside in the gallery, Carew hears the housekeeper, Mrs Polke, approach, her tread is heavy. She meets the old man going the other way. He hears their whispered conversation, short but angry. Must there always be people whispering about him?

It's not right, sir – not fitting—

He cannot make out the old man's reply, short and muttered. But Mrs Polke makes no attempt to keep her voice down.

Not right, sir, it's in the blood. No good will come of it.

His eyes flicker back towards the older boy. Ralph has been watching him all this time. Carew cannot read the expression in his eyes.

❧

It's not right, sir, it's in the blood...

Old Polke. How many years has it been it since he thought of her? In the moonlit room, the present-day Carew almost smiled. Never was one to mince her words, was old Polke.

Was this his first memory? He was fairly sure it must be. It was certainly the first one that makes any kind of sense. Before that there were only flashes of something that he does not understand. A vague impression that he was hiding somewhere for a long time, of fire and ice together. But these memories were like trying to make sense of a night of drunkenness, he sometimes thought, and just as unprofitable.

Of one thing he was sure, however: he was never taken to sleep in the old man's bed again.

He took one last look at the sleeping woman and her child, and then drew the bed curtains gently. Outside the window a barn owl dove past on silent wings. He, who was once so in tune with every last wild creature on the manor lands, had a notion that it would be heading towards the woods on the hill. He wondered if Moocher was still there at the Drover's Path, or whether he had become bored with waiting and had moved on.

I've come to settle an old score.

The words had slipped out, catching him unawares. He'd said too much, that was for sure. People were hanged for less than he was about to do. But an old vagabond like Moocher, he reasoned, who would listen to him?

The moment had come. He couldn't put it off any longer. He both longed for, and dreaded, what he might find. Carew put his hand to his belt, felt the row of knives, tested their sharpness against his thumb, and then made his way quickly back down the stairs, and out into the cold night. There he doubled back to his hiding place at the parlour window.

He didn't have to wait long. No sooner had he settled himself than the door from some outer room opened, and into the parlour walked a man.

At the sight of him, Carew had the sensation of something hard and sharp twisting between his ribs. At first he thought that his eyes must be deceiving him. When the door opened, he had moved back instinctively so as not to be seen, but now he leant forward again, almost pressing his nose to the window so as to get a better look. Could it really be? Surely not – it was impossible.

Like the house itself, he was so much smaller than Carew remembered: an old man, dressed in black. His hair, what remained of it beneath his old-fashioned cap, was white. He walked slowly, his shoulders stooped.

The old man made his way to the chair by the fire and lowered himself into it. The two lurchers thumped their tails on the floor, but carried on sleeping. A log shifted in the grate, making the sparks fly. Only the little black-and-white cur stood up; she was a little unsteady now, one of her legs dragging behind her stiffly. She went up to the old man and pushed her greying muzzle into the palm of his hand.

Carew leant back against the wall. He had been holding his breath, and now let it out slowly. So it was true. His eyes were not deceiving him.

It was not Ralph after all. It was the old man.

Old man Pindar is still alive. . .

Dear God.

That changed everything.

The White Horse Inn,
Marlborough,
Wiltshire

The Feast Day of St Herbert, 30th day of October, 1611

Loving brother etc.

Further to my last, I write this addendum in some haste.

News has just reached me that there has been some kind of disturbance at the old place. Richard Pitton, our steward, has sent word that I should return there without delay, although the miserable fool who brought the tidings gave so garbled an account of the events that I hardly know what to tell you.

All I can gather is that our people (God's blood, brother, a more credulous and ignorant lot it would be hard to find) say they have seen lights up at the Drover's Path. Faint glimmerings like will-o'-the-wisps. They say that a man, a stranger to these parts, and a dog have been seen walking the fields there, but so far no one has been able to apprehend them.

Our father is in a state of much agitation, although exactly what the old man has either seen or heard the fool was unable to say. Only that he seems so much agitated that he will not keep to his bed, but stays in his parlour by the fire, day and night, and when they try to carry him upstairs, he does refuse, ranting and raving, like a veritable madman, and calling upon us – upon his sons – to succour him.

It seems I have no choice but to return to the old place myself again on the morrow. Our party – de Caus and the young Lord Nicholas and I – are still at the inn at Marlborough, so at least we have not far to go. I must put off my visit to you at Bishopsgate a little longer it seems.

I will write to you again when I have news.

Your dutiful brother,

Ralph Pindar

Postscript
I know what you will be thinking; that it is that cozening scoundrel John Carew come back to the old place to plague us all. You had better hope that it is not. You do not need me to tell you what the penalties are for poachers and vagabonds in these parts. And if it is he, and it can be proved upon him that he has stolen even half a coney from our lands, I will not care if he has come back from very jaws of death, hanging will be too good for him.

Post-postscript
My friends tell me my good sister, your wife Celia, is much visited by ladies of the Court.
    Chapeau, brother.
    I confess I did smile a little to hear that.
    Who cares if they do dine out upon her notoriety?

SIXTEEN

Carew

*Events occurring at Priors Leaze Manor in the country
of Wiltshire.*

B UT RALPH, IT TURNED out, was not the only one
with murder on his mind.

For several days after his return to Priors Leaze, Carew
had hidden out in the barn trying to work out what to do.
That the old man should still be living was the one thing
that he had not bargained on when he took it into his head
to come back to the old place. He had assumed – quite
wrongly, as it turned out – that it would be the younger
of the two Pindar brothers who would be in possession
of the manor now (since Paul, so far as he knew, was still
living in Aleppo). So when he had looked in through the
window that first night, had seen the old man himself
come into the room, settle himself down by the fire with
his dogs, Carew's heart had turned over in his chest. His
first impulse had been simply to throw himself at the old
man's feet.

*It is I. John Carew. The boy who ran away. Dost thou not
remember me?*

But it did not take more than a moment's reflection to
realise that this was a luxury he could not afford. To do so
would be to forfeit completely his hard-earned advantage:

those three days and freezing nights shivering with Moocher at the top of the Drover's Path while he got the lay of the land; his careful arrival, unseen by anyone, under the cover of darkness. If he went to the old man now he could hardly ask him not to tell anyone of his return, and it would only be a matter of hours before everyone within the manor bounds knew of it.

Besides, what would he say?

I've come to kill Ralph, and no one must know I am here.

There would be a certain pleasure in voicing the words, but if there was one thing of which Carew was certain, it was that the element of surprise was vital to his plans.

He was not sure how long he had spent looking in through the window that night. Long minutes, perhaps even hours, had passed. He wondered at how frail the old man had become. His movements were slow, the skin of his face and hands had turned that curious colour of the very old, chalky, almost bloodless, as though his life were slowly seeping from him and it was just a shadow self that remained.

And another thought had occurred to him. After so many years of absence could he really just turn up? Could he really just walk down the garden path and knock on the door? The possibility occurred to him that the old man most likely thought he was dead. Perhaps they all thought he was dead. Had Paul written to him? Or Ralph?

Soon, it would soon be the Feast of All Hallows. He wondered if they still kept up the old customs: decorating the hall with greenery; leaving food on the lintels of the houses; lighting fires to guide the souls of the departed back home, just as they used to when he was a boy. A younger, more mischievous version of himself would have thought it a great jest to wait until the feast day itself before showing himself:

Here I am, John Carew, see! I am come back from the dead, tra-la!

He saw himself leaping from the pie, as it were, like a blackbird or a crowd of starlings, one of those banqueting tricks from the days of the old Queen that he used to hear talked about in the manor kitchens, tricks to startle and amaze.

But the older Carew knew better than to frighten the old man so.

At first, so that he could be sure his presence at the manor was not discovered, Carew took to sleeping by day and roaming the house after dark, just as he had on the first night. It did not take long for him to pick up its rhythms. The place was so much changed that at times it felt to him as though there were barely a pulse.

Did anyone come to Priors Leaze these days? Since Ralph's brief visit, there had been no callers of which Carew was aware. An air of such quiet hung upon the place it was almost unnatural. For a large part of the day the old man sat dreaming; he talked to his dogs, made pictures in the fire. Twice a day the girl brought him his mess on an old-fashioned wooden trencher: a pitcher of small beer, bread, cheese, watery pottage. The diet was unvarying, but the old man did not seem to mind. He gave most of it to the dogs.

He did not sleep much. He spent little time in his own chamber – perhaps the stairs were too much for him now – but sat up most of the night in his chair by the fire. There he dozed fitfully, muttering in his sleep, his dogs around him. Carew sometimes imagined that it was his own name he could hear on the old man's lips, but the words were always indistinct

The dogs were used to Carew now. They would stir when he approached, but did not growl or fuss. His own dog Robin followed him like an adoring shadow on her stiff legs, as if she were afraid to let him out of her sight. Sometimes, when the old man woke, he would cock his head as though he were listening for something, but he soon dozed off again. The old man was almost blind now, but his hearing was still sharp, and he had that curious sixth sense that sometimes comes with ailing sight. When Carew came softly into the room to hide in the cobwebby shadows or behind the tapestried arras, the old man had a way of tilting his chin, of turning his face this way and that, as though he could feel the unseen presence, the subtlest vibration along his skin.

Sometimes Carew took up a position in the window casement. He found that he could sit there very still, his knees pulled up to his chin.

Several times he felt his resolve falter; several times he almost ran to him. What would he say to him? What *could* he say?

It is I. John Carew. The boy who ran away. Canst thou forgive me?

Apart from the sleeping woman, whom he now knew to be a servant, the dogs seemed to be the old man's whole world. The fact that Robin would no longer stay at his side troubled him greatly.

'Robin, where are you, girl?' The old man would put his hand out, and she would push her grizzled muzzle into his outstretched palm. 'Why won't you settle, foolish creature?'

He pulled her ears, feeling the once-silky fur beneath his fingers, fed her a titbit, a rind of cheese from his supper plate. She accepted it humbly, thumping her tail, and then followed Carew out again, her nails clicking on the flag-stones, leaving the old man staring sightlessly after her in the dark.

Alone except for the skittering of mice in the wainscot-ing, Carew roamed the darkened rooms. The small parlour where the old man now lived was no better than the rest of the house. Carew remembered it from his boyhood, could recall the clean smell of beeswax and lavender and the old-fashioned country habit of laying rushes on the floor. In those days the wooden wainscoting had been hung with a tapestry arras which showed a hunting scene, lords and ladies in green and scarlet clothes, a stag, dogs baying. The sumptuousness of its colour, its pictures, had been dazzling to the young Carew's untutored eyes.

Now the arras hung from the wall in tatters. A layer of dust clung to it so that the colours hardly showed in the dark room. When he inspected it, he found that the edges had been shredded by mice. The room had a sour smell, of old dogs and decaying flesh. There were mice droppings on the old man's supper plate.

How could his sons – Paul and Ralph – have allowed this to happen? Carew felt rage rising in his gorge. He could forgive neglect of the house, but neglect of the old man, that was another matter altogether. That he could not forgive.

Paul and Ralph: where were they now? He went upstairs so that he could examine their portraits once more.

Ralph stared straight back at him: *Lay one finger on me, kitchen boy, and I will crush you like a worm. Take that, kitchen boy. And that. Take that, you snivelling little rat-catcher. Take that and don't forget your place.*

And suddenly he is a child again. He is the kitchen boy, his head ringing and buzzing from where Ralph has banged his head on the stone kitchen floor. For which particular misdemeanour, Carew – looking back from this great distance – cannot now rightly say. Ever since they were small children – that is, ever since Ralph's father had brought him to Priors Leaze, a half-starved child who had had to be smoked out like a feral dog from the empty cottage – Ralph had made the rules. But lately Ralph has been away. To London, Carew has heard tell, staying with an uncle to whom he was to have been apprenticed. Clearly the visit has not been a success for now he's back – Carew observes, his ears ringing – bigger, fatter and nastier than before.

The older boy's face looms over his own, his fleshy features distorted. It's Ralph a-right. His fleshy body, stuffed with sweetmeats and sugared fruits, has always seemed to Carew to have no bones, as though he were made of pastry dough. But now there is something different about him, some subtle change, Carew cannot quite work it out.

At this angle, Ralph's cheeks, already running to flab, puff outwards, merging with his too-fat neck, giving him an uncanny likeness to a toad that Carew had once found in the bulrushes by the lake. Carew had kept the toad in a box, fed it with slugs and worms from the garden, until Ralph, who had somehow, despite Carew's best efforts to avoid him, tracked him down to the secret place where he kept his prize.

When he next went there it was to find the box open on its side, the creature gone. He knew at once that it was Ralph's doing, hoped against hope that the creature had escaped, but he found it soon just a little way off: a pulse still throbbing in its neck, one leg twitching as though trying to escape his tormentor, but already its eyes were glazing over with the grey film of death. The creature's innards, crimson and white, glistened over the grass where the older boy had stamped on it with his foot.

It had occurred to Carew that leaving the creature there, not quite dead, had been a deliberate act. That Ralph had left it there on purpose for him to find. He had always known that Ralph was bad, that Ralph must be avoided wherever possible. The whole of his life at the manor has been coloured by these facts, but this act, this piece of deliberate cruelty, is something that he has yet to process. At the back of his mind is the beginning of the thought, which will not for some time be fully realised, that Ralph would like to do the same to him.

Now, with his head still buzzing from where he has cracked his skull on the kitchen flagstones, the thought coalesces fully for the first time, takes shape and flies. And with it, hard on its heels as it were, rushes another, more troubling one.

There is something else that Ralph would like to do.

Like tumbling doves, the two thoughts lock briefly, fly apart again, feathers tearing the air.

In a vain attempt to push this new thought away, the fatal words come spilling out, unbidden.

You look like a toad, so you do, Master Ralph!

As he says the words his throat is dry with fear.

Master Ralph looks just like a great big fat toad!

Although how he gets the words out he does not know. Ralph has manoeuvred himself so that he is now sitting astride him on his chest, crushing all the air from his lungs.

There is a pause. For a moment both boys are still. Their eyes lock.

What's that you say, kitchen boy? Ralph's head is cocked ominously to one side.

Carew knows that this is the moment he should back down. He knows it because instinctively he has always been able, with the subtlest of calibrations, to calculate just how far he can push Ralph, and still come back from the brink.

But this time… this time he can't, he really can't. Perhaps it's not Ralph who's changed; perhaps he is the one who's different. The devil is in him, whispering in his ear: *He's a toad – a toad – he's nothing but a hideous great toad—Say it, John. Say it*.

So he says it again. He can't help himself. He is dizzy, and not just from the blows on his head. A beautiful feeling – although he cannot put a name to it – of release, of euphoria, is coursing through his veins. Even if he dies now, which he quite likely will, it will have been worth it, just to see Ralph's face.

When he does try to speak his breath comes in short rasping bursts.

Master Ralph is – a – great – big – toad – a – great – big – fat – toad—

It is a declaration of war.

A war from which, this time, there will be no going back.

But at first, to his surprise, Ralph seems not to react. He looks down, almost pensively, at the kitchen boy lying beneath him. A gob of spit is slowly gathering on his bottom lip. It hangs there, glistening. His face looms over Carew's, closer and closer. When he guesses what Ralph is going to do, he begins to turn his head, furiously thrashing from side to side, but it is no use. The warm wetness of Ralph's spittle drops on to his cheek.

That's dis-gusting! His voice is a thin wheeze.

Ralph snickers, jiggles his hips to and fro. In this position his weight, which is normally his greatest disadvantage, easily trumps Carew's superior nimbleness and strength. In this position he is the helpless and inferior supplicant that Ralph wants him to be, a role that Carew, although he is only the kitchen boy, has always resisted with every last drop of resourcefulness he can muster.

Ralph gyrates his hips again, more knowingly this time.

Carew squeezes his eyes shut, tries not to feel the older boy's flesh pressing against him through the thin material of his hose.

When he opens them again, Ralph is still looking down at him. There is an odd smile on his face, an expression that Carew has not seen before.

Open your mouth for me, kitchen boy.

What's this? Carew, expecting violence – a language he understands – feels his eyes widen in dismay. For some reason that he cannot yet fathom, this is worse than any beating Ralph might inflict on him.

That's. . . that's disgusting!

Ralph snickers again. Bends forward as he marshals another glistening bauble along his bottom lip.

I've got something for you. Open your mouth, I say. . .

No! Almost too late, Carew realises his mistake and snaps his lips shut.

Do it!

Nnnn!

A second sticky gob of warm wetness falls against his face.

A feeling of panic fills Carew now. He can barely breathe. He has had fights with other boys before – indeed, it could be said that his whole life has been one long fight – but never one like this. He does not know the rules for this kind of engagement. Ralph is so close now he can smell him – smell his breath, the sweat beneath his arms. His odour is a curious one; both sweet and rank at the same time, like a soft cheese on the turn. For some obscure reason this is worse, far worse, than any physical pain. His helpless proximity to Ralph at this moment is pure torment. He can't stand to have the smell of Ralph in his nostrils, or feel the spread of his fat buttocks grinding against his groin—

For the feeling of Ralph's buttocks against his groin is more insistent now, he tries to shut his mind against it, to push the feeling away. But it's getting harder because all this time Ralph is rocking his hips back and forth, back and forth. . .

Open your mouth. Do it!

No, you great fat toad, it's disgusting – you're disgusting. . .

Not half as disgusting as you are, you snivelling scrawny little rat—

Another gob of spit lands nearer its mark this time, at one corner of his mouth. He is desperate to rub it away – rub all feeling of Ralph away – but his arms are still pinned hard by his sides. And besides, to his shame, the first inklings of a much more pressing indignity are beginning to intrude upon his consciousness.

You're going to say it for me, kitchen boy. Ralph's voice quavers slightly.

No!

Say after me, my mother was a whore – he is almost singing the words – *my mother was a witch and a whore. . .*

And they are back in the old familiar territory again, dipping back suddenly into the old childhood refrains and torments, but this time Carew barely hears him, so intent is he on the urgency of the matter at hand. He shuts his eyes, dreams of icy water, of red-hot coals, of biting ferrets, poisonous adders, stinging spiders – of anything at all that might restore him to his normal state. But, too late—

Ooh! Ralph purses his lips together. *And what have we here. . .?*

Carew feels the panic rising in him. What have they done to him! This isn't Ralph! This is a Ralph he has never seen before. A boy player playing a part that, quite frankly, is beginning to terrify him. In the wan kitchen light

Ralph's lips glisten, plump and red like a girl's. The sight of him – of them – makes Carew want to scream but, as in a sleeping nightmare, when he opens his mouth, not a sound comes out.

And what have we here, little John? Another exploratory grind of the hips. Then a titter. *Not so little any more, I see.*

As involuntarily as the other thing, Carew feels the blood rushing to his cheeks. At that moment he feels a shame so profound he thinks he might die of it.

Ooh! Fie, you blush like a maiden, Johnny.

Stop it!

Why should I? Another titter. *When you're enjoying it so much. . .*

Please! But as soon as the word is out, he knows he has made a mistake. There is another pause, more ominous this time. That same odd look passes over Ralph's face.

What's that, kitchen boy? The boy player cups his hand around his ear. There is something grotesque about the movement. *What's that you say?*

You heard. . . If Carew had the breath, he would spit in his face right now.

No, no. . . Still cupping his hand to his ear Ralph shakes his head. *I really don't think I did.*

And of course Carew knows exactly what Ralph wants. He wants to hear Carew beg. As if reading Carew's mind, Ralph says, *Go on, beg me. I want to hear you beg me to stop.*

He knows that Carew would rather die. But Carew is not ready to die, not just yet. Lying on his back, he looks around desperately. At this afternoon hour the kitchen is deserted. To one side of him the fire in the hearth is damped down to burning embers; on the other side are the doors to the store cupboards and the distilling room. High up on a shelf behind Ralph's head, rows of copper pans – the ones Carew himself has scoured only that morning – glister faintly in the thin winter light. Irrelevantly, he sees the long black thread of an old cobweb stirring in the rafters.

Even if he were able, he will not cry out for help, not even now, would rather cut out his own tongue than do that – Ralph knows this – but all the same, at any other time, succour in some form or other might have come. But there is no one. The flagstoned floor is icy against his back.

All right then, have it your own way, kitchen boy!

And the next moment Ralph is on top of him. He is lying face down over him and covering Carew's mouth with his own. Carew can feel his probing tongue, soft and wet, trying to force its way in between his lips; he is half-biting him, half-kissing. One hand is groping against his thigh.

But now, with his weight more evenly distributed, Ralph has given away his only advantage and Carew wastes no time in pushing out from under him. For a few minutes the two boys roll together on the ground biting, scratching, gouging, kicking, like two curs together. No rules now. How the fur flies! This is not the first time he has fought Ralph, but never before has he been so aware of the profound intimacy of it. Never before has he been so acutely aware of the other boy's body pressing down upon his own: his heavy flesh, Ralph's breath in his ear, the smell of his hair, his sweat. As they writhe together on the floor, he cannot tell at what point his body ends and the older boy's begins. Is it the sound of his own raw breath or Ralph's that he can hear gasping and grunting?

And then the knife.

He cannot remember now whose knife it was. He only remembers himself sitting astride Ralph – *who's going to beg now, toad boy?* – he actually has his hands round Ralph's fat throat, his thumbs are pressing down into that pile of loathsome lard whence a satisfying bubbling sound is coming... when suddenly there's a knife at his own throat.

He feels it rather than sees it: a prick of steel, a cold blade pressing into his windpipe. He knows then what death looks like. Death is Ralph's face. The face of a boy not much older than he: sallow of skin, fleshy of feature, a face so distorted with passion that there is a kind of madness there.

It is a moment of complete clarity. He knows that this time Ralph is going to kill him.

And then Ralph's arm is lunging upwards, and there is a flash of something near his ear, and then he is sliding to the floor. He does not remember feeling the blade cut his face. At some point, instinctively he flings one arm across his neck to protect his throat – Ralph has watched the pigs being slaughtered in the farmyard, he knows how it's done – and with the other he must have raised his hand to cover Ralph's hand, crushing it, the blade inside. He can read Ralph's thoughts so clearly at this moment he has almost become the other boy; the two of them seem to merge, to inhabit, however briefly, the same body, two in one. Carew has never known anything like this. He knows, with every fibre in his body, that Ralph is trying to kill him, and yet what he feels at this moment, perhaps for the first time in his life, is. . . love.

But then there is blood. A great deal of blood. And the sound of Ralph screaming.

After that Carew's memory is a little hazy. He remembers a terrible commotion in the kitchen, voices shouting, the sound of running feet. The old man is there, trying to pull them off one another, although at first they are stuck as fast as two ticks, and it's not until someone throws a pail of water over them that they are finally prised apart. They separate, sneezing and trembling like a couple of farm curs.

Now, so many years later, Carew stared at the portrait again.

Lay one finger on me, kitchen boy, and I will crush you like a worm.

Not any more, fat boy. Carew, contemplating his childhood companion, almost smiled.

Rafie. I'm waiting for you, sweet Rafie. Come home soon.

He took a knife from his belt, and in the candlelight pressed the tip against one of the folds in Ralph's painted neck, with a quick flick of the wrist he scored through the canvas, left to right, hard and deep. A merciless butcher's cut.

Splayed. Skinned. Spatchcocked.

SEVENTEEN

Carew

Events occurring at Priors Leaze Manor in the country of Wiltshire.

H AD JOHN CAREW REALLY come home with the intention of killing Ralph? Or was it just a young man's *braggadocio*, the old Carew swagger, that made him tell himself this was so? There was no doubt that the thought of it had sustained him on the long journey home: the sweet thought of revenge for the cruelties and indignities meted out by his childhood companion. But now that he was back at Priors Leaze, his position was altogether different from the one he had imagined.

With the old man still alive he knew he could never kill Ralph, even if it were practicable to do so. Carew had known the very instant he had seen old Pindar through the window that he would not be able to go through with it. For a son to die before a parent was against Nature, and besides, he reasoned, killing was too good for Ralph. All the drownings, impalings, slicings and throttlings of his wildest imagination, he would have to put to one side. And somewhere, deep in his calculations, he knew he had to think of his own scrawny skin.

But if he was not actually going to kill Ralph, then he was going to have to think of some other, more subtle torment.

But first he was going to have to fetch Ralph back to the manor again. And to do that he was going to need help.

On an upper platform in the barn Carew had made himself a hiding place. From here he watched the comings and goings at the manor carefully. The barn faced on to the courtyard on the kitchen side of the house, and by knocking out some of the soft wattle between the beams, he fashioned for himself a spyhole.

The household was much reduced, that much was already clear. Very occasionally some men from the village came and went on farm business. They led the cows out to pasture from the byre. Old George, young George, Quentin and Peter: with a small pang Carew recognised them all as the old man's tenants. In the courtyard, the mud and muck from the byre lay ankle deep. The men had tied dried straw around their ankles and lower legs, country-fashion, binding it with twine. But they never stayed long, and Carew soon dismissed them from his plans.

If he were going to find help, it was going to have to come from closer to hand. Apart from the old man himself, only the one servant, whose name Carew now learnt was Alice, and her toddling child, aged two, lived at the manor now. During the day another girl, Anne, joined Alice. Both were raw-boned Wiltshire girls; sisters he reckoned.

From his spyhole in the roof of the barn, Carew looked them over carefully. As the raw material with which to put his plan into effect, they were not much, but Carew recognised they would have to do.

Alice was the dreamy one, not a bad looker. Her hair was soft and feathery, the exact colour of the pelt of a baby mole. Anne was an older, meatier version of Alice. Heavy breasts, thick waist; her upper arms, red and mottled, were roughened from work. It was Anne's job to tend to the cows, to milk them morning and evening, and take them out to pasture, to feed the chickens, and take slops to the pigs. Alice's task was to look after the old man and his dogs, and to tend to the laundry and the cleaning. Most of the time they did neither but flirted with the men, or sat gossiping by the kitchen fire.

If he were going to have either one, Carew thought idly, it would have to be Anne. Alice was the prettier of the two, but he knew the type: she was the one most likely to give herself airs, imagining that some tribute was due to her looks. A day or two of cajoling at the very least, and he had no time for that just now.

Plain Anne, on the other hand, was another kind altogether. He knew this type too: admiring, grateful – he had always liked the grateful ones – they went at it with a will. Carew lay back and closed his eyes, testing the temperature of his body. He tried to imagine the feel of the girl's flesh against his hands, the cool of her buttocks against his thighs as he pressed down over her, his hand on the small of her back, the warmth between her legs. It had been so long since he had a woman. All that flesh. He could lose himself in Anne's flesh, he thought, for a while anyway, or perhaps it was just the similarity in their names that attracted him.

Anne. Annetta.

Annetta. His woman.

Perhaps a coupling with Anne would blot out just for a moment the perpetual feeling of loss. Only three letters between them after all, he encouraged himself. If he kept his eyes closed, perhaps? He lay back on the straw and tried again. Imagined himself giving her a slap or two, watching the smarting red outline of his hand appear on each of those pale moons. His quicksilver mind soon had her at his mercy, trussed up like a woodcock, ready for the spit. In his mind's eye he held her there, musing; and then found his mind drifting again. He tried to imagine the sounds she might make as she bent for him over a convenient hay bale; a kind of lowing, like a young calf or perhaps an indignant chicken cluck... But no. *Fanculo*! What was wrong with him? This was not the moment to digress. Carew pulled himself back to the job at hand. He felt himself stirring, briefly. But no. Nothing doing. Even though it had been a long time since he had a woman, somehow, he no longer had an appetite for it. He was at a loss to explain it.

He had had other women, of course, many times, since he left Annetta in Venice. In Genoa, Marseilles, Lisbon: the docks were always full of women, they swarmed with them like rats; young ones too, although Carew always felt more of an inconvenient pity for them than desire. There had been a lady's maid in Ragusa with whom he had coupled up against a wall. Another in Naples. But it was someone else's face he always saw.

If he lay quite still, with his eyes closed, he could imagine Annetta next to him.

They are close together, not quite touching, just their little fingers entwined. They are looking upwards. Overhead the sky is blue. Larks are tumbling somewhere high out of sight in the blue empyrean. He turns his head a little, sees her face out of the corner of his eye: the pure, high bridge of her nose, a small mole, like an exquisite beauty mark, on her right cheekbone. Or was it her upper lip?

If Carew was afraid of anything it was that one day he would not be able to conjure her to him at all. He had to concentrate hard these days, just to hear the sound of her voice.

Santa Madonna, *John Carew, can't you remember any-thing!* She rolls over so that she is lying on her side, facing him. *And what are you smiling for?* He can feel the warmth of her body, her breath. She draws a finger softly down the side of his cheek. *And leave that poor girl alone, or you'll have me to answer to,* capito?

He had wanted her in a way that he had never wanted anyone else. She was bossy, defiant, opinionated. She would never do as she was told. Had ruined him, for ever, for all other women.

But you cannot be in love with someone who's dead. Who had said that? And besides, what did they know?

It was not long before he became bored with hiding. When the men left for the fields and the two women were on their own, he reckoned it would be safe to come out. During his first few days back at the old place he had been careful to venture out only under the cover of dark-ness, but now that he knew what their movements were, he allowed himself to make quick forays into the house in daylight. But soon he grew bold. Once, he went into the kitchen and was nearly caught by one of the sisters coming back unexpectedly. When he heard the scrape of the latch being pulled up, he only just had time to dart out of sight into the distilling room.

'Ye seen my pattens, sister?' It was dreamy Alice calling.

A voice, muffled but distinctly snappish, answered from somewhere in the yard.

'Well, keep your hair on. . . I know I left them in here somewheres.'

He could hear her moving around as she hunted for the missing shoes. Then the latch banged again and the room fell silent.

Carew emerged slowly from behind the cobwebby door.

The sight of the kitchen in the daylight disgusted him even more than it had done on that first night in the dark. There were the same gnawed bones and unscoured pots lying in the fireplace. Grease had spilled from the dripping tray, congealing on the floor like candle wax. The lid was off the milk, and there were mouse droppings around the bread crocks. Several dog turds, hard and blackened with age, clustered beneath the table.

And there, in a corner next to some old sacks, he spied the missing pattens.

In almost all other respects, Carew's standards were not high, but when it came to kitchens – to this kitchen in particular – it was a crime he could not forgive. He remembered Mr Bull, the mountain of a man who ruled the kitchen kingdom between these walls when Carew was a boy. The aptly named Mr Bull, built – ha, ha – like a bull himself, no neck, giant shoulders, whose little pink lashless eyes could see round corners and through walls; whose very breath always seemed to the young Carew to steam from his nostrils if all was not exactly as pleased him; if every last pot, pan, copper and dripping tray were not shining like the burnished sun; if he could not see his own face in the polished flagstones. . .

Carew looked around the room again. The old man might be almost blind, but he was not yet entirely in his dotage. Who had hired these women? Carew would not trust them to lick his boots. On second thoughts, perhaps he *would* get them to lick his boots. He thought of the old man, of the mice droppings on the dirty trencher, and felt his rage rising again. His first thought was to smash something. His second: to drag the two women in by their slatternly ears and force them to clean the place on their hands and knees. Then suddenly he heard the sound of approaching footsteps on the stones outside. No time to lose. Carew grabbed the pattens from the corner and placed them in the middle of the table. Then he reached beneath the table, scooped up two dog turds, placing them neatly, one in each shoe; whisked nimbly back into the distilling room, half closing the door behind him.

This time it was Anne.

Carew watched her through a small crack in the door. She saw the pattens immediately.

'They're right here on the table, you daffy wench.'

'They're not I tell you, I looked in there—' Alice, wrapped in a shawl, poked her head around the door. When she saw the shoes she stopped in mid-sentence. 'Well, they weren't there a minute ago, I swear.'

'You know sometimes I despair, I really do.' Anne went to retrieve the shoes, and saw what lay inside them. 'By all the saints, sister—' She picked them up gingerly, thrust them out for Alice to see, '—what d'you call this?'

She held up the pattens, the dog turds nestled inside, and for a moment they both stared, uncomprehending.

'But... that's a horrible thing to do, that is,' Alice gave her sister a slap on her bare arm.

'Ow!' Her sister turned on her indignantly. 'Don't be daft, it weren't I. Why would I do something like that?'

'Well, someone must have done it, and I know it weren't I neither.'

'And it can't have been the old man...' Alice's brow puckered doubtfully, '...d'you think?'

'Don't be daft, he hasn't been in here these last three years.'

'One of the men? Young George?'

'No, it weren't none of them. They've been out at One Hundred Wood these last two days.'

'The little 'un?'

'Now that really *is* daft.'

'Then who. . .?'

A tremulous silence filled the room.

When no answer suggested itself, they stared at one another with rounded eyes. The unfinished words hung in the air, heavy with meaning. Each knew what the other was thinking, but neither wanted to say the words out loud, but from the look on their faces Carew knew immediately. He wondered what they called them these days: little people, fairies, elves?

Behind the kitchen door Carew was grinning so hard his cheeks ached.

After this, he lost no opportunity to plague the two sisters. They were such easy prey it was hardly sporting, but Carew could not stop himself. It was as though he were a boy again. He hid objects and then repositioned them again in strange places, opened and closed the barn door, tipped over the milk pail.

Before long Anne refused to go into the barn unless Alice went with her; soon the two women were too frightened to go anywhere without the other. At night they took to putting a dish of bread and milk on the kitchen doorstep.

Soon Carew began to think of other, more inventive ways to plague them. He considered taking the child and rematerialising it somewhere strange – the barn roof, perhaps, or one of the attic rooms – only he couldn't think how to keep it quiet in the meantime. Entertaining a dribbling two-year-old was not Carew's idea of fun.

From his hideout Carew had observed the child carefully: a stolid, slow-witted creature, who wandered round the farmyard chewing on a piece of stale bread. Still in long skirts, it was impossible to tell whether it was a boy or a girl. But it was not so much the child's sex as its curious status that puzzled Carew. He wondered if it were defective in some way, but after a while came to the conclusion that it was merely neglect that ailed it. He had assumed that the servant Alice was the child's mother, but after a day or so of watching them all, he began to think that she must be minding it for someone else. She did not neglect it exactly, but maternal solicitude was distinctly absent.

One afternoon, he came face to face with the child in the barn. It stared up at him, a slight cast over one of its eyes.

He crouched down to get a better look.

'Come here, I won't bite.' He examined the child gently. 'You're a right mess, you are.'

Two rivulets of green slime ran from the child's nostrils; the skin on its arms was red and flaky, and there were open sores where it had scratched itself.

'What's your name, then?' The child stared back at him, silent, incurious. 'All right, be like that then. See if I care.'

It occurred to Carew that perhaps the child did not speak because no one ever spoke to it. Its cap and skirts were filthy, but when he looked closely he saw that they were trimmed with lace. The stitching on them was exquisite. These were no country clothes, that was for sure. Some nearby gentry had put their infant out to wet-nurse, and forgotten about it. Carew picked up the hem of the child's pinafore and ran it between his fingers.

'Nice bit of lace you've got there,' he said conversationally. He had not seen lace of such fine quality since he lived in Venice. 'Nun's work, if you ask me.' He looked at the child solemnly. 'I could tell you a thing or two about nuns.' Carew gave a sigh. 'But listen to me, rabbiting on – bad as Moocher.'

It occurred to him as he spoke that it had been days now since he had addressed a word to another human being, but still the child said nothing.

213

He closed his eyes briefly, and with an effort, he summoned Annetta to him again.

Shall I do it?

Santa Madonna! She rolled her eyes, *Just do what you have to do.*

'Well, I can't sit here like a gossip.' Carew opened his eyes again. 'And nor can you – you've got work to do.'

He pulled the child to him and deftly untied the ribbons at the back of its pinafore. 'Well, at least they feed you, I'll say that for them.' Against his hands the child's body was like a suet pudding. 'Off you go now,' he murmured, not unkindly. Carew turned the child round, gave it a little push in the direction of the open barn door.

'Tell them it was the fairies what did it.'

On the Eve of All Hallows the girls went to church. From his spyhole in the barn, Carew watched them depart, decked out in such small fineries, as they possessed: a cape of loden green for Alice, a new ribbon for Anne. Somehow they had brushed the mud from their skirts. They swung the child between them, fears of elves and hobgoblins momentarily forgotten.

Carew knew exactly the route they would take: through the farmyard and past the lake, and then through fields, across the stepping stones at the bottom of the field, and then over the stile. The hems of their dresses would soon be wet with dew.

From the window in one of the upstairs rooms Carew looked out at the little church, heard the bell tolling from the squat tower. How long since he himself had been anywhere near a church? It was the sound of his childhood, familiar, almost comforting. For a brief moment he allowed himself the luxury of imagining Annetta here with him. In his mind, he walked her to the altar on a fine

May morning, her hand in his, her dark hair braided with flowers—

Christos! What kind of a fool was he to think he could ever find that kind of happiness?

He pushed the thoughts away.

That morning there had been a mist in the valley. Now it clung to the hillside, hovering like spirit matter over the black water of the lake. It was set to be another fine day. Carew looked up in the direction of the Drover's Path and wondered if Moocher were still there.

When he turned his sights back to the church, he could see the straggle of people making their way through the wicket gate by the old yew tree. For a moment he had the wild notion that he should just stroll up there and join them all.

He imagined himself pushing open the door, feeling the sudden drop in the temperature of the air as he went in; imagined the smell of incense; the whitewashed walls with its pictures of the Virgin and all the saints, and on the back wall the picture of the devil, painted blue and red, dancing in the flames. In his mind's eye they were all there, his childhood companions, even Paul and Ralph. They turned, nudged one another, stared at him round-eyed.

A thin whisper seemed to pass over them, just as it had the first time he went there, all those years ago. He could still feel the old man's hand at his back.

It's him, that's the one. It's her *boy. The one they burnt at Starling's Roost, the one who's still burning most like.*

The one who burns in hell.

EIGHTEEN

Celia

Bishopsgate.

S HE WAS NEVER EXACTLY sure when the first small
cracks and fissures in her relationship with Frances
Sydenham began to appear.

Sometimes she thought it had been talk of the diamond
that had given her the first warning signs; later she realised that it was Annetta who had caused the first serious
breach between them.

They had been sitting in Celia's gallery one autumnal
afternoon, and their conversation had turned to the first
visit, to the *miladies* Peters and Ormiston.

'At first I thought they were speaking another
language,' Celia recalled. 'I couldn't understand them
at all.'

'But they are *Scots* ladies, of course. You mean you
couldn't tell? Don't tell me you have never heard a Scots
accent before, you *puur wee thing*?' Frances took one of
Celia's cushions and threw it at her playfully.

'There were not so many Scots in Constantinople or
Aleppo of whom I ever heard tell.' Laughing, Celia batted
the cushion away.

'Well, you must get used to it, there are scores of them at
Court these days.' Frances sank down on to the cushions

on Celia's divan and stretched out luxuriously. 'They came to London with His Majesty.'

Celia tried to look interested, but the Court of King James, she thought privately, had about as much to do with her as... well, as Lady Sydenham with the House of Felicity.

She looked over at Frances, and it occurred to her that, sprawling upon the cushions, she did not look at all as a respectable Ottoman *khatun* should look. *Oh, no*, Celia thought to herself in amusement, *not at all.*

Madonna! She could hear Annetta's scathing voice, *You do not lie there as though it is your* bed*!*

She wondered about explaining the indecorum of this to Frances, but some instinct made her think better of it. She put her hand to her mouth to hide her smile.

'Do I amuse you?'

Frances, in turn, was looking at Celia. Her head was upside down and from this angle her eyes appeared narrow and calculating. At first Celia had missed the subtle change in tone.

'No, not at all,' she answered easily, her head bent over her work. 'It's just that you have never sat with me like this before. Like this I mean.' She indicated the divan. 'Like a true Ottoman lady, a *khatun*.'

'Well, child, some of us don't have time to lie around all day.'

The barb hit home.

After a moment's hesitation Celia replied carefully, 'All the same, it is comfortable, is it not?'

'Yes, indeed, barbarously so.' Frances pulled herself slowly upright again, smoothing down the folds of her dress. 'Barbarously so.'

It was quite clear to Celia that she had made a mistake.

'It is so easy to forget with you, my sweet Celia.'

'Forget?' Celia looked up, puzzled, 'Forget what?'

'Oh, you know...' Frances replied, waving one hand about her in a vague gesture. 'How long you were away from us.'

She selected another of the cushions, and threw it, a little harder this time.

'Imagine not knowing how a Scots lady speaks. It may interest you to know,' she added, 'that there is a *Scots* King on the throne of England these days.'

'Well, of course I knew *that*.' Playfully, Celia threw the cushion back. It struck the side of Frances's head, and the silver thread embroidered on the velvet caught at one of her earrings.

'You fool!' Frances shot Celia a look that was positively venomous.

For a moment Celia was so surprised she could say nothing. 'Are you hurt?'

'You little fool!' Frances said again, putting her hand to her ear, 'You should have more care—'

'Your earring... forgive me... are you hurt?'

Frances turned away, abruptly rubbed her ear, and hooked the earring back into place. When she turned back to Celia again, she seemed, just as suddenly, her old self once more.

'It is no matter, nothing really.' She took Celia's hand and squeezed it. 'I am sorry I spoke so roughly. Come, let us be friends again.'

'Of course,' Celia murmured. 'Friends.'

She bowed her head over her work again, but the camaraderie between them was beginning slowly to leech from the room. For some time the two worked away in silence. Frances was a dexterous sewer, but Celia had the impression that she did not much care for this kind of work. She herself was embroidering the figure of a bird in fine silver filigree on a piece of black velvet, yet another custom that she had brought back with her from the East. Normally Celia was a swift, neat worker, but something about this last exchange unsettled her.

Frances's words hung over her like wasps buzzing over rotted fruit. She had called her a fool! In her own house! The discourtesy seemed to weave itself into Celia's work: the lines she sewed became uneven; her threads tied themselves in knots, and finally snapped. When she pricked her finger she cried out and a drop of blood fell on to her white lace sleeve.

Immediately Frances was all solicitousness. 'Ah, now you have you hurt yourself. What a pair we are! Here, take this...' She handed Celia her handkerchief, an exquisite wisp of Flemish lace.

Sucking her pricked finger, Celia shook her head. 'It will only spoil.'

'Don't be a *goose*, take it.' Frances was still holding out the handkerchief. 'I can see that you have drawn blood, and it's really no matter—'

Celia stared at her, 'What did you just call me?'

'Why – nothing.'

'You called me "Goose"—'

'Perhaps I did. What of it? I was only jesting...' she said, almost sulky. 'You are so overdelicate these days, Celia, I hardly know you.'

Celia looked down at her pricked finger.

'Annetta always called me Goose.' She pressed the pad of her finger and squeezed it so that another drop of blood flowed out. 'It is curious to hear her special name for me on someone else's lips, that's all.' And then in case Frances had not quite understood, she added, 'Annetta was my companion in the House of Felicity. In Constantinople.'

'You mean the little nun?' Frances said, a little too quickly. 'But I knew that, of course.' She took out a pair of tiny golden scissors from her workbox and snipped at some stray threads. 'Don't look so surprised. Your husband warned me only a few days ago that you are expecting her. I understand that she is to come here, to live with us at Bishopsgate.'

Celia felt a stab of irritation. Paul had told her about Annetta? If he had done so why had neither of them mentioned it to her before now? In any case, surely it was up to Celia herself to do that? This was not the first time they seemed to have been conferring behind her back. The phrase 'live with us at Bishopsgate' hung ominously in the air.

'Yes, she is coming to stay with me here at Bishopsgate. To live here, indeed, if she cares to, for as long as she likes.' Trying not to emphasise the word 'me' too much, Celia bent her head over her work again. Why was she finding it so difficult to have this conversation? This was her house, and she could invite here whomsoever she pleased. After everything they had been through together in the House of Felicity – she and Annetta – no one could possibly understand the bond they had, not even Paul, and she saw no reason why she should have to apologise to anyone for inviting her. But that was what Frances was making her feel. Celia's neck and hands were damp with angry perspiration.

'But of course I knew that. Although why I should hear it from him, child, and not from you I have no idea.'

This second barb was lightly dealt, but a barb nonetheless. Frances's tone of voice when she said 'little nun' rankled deeply.

'Annetta comes here as a Venetian lady, just like any other.' Celia's silver needle flew angrily in and out of the velvet fabric.

'A lady?' The expression on Frances's face indicated quite clearly how very much she doubted that that was the case. 'How so? She is a religious, so I'm told, and always was. I also seem to remember Mr Pindar telling me she had never taken full orders—'

'—which is why it has been possible for her to leave her convent in Venice. She returned from Constantinople with a large dowry—'

'—and the convent, your husband gave me to understand, seemed to want the dowry rather more than they wanted her, yes, I know, I know—'

'—then he will also have told you, since he was in such a telling mood.' The palms of Celia's hand were by now so clammy with rage she could hardly hold her needle, 'that if it were not for her I might not be here at all.'

But Frances was doing her usual trick, Celia now realised, of appearing not to hear when someone suggested something that might thwart her.

'So if she never took full orders...' she was saying thoughtfully, 'that would have made her either a novice, or perhaps indeed, she was one of the convent's servant-nuns? And from what I hear, it is most likely to be the latter, if I am not much mistaken.'

And since when did you know so much about these things? Celia wanted to shout at her, but she did not trust herself to speak. This was almost a worse insult than the disdain with which Frances had uttered the words 'little nun'. Annetta, who had risen to become the Ottoman queen's right hand, one of the Valide's most trusted and loyal servants. Annetta, a woman of the very highest status and respect in the House of Felicity, not because of an accident of her birth, but because of her own talents and endeavours. Annetta, who after the Valide's death and her own manumission, had been offered the hand in marriage of no fewer than three Ottoman viziers, but had chosen instead to take her dowry back with her to the convent whence she had come. And now she was to be relegated to the status of a mere servant! Celia was so outraged she hardly knew what to do with herself... But there was worse to come.

'But my dear Celia, forgive me for saying so – and I say this as a friend – but a convent servant is hardly a suitable companion for the wife of Merchant Pindar of Bishopsgate, do you think? Most especially now.'

'Now?' With an effort Celia swallowed her rage. 'How so?'

'Now that you are in so unusually fortunate and exalted a position, considering your natural station in life.' Frances's head was bent over her sewing. 'Which, let us not forget, is not even that of a merchant's daughter, but the child of a mere sea captain, if you will not mind my saying so. And now you have the very highest ladies in the land, women of rank and title, coming to call on you, and as if that were not enough, there is every likelihood that you are soon to be invited to Court and, who knows, might even one day be presented to their Majesties. And you, Celia, a mere sea captain's daughter...' she said again, for emphasis.

Celia regarded Frances Sydenham coldly. She was so smooth, so sleek, so perfectly poised, so in command of her – Celia's – own household.

Is it quite wise to let her govern you so?

Of late, Annetta's imagined words kept coming back to her. And now she knew the answer. No, she had not been wise. Not wise at all.

Celia put her work down. 'I think you do forget yourself, Lady Sydenham.'

Frances did not reply to this, but nor had Celia succeeded in shaming her. She merely put her work down, as Celia had, and for a few moments the two women stared at one another over the dusk-filled room.

'Shall I call for the lamps,' Frances said at last, 'it is almost dark?'

'Not just yet, I thank you. I will call for them when I am ready.'

For a moment Frances said nothing. Then, 'How I wish that it had ever been in my power, when I was Sir Aubrey's wife, to be so extremely useful to my husband's advancement as you now are to yours,' she said. Leaning forwards to put more charcoal on the little brazier, she blew into the coals making them glow red and bright.

'So you say,' Celia replied, 'but I cannot recall my husband Paul ever saying so to me—'

'It is fortunate indeed that you have me to advise you, for I do believe that you are quite a child in these matters, Celia, quite a child. Do you really think that you can manage this house without me?' Her voice was quite gentle as she said this. 'You know you cannot.'

For another moment Celia remained quite still. There was so much she wanted to say, but she could not seem to put the words together. She became aware of a strange smell filling the room. She put her fingers to her temples. Her head was so full of rage that she thought her skull might burst. It was as though all the unspoken thoughts and desires and memories of the past were swirling inside her head. One of her curious ideas came to her: what would the inside of her head would look like if someone were to take a knife and slice off the top? She imagined her thoughts clogging her skull like detritus, like dead leaves, like black slime.

'So how, exactly would you advise me. . .' she began.

But Celia never learnt what Frances would advise her. The smell grew stronger, and she was filled with a sudden nausea, and a wave of such great faintness came over her that she was almost overcome. It was the smoke from the brazier, and it was making her feel quite ill. She stood up shakily, and went over to the window. Her intention had been to open the window casement to breathe in the fresh air, but without her stick she was clumsy, and in her haste she tripped up over one of the carpets. The last thing she remembered was falling and hitting her head against the window casement with a sickening bang.

She had been dreaming about Annetta and the House of Felicity when she woke at last.

She was lying in the centre of an enormous bed, drapes of rose-coloured Venetian silk half drawn around it. There was a curious sensation in her limbs, which felt heavy and boneless all at once. When she looked up she saw a water mark in the silk canopy and a great quantity of papers pinned to the linings of the curtains. There was a faint odour of new wood, and pink gilly-flowers in a vase of bright blue faience in the casement window. The room beyond was light and airy, the closet of a fine lady. It was several moments before she real-ised that it was her own. She sunk back again, eyes closed.

And now, still skimming just beneath the surface of sleep, she realised that she could hear two voices.

'What did she say?'

'It sounded like a name.'

Had she been talking in her sleep?

Two people were standing at the bottom of the bed, speaking together in low voices. One was Paul. The other was Frances Sydenham.

'She's calling for her friend Annetta.'

'I thought she said Ayshe?'

'Ayshe was her other name, the one they gave her when...' Paul's voice trailed away as he searched for the words, '...when she was in Constantinople.'

Paul would never talk about Celia's time in the House of Felicity if he could help it.

'Oh, you mean the one who was – confined...' To signal her understanding, Frances Sydenham gave a delicate cough, '...at the same time as she? The one who is coming to live here?'

'The very same.'

When Celia opened her eyes a crack she could see that the two were standing very close together. Whenever Paul spoke, Frances leant towards him, hanging upon on his every word.

'Poor creature,' she heard Frances say. 'She is like a little broken bird. Does she often have these dreams?'

'At the beginning, yes, very often. But later not so much,' he frowned, 'although of late I have noticed an increase...'

'Perhaps the thought of her friend coming has unsettled her?'

Celia kept her eyes closed so they would not know she was awake.

'I have hopes that this lady's visit will do a great deal of good.'

'But if the dreams, as you say, have returned...' Frances murmured, '...surely that cannot be beneficial?'

'On the contrary, I think it will do her all the good in the world.'

'You are right, of course, of course,' Frances agreed immediately. 'How I pity you,' she sighed, putting a consoling hand on his shoulder. 'How hard it must have been for you these last years.'

Celia had heard enough. She stirred, opened her eyes.

Paul came over quickly to her side of the bed. 'Well, good morrow, sleepy head!'

'Paul. . .' With an effort she reached out a hand towards him; he took it in his and squeezed it. 'What happened?' Her eyelids felt heavy and her head ached.

'You fell and struck your head.'

'I fell?' Celia put her hand to the back of her head, where there was a lump the size of a pigeon's egg. 'Why—?'

But it was beginning to come back to her now: the smoke from the brazier, the curious smell in the room. And the insolence of Frances Sydenham.

'You fainted.' Frances sat down beside her on the other side of the bed, her expression all concern, 'and hit your head when you fell – such a severe blow, you poor, poor creature.' She took Celia's other hand. 'I have been so worried. . .'There was a catch in her voice.

'We gave you a sleeping draught, do you not remember?'

A sleeping draught! No wonder she was having difficulty opening her eyes.

'How long have I been asleep?'

'A whole day and a night, sleepy head.'

'*What?*' Celia sat up, aghast.

'Lady Sydenham is quite an apothecary in her spare time.'

'But a sleeping draught – for a bump on the head – was that really necessary?'

'But of course.' Frances was nodding sagely. 'As Galen himself has said, sleep is the greatest healer.'

'You were talking in your sleep just now,' Paul said.

'Was I?'

'You were calling for Annetta.'

Celia looked up at Paul. 'She's still coming, isn't she?'

It seemed to her just then that it was terribly, terribly important that Annetta should still be coming.

'But of course, why shouldn't she be?'

'Lady Sydenham...' Celia took her hand away

'I am here, my sweet child,' Frances murmured consolingly. 'Tell me what I can do for you?'

All of a sudden the very thought of Frances calling her 'my sweet child' made Celia's skin crawl. *You presume too much, my lady*, she thought. *I am not your sweet child. I am not anyone's child*. All the same, she forced herself to smile up at Frances with all the sweetness she could muster.

'Forgive me, but... would you mind?' Celia glanced towards the door. 'Of your courtesy?'

Her meaning was plain, and this time Frances could not ignore it.

'But of course, as you wish.' She turned tail and swept from the room, her skirts billowing behind her.

Celia watched her go. She had a feeling she would pay for this later, but for the moment she did not care. When the door closed behind her, she turned to Paul.

'Was I discourteous?'

'No.' Paul too had watched Frances go. 'But you know she is only trying to help.'

'Yes, she has been most helpful,' Celia said. 'All the same, I wish she would confine herself to her own closet.'

'I should order you a sleeping draught more often.' Paul was amused by the unaccustomed tartness in his wife's tone. 'I see that sleep has done you good.'

'I believe it has. Paul... has Lady Sydenham told you her plans?'

'So she is Lady Sydenham again now, is she? What happened to plain Frances?' When Celia did not reply he said more seriously, 'Her plans for what?'

'For when she takes her leave of us?'

'Why? I thought you liked having her here? That she was a help to you?' And then, mischievous suddenly, 'Tell me, is it the *miladies*?'

'No, not the *miladies*, I do not complain about them. . .'

Then of what could she complain? That Frances Sydenham was learned? That she read books, sometimes even Latin ones? That she seemed to understand Paul's business affairs, even to relish them, when she – Celia – could not? Even Celia could see the absurdity of that. And if she were to complain about it she knew he would think her quite mad. Most men would not think any of these things suitable accomplishments in a woman at all, but Paul? He was so unlike other men in that respect. . .

So what, then? That she leant too close to him when they talked? That she hung upon his every word? That she had become afraid – afraid in the very quick of her being – that he had begun to confide in Frances more than he did in her?

What else might she be better at?

Oh, sweet Jesus! She felt a sharp constriction, first in her chest and then between her shoulders. *Please, no!*

All these things – which before had been mere ghosts of thoughts, whispering at the furthest edges of her mind – had now taken solid form. The pain of them was a sharp, physical thing between her shoulder blades, as though someone had strung her up from the ceiling on meathooks.

And now there was something else she must articulate. . .

'Paul?'

'Yes, my own?' He picked up her hand and held it to his lips.

'Frances put something on the brazier. I remember now. When she thought I was not looking she took something out of her pocket and burnt it, something in a small blue packet – I know not what – it was the smell that caused me to faint, I am quite sure of it.'

'Yes, she told me.'

'She *told* you?' Celia could not believe she was hearing this.

'She told me she had been burning some sweet herbs to purify the air. There is still some dampness in your gallery. She has been very much afraid that it was the smell that made you nauseous.'

'She did it deliberately. To make me sick.'

'No, Celia, she did it to take away the effects of dampness, which can be severely injurious to the lungs,' he explained, still patient. 'I have never known anyone else think so constantly of someone else's health and comfort.'

'She pretends to, but that is what it is, a pretence. I do not think the lady wishes me well, I do not think she wishes me well *at all*—' Her words came tumbling out.

'Now you are imagining things.'

'No! I am *not* imagining things.'

When they looked at one another, their gaze was at once tender and hopeless. *We are like two people in a shipwreck*, Celia thought, *waving to one another from opposite shores.*

She knew she must try again. 'You must believe me—'

'Very well.' Paul sat down next to her again. 'Give me one instance, just one, which in anyway proves this accusation, and I will get rid of her immediately. But if, when we look clearly at the facts, that cannot in fact be done,' he added sternly, 'then I ask that you behave towards her with the courtesy and decorum that any guest in this house deserves.'

'I don't like the way she talks about Annetta. I am sure she machinates to keep her away from me—'

'That's absurd,' Paul said in a very low voice. 'What does she say about her?'

'She calls her a servant-nun.'

'Annetta *is* a servant-nun. Or was. Both before and after Constantinople.'

'But that's not what she is to me!'

'It is, alas, what she will be to everyone else who comes through our doors. You will have to do better than that.'

'I know, the apple coddlings! I never thought on it till now. *Now* it makes sense. On our very first day here you ate my apple coddling, and became ill shortly after – don't you recall?'

'That was a recurrence of an ague I first had in Venice, and nothing to do with apple coddlings,' he said patiently, 'no matter what that want-wit of a physician might have said. What else?'

'She keeps trying to find out about the Sultan's Blue. She wants me to wear it when the *miladies* come—'

'Is that the best you can do?'

'*Is that the best I can do*? Oh, Paul!' She looked at him in dismay. 'Has she blinded you so completely?'

'Half of London want to see you wear the Sultan's Blue. It is perfectly natural for her to be curious about it – everyone else is. I would be more suspicious if she never mentioned it at all. Lady Sydenham is nobody's fool.'

'Monstrous! So you side with her now, do you?' It seemed to Celia at that moment that Frances Sydenham had inserted herself between them like a silken bolster, down the very middle of their marriage bed. 'There, I have my proof! In a nutshell—'

'Side with her?'

'Against me!'

'Of course not! I just can't have you imagining things.'

231

'I am *not* imagining things.'

'After everything she has done to help you – to help us – this is not worthy of you, Celia, not worthy of you at all.'

'So you *do* take her side against mine!'

'I do no such thing.'

'Are you in love with her?'

'*Christos*! Celia, what has got into you?'

Just then there was a knock on the door.

Paul, in his anger, was about to shout at whoever it was to keep out, when the door opened and Frances Sydenham came in again.

'You have a visitor,' she said to Celia. There was a pinched look around her mouth.

She stood aside, and there, in the doorway behind her, stood a person Celia was quite sure she had never seen before: a little grey-haired woman in a shabby, mud-splattered travelling cloak.

'She says her name is Annetta Scabbūri.'

NINETEEN

Annetta

Bishopsgate.

F OR A FEW MOMENTS it had been exactly as both
of them had imagined.

'Annetta!'

'Goose!'

They flew into one another's arms.

'Can this be? Are you really here?' Celia took a step
back, holding Annetta at arm's length. 'Am I dreaming?'

'No, it's not a dream, I am here – although I can hardly
believe it—'

'Nor I.'

Later that afternoon, alone at last in Celia's chamber,
they had hugged and kissed, and then hugged one another
all over again.

'I want to know everything, *everything*!'

'And I – but wait, let me look at you, you are walking
again. . .! Your legs?'

'Quite healed.'

'Glory be.'

'Do you remember?'

'That night, before they took you away? How could I forget?'

'I want to hear what happened to you in the Palace of
Sighs.'

'And I want to hear how you stole the diamond—'

'And about Aleppo—'

'And the convent—'

'About your husband!'

'About the Valide and the three viziers!'

The two women gazed at one another, half-laughing, half-crying. Half-afraid of what they might see; of what they might hear. For the moment neither of them dared to bring up John Carew's name.

'You look just the same,' Annetta said quickly.

'And you – you too are. . . just the same.'

Brave words, but Celia's glance slid away from Annetta's face as she spoke them. Annetta – *so changed*, was all she could think, *so very changed*! She was shocked to think that at first she had not even recognised her. So much smaller than Celia had remembered: she stooped as she walked like a woman twice her age. Her long illness had turned her skin sallow, and streaked her dark hair with grey. But she must not let her see it, no, not for anything in the world.

For a few moments Annetta allowed herself to be comforted by these words. She searched Celia's face, as though, by some trick of memory, her old self might somehow be reflected back at herself in her friend's gaze.

'Am I – really?'

'Exactly so. A little thin perhaps,' Celia said, squeezing Annetta's arm. 'Sea voyages, you know, they do that. . .' Her voice trailed away. 'My husband complains that I am become thin as a wraith each time we set to sea.'

'You always were a liar, Celia Lamprey.'

'It is the truth, I swear it.'

'It is the most terrible falsehood, and you and I both know it.' Annetta put her hand to her cheek. 'Alas, the plague is no great beautifier. But you, Celia, you have not changed at all.'

And it was true. Here was Celia at last, almost miraculously unchanged by the years and the misfortunes that had separated them. The very same Celia: gentle, affectionate, her hair shining reddish-gold, her beautiful skin still unlined. And yet... and yet... there was something troubling about her that Annetta could not quite put her finger on.

'Now you are the one telling falsehoods. It must be ten years at least?'

'Eleven, by my reckoning.'

Celia walked to the window and stared out at the rain. She stood there for a few moments looking out, small and stiff in her English clothes, like a little *infanta*.

'When I lived in Aleppo, in the heat of summer, how I used to long for the rain,' she said now. 'English rain falling on English grass. That would have been to me then like very heaven. *In England it would be different*, we always said that.' She passed a hand over her eyes, as though rubbing away some thought. 'But now you are here, my dearest friend.' She turned to Annetta again, 'and *that* is my very heaven, my very seventh heaven of delight.'

For Annetta, however, her first few days at the great house in Bishopsgate were very far from being any kind of delight.

It had all started, most inauspiciously, with the upsetting of her bed.

She had been woken, very early on her first morning, by a bad dream. In her dream she had been standing at the head of a country lane at dusk, a very steep place, like a tunnel, with the branches of many trees crowding overhead. In her mind's eye she had been stumbling down it, trying to reach someone, or something, but the path grew narrower and darker, and narrower and darker, and all the time the colours around her were fading, seeping into one another and dissolving. Not into blackness, which would have been too definite a thing, but into a terrifying absence of colour, where there was nothing but billowing shadows, and she knew that if she went any further down the tunnel, she too would simply dissolve.

She sat up with a great cry.

When Celia had helped her to undress the night before, they had drawn the curtains around her bed so closely that not even the smallest finger of light could penetrate the drapes, and now she was filled with panic, not only because of her dream (a dream of ill omen if ever she had had one) but because of the darkness all around her, a darkness so profound that she was not even able to see her own hand when she put it to her face, and for a moment she was filled with such terror that she hardly knew who she was.

When she had lain dying of the plague at the *lazaretto* on the island of Santa Maria di Nazareth, Annetta had known it to be the case that the sick were often buried before they were dead. Everyone who came there knew it. Somehow they had all heard the stories. You could smell the fear, above the stench of pus and rotting flesh and excrement-filled straw: a solid wall of odour so powerful that grown men had been known to faint dead away just by breathing it.

There had been a young woman who had died on the floor next to her: Eufemia, a little servant-nun, a *conversa* from the same convent as Annetta, hardly more than a child. Except that she had not been quite dead. Her eyes had still been open when they came to take her away. Annetta had known that the *conversa* was not dead because the eyes of the dead do not follow you on their way to the grave in the way that Eufemia's had done, or not that she had ever heard tell. She often thought about Eufemia, wondered what had become of her, wondered if she had known what was happening to her, when she was buried alive in the pit full of suppurating bodies, and if she, Annetta, would ever be quite free of the memory. She had been too weak to cry out, to stop them taking her. The thought haunted her still.

What kind of a name could you give to a place such as that, she had often wondered?

A place where not dying was worse than death itself.

And now Annetta was to be shamed in front of all of them, and this was the reason. When she had woken from her dream of ill omen into a place that was black and airless and hot, with something heavy pressing down on her, for a moment she had believed herself to be trapped there, suffocating, with no way out, her nails clawing at the walls, her breath slowly getting shallower, her life seeping away, just as it must have done with Eufemia. And in her panic she had almost pulled the whole bed down on top of her, canopy, curtains and all. And now she was afraid that the household would be whispering about her; and that woman, the *milady* Sydenham, would be looking down at her in that superior way of hers, although she took great care to pretend otherwise.

Milady Sydenham. Who was she exactly? Not even so great in height as Annetta herself, who was not a tall woman, but still managing to look down her nose at you.

Oh, you mustn't catch a chill, Sister Annetta, after your long journey and all. Please, I entreat you, Sister Annetta, have my chair; here, let me move it for you, just a little closer to the fire. Please, I beg you, let me help you to some refreshment.

But Annetta knew an enemy when she saw one. *Milady* Sydenham's lips had said one thing, but her eyes had said something quite other.

A little chicken gizzard is easy to digest, and will be quite good enough for the likes of you.

Come sit in the best seat by the fire, and take a tumble into it while you're about it.

Of course, she did not actually say these things, but Annetta could see she was thinking them.

It did not help that she found herself alone on that first morning in Bishopsgate. Apparently it was Celia's habit to break her fast in her own chamber, and the Sydenham woman – taking Annetta to one side and speaking gravely to her as though she were speaking of someone who was ill – was sure that Annetta would not want her disturbed, although what it had to do with the Sydenham woman Annetta was at a loss to know.

Now, as she made her way down the staircase, the house seemed even bigger to her that it had the previous night. Celia, the mistress of all this! Had she made a mistake in coming here? Celia was now a wealthy merchant's wife, a woman of the world, with friends like this *milady* Sydenham, who was so clearly a person of rank.

What would she want with someone who was no one?

The night before, she and Celia had clasped one another and wept, and looked into one another's faces and wept again. But all that time, over her shoulder, Annetta had seen the figure of the Sydenham woman, remote, smiling, pinked and primped like a *contessa* in her silks and her lace; her expression a mask of politeness, not quite concealing the thoughts that lay there: *Who is this person, and what are we to do with her? What does she want with us? Or we with her?*

Later, when she and Celia were alone, she had put on her bravest face. But now, in the cold light of day, Annetta knew how they must all see her: a woman without family or connections, a woman who was no longer young. And at the edges of her mind lingered another more distressing thought: what would *he* say if he could see her now, her once vivid presence turned to shadow?

He. John Carew. The *monachino*. The seducer of nuns.

John Carew would laugh to see her now, she was quite certain. Laugh to see how thin she had become, scrawny as a barnyard chicken, chest like a griddle pan. No meat on her at all these days. What would he want with her now? What would he say? He would laugh at her, she was sure, and wonder why he ever thought he loved her.

Give me something to live for, she had said to him. And he had. In the *lazaretto* she used to imagine he was coming for her. Would sometimes, in her delirium, think she saw his face. She willed herself to stay alive by telling herself stories. That one day they would find one another again; they would marry, have two children. A boy and a girl. They would call the girl Celia, and the boy John. But then, much later, she had only to catch sight of herself in the glass and she knew that whatever hopes had kept her alive, it was all over for her.

Now, as Annetta stood at the top of the stairs, her hand on the balustrade, she heard the murmur of a man's voice saying the household prayers. There was nothing for it: go down the stairs she must. On the landing of the floor below, a flat grey light seeped in through mullioned windows. A Turkey carpet had been thrown over a table against a window. Dust motes sparkled like tiny angels' wings.

Madonna! The Pindars' house was big as a *palazzo*; Celia must employ two dozen servants at least. Annetta tried, of course, not to be impressed. But when she looked down the great oak staircase, it was with a vertiginous feeling. Was she meant to take these stairs? She hesitated. They seemed far too... opulent, for the likes of her.

The man's voice ceased, and in its place came a scraping of benches, a sudden hum of voices, and a clatter of plates and knives, the sound of the household breaking its fast.

Annetta arrived at the doorway at last and looked in.

Two trestle tables had been laid for the household breakfast. Her gaze alighted immediately on *Signor* Pindar; next to him was the insinuating Sydenham woman. The two were sitting together at one of the tables, the servants grouped at the other. In front of them were churns of milk and soft white manchet bread of the kind that is flavoured with cinnamon. On the dresser had been placed a variety of meats: a plate of quails' legs, a fricassee of chicken, and some kind of pie with a latticework of pastry. Annetta's quick gaze took in everything. Clearly every day was a feast day in this house. *Signor* Pindar was eating with a will but the lady took almost nothing. She looked paler than Annetta remembered, and she was not eating her food, but playing with it, making little pellets from the bread by rubbing it between her fingers.

Well, she could not stand here all day. Annetta gave a little cough. The *Signore*, Celia's husband, stood up to welcome her immediately, but it was the lady who got to her first. In front of the assembled household *milady* Sydenham questioned Annetta about how she had slept, how long and how deeply, whether the feather bed was comfortable, whether the linen was sufficiently warmed and aired. Annetta, a woman entirely unused to public gaze, answered her questions gruffly, her gaze fixed to the ground.

Lady Sydenham would like to give the impression that nothing had been too much trouble for their new arrival. She was afraid that the room they had put her in might be too noisy? Too hot? Too cold? Annetta, in return, was obliged to divulge that she had been most perfectly comfortable. Great heaven, after a journey like that she had slept like the dead. When Annetta realised what she had said she almost smiled. For a few moments she was surprised, almost at risk of being gratified, by so much solicitude.

But these warm feelings did not last long.

'And – please – Sister Annetta, do not concern yourself one bit about the broken bed.'

'The broken bed?'

Annetta felt *Signore*'s gaze upon her; could see immediately that this was the first he had heard about it.

'What happened to the bed?'

'Oh, it is of no account,' Lady Sydenham said easily, 'of no account at all. I'm so sorry I mentioned it. I don't suppose, coming from a convent, you've ever slept in a bed such as this, have you, Sister Annetta? One with drapes around it, I mean.'

Although she kept her gaze fixed steadily on the ground, Annetta's face was aflame.

I don't expect you've ever seen such valuable furnishings, silken canopies, and silver plate as we have here. The bed hangings alone, woven specially from worms in Damascus, the ones that are lying ripped up and torn in your chamber upstairs, must have cost fifty ducats – but please, I entreat you, Sister Annetta, do not give it another thought.

The lady did not say these things of course, she merely smiled. It was a smile that was meant to be sympathetic, but Annetta knew in her bones that it was full of deceit, like a cat that has scratched and drawn blood, and then rubs itself, purring, around your legs.

Annetta turned on her. 'Of course in my convent they made us sleep on broken glass – it so wonderfully mortifies the flesh.' She laced her fingers behind her back to stop herself from trembling. 'And I am not your sister.'

Had she really just said that? *Oh!* she thought, *me and my sharp tongue!*

But she must have said it, or something very like, for the silence that followed was long and awkward. *Signor* Pindar and the *milady* exchanged glances. A little shiver of laughter ran down the servants' table. The servant girl Nan, who had brought her basin of washing water early that morning and doubtless had been the source of the tale of the broken bed, put her hand to her mouth. *Well*, Annetta thought, *that tells you something, does it not?* Her quicksilver mind was alive to the smallest signals that would tell her how this household worked. Lady Sydenham, it was immediately clear, was not greatly loved.

The barb was perfectly aimed; the lady silenced. Annetta thought she would feel steadied by this little triumph, now that she had showed them all that she was neither so little nor so insignificant as she looked, but the feeling lasted only a moment. To her shame, she could feel her eyes pricking with tears.

'What I mean is. . .' Her voice caught, as though something were lodged in the back of her throat, and she was obliged to clear it several times before she could get the words out, '. . .what I mean is, I am not a religious any more.'

Aware that everyone – the male servants, the *Signore* himself – were all looking at her, Annetta was in torment.

'Then what shall we call you, madam?' *Signor* Pindar spoke to her gently. She knew that he had seen her distress and was trying not to notice it. *He is kind,* she thought. And it was his kindness that almost undid her.

'Shall we call you Mrs Annetta?' he ventured. 'Or perhaps Madam Annetta?' He glanced across to the other woman. 'We have Lady Sydenham, so it is only right that you should be Madam Annetta.'

Then he took her by the hand to lead her to her place at the table and seated her next to him, as though she were quite as fine as any other lady.

'You are most welcome, madam.' He spoke the words very clearly, so that the whole household could hear him, and they should not mistake her status in his household. Then he took her hand and brought it to his lips, and when she tried to pull her hand away, he held on to it, clasping it between both of his, and would not let it go.

'You are most welcome,' he repeated, and the sound of his voice was like a balm to her sorry soul. 'It must – it will – at first feel strange to you here, madam – after all these years.' He spoke hesitantly for such a great man, and the thought was strangely comforting to her, 'and after everything you have been used to, but – I wish – I want you to know – we both do, Celia and I.' He was still holding her hand between his, 'and indeed you *must* know – you are not a stranger here. You are our most honoured guest. You are among friends.'

And in that moment all she could think of was how familiar his voice sounded.

Do I not know you? She found herself thinking. *You and I,* Signor *Pindar, have barely met before this moment, and yet – do I not know you?* But the notion vanished almost as quickly as it had arisen.

'I thank you, sir,' she said, when she ventured to look up at him at last, 'with all my heart.'

Their eyes met and they smiled at one another, and she knew in that moment what she had not known before, which was that all her misgivings were in vain. That she *was* among friends, and had been right to come here after all.

And with it an absolute certainty that if anyone could help her find John Carew again, it was he.

A realisation that hit her like a gift from God.

TWENTY

Annetta

Bishopsgate.

A LAS, THESE COMFORTABLE FEELINGS did not
last.

At about midday they sent word to Annetta that
Merchant Pindar desired to talk over a business matter
with her in the great gallery. She was taken by a servant
to the same first-floor withdrawing room that she had
passed on the *piano nobile* earlier that morning. The room
comprised a long gallery running the entire length of the
house, with windows looking down over a gatehouse and
the street beyond.

She went in and walked slowly along its length.
She took in the silk hangings, the marble fireplace,
the window casement with its velvet-lined seats.
By the saints, Celia's house had more treasures in it than
the Doge's Palace. Annetta had never seen such things,
not even in the House of Felicity. And yet, she could not
get over this feeling of... what?... of melancholy suffus-
ing the place.

There were eddies and currents in the house that she
did not yet fully understand.

From the window casement there came a low droning
sound. A bumblebee, awoken by the autumn sun, was

bumping up against one of the glass panes. It flailed and spun before dropping exhausted on to the lintel. Its sad buzzing only served to emphasise the quiet of the house.

And that was it, now she had it: the quiet. The house was full of people, and yet they barely made a sound. There should be laughter, and the sound of children playing in the garden and small footsteps running overhead, but instead all Annetta could hear was silence: a silence that hovered over everything – silver, porcelain, Turkey carpets, all the treasures in Paul Pindar's gallery – like a mantle of dust.

She went over to the window. In the road outside a cart came rumbling past. Looking down, she saw the servant girl Nan come out of the gatehouse. She stopped briefly to speak with the gateman, and then jumped nimbly on the back of the cart. *Well, she certainly seems to get around*, Annetta thought.

Against the wall on either side of the window were two huge cabinets made from black wood. A hunting scene had been inlaid into the woodwork with ivory pieces. When she opened the doors she saw that top half of the cabinet consisted of many little drawers, each with its own tiny handle. Fascinated, she began pulling open the drawers one by one. In each she found a gemstone lying in a bed of silk. Some of the stones were loose and uncut, others richly worked and engraved, offset by gold or silver settings. In one she found a spinel; in another a cameo carved with the head of a man, his brow garlanded with leaves; in a third, a lump of amethyst carved with two naked figures, a man and a woman. They looked old, but she did not know how old.

The little drawers opened and closed smoothly, their runners rubbed with beeswax. Beneath the top section was another drawer, slightly larger than the ones above. When she saw what lay there Annetta's mouth fell open with surprise. Inside, thrown carelessly together were handfuls of jewels: a little enamelled scent-bottle set with gemstones of different colours, red and green; any number of golden chains set with enamelled knots, stars and scrolls; rings and earrings and pendants set with coloured gemstones. Among this tangle of chains lay a hatpin fashioned from an enormous baroque pearl the size of a quail's egg. The pearl was in the form of a ship, complete with a tiny golden sailor sitting in a tiny golden crow's nest, its rigging fashioned in gold filigree. No jeweller or goldsmith on the Rialto could have a more exquisite collection. Annetta looked at them in amazement: did they have no fear of thieves in this country? Shouldn't they be kept, at the very least, in a strongbox? But here they all were, strewn almost carelessly together.

She was taking out the pearl and gold hatpin to take a closer look at its workmanship when she became aware of someone standing behind her. Thinking it was the *Signore* come to find her at last, she turned round.

When she saw who it was her face fell.

'Oh,' she said, 'it's you.'

Madonna, the woman was everywhere, like a bad smell. There had been no sound, not even the faintest squeak of a floorboard, to announce Frances's presence. How long had she been there? Caught unawares, Annetta had no time to put the pearl hatpin back in the drawer. Instead, her fingers closed around it and she put her hand behind her back, then immediately regretted it, cursing herself for not having the presence of mind simply to put it back. And now – *cazzo!* – she was stuck. There was nothing to be done but to hold on to the pin until the lady moved away.

If Lady Sydenham had noticed her dilemma, she gave no sign. 'I hope I didn't startle you?'

'No.'

Annetta regarded Frances warily. In the convent her fellows had been either worldly aristocrats, who thought themselves too grand to speak to her at all, or peasant girls, simple as children. This Sydenham woman was neither. There was something about the *milady* she found deeply unnerving.

'Don't look so alarmed, madam.' There was the faintest hint of amusement in Frances's voice. 'I am sure Merchant Pindar has no objection to you walking in his gallery.'

Annetta considered these words carefully. Did she mean to sound so superior? Or could it be that she was trying to be kind?

'It is a beautiful room, is it not?' Although this was said with an encouraging smile, her words grated on Annetta's already raw nerves.

What kind of a fool does she take me for? Does she really think she can charm me with a few threadbare words? There was a time when I might have fallen for this, but not any more. I will not be won so easily.

'The cabinets are particularly beautiful, do you not think? The ones with the hunting scenes?'

Annetta regarded Frances in hostile silence. The pearl, which had been smooth and cool to the touch, burnt into the palm of her hand.

Frances, by contrast, seemed not in the least put out. She fitted into this room, into this household, in a way that Annetta knew she never would. Her lace collar, snowy white, fell around her shoulders in perfectly laundered and starched points; her hair curled at her forehead, just as it should. Her dress of black-and-white striped silk gleamed as she walked. She was not beautiful, but there was something about her that drew the eye. *I had that once*, Annetta thought. She remembered her own early days at the convent, her delight in breaking the rules with her jewels and her gold chains, her petticoats of shot-gold tulle, the trimmings of finest *Point de Venise* lace. There was a time when she too had delighted in fine clothes. *But look at me now*, she thought, *an old woman in a shabby and ill-fitting robe, my linen sour from the voyage, my hair and skin still tasting of sea salt.*

And she felt such a rage towards this woman standing there, so cool, so superior, she could hardly breathe. *She* was the one who had come here to be Celia's companion: had her position in the household already been supplanted? She looked her over again. *What would it take,* she wondered bitterly, *to ruffle that perfect surface? Did she ever sweat? Or itch? Or bleed? Let her spend a summer of raging heat and plague on the lagoon,* Annetta thought, *let us see how she looks then.*

And yet there was something about her, some disquiet lying beneath that tawny surface. There was a stillness about her that was not entirely natural. Over the black-and-white gown she wore a loose-fitting jacket of yellow grosgrain silk. Her face, it seemed to Annetta, was all politeness, but there was something febrile in her gaze.

Her eyes, those curious slanting eyes, were quick and darting.

The eyes of someone who had done battle. *Who knew?* Annetta found herself thinking. *Perhaps she was still.*

'If you are quite finished, Sister—?'

'I am no longer a *suora*,' Annetta snapped. 'The *Signore* said I am to be Madam Annetta now.'

'But of course.' Frances, ever courteous, bowed her head in acknowledgement. 'Forgive me, madam.' If she found Annetta's tone insolent she gave no sign of it. Instead, she put her hand on the door frame, as though to steady herself, and Annetta saw that she was holding a handkerchief in one hand.

'If you are quite finished here, madam, she will see you now.'

Annetta's eyes widened. *And just who do you think you are? Celia's gatekeeper? I don't need you to tell me when I can and cannot see her.* But she could not leave, not just yet, not unless she took the pearl with her. She should just put it back in its little drawer right now, with a flourish; should assert her perfect right to have looked at any of the treasures in these drawers. She had only wanted to look at it. But something told her it would be unwise to let the *milady* Sydenham see even that.

'Who?' she said, her hand still behind her back, although she knew quite well of course, who was meant. 'Who will see me now?'

'Mrs Pindar, of course.'

Mrs Pindar! Was she doing this on purpose? Everything she said seemed calculated to play on Annetta's fear: that she was not really wanted here at all; that after all these years Celia was not her Celia any more, but someone else.

'She – we – have visitors today.' Frances was at once confidential and apologetic. She took a step into the room, and seemed about to come towards Annetta, perhaps to usher her out, when something stopped her. She looked around and her eyes lit upon a bowl of quinces on the dresser.

Her nose wrinkled.

'*Ah* – forgive me. . . the smell.' She stepped back and put her handkerchief to her nose, and then stood for a few moments breathing deeply, her eyes closed. 'Something about the smell of quinces that I cannot. . .' She tailed off vaguely. 'They do not agree with me. . .'

And then the moment passed and she was herself again.

'Madam Annetta, we have visitors today.' Her tone was a little firmer this time, as if she were speaking to a child. 'Some ladies – Lady Peters and Lady Rich – they are coming to call.'

The names, of course, meant nothing to Annetta, but by the reverential way that they were spoken, their importance was made quite clear.

'We thought you might prefer to rest, Sis— Madam Annetta,' she added, in her soft voice, 'after your journey?'

Her meaning was obvious. The visits would not include Annetta.

Across the room the two women held one another's gaze. And at that moment the sun came out, and a blade of light came slanting through the window. It fell across the floor between them, slicing the room in two.

Lady Sydenham was about to leave the room, when she paused, turned to look over her shoulder.

'Mrs Pindar... she is not strong. But of course you already knew that.' Frances dabbed at the corner of her mouth, holding the handkerchief there for a few moments before tucking it back in her pocket. 'Oh, and I almost forgot. Mr Pindar sends word to say that he cannot see you today, alas; he has been called to the Exchange on business. I expect he will meet with you some other day.'

She turned, smiled. The sun had gone in now and in the grey English light she looked very pale. 'I think we shall be friends, shall we not?'

'*Ma certo*,' Annetta answered, her eyes narrowing. 'But of course.'

TWENTY-ONE

Annetta

Bishopsgate.

'WHO IS SHE?' As soon as Celia's visitors had gone, Annetta burst into her room.

There was no need to ask who 'she' was.

'Lady Sydenham?' Celia said, giving Annetta a hug. 'A friend. Why do you ask? Surely that much is obvious.'

'A friend?' Annetta found it hard to imagine the *milady* Sydenham being anyone's friend.

'She sailed with us from Antwerp to London. She is the widow of a Muscovy Company merchant of my husband's acquaintance.'

'A widow?'

'Yes, she is but recently widowed.'

'If she's what you call a friend these days,' Annetta muttered, only half to herself, 'small wonder you hide in your room like this. Everywhere you turn there she is, like a bad smell...'

Celia began to laugh.

'I don't see what's so very funny about that?'

Celia put her arms round Annetta and kissed her again. 'You really haven't changed have you?' And then, more seriously, 'Come, tell me, has she done something to you? Said something?'

'Nothing,' Annetta said, sullen.

Not yet. But I know an enemy when I see one. The servants take their cue from her. They treat me as though I am of no account—

'Must you pace up and down like that? You are making my head hurt. Here, come and sit beside me.' Celia patted a space in the window seat beside her. 'Tell me, how did you sleep? Did you breakfast well? Have they been looking after you?'

'Everything is quite... perfect.'

Pride prevented her from mentioning the small failures of attention. How the water they had brought her for washing that morning was cold; how her body linen had been returned to her still soiled. That while Celia sat here being waited on hand and foot, she had been obliged to empty her own slops. The humiliation of the broken bed...

She looked out of the window. '*Madonna*, can it really be raining again?'

'It rains a great deal here and the sky is always grey. You must get used to it, you know.'

'But you are so very... comfortable here, are you not?' Annetta looked doubtfully around the echoing room. Now who was telling falsehoods? A more comfortless room she had never seen, not even in the convent. Even the bed – so very big, so very pink – had an almost threatening look about it. But it would not do to say so; even Annetta, with her sharp, plain-speaking ways, could see that.

'Your house and garden are... so very fine.'

'Thank you. My husband made them,' Celia said flatly, as though the thought gave her no pleasure.

'No wonder you have visitors... those two fine ladies I saw arriving in their carriage just now. I am not surprised they like to come here.'

'You saw them?' Celia picked up some sewing which had been lying next to her on the seat.

'From my window. Are they...' Annetta searched for the right words, '...your friends?'

She pictured the two women: large English ladies with ruddy faces and big bones. The thought of them being Celia's friends almost made her smile.

'The *miladies*? Great heaven, no.'

'The *miladies* – is that what you call them? But if they are not your friends, then why do they come?'

'Lady Sydenham brings them,' Celia, busy at her work, snapped off a thread. 'It gives her pleasure, so I oblige her.' She did not meet Annetta's gaze. 'And besides...'

'Besides what?'

'She – we think it will help my husband.'

Was Annetta imagining it or was Celia blushing? A pink flush had appeared at her neck and round her ears.

'It is the fashion to come here. *I* am the fashion, or so I am told.' Her fingers darted over the silk stuff she was sewing. 'They have heard that I was once *Gözde*, a favourite of the Sultan. They have no idea what that means, of course; but it amuses them. It even, I think... excites them.' From Celia's tone of voice Annetta could not decide whether this pleased or displeased her. Her glance slid sideways towards Annetta, and then away again quickly. Then she added, with unexpected vehemence, 'They think, all of them, that I am a fool; some kind of want-wit who does not understand what's happening.'

Annetta put her hand into the bag of coloured threads, red and yellow and blue, felt the tangle of silks smooth against her skin.

'And... do you?'

'I understand perfectly how much it will help my husband – bring him to notice at Court.' Celia stabbed her needle into the canvas, put her embroidery down, and rolled her neck as though her shoulders were hurting her. 'It will help to advance him in the world.'

Annetta looked around at the immense silk-lined room. Outside at least six gardeners laboured in the rain, planting *Signor* Pindar's new orchard; and here was his fair *Signora*, stitched all over with pearls and looking as though she supped every day on larks' tongues. *He seems quite well enough advanced to me* – the words sprang to her lips, but she caught at them deftly before they could escape, and stuffed them back inside their box.

'And. . . so. . .' she said slowly, 'does it? Is he now more "advanced", as you say, although quite what that means I don't know.'

'We have an invitation to the masque at Court. I am to meet the Queen.' Celia gave a sigh, as if the very thought of it wearied her. 'Lady Peters and Lady Rich brought us the news this very day. We will gain favour at Court. It is beyond Frances's wildest dreams.'

'Do you mean that Sydenham woman?' Annetta said the words as though she had tasted something sour.

Celia bent down over her work again, her shoulders tense. 'I do.'

'A very paragon then, your Lady Sydenham.'

'What's that supposed to mean?'

'To so rejoice so much in someone else's advancement.'

There came a knock at the door. It was Nan come in to light the lamps and lay the fire.

'Come in, Nan,' Celia spoke to her kindly. 'But those are tallow candles; do you not remember me asking you to bring me the wax?'

'The lady gave me these to bring,' the girl said flatly, keeping her gaze on the floor.

'Very well then,' Celia said mildly. 'Tomorrow. Just carry on here for now.'

She turned to Annetta again. 'I was telling you about Lady Rich and Lady Peters, and our invitation to the Court Masque, was I not?' Celia was no longer bending over her embroidery, but looking steadily at Annetta. 'Great heaven, is it not warm in here today, Ayshe?' she said, fanning her hand over her face.

Ayshe? Annetta looked at her in puzzlement. Their conversation had taken a very strange turn. It was not warm at all, it was positively chilly in Celia's bedchamber. And she had no idea what a Court Masque might be, and cared even less. She saw Celia glance quickly at Nan again and back again. Once more she fanned her face with her hand. Ah, now she understood! How strange it was that the lessons of the House of Felicity should be so ingrained, even after all these years.

'Oh yes,' she said, following Celia's cue. 'The Court Masque, please tell me more, I am so interested to hear about it.' She rolled her eyeballs at Nan, who was kneeling at the fire with her back to them.

Celia put her hand to her mouth.

'It is such an honour, you cannot imagine,' she said when she had steadied herself. 'Lady Rich and Lady Peters brought the news just this morning. To be so noticed by their Majesties! We will gain favour at Court. It is beyond my wildest dreams.'

Nan took an unconscionably long time about her business. She dropped things, fumbled, laid a fire that smoked and had to be laid all over again. But eventually, she left.

Annetta's skin was crawling with impatience. She went to the door and opened it a crack, but Nan was nowhere to be seen.

'You think your servant is listening to our conversations?'

'Well, you saw her just now. Ears flapping like an elephant. And I know she reads my letters...'

'Then you should dismiss her.'

'There is someone else I should like to dismiss even more,' Celia said fiercely.

'The Sydenham woman?'

Celia put her hand to her cheek. 'Annetta, what can I do? I let her stay and now she won't leave.'

'It is your house, Goose, surely you can do what you like. If you want her to go, she must go. Who is she really?'

'She is supposed to be a widow, but she does not behave like one.' There was no pretence now that Frances was a friend. 'I have never seen so much as a tear, and she never wants to talks about him.'

Celia explained how she had travelled with them from Antwerp, and her initial kindness in helping her to manage the house in their first few weeks at Bishopsgate; then about the endless visits; and finally about the incident with the brazier.

'She put something, a powder of some sort, on the coals, I'm sure of it.'

'But why?'

'I think she wanted to make me ill – it did make me ill! For all her pretence, for all her sweet words, she does not wish me well, Annetta, of that I am quite certain.'

'What does your husband say?'

'He won't listen to me. Last night, just before you arrived, we quarrelled. He thinks I am imagining it, but I *know* I am not. I saw her do it, she had a packet made from blue sugar paper.'

'And he won't take your word?'

'No.' Celia looked stricken. 'She has tricked us both into trusting her. And – he sides with her, Annetta. I don't know what's happened to him. It is as though he is bewitched. I've seen them standing together, so close, too close – I am sure she wants him. I have even begun to imagine that she wants the diamond. You can't think how often she plagues me about it.'

'Then we must find a way to get rid of her.' Annetta thought for a moment. 'I am sure you are right not to trust Nan. She is the *milady*'s creature, I am quite certain of it. I know that Nan sleeps with her in her room; I have already seen them several times whispering together.'

'Can you watch them? Find out what you can? If we can prove something, anything, it will be a thing of the moment to get rid of her. If not she will find a way to stay on, I know it.'

'It would be my pleasure.'

Later, when Annetta returned to her room, she thought about everything that had passed between Celia and herself. She thought about the Sydenham milady, and the strange state of affairs between Celia and her husband, of the feeling of pervading melancholy that suffused the corridors and galleries of the house. What would John make of it all, she wondered.

John? John Carew? Annetta whispered his name into the lonely room, as if by naming him aloud she could somehow draw him to her. She had agreed to watch the widow, and her maid, Nan, for Celia, but the secrets of the house at Bishopsgate were not the reason she had come here.

She had come here hoping to find John Carew. She had come here for love. Love? Was that what this madness was?

And her thoughts turned inwards again, and she was back there, back in the silvery, dew-jewelled garden at dawn. And the arms of the stranger, the intruder, were around her and she was fighting him – twisting and turning, and biting and clawing at him with her nails – but he did not let her go, he would not let her go, and she could feel him, the whole length of him against her body. She could feel the unfamiliar strength of a man, the texture of sinew and muscle and bone, and his breath against her neck, and even the very smell of him, sweat and leather, the merest hint of which, for ever after, would make her hunger for him. And despite her terror she had felt an erotic charge so powerful she thought she might faint.

And sometimes, in the depths of her most secret mind, she would imagine him forcing her right there and then on the dew-strewn grass; and other times whispering some tender thing in her ear, or kissing her neck, or trailing his finger, soft as a dandelion clock, down her cheek, and she would pull up her dew-sodden shift to her waist, and lie down on the ground and open her beautiful thighs for him, like the cheapest curtezan in Dorsoduro, for there was no act of love so debasing, so humiliating, that she would not have agreed to, unhesitatingly, with the helpless love of a dog for its master, if only to feel his arms around her once more.

TWENTY-TWO

Carew

Eve of All Hallows, 31st day of October, 1611. Events occurring in and around the Priors Leaze Manor in the country of Wiltshire.

UNTIL NOW, HE HAD never been back to Starling's Roost.

It was only a short walk across the fields, and so once he was quite sure that everyone was safely in church, he called Robin to him and set off. The morning mist was gone; the grass was criss-crossed with spider's threads. Tiny dewdrops clung to them, making them sparkle like gold and silver threads. He passed the strip of water that was once, in some long-forgotten time, a moat. On its black waters were two white swans, their feather, like angels' wings, luminous with trapped light.

He looked around for the spot where he had found the toad. He thought he could remember a tree, the old trunk of an elder, and a rock nearby, but he could not find either. Strange how the memory plays tricks. Everything was exactly as he remembered it, and yet at the same time, quite different. When he looked back at the manor, it seemed to list slightly to one side, as though it were sinking into the ground.

As he walked he looked up to the crest of the hill where the Drover's Path began and where he had left Moocher. From somewhere up there, out of the corner of his eye, he caught a flash of something glinting, the sun catching at a blade of steel or a piece of glass. Could it be that the old man was still hiding out up there? Was he watching him, perhaps? Carew was half tempted to climb the hill and winkle him out – he had been too long without human company, and at this moment even a conversation with Moocher would be better than nothing – but he knew he must not be distracted from the job in hand.

He kept walking. These were the fields and copses where he had grown up; the terrain was so familiar to him that his feet seemed to find their own way. Like everything else, the landscape seemed so much smaller, the way so much shorter, than he remembered. He stepped so lightly that his feet left no trace, not even a footprint in the dew. He breathed in deeply. It was a dream of a day: crisp and clear, with a faint smell of wood smoke in the air. The late autumn leaves blazed with colour. He knew that if he climbed to the top of the Drover's Path, he would be able to see as far as the next valley, as far as Salisbury even. On a day like this, if you knew exactly where to look – a notch in some woods on the furthermost ridge – you could see the top of the cathedral spire. And even the smallest sound carried for miles on the still air.

He came upon it quietly.

The burnt-out cottage stood on its own in a small clearing in the woods. In the years he had been away, vegetation had grown up around its ruined shell. Alders pushed their way up through the collapsed roof; a tangle of brambles and bindweed, with its feathery autumn heads, sealed the windows. A little way off a heap of stones marked the spot where the well had once been.

The blackened front door still hung from its hinges. When Carew pushed his way in he saw that there had, at some stage, been a rudimentary effort to inhabit the space. Someone had built a fire in the middle of the room; some cooking implements lay around; the mouldy remains of an old jerkin, a single boot. A vagabond like Moocher most likely, trying to avoid the stocks, or a soldier making his weary way home from the wars. Only strangers would dare come here now.

Rot and decay were everywhere. He kicked at a blackened beam with his boot, and again at something that might once have been a table or a chair. When he looked up into the blue sky, he saw a bird, a hawk or a buzzard, slowly circling overhead; heard its faint mewing cry.

Carew wondered if he too should build a fire. Today of all days it would be a fitting thing to do. Later on, when it grew dark, there would be many fires in the valley, lights to guide the souls of the dead. But there were no ghosts here; not even today, on this day of all days. If the dead ever walked abroad, he thought, it would be now. But looking around him, he could see that there was nothing here for him after all. Every trace of her had been wiped off the face of the earth.

His mother: what had she been like? He had grown up believing that she was a witch, but what did he know of these things? He was only a child. The things he remembered were quite ordinary: her working in the garden, or singing, or wearing a crown of bindweed on her head. Sometimes men visited her, and afterwards he thought he could hear her crying. Sometimes Carew thought he could remember the night they came for her. It had been in midwinter, on the feast day of St Thomas the Apostle, one of the 'rough days' when the men of the village beat the bounds, with firebrands and drums and whips, not to call the spirits of dead as was the custom at All Hallows, but rather to chase them away, cleansing the parish of dark spirits. The young Carew had had the impression of a great noise, a banging of wooden spoons against pots and pans; and of colours, orange and black; of a roaring sound, and flames that jumped so high they seemed to lick the sky; of men's voices shouting, and another voice – his mother's voice – telling him to run.

And among them all, a familiar boy's voice, piping and clear. *Burn the witch, burn the witch.*

But then suddenly his memory seemed to yield. He had a notion that he might have hidden in the well for a time – he had a vague impression of clinging to something wet and damp, of trying not to fall. After that he knew he had hidden out in the surrounding woods for a long time, he was not sure how long, some weeks, months even. He knew they had tried to catch him, but he was too quick for them, even then. When they came looking for him and tried to flush him out, he had climbed up into the trees where the dogs would not smell him; he even learnt to sleep there, in the crook of the branches. At night he could hear the badgers grunting and shuffling like old men, heard the foxes' hoarse bark. In the day, from his treetop eyrie, he watched the deer moving through the pale green light of the forest, nibbling on the bark of the trees. He lived by digging for worms, picking nuts and wild fruit, rabbits that even then he had been able to snare. He was so hungry that he ate the flesh raw. Sucked on handfuls of wild grass.

It had been old man Pindar who had coaxed him out in the end. Found him living, a feral creature, in the burnt-out remains of the little house. Carew smiled to himself. Strange how he had seemed old, even then. The old man took him in. Who else would have had him? He was like a wild animal, a half-starved woodland sprite, covered in deer ticks and with a head full of lice.

Had he mourned his mother? Had he wept? Looking around the burnt-out cottage, Carew realised that he felt nothing. After all these years, there was nothing that could penetrate the carapace he had grown around his heart. He wore it like a badge of honour. When he thought of himself as a child, all he could feel was a kind of distant curiosity. If he had learnt anything at all in the intervening years, it had been to stare unflinchingly at the past. Did they kill her before they burnt her? Had they defiled her body? Perhaps they had hanged her first, strung her up with a rope from one of the beams of the house before they locked the door and set fire to the thatching. It did not seem strange to him that he could ask these questions, that they did not even make him flinch. He had seen enough hangings and burnings in the years since, so he knew how it was done. How he had laughed with the crowds as the body of some poor devil twitched and jerked on the end of the rope; gone home with them, in holiday mood, the smell of burning human flesh still clinging to his hair and his clothes.

But at night, since he had been back at the old place, he had had the same dream. It is the night of his mother's death: there are orange and black shadows, the roar of flames, and the sound of men's voices. It is all there, what little he remembers. And in his dream he is fighting someone. He has his arms round him; they wrestle together, like Jacob and the angel. They struggle and struggle; he can hear his own voice, ragged and gasping, as he strains to hold on to him; and he can hear his opponent's breath, feel his flesh pressing against his own. He is struck each time by the curious intimacy that is between men when they fight one another.

In his dream he hears a voice. And then, at last, a face. And he realises that it is not one of the men he is fighting, but Annetta. They are in the garden of the convent on the lagoon where they first met all those years ago. Only this time it is she who is struggling to hold on to him. She is holding him, cradling him in her arms. She is whispering in his ear.

By all the Saints, John Carew, she is saying to him, *put it down.*

Put it down, she is saying to him in her beautiful voice, *all is well, you can put it down now.*

And her voice seems to be coming from some still, deep place. And suddenly they are not fighting any more, but embracing. And in his dream he feels... he feels... the truth is Carew has no words to describe how he feels. All he knows is that it is as if all the broken pieces inside him have been put back together. And it is she who has done this for him.

How he wished she could be here with him now. He would like to have shown her the place where he grew up, even if it was a burnt-out ruin. He sat down with his back to one of the blackened walls, watched as his dog Robin rooted around in the bushes a little way off. Suddenly she stopped, stood still, and pricked her ears as though she had heard something. He heard her let out a small growl: a deer or a rabbit, no doubt. Carew was so sure that no one ever came to Starling's Roost that he paid the dog no heed, and so did not see the face of Moocher – his eyes fixed, sly – peering out at him from behind a tree.

Instead, with his face turned to the sun, he fell into a reverie. *Christos, woman,* he said to Annetta, *what have you done to me?*

I don't know what you are talking about, John Carew, she had said, in that definite way of hers.

You have a lot of lip, woman, for someone's who is dead.

Dead?

Yes, dead. Christos, *it's been seven years. Is there nothing that will shut you up?*

A pause, and then, *How do you know I'm dead?*

A little matter of the plague, or had you forgotten?

Of course I remember. How could I forget? But how do you know I'm dead?

I came to find you, but you sent me away.

Madonna! *Not still harping on about that!* She rolled her eyes. *No good both of us dying. What would be the point of that?*

Would have been better if we'd both died, he said gloomily.

Oh, well, that's just typical.

Typical?

Typical of a man to think only of himself. A pause. *And don't look at me like that; you think I sent you away for your own good? The* suoras *were dropping like flies all around me. It wasn't a pretty sight, I can tell you.* She looks at him, and he can see the longing in her eyes. *I sent you away so that I would have something to live for,* capito?

Stop. Hold it right there. He would like to play this last part over and over again.

In the shelter of the wall it was almost warm in the sun. Carew stretched himself out on the grass, his head cradled in the crook of his arm. Sometimes, in that small space between waking and sleeping, he can catch a fleeting glimpse of Annetta's face as he had last seen it. He can picture the room in which they had been standing: the refectory of the already deserted, plague-ravaged *convento*. High ceilings, dark panelling, a simple crucifix affixed to a whitewashed square. There are dirty cloths still on the tables; the remnants of some hastily abandoned meal scattered across the trestle tops. He remembers the way the sparrows flew in and out between the high rafters, swooping down to take crumbs of bread, and how shrill their chatter sounded in the heavy silence of the abandoned room.

Across the centre of the room lay the smouldering remains of a line of partially burned straw, an ineffectual attempt on the part of those few remaining souls to chase away the pestilence. Everything about the place spoke of death. And now, in an enormous effort of will, he can just conjure up the sight of her. In his mind's eye he watches her; she makes her entrance into the room at last. She wears the black robe of her order, but her head is uncovered. She looks pale, but otherwise unharmed. She does not seem particularly pleased to see him.

You told me I was mad to come, he whispered into the autumn sunshine.

Well, what did you expect? You came into a house of plague, she almost snapped at him.

I came to find you.

Don't come complaining to me; it's probably what saved your life.

Say it. Say it again for me.

I sent you away so that I would have something to live for.

And – did you? When she did not answer he went on, *I came back for you—*

—here we go, I thought we'd been over that—

Will you stop interrupting me, woman? he said, impatient now. *I mean I came back for you a second time.*

But you didn't find me?

I didn't find anyone. The convent was deserted. There was only a gatekeeper, I don't know his name. He told me that all the nuns had died in the plague; all but a handful, perhaps two or three – he didn't know how many. He said they had been transferred to another convent of the same order, he did not know where, except that it was not in Venice.

So what did you do?

I went to try to find you. I tried everywhere. I even went to the lazaretto.

To this she did not reply.

Well, he prompted her, *say something.*

Santa Madonna, *John Carew, don't you ever listen?*

Well, no one else gets to talk much around here—

I said how do you know I'm dead? she interrupted him.

No one ever came out of a lazaretto *that I heard.*

She said something in the Venetian dialect that he did not understand.

Better mind that tongue of yours, woman! What will the suoras *say?*

Oh, I don't worry myself about them, she answered, grand as a duchess.

I remember. Carew tried to stop the smile from entering his voice. *It didn't sound very ladylike.*

But I am no lady, or not in your world; you should know that by now.

True enough, but must you sound as though you learnt to speak in a brothel?

But I did learn to speak in a brothel.

Christos!

Christos? *Why are you always saying that?*

Christos, *if that isn't just my luck. After all that time and you have to go and be another bloody witch.*

She was so beautiful, she took his breath away.

How so?

Well, look what you've made me do. Who else could make me talk to myself like this? Seven years later and I'm still talking to myself.

TWENTY-THREE

Carew

Events occurring at Priors Leaze Manor in the country of Wiltshire.

C AREW'S RUSE TO GET Ralph to return to Priors Leaze took effect more quickly than he could ever have hoped.

After his visit to the burnt-out cottage, he had arrived back to find that a carriage with a crest of arms on the door, freshly drawn in crimson paint and as rare a sight in this rural Wiltshire backwater as a meteorite fallen from the heavens, had arrived at the weed-choked front door. A train of baggage wagons – Carew counted seven of them in all – were lined up in the lane behind. The axle of one had broken in the mud and was blocking the rest, and the place was in turmoil. The carters were roaring at one another; liveried servants swarming around them like ants in a sugar bowl. The commotion could be heard from two fields away. Carew took up a hiding place behind the orchard wall, astounded to find that an entourage of such great size should have arrived in the short time that he had been gone. He must have been at Starling's Roost longer than he thought. As he watched, a woman was being helped from the carriage by one of her maids. She was swollen-bellied and held a handkerchief to her mouth.

More interesting still to Carew was the sight of the man who emerged from the carriage behind her. Even from a distance, his form was familiar. For one wild moment he imagined it might be Paul – something about the way he stood, the angle at which he wore his hat – and Carew almost broke cover and started to run towards him, but then another thought occurred that stopped him in his tracks.

Retreating behind the orchard wall, he looked again, more carefully this time. The figure looked like Paul, but now he could see that it most definitely was not him. Whereas Paul's figure had always been narrow and compact like his father's, this man was large-boned and generously fleshed. Whereas Paul, no matter what the fluctuations in his fortunes, had never deviated from wearing sober merchant black, this man was dressed in a suit of rich velvet; a short cape of a contrasting brocade was thrown over one shoulder. Even from a distance it was possible to see the glint of jewels on his fingers and pinned to his cap.

Well, well, Carew thought, that's him.

Ralph.

I'd know you anywhere.

Strangers at Priors Leaze! A group of curious onlookers from the village lined the road, and were watching these apparitions with as much awe as if they were savages from another world, or had stepped from pages of a chapbook. Carew gave silent thanks for the commotion. In the confusion and the press of people he was far less likely to be noticed. Ralph's people would assume that he was a Priors Leaze servant, while anyone from the village, so long as they did not get too close a look at him, would assume he was one of the visiting entourage. No point trying to hide from anyone now.

Carew had dreaded seeing Ralph again, but now that the moment had come, it was not at all how he thought it would be. The days of skulking in the barn were over, and the thought filled him with elation. There seemed to be more blood flowing through his veins; his pulse quickened. A voice inside his head, the voice of reason, begged him to wait, begged him not to do anything rash, anything he'd regret.

A voice that was as easy to ignore as it always was.

He stood up, pulled back his shoulders, and walked straight into the courtyard.

'Here, let me help you with this.' He went as if to take a bundle from the nearest cart.

'Ho! You there! Who told you to take that?' A man dressed in a steward's livery was standing on the back of one of the carts looking down on him. 'Those are the linen baskets. It's just victuals that need taking in.'

'You're not stopping then?'

'Think his Lordship would put up in a hole like this?' The servant, a big broad-shouldered fellow with red hair, gave Carew a disdainful look.

'It was good enough for His Nibs when he was growing up.' The words were out of Carew's mouth before he could stop them. 'Too good, if you ask me,' he muttered under his breath.

The man's expression curdled. 'What's that, you idiot?' he growled at Carew.

'I said, nothing be too good for our own Master Ralph, God save him.'

Jesu! He'd only been doing this a few minutes and already he'd found someone who needed a good kicking. Carew liked a fight as much as the next man, but even he could see that to pick one now would not be the best way to melt into the crowd.

'You'll not be stopping long then?' he enquired. 'You'll be on your way to London, I take it?'

The man stared down at him with an expression that was half-annoyed, half-puzzled. He managed to convey the impression that it was an affront to his pride that a country yokel such as Carew should address him at all. He stopped, put his hand to his eyes to shade them from the low autumn sunlight. 'Don't you ask a lot of questions.'

'Don't mean no disrespect—' With an effort, Carew arranged his features into what he hoped was a subservient smile, '—sir.' The word, applied to an uppity steward, almost choked him, but it seemed to have the desired effect.

The man was mollified. 'If you must know, we're on our way back to London from Lord Nicholas's place at Salisbury. Got to get to Richmond for Her Majesty's new masque; his Lordship's to take part in it, so they tell me, but at the rate we're going we won't be there before Twelfth Night,' he grumbled. 'Wouldn't have stopped here at all if it weren't for your bleedin' Master Ralph,' he added. 'Some trouble with poachers, or some such. Although why his Lordship should concern himself with poachers, his own or anyone else's, is a mystery to me. Took us back on ourselves, and right out of our way, and now look.' He indicated the cart with the broken axle stuck in the mud.

'Poachers, of course.' Carew nodded sagely, still hovering. 'Our Master Ralph, he don't like them at all.'

Meanwhile, his thoughts were on fire. Poachers? At Priors Leaze? That was news to him. Carew was quite certain that he had left no traces at all of traps or snares, either up at the Drover's Path or at Starling's Roost. But perhaps this was merely the explanation Ralph had chosen to give. After all, he would have had to tell them something: as excuses went, a pair of ignorant country housemaids complaining about fairies might have seemed a little thin, even for Ralph, to justify commandeering some grandee's carriage and baggage train.

As for the rest of it: a Majesty's masque in Richmond? A Lord Nicholas with a place at Salisbury: who was he when he was at home? So much information – coming all at once – roared through Carew's veins, warming them like aquavit.

'I expect he'll be glad to see his old father too?' Carew said, still hovering. Might as well be hung for a sheep as a lamb. His face felt as though it might explode with the effort of so much subservient smiling.

The steward looked up sharply from the complicated knots that he had been picking at. 'What, you still here?' He put his hand up to shade his eyes from the sun again, squinting down at Carew as though he were still having difficulty seeing him. 'You're jesting, ain't yer? No love lost between the two of them. But I don't suppose you need me to tell you that.' He went back to his knots, conversational suddenly. 'Son wants to pull the old place down; father says over my dead body; son says, so why don't you get a move on, you're almost dead anyway, old man, I want my new mansion; father says, well I ain't in my coffin yet, sorry to disappoint you, and besides, there's others in the picture what have rights to my property alongside you; son says, but they're dead and gone and ain't never coming back, just sign these papers old man, and I'll take care of the rest; over my dead body, father says again, I don't trust you any further than I could. . .' Warming to his story, and to his chance to show off his superior knowledge, the steward glanced up again, but his interlocutor was nowhere to be seen.

'Ho, you there!' He called out, looking around for him vainly. 'Don't you want to know what the father says? I heard it all straight from your master's housekeeper, the strange one with the eyes. Nice line in listening at keyholes does that one—'

But Carew had heard enough and had already slipped away, passing unnoticed through the milling crowd and into the house.

Inside, there was an equal state of confusion. In the kitchen, he came across Anne and Alice, standing with their backs against the wall, the child pressed up between them. He watched the faces of the two girls carefully, but he need not have worried. Neither of them showed even the smallest flicker of recognition. In fact, they seemed barely to register his presence at all, but stared past him to a third person, a woman Carew had never seen before. The woman, who was dressed in the livery of a better class of servant, was walking round the kitchen opening and closing cupboard doors, peering into the food chests and turning out drawers. Her lips were compressed into a thin disapproving line. She looked around at last.

'*Ach*, so; there you are.' Her gaze swept clean past Carew and came to rest on the two girls instead. 'Alice and Anne, is it?'

Her collar was white and crisp; her eyes were very cold and blue, and reminded Carew of a kind of dog he had once seen belonging to a merchant of the Muscovy Company. She had a faint accent that he could not identify – Netherlandish perhaps? – a faint sibilance that marked her as a foreigner.

'Well, is it, or isn't it? Speak up.'

One of the girls – Anne – opened her mouth as though to say something, but no sound came out. She looked like a rabbit that has been hypnotised by a snake.

The woman's strange pale gaze swept the room again. This time, it came to rest upon the child.

'*Ach*, and so there he is, the little one.' She made a barely audible sound – *tsk* – with her tongue against her teeth. 'If you would hear my counsel, I'd get the child cleaned up quickly, before your master asks to see him.'

She turned back to her inspection, and the two girls crept away, pulling the child behind them.

Trying to look busy, Carew followed them out, and went to try to find the old man. He arrived there to find the parlour empty. Suddenly, he heard voices approaching from the direction of the hall. If anyone were to come into the parlour now, he would be discovered. Carew did the only thing possible: he slipped into his old hiding place behind the arras.

Immediately, he knew he had made a miserable mistake.

He listened again. The voices grew louder, paused at the threshold of the room. For a moment he allowed himself to believe that they would not come in, but then he heard the unmistakable sound of heavy footsteps entering the room. *Fanculo*! He was trapped, like a ferret in a hole.

It was dark behind the arras, and the narrow space had a peculiar musty smell of old wool and dust. As a boy it had been easy for Carew to hide here; it was not quite so easy as a fully grown man, for all that he had become thin a gnawed bone. All the same, he told himself, it should be possible to remain here undetected, for a while at least – so long as he did not either breathe or blink. Extraordinary to say, but the hole that he made all those years ago was still there; a spot of light was shining at shoulder-height through the mouse-nibbled tapestry. Cautiously, Carew bent down and put his eye to the hole.

Three men had come into the room.

The first was soberly dressed in a scholar's or a lawyer's black and dun robes; the other two were apparelled so outlandishly that it was a moment or two before Carew could take it all in. The second man, and the youngest of the three, was wearing a waistcoat of embroidered and padded silk, and silk stockings with clocks at the heels; his head peeped from the folds of a vast lace collar. On his feet were red silk high-heeled shoes decorated with pompoms.

The third was the man in green.

'I don't give a damn,' the man in green was saying over his shoulder to a fourth person, a servant presumably, hovering just out of Carew's field of vision. 'Tell them to bring the brat at once. I want to see it now, and I've no mind to be kept waiting.'

The speaker had his back to the arras. He walked over to the window and then, catching sight of himself in the panes of glass, stood there for a moment, legs astride, regarding his own reflection. He pulled off his gloves, two great gauntlets of gilded leather, and straightened the plumes on his hat. There were jewels on his cap and on his thumbs of which the Great Turk himself would not be ashamed.

Like his brother Paul, Ralph Pindar was a man now well into his middle years. The fat boy had become a fleshy man, paunchy even, although his flesh became him in a way that Carew found surprising. Merchant Pindar the younger was clearly, and in every way, a man of substance. His very presence sucked air from the room.

Ralph turned from his own reflection at last, and as he did so, his eyes lit upon the arras behind which Carew was hiding. Although Carew knew he must have been imagining it, for a moment it was as if their two gazes locked. Carew's eyes snapped shut. He had an odd notion that to keep them open would be to create two beams, emitting light or some other strange force – some kind of evil catnip, perhaps – that would pull Ralph's attention to him, wherever he was.

He forced himself to breathe – slowly now, very slowly – wondering all the while what would happen to him if he were discovered. He had been in some scrapes before now, but this. . . this topped everything. It had been. . . years. How many years: ten? fifteen? *Jesu!* What was the matter with him? However long it was, it was not nearly long enough. What was he thinking? He had hidden out at the top of the Drover's Path with the express purpose of making absolutely sure that he had the lay of the land in every last detail before he encountered Ralph again, and here he was walking right in and offering himself up like suckling pig with an apple in its mouth. . . In his mind's eye, it was as though he could hear someone, anyone, Paul most probably, berating him – *yap, yap, yap* – just as they had done all his life. At that precise moment, he could box *himself* over the ears.

But he could not seem to help himself. Ralph had been at the manor only five minutes and he, Carew, had become the kitchen boy again, hiding from him like a cowed dog.

Sure enough, the sound of Ralph's footsteps were coming closer now, but just then a woman servant – Carew could not see which one – brought in a plate of food, although judging by the way she scuttled off again like a frightened beetle, he guessed it was either Anne or Alice, and the footsteps retreated. Then came the sound of a bottle being opened, and of liquid – wine or small beer – poured into glasses.

Then the door opened again, and the housekeeper with the pale eyes came in, pushing the child in front of her.

'Sir?' She looked at Ralph enquiringly. 'You wanted to see him?'

'Yes, bring it here.'

She tried to coax the child into the room, but at the sight of Ralph standing there, legs astride, it pulled back, afraid suddenly.

Ralph gazed down at the child impassively. 'Still snivelling, I see.'

The housekeeper put her hand tentatively on the child's neck, as if to calm him, but to no avail. He hid his face in her skirts and began to bawl.

'He's frightened of you, that's all.'

'Of course it's frightened of me. It's frightened of everything. Well, it's still alive, that's something I suppose.'

'Perhaps if you—' she began, but Ralph was not in the mood to listen.

'Enough, take it away.'

Without another word the woman spirited the child back to the kitchens.

Carew had been curious all this time to see who Ralph was nowadays, who he had become. As he listened to this conversation he knew the answer: the bullying boy had become an arrogant, brutish man.

'Look at this – this moth-eaten old tapestry has been here since I was a boy.' From the sound of his voice, Carew could detect that Ralph was very near the arras again. It was the same voice he remembered from when they were children, but different: a man's baritone, deeper than he had imagined. 'I've half a mind to pull it down right now.' Inches away from his face, the tapestry blew inwards as Ralph ran his hand down it.

'Disgusting thing – positively verminous.'

The arras billowed again, closer still to where Carew was standing. His face was sweating like greasy cheese.

He knows I'm here, the thought occurred to him. *He's just toying with me*. A taste of bile rose in Carew's throat.

For a moment it was as though his brain had frozen over. It was all he could do to stop himself breaking out from behind the arras and making a run for it, but it was too late now, even for a plan as imbecile as that.

But, incredibly, the next moment Ralph had moved away. Carew could hear his footsteps recede, and then the sound of logs being kicked in the fireplace.

'And so, Monsieur Pindar, just how long will this business of yours take?'

It was the older of Ralph's two companions, the man in the black and dun robes, who spoke now. From his hiding place, Carew could see him walking around the room looking for somewhere to sit; he pulled out a handkerchief and placed it on a chair before sitting down. 'And may we not give the respects to your father now that we are here?'

'You're jesting, I suppose, de Caus?' The younger man in the group now gave a high-pitched little snort of laughter. 'Mr Pindar and his father quite detest one another. You keep him locked in the attic, don't you, Rafie?'

'My father is indisposed,' Ralph said. 'They tell me he is resting in his chamber, and asks to send his deepest regrets that he is not able to receive you. My Lord especially.' He gave a curt nod in the young man's direction. 'No doubt fearing to be blinded by your most noble – and sober – visage.'

'My point, Monsieur Pindar, is are we to lie here tonight, or press on to the next coaching inn?'

'Great heaven, you don't expect me to spend the night here, do you?' the young man said in alarm. A lock of hair had fallen over his eyes; he brushed it to one side with the back of his hand.

'Why, my dear Lord Nicholas, are you afraid of phantoms?' Ralph put his hand to the boy's face, pinching his earlobe between his fingers. 'I thought it would be worth spending All Hallows' Night here at Priors Leaze, just to hear you squeal.'

'For God's sake, Ralph.' The young man pushed his hand away. 'How I wish you wouldn't do that.'

'Oh, but why, my sweet young friend, when I like it so. Your cheek is so very girlish and soft.'

'Oh do shut up,' the young man said mildly, taking himself off to the other end of the room. 'Tell him, Salomon,' he appealed to the Frenchman. 'Tell him we must move on.'

'It is only twelve of the clock, so if your business could be speedily conducted, monsieur, and if my Lord wishes to travel onwards today, it can very soon be arranged,' de Caus said, with the weary air of someone trying to keep the peace. 'But I'm sure her Ladyship, for one, is grateful to be breaking the journey, even if it's only for a few hours.'

'My Lady Nicholas is feeling bilious.' Ralph refilled their glasses. 'And mark my words, my Lady will continue to feel bilious wherever she is,' he said, laying a heavy hand on the young man's shoulder. 'It can make no difference to her whether we stay or go. I have some business to attend to here, and then we will be on our way.' He kicked at a dried-up dog turd with his boot. 'D'you imagine I want to stay here any longer than I must?'

'I really think it should be his Lordship who decides in this matter; they are his father's carriages we travel in, after all,' de Caus said firmly. There was a weariness to his voice that suggested this was an argument that had already been rehearsed several times. All three were clearly much on each other's nerves.

'My wife finds the swaying of the coach disagreeable,' the young man said, swallowing his wine and holding his glass out for more. 'Can you blame her? It's all your fault, Pindar, all this inconvenience just for a poacher. I don't understand it, why cannot your steward take care of it?' He walked over to the far side of the room and, sitting down in one of the window seats, closed his eyes. 'I can't say that the carriage doesn't make me feel bilious too. It's very heaven to be out of it for a while.'

Now that he was sitting at the window, the young man – Lord Nicholas – was for the first time directly in Carew's field of vision. He was even younger than Carew had supposed: a youth of perhaps no more than nineteen or twenty. He had dark hair and a pale complexion. His chin was almost hairless, with just the faintest trace of down on his sulky upper lip. But it was his hands that most drew Carew's attention: hands like a girl's, so white and smooth it was quite clear that they had done nothing more strenuous in their whole life than wield a toothpick.

'Sweet *Jesu*, everything makes your wife bilious.' With cheerful indifference Ralph picked up a leg of cold chicken from the plate on the table and began to eat it. 'And – she – seems – to – find – almost – everyone – disagreeable,' he added, through mouthfuls.

'Well, she certainly finds *you* disagreeable,' Lord Nicholas said, his eyes still closed. 'And she's Lady Nicholas to you, Rafie, you should know that by now.'

'No need to be so snappish.' Ralph threw the gnawed bone over his shoulder. It landed near the fraying arras, almost at Carew's feet. Now Ralph was holding up a second leg between two fat fingers, looking at it with an expression of disgust. '*Christos*, the fowl become scrawnier every time I come here.'

'Only because your appetite gets bigger.' Carew's gaze swivelled to take in the young man. 'Why, Rafie,' he was saying, pushing the lock of hair off his face again – 'I do believe your nice new doublet is already fraying at the seams.'

Carew saw Lord Nicholas exchange a quick glance with de Caus.

'Great God, Salomon,' he added, pressing his point, 'what trencher habits our merchant friends do have. I'm almost ashamed of them.' He turned to Ralph again, his face flushed. 'You'll have to do better than that if you are to come with me to the masque.'

'That's not what I heard,' Ralph said, still chewing on the chicken bone with the greatest unconcern. 'I hear that their Majesties' masques are the very last word in drunkenness and dissolution.' He looked up with a grin. 'I'm imagining we will both fit in there nicely.'

'Oh, what do you know,' the young man said with a sulky expression. 'Prince Henry has a very different view, mark my words. Good heavens, Ralph, do you *ever* stop eating?'

'And do you ever stop whining?' Ralph seemed thoroughly good-humoured now, grinning and wiping the grease from his chin. 'You should eat more.' He gave the young man a steady look, 'or there'll be nothing for your wife to get hold of.' He took a slug of wine. 'Eat more and drink less, that's my advice,' he added, smacking his lips, 'you know how foolish it makes you.'

'Don't remember asking for your advice.' Lord Nicholas gave a dainty hiccough, and then, wrinkling his nose, 'Faugh! How many dogs does your father keep. It stinks like a hunting kennel in here.'

'Have no fear; we won't stop here any longer than necessary. De Caus, I beg you.' Ralph waved at the third man. 'Come along with you, you tight-arsed Frenchman, have something to eat. Our young friend would not want

284

us to stand on ceremony – would you, Nicky?' He seized the bottle from the table and poured out a beaker of wine.

'We should pity her Ladyship.' De Caus, who had not moved from his chair, was looking at Ralph as though he were a particularly repellent form of insect life, 'in her condition, my wife, she was always the same – *très malade* – it is not at all surprising.'

'Well said, de Caus. At least you have a heart. Unlike some people I could mention.'

'Why, are you suggesting that I have no heart? When no one on this earth should know better than you that I am all heart?' Still chewing, Ralph looked up from his plate with small, hard eyes. 'Am I not,' he said with careful deliberation, 'my dear Lord Nicholas?'

'My wife complains that I do not keep company with her when you are around.'

'Well, if she's in a condition again, as Mr Waterworks here so delicately puts it, then clearly she has been keeping company with someone. . .' Ralph threw the second chicken bone over his shoulder, where it landed close to the first at the foot of the arras. There was a small, nasty pause. 'Even if that someone is not you.'

'Monsieur Pindar, I really must protest—' De Caus got to his feet.

'Oh, keep your hat on, you old French fart.' Ralph jabbed his knife in de Caus's direction. 'You see, what did I tell you?' He turned to where Lord Nicholas was sitting, one long slim leg crossed over the other, yawning and picking his fingernails. 'Always complaining. Mr Hydraulics here is as bad as your lady wife. I *told* you to leave them behind, but would you listen?

'Salomon does what he likes,' Lord Nicholas said with a small hiccough. 'But Lady Nicholas. . . make her miss the masque? How could I, poor creature?'

'She's your wife.' Ralph turned and spat over his shoulder on to the floor. 'She must do as she's bid.'

'And does *your* wife always do what she's bid, Monsieur Pindar?'

'I have no wife, de Caus,' Ralph said, sucking on a third chicken bone thoughtfully and then spitting out a piece of gristle. 'But if I did, rest assured she would do as I told her.'

'Rafie with a wifie!' Lord Nicholas looked up from examining the clocks on his stockings and gave a little scream of laughter. 'What a thought! Pity any poor creature insane enough to betroth herself to him, wouldn't you say, Mr de Caus?' His tone was confidential, but his gaze was fixed on Ralph. 'For all his great fortune.'

'I'll just let you spend my money instead.' Ralph's blue eyes, small and icy, looked up from his plate and came to rest on the young man. 'After all, my Lord Nicholas, you do it so well.'

At that moment there came the sounds of voices shouting and dogs barking just outside the parlour window; such a commotion that it drew all three men to the window.

'Well, gentlemen,' Carew heard Ralph say. 'It seems as if they've caught our poacher. Shall we have some sport? Wait here, and I'll have them bring him in.'

Lord Nicholas and de Caus watched him go.

For a moment there was silence; then the Frenchman began to pace around the room.

'*Insupportable. . . insupportable. . .*' he muttered to himself, before turning to the young man with sudden vehemence. 'Forgive me, my Lord, but what would your father say if he knew that you let this. . . this. . . person. . .' He hesitated, searching for the right words, '. . . direct you so?'

'Rafie? Oh, you mustn't mind old Rafie.' Lord Nicholas turned from the window. 'But no more talk of fathers, I beg you; you know how nervous it makes me.' Swaying slightly, he walked over to the table, and Carew could hear the sound of more wine being poured. 'You forget, de Caus, it is my carriage we ride in. I will give the orders to go or stay as I please.' He seemed to have a good deal more authority with Ralph out of the room. 'But best let Rafie get his business over with. Besides,' he added, 'if they really have caught the poacher it might be good sport, what do you say? Do you suppose they'll set the dogs on him?'

The Frenchman was not interested in poachers.

'A merchant, at court?' he was saying. 'Is this possible?' He shook his head. '*No, no, no, no, no... incroyable.*' And then, addressing himself to Lord Nicholas again, 'In France, you understand, this would never happen.'

'We're not in France,' the young man said with a yawn. 'And I notice that, de Caus, you are at Court often enough.'

'Respectfully, this is not the same thing at all. I design gardens and waterfalls and moving statues. I interpret the writings of the ancients – of Vitruvius and his treaties on hydraulics. I am but the most humble servant to eminences such as your father and Prince Henry and Her Majesty your Queen. When I find myself at court I know very well that I am there because of my expertise, because I can be of *use*,' he added, shrugging his shoulders, 'not for – how do you say it? – the pretty colour of my eyes.'

'And what makes you think that Merchant Ralph is not useful? I got myself into some scrapes, you see. At the university. There's a group of us who liked to play cards – and I got in deep. And Rafie, you see, he understands little things like that.' Lord Nicholas's expression now turned sulky, 'unlike my good father. So you see, he pays my gaming debts when my father will not.'

There was a short silence.

'You mean you owe this person money?' de Caus said gravely, and then, faintly, '*Tiens... encore plus incroyable.*'

'I don't *owe* him anything,' the young man said coldly. 'He takes care of my gaming debts, that's all.'

There was another small silence.

'A man like that... I doubt very much it will be that simple; trust me, he will extract a price from you, somehow or other,' de Caus said, with an effort at patience. '*Ne croyez-vous pas?* You should take more care, my Lord, with whom you associate. Does your father know you keep company with this person?' He took one look at Lord Nicholas and shook his head, 'But no, of course he does not.' De Caus went over to the table. 'And this person wants me to design a garden for him here... *impossible, impossible,*' he muttered to himself. 'I think, after all, I will take some wine.'

'Well, I'm not going to apologise for it. Everyone knows Ralph Pindar is... what he is. But he's rich, don't you see. Debts like mine don't mean anything to him. Just go along with him, can't you?' The young man sat down in the chair that Ralph had so recently vacated and put his feet upon the table. 'What you should know is that they let just about anyone attend the masques these days, or so my father says. You should hear him... "It wasn't like this in the old days, in the days of the old Queen, God rest her most Glorious Gloriousness."' He spoke in a high nasal voice that was meant to imitate his father. '"*She* knew better than to shower any old Tom, Dick or Harry with honours, God Rest her Gloriousness." In fact, she didn't give so much as a knighthood to anyone.' He drained his cup, and then added, with a small hiccough, 'most especially anyone from Scotland.'

When he put his cup to his lips again, his hand trembled and some of the liquid spilled down his embroidered waistcoat. The young man was now extremely drunk.

'You should not speak so about her late Majesty.' De Caus was looking at him with a shocked expression, 'nor your most noble father.'

'God's blood, de Caus, you sound just like him. You're not my tutor, you know. D'you think I give a damn what you think?' Lord Nicholas gave another titter that made Carew want to surge out from behind the arras and slap him. 'You don't matter – *you* are no one around here,' he added, aggressive suddenly.

He leant back in the chair again and closed his eyes. 'I saw her once, you know, the old Queen. Father took me to Court when I was just a boy. She was lying on a great pile of cushions, with her wrinkled old dugs half hanging out; only two teeth in her head; breath that stank like something rotting in a charnel house.' He gave a small shudder. 'I should know, she made me come over and kiss her hand.' He wrinkled his nose. 'And now a knighthood can be bought for thirty pounds. Imagine! A vulgar little knighthood. Thirty pounds! The King – God save his Gracious Rickety-Legged Majesty – practically gives them away to anyone who can afford it, no better than prizes at a coconut shy, and naturally enough every last money-grubbing little merchant thinks he should have one—' He looked up at de Caus with bloodshot eyes, '—and that of course includes dear Rafie.' He gave another little titter. 'Except that so far the prize has eluded him. Dear me, that makes him *very* annoyed. But what *can* he do?'

De Caus, shooing one of the dogs away from the plates of food, did not reply.

'I'll tell you what he can do: what he can do is be generous to me.' Lord Nicholas stretched out his long legs in their white silk stockings. 'Robert Carr, the King's favourite, is well known to me. Prince Henry too. We are exactly of an age. Merchant Ralph imagines that I will introduce him into Court circles. I have the entrée, you see. So I am useful to him, or so he thinks. Do you really think he would pay my gambling debts otherwise? You see, de Caus, I understand his game rather better than you think.' He turned to the older man with a look that was half-cool, half-challenging. 'How much do you know about our Court?'

When the Frenchman still made no reply he went on. 'Look at me. I am young, and I am handsome, am I not?' he said. 'Oh, don't look at me like *that*, de Caus, these days it's the way to get ahead. His Majesty likes to be surrounded by pretty young men. The King, it is well known, has never taken a mistress – or a mistress who is a woman, that is. Some say he despises women; young men are all the fashion, these days. And Rafie here – well, he imagines he is going to use me as bait.'

He shot de Caus a look that was anything but innocent.

'Bait? I don't understand. *Qu'est-ce que ça veut dire...* bait?'

'He imagines that he is going to use me to get the attention of the King.'

There was a thoughtful pause while de Caus digested this information.

'And have you considered the consequences if he should succeed? For yourself, I mean.'

'I can imagine worse things that being His Majesty's favourite. It might be nice to be somebody's favourite. After all, I'm better looking than that Robert Carr, everybody says so. And you've seen how everybody sucks up to *him* these days; it's enough to make you vomit. And if I were made favourite everyone would have to suck up to me – even Father...' He paused as this delightful thought sank in.

'I can only admire your candour.'

'I have no illusions. It's all Rafie thinks of: preferment at court, a knighthood, a coat of arms. But so far alas—' Lord Nicholas clicked his fingers into the air, '—*rien*! It has eluded him. He's in a great big chafe about it, I can tell you.' He tilted the chair on to its two back legs, 'but then that's old Rafie for you, always in a chafe about something.'

'It seems a most uncertain plan.'

'Ah, but that is only the beginning. His brother has just this moment arrived back from the East, you see, with a diamond as big as a duck egg. Pindar's Great Diamond, they are calling it, surely you've – oh!' Like a boy player he clapped his hands over his mouth theatrically. 'Oh, I was not supposed to mention his brother, and most especially the diamond, to anyone. How. . . foolish of me.'

'I think I have heard talk of this brother. Would that be Paul Pindar, of the Levant Company?'

'The very same.'

'But. . . this Paul Pindar has a reputation as a scholar and a man of letters—'

'Not much like our dear Rafie then—'

'—and as a collector, too. *Mais oui*. . . of gemstones, yes, but of plants among other things. Yes, yes, I have heard of this other Pindar. He is the one who is building that great house and garden in Bishopsgate. But is it possible that this Pindar, and this one.' He jerked his head in the direction of door, 'are brothers?'

'Ralph hates him, of course, but then Ralph hates just about everyone.'

'But there was something about this other Pindar, was there not?'

'He made a fortune – but then lost it playing at cards. Made another one out in the East, and now he's home again, even richer than his brother, so they say.' Lord Nicholas grinned. 'Imagine how that annoys him.'

'Maybe all this is as you say. But what I don't understand is what has the diamond got to do with this knighthood he so desires.'

'We all know how His Majesty likes to...' Lord Nicholas paused for effect, '...collect.' He drained his glass. 'And His Highness Prince Henry, too. They are as fond of gemstones as they are of your gardens, Mr de Caus, or Mr Inigo Jones's masques. So, you see, if he is to get the King's attention, this is his moment.'

'But you say this diamond belongs to his brother?'

'Oh, you mark my words.' Lord Nicholas laughed unpleasantly. 'He wouldn't let a little thing like that get in his way.'

Just then there came the sound of another disturbance outside the window: cries and hollers, and dogs barking in excitement.

'Can you hear that? Something's happened.' Lord Nicholas jumped up and went over to the window, craning his neck to get a better look. 'Yes, here they come now. They've caught someone. An old man... an old man hung all about with pots and pans like a tinker... What'll they do to him, d'you suppose? My father always makes sure they hang for it.' He put his hands against the window-panes, his whole body tense with excitement. 'D'you suppose Ralph will do the same? Five guineas says he does. That'd be good sport, wouldn't it, de Caus?'

Carew heard these words with dread. Moocher! They had caught Moocher! That addle-brained, moon-crazed old rat-catcher! In his hiding place behind the arras Carew was now in double torment. Dear God, he was going to box that grizzled old head of his so hard he'd hear bells for a month. Carew knew in the depths of his very soul that if Moocher should be made to talk it would be the end of it for both of them.

What in the name of God would Ralph do now?

TWENTY-FOUR

Paul

Bishopsgate.

E VERY NIGHT NOW HE found himself looking at the diamond.

When all the household was asleep, he would go quietly in his stockinged feet down to the great gallery and take it from its hiding place. Each night he followed the same ritual. Unlocking the doors of the ebony cabinet, he would carefully slide away the mirrored section in the middle, and take out the diamond from its secret drawer. Then he would quickly reassemble it, so that if anyone were to come upon him unawares they would never guess what the cabinet contained.

He knew it was dangerous to handle the stone so often, but he could not help himself. He would sit by the fire holding it up to the flames, watching the light refracted in it, losing himself in its beauty. At these times the room seemed smaller and more airless than it did during the day. The candlelight shimmered and glistered against the ebony doors of the cabinet, making pictures – eyes, faces, grinning lips – in the darkest recesses of the room.

The time was coming, very soon now, when he would no longer be its custodian. Each night as he held the stone in his hand, the thought became harder and harder to contemplate.

It occurred to him that perhaps he should keep it after all. And at the same time he had a feeling that if he did, something at the very centre of his life would not hold.

Paul was sitting like this when he became aware of a figure standing in the doorway. He knew immediately who it was even before he looked up, and half-realised that he had been waiting for her to come to him again, and that this was the reason that he stayed up so long, and so late. There was no longer any pretence from either of them that she had come looking for Quirkus.

There was no time to hide the diamond this time, so he closed his fingers over it instead, concealing it in his fist. Looking up, he found himself saying the very thing he had determined never to say: 'Lady Sydenham, won't you come in? Please, do me the honour of sitting with me a while?'

Most women would have made some show of reluctance, at the very least have shown some small display of hesitation, expressed some concern about being surprised in the middle of the night, but not Frances.

Frances Sydenham was not a woman to waste anyone's time. There was the most admirable energy and clarity in everything she did. She walked in now with her candle held high in one hand, her skirts pinched between the fingers of the other. Holding herself very upright, she moved with the air of someone carrying out a visit in broad daylight to a fellow matron of impeccable rectitude and respectability. There was something queenly in the way she proceeded across the floor and waited for him to pull the chair out for her. Quickly, he hid the diamond in his pocket.

'So, tell me,' she said, without preamble, settling herself down in a rustle of silk, 'is it true what they are saying at the Exchange about Pindar's Great Diamond?'

This was not at all what Paul had been expecting. 'And what do they say at the Exchange?'

'I hear there is only one topic of conversation these days. Pindar's Great Diamond. But you know that, of course.'

He got up and went over to the dresser where he had placed a bottle of muscat, a gift from a Levantine merchant of his acquaintance, and without asking poured them both a glass.

When he did not a reply immediately, she pressed him. 'Come, every last apprentice in London knows about it.'

He took a mouthful of the wine, and then another. He was aware of its effect almost immediately, a warm, glittering sensation, like diamond dust along his veins.

'Would you like to see it?' The fatal words were out before he could stop himself.

'There is not a woman in England who could refuse such an offer.'

'Then your wish is my command. I present to you. . . the Sultan's Blue.' Slowly, like a conjurer, Paul pulled the diamond from his pocket, and opened his fingers, one by one. The diamond, three hundred carats of blue starlight, glowed like a living thing in the palm of his hand.

He heard her small intake of breath as her eyes lit upon it for the first time. 'So it is true then; it really does exist—'

'Why, did you think it a traveller's tale?'

'I. . . was not sure. May I?'

She put her hand out, but he pulled his hand back quickly before she could touch it.

'Have you gone mad, madam? I should tell you, there are those who believe that there is a most powerful magic contained in here.'

'A magical stone?' Frances, picking up easily on his game, put her hand to her mouth. Her dark eyes sparkled.

'A most powerful magic. I can hold it, because – for the moment at least – the diamond is in my keeping. There are some who believe that it will bring *mala sfortuna* – bad luck – to anyone else.' He held the stone out to her again, only this time with a hint of a challenge. 'But you – you, my lady – seem to me like a woman who might take her chances.'

Frances glanced up at him quickly, as if not sure of his meaning, but was reassured to see him smiling.

'You have found me out.' She smiled back at him. 'I for one have always believed in taking my chances – but perhaps not this night.'

She sat back in her chair, raised her arms languidly over her head, like a cat stretching.

'You say the diamond belongs to you. . . for the moment? Does that mean you will sell it after all?'

'There are many legends – one of them is that the stone must never be bought or sold. When the time is right, the diamond will move on, or so it has always been believed. And that there's no point asking why, or trying to prevent it.'

'Then I predict much desolation at the Exchange.' Raising her glass to her mouth, she looked at him thoughtfully over its lip. 'But these are gossips' tales, surely? And not a little convenient if the keeper of the stone does not wish to be parted from it.'

'Perhaps, but I for one have never felt able to take that chance.'

'Then it is a magical stone indeed.'

For a moment Frances said nothing more, but began to take the pins from her headdress distractedly.

'And is it true – and now I see that it must be true – that you won it in a game of *primero*?'

'You'll be telling me it was in Zuanne Memmo's ridotto next, and how many were the players, and for how many days and nights we played—'

'Now you are making fun of me!'

'Only a little.'

'Then I must hold you forfeit.'

As her headdress came loose at last, she took it off and shook out her hair, so that it fell down her back, very black against the whiteness of her neck.

'You have but to name it.'

'Anything?' A small dimple appeared in Frances's right cheek. 'That is temptation indeed. Very well, let me see. . .'

She leant back again. Thoughtfully she raised her arms up and piled her loose black hair on top of her head. Then she shook her head. 'Ah, no! I am too stupid ever to think of new forfeits.' She gave a small sigh, 'so it must be the old one, I suppose. You must drink your wine down. All of it.'

'All of it?'

'All of it, if you please, and without spilling a drop.'

'You are a hard taskmaster.' Paul drained his glass. 'There, are you satisfied?'

'By no means.'

'What, not satisfied? And so big a cup!'

'I said, without spilling a drop. And you, sir, did spill more than a drop,' she said, the dimple appearing in her cheek again. 'I did distinctly see at least two fall upon your doublet.'

'You did?'

'Aye, so you must drink your fill again.'

'Take care or you will get me in my cups.'

'What, a little nursery game?' Laughing, she pulled a strand of hair forward, winding it around one of her fingers. 'As if a little draught or two of wine could get the better of such a one as you.'

'I've had my apprentice days, it's true, but I can assure you those times are long gone.'

'Nonetheless, a forfeit is a forfeit.'

'Then so be it.'

As Paul drained his glass for the second time, the melancholy shade of Parvish came to him, wagging his finger. *The widow Sydenham.* He could hear her name on the old merchant's tongue, his tone of voice quite enough to convey his distaste: the fashionable dress, the dishonouring whiff of her learnedness. If Parvish could see them conversing together in the dead of night... but, at that moment, what did it matter what Parvish thought?

'So if you are not to sell it, then what—'

'My task is to keep the diamond safely until I can pass it on to its next custodian.'

'You would just *give* it away?'

'Yes, I intend to do just that. Who could put a price on such a thing as this?'

She leant towards him again and this time she was so close that he could see the sheen of the firelight on the skin of her neck. He resisted the impulse to pull her towards him, to bury his face in her hair, to smell her odour of female sweat and some dark flower, violets or iris—

'And that person, I surmise, has been chosen by you?'

'You ask a lot of questions—'

'—ah, so you *do* know who it is! And now it is I who has found you out.' She sat back in her chair, and as she did so he saw one foot kick out from beneath the hem of her dress, and then, in a fluttering of silken layers – did he imagine it, or did he really see? – the pale curve of her stockinged calf, the small hole in the black silk—

'Come, tell me. This is a mystery indeed. You know you can confide in me. Besides, who would I tell? Who is he?'

'What makes you think it is a "he"?'

'Ah, so we are to play at guessing games are we?'

As though she could no longer bear to remain seated, Frances jumped up and went to stand by the fire.

'Have pity, no more games. I have no doubt that you could outguess me in a moment – and can only trust to your honour that you will not try.' Paul was aware that the wine he had just drunk was now roaring through his veins. 'But tell me, what else are they saying at the Exchange?'

'At the Exchange they are saying that it is only a ploy, and that you will surely change your mind. They say that Prince Henry has spent seven thousand pounds on gemstones alone this last quarter.' She let this idea hang in the air between them, 'which only serves to make His Majesty all the more desirous of it. It's common knowledge that there is much rivalry between the two in these matters, and little love lost. It must occur to many that there would be a real chance of preferment if they were able to present the King with such a gift.' She looked at him curiously. 'And you are telling me that you would throw away your natural advantage? And for the sake of. . . a woman? She must be a great lady indeed.'

'Preferment at court would be of no interest at all to this particular lady. She has come to these shores on quite another mission, I believe.'

'You mean – the little nun? Celia's friend.' He saw an expression of utter incredulity pass over her face. 'Surely not. . .?' But one look at Paul's face told Frances immediately that she was right. 'Ah, but now see what I have done. I had thought all along that it was Parvish, but now I see. . . forgive me, I have made you tell me what you wished to conceal. It was not my intention. We women, you know, we cannot help ourselves. We are eternally curious. Ah, don't look like that, if there is one sorry skill that I have in this world it is that I am good at keeping secrets.' And then, as if to change the subject, she put in quickly, 'One confidence deserves another. I can tell you are wondering how I know so much of what goes on at the Exchange.'

'Yes, I do confess it.' And it was true that Paul could not be but struck by the information she seemed to have at her fingertips.

'During his illness my husband – the late Sir Aubrey – had me deal with all his correspondence and business affairs. I learnt a good deal. When he became sick, there were many months when I wrote all his letters—'

'A poor pastime for a woman.'

'To the contrary, I liked it very much. Does that thought surprise you?'

'No. I find it. . . intriguing.'

'Most men are of another view. Although in Antwerp when I was living there, I knew many women who helped their husbands in this way. She-Merchants. Wives, and sometimes widows, too, would trade in their husbands' names, and they did it very well.' She looked down at her glass. 'Some had better heads for figures than their husbands did – I put myself in that category – although we had to take care we were not found out—'

'Hide your light beneath a bushel?'

'You see my point exactly.' There was a pause. 'But then you always do.'

When Paul did not reply, she went on easily. 'I love what is new,' she said, holding his gaze just a second too long, 'and I think, Merchant Pindar, that you do too.'

Desire to have her was raging in him now. He knew then that they were at the very brink of something, that if they did not pull back now, there would be no returning from that place; that whatever it was that was done now, would be with him for ever, never to be undone.

He turned away and stood, not moving, with his back to her; hoping, as he did so, that she would take this as a sign not to come any closer. And at the same time willing her to come. He felt rather than saw her move towards him; heard the faint scrape of her silk hem as she moved, like rain on grass.

'Won't you pour a glass for me?'

She was standing so close behind him that he could feel the heat of her body.

He took a mouthful of wine, rolling it slowly around his tongue. He swallowed, felt it burn along his throat, into his chest.

'Why, do I forget my manners, Lady Sydenham?'

'You do.'

'If you surprise a man in the dead of night like that, then you have only yourself to blame.'

'It's true, I blame only myself.'

She put her hand out, so that her fingers rested along his arm. She held them there, feeling him, his hard spare flesh. Her touch burnt him through the cloth. Still without turning around Paul picked up the flask again. He poured more wine, a few drops of it spilling on to the white damask cloth.

'Your hand is shaking.'

'You are mistaken.'

'I think not—'

They heard it at the same moment. The squeak of a floorboard. They flew apart, just in time.

The small, stooped form of Annetta stood in the doorway.

'I thought I heard voices.' She looked from one to the other of them. 'I do so hope I am not interrupting?'

TWENTY-FIVE

Carew

Events occurring at Priors Leaze Manor in the country of Wiltshire.

C AREW WAS STILL HIDING behind the arras when Ralph returned.

'We heard more shouting. Is that him, the old man?' Lord Nicholas, turning to Ralph, was quivering like a dog before the chase. 'Is he the poacher? What'll you do with him?'

The prospect of some cruel sport, of drawing blood had sobered him.

To this, at first, Ralph had said nothing. Instead, he walked to the window, and stood there with his back to the room.

'Well, they've certainly caught someone,' he said at last. 'Strange-looking fellow; says he's a rat-catcher by trade.'

He spoke so quietly that Carew knew immediately that something had changed. His tone was different. Thoughtful. Ralph at his most dangerous.

'It appears that this old man has been hiding out in the barn these last few days; some of the people here have suspected as much.'

'Are there others?'

'The old man swears he's on his own, but I don't know. . .' Ralph's voice tailed off, still thoughtful. 'He says he was a player once, at Blackfriars. Perhaps we should take him with us.' He turned to Lord Nicholas and de Caus. 'I wonder, do their Majesties still keep fools at Court? Other than the Scots, that is.'

Carew heard these words with a sinking heart. Moocher! That moon-crazed old rat-catcher! What had he been thinking, to allow himself to be picked up as a poacher and a vagabond? The lure of a nice warm barn must have been too much for him. As Carew knew only too well from his long months on the road, sometimes even an Assizes jail was preferable to the bitter cold and the frozen mud of the fields and hedgerows as winter closed in. The trouble was that Moocher had not reckoned with Ralph. Neither of them had reckoned with Ralph.

'They found this on him,' Ralph said, placing a small round object carefully in the centre of the table.

'Dirty old thing, it's not worth thrupence,' Lord Nicholas complained.

'To the contrary, *une tres belle poche*. . .' de Caus said, picking it up and looking at it with interest. 'A lady's pocket. And a fine one. Ottoman work, if I am not mistaken.'

'That's is exactly what I would have said.' Ralph stood looking at the pocket intently. 'A strange thing,' he added slowly, 'for a vagabond dressed in rat-skins to carry around with him, wouldn't you say?'

'There, what did I tell you! He is a thief!' Lord Nicholas said. 'Is there anything inside?'

Ralph pulled at the silk drawstrings and shook the purse out. 'A few Venetian coins. Worthless.'

'Then he must have sold whatever else was in there,' Lord Nicholas put in, 'or spent it.'

Ralph turned and gave him a despising look that said, *What, you imbecile, in these parts?* But he restrained himself and said instead quite levelly: 'Why do you not ask him that yourself?'

Two men came in, carrying Moocher between them, his legs dragging on the floor behind him. The men – the Pindars' steward Pitton and another man from the farm – tried to make him stand, but every time they took their supporting arms away, Moocher fell to the floor. Eventually, uncertain what to do, they left him there, moaning softly to himself. There was blood coming from a blow to the side of his head, and one of his eyes was swollen.

If he had not known it was Moocher, Carew would not have recognised the muddy, bloodstained wretch before them. They had stripped the old man of his rat-skin coat and the vagabond motley – the belts and pieces of string with the traps and pots – hanging from it, but even if he had been wearing it, Carew would scarcely have recognised him. He no longer looked like the big man that Carew remembered from the Drover's Path but seemed to have shrunk to a man half his size beneath the blows that had already been dealt him.

'What have you to say for yourself?' Ralph put the toe of his boot to Moocher's face and turned it towards him. 'You've been poaching on my land, and you're going to hang for it, old man.'

When Moocher did not reply, Pitton spoke up.

'Swears blind he never caught anything on your land but vermin, sir, rats and squirrels and the like. But my men say they know different. They say they've seen signs that someone's been trapping out in the West Woods, near Starling's Roost. Definite signs.'

'Where did you find him, in the barn?'

'No, sir, he was picked up wandering in the fields, gleaning the last of our winter wheat. He swears he's never been near the house until now,' the steward said, 'or the barn.'

Ralph leant over, swinging Annetta's pocket in front of his face. 'See this, old man? Where did you get it?'

At that moment there was a groaning sound, as Moocher tried to speak, but the words came out so indistinctly that it was impossible to understand them. 'I din' mean to. . . I din' mean to do it. . .'

'Didn't mean to do what?'

But all Moocher could do was repeat the same phrase.

'He's lying.' Ralph looked down at him. 'Of course he's been here. I thought you said that things have gone missing: bread, cheese, a flitch of bacon?'

'Yes, sir, but we didn't find any of those things on him, sir. Only wild food. Brambles and cobs and suchlike.'

'What about the two maids who look after my father – what are their names?'

'Anne and Alice, sir.'

'You've questioned them, what do they say?'

'They say that it's a sprite that took them – one of the fairy folk. A spirit that walks only at night.'

'But it's not just that, sir,' the other man put in. 'They say they've seen all manner of things. The dogs behaving strangely. The child, too. Shoes that vanish into thin air and then reappear again somewhere quite different. Articles of clothing coming undone. But they say they've never seen this man before. And on that they will not be foresworn.'

'And you say he's come down from the Drover's Path? You are quite certain?'

'That's what he said when we picked him up. The fellow is quite crazed. Ranting. Says. . .' He hesitated, '. . . says he's. . . seen things. . . up there.'

'Seen things? What kind of things?'

'Couldn't rightly say, sir.' Pitton and the other man exchanged an anxious glance. 'Like I said, the fellow is quite moonstruck.'

Moocher, who had crawled to the corner of the room, was still mumbling. 'Din' mean. . . Din' mean to, I swear. . . it were jist an accident.'

'What didn't you mean to do?' Ralph was shouting at him now. 'Oh, what's the use.'

He went to stand by the window again, looking out over the fields and then the swell of the downs rising behind; the wooded crease in the hillside that was the Drover's Path. Shadows, black and violet, were lengthening in the chill afternoon. A harvest moon, huge and yellow, was rising on the horizon. Behind the black furze of Starling's Roost, the birds circled and cawed, preparing to settle for the night. Their sound, thin and eerie, carried on the still air.

An uneasy silence had fallen upon the room. It was clear to all of them that it was too late to travel on now. The business with the rat-catcher had delayed them.

Just then the dogs entered the room again, their nails clicking against the stone floor. They approached the arras, and began to pick over the chicken bones thrown there by Ralph. Sensing a presence, one of them went over and sniffed at the old tapestry, putting her nose into the gap between the arras and the wall. Was his own dog Robin among them? Carew hoped against hope that she was not. If Robin were among them, he was done for – but even as this thought crossed his mind, he saw the tip of her nose, then her grizzled old muzzle, appear in the gap between the arras and the wall behind him. And he knew, with a sinking heart, from the slight movement in her body that she was wagging her tail at him adoringly.

When Ralph looked round, his eyes fixed upon the dog immediately. 'Look.'

'What?'

'The dog.'

'What about the dog?'

'She has found something behind the old arras – something, or someone—'

'What do you mean?' Lord Nicholas said in a frightened whisper.

'Who's there? Come out, whoever you are—'

For a few moments no one moved.

Over the brow of the hill, at the neck of the Drover's Path, a flock of starlings was careening through the air, thousands upon thousands of birds on the wing, bending and twisting as one, until the sky was black with them. And in the distance, up the valley, there could now be seen faint pinpricks of light as the fires were lit for the feast of All Hallows, lights to call the dead home, guiding them through the cracks between two worlds.

'Why did we come here?' De Caus drew his cloak round him. 'This is a godforsaken place.'

Instinctively, the three men had moved closer together.

'Pull it down. Pull the arras down. Find out who it is.' Lord Nicholas's voice was shrill. 'For heaven's sake, Ralph, what are you waiting for?'

'I can see him. . .' Ralph's expression was dazed. 'I can see him – he's here – he's behind the arras. . .I can see him looking at me—'

'What do you mean?' Lord Nicholas looked at him in terror. 'Who is here?'

'*He* is here.'

'Who is *he*?'

'He, Carew – John Carew – they said he'd come back. . .' Ralph pointed a finger at the wall. 'He's there – I can see him – I can see the whites of his eyes. . . he's been there all along, hiding from us just behind the arras—'

De Caus and Lord Nicholas exchanged glances.

'*Je ne comprends pas—*'

'Nor I, he has gone quite mad. *You* do it, de Caus—'

'Do what?'

When the Frenchman hesitated, the young man began to scream at him, 'For pity's sake, de Caus, just do it – pull it down!'

'Very well.' The Frenchman walked to the arras and grasped the fraying material with both hands. It came away as easily as if it were made from nothing more substantial than leaf mould, and fell with a sigh to the ground.

The three men stared.

Into the shocked and silent room the only thing that could be heard was de Caus's voice. 'There you are – see – *rien – rien de tout* – nothing there at all but a pile of old dust,' he said, adding with an attempt at levity, 'a *phantasm*, monsieur, nothing more. A mere *phantasm* of your mind.'

Only Moocher, forgotten and unheard, was muttering, 'I din' mean to do it. . . I din' mean to kill him. . . t'were an accident, I swear.'

Priors Leaze Manor

The Feast Day of St Hubert, 3rd day of November, 1611

Most excellent brother,

What I am about to recount will astonish you, and indeed, no one is more amazed that I should find myself penning these words than I.

In short, the stranger who has been seen in these parts has been apprehended. An old man, a rat-catcher by trade, was picked up in the fields. Before he came here it seems he lay for some days at the top of the Drover's Path, a fact that, as you might imagine, has caused much wonder among the common folk here, who have gathered to look at him as if he were Lazarus himself, returned from the dead. If a comet had descended among our people, I swear it would scarce be less of a wonder to them, for all that he is old and stinks like a nest of mice.

These details I would not trouble you with were it not for the fact that when Pitton questioned him, he claimed to have travelled the road for some days with a man whom he believed was heading for the manor lands. He too lay out at the Drover's Path. What has become of this fellow he cannot say, only that some days ago he disappeared and he has not seen him more.

This man, his companion, he describes as being of middling height, with dark hair that falls around his face, and a somewhat scowling look about him; clothes much travel-stained, but which had once been good; a belt on which he kept many knives. Sweet Jesus, I hear you say, half the knaves in England look like this, but there is more. It seems the man was not a talker, and was reluctant to divulge much information about himself, despite the old man's best efforts. But this, such as it is, is what he was able to discover.

The man's master had been a merchant, with whom he had sailed the high seas for many years, but he told the old man he had parted company from his master some years before and was only now returned home. The old rat-catcher, who goes by the name of Moocher, formed the very strong idea that his companion had a connection to the manor, although now that he had arrived he seemed unaccountably afraid to approach it.

Said he had the impression that he had come here to find something, or someone, although he could not say what, and no amount of whipping or nights in the stocks has been able to get him to say any more. If he knows the man's name, he is most determined not to say it. I took the whip to him myself in the end, until Pitton stayed my hand, and said I would kill the old fool if I went on, and t'were better to wait for the hangman's noose.

Now the old fool licks his stripes and weeps most piteously, a-feared that his testimony will cause his sometime companion to hang beside him.

Which, most surely, when we find him, he will.

In short, brother, could it be that John Carew is returned after all? Our father is most entirely convinced of it. Although he has not seen him bodily, he believes he has heard John's voice speaking to him, and that he has given him many other signs besides. He rambles about the dogs, says that at certain times they become restless as though someone is in the room, but they do not bark, as they surely would with a stranger.

But for all this, no one else at the manor can say they have seen him. There are signs that someone has been hiding out in one of the barns, and all manner of curious portents besides: food stolen from the kitchen; a child's costume turned widdershins. The two women who keep house here have been so affrighted that only the direst threats have convinced them to stay.

I do confess to you to being somewhat womanish about the situation myself. Do you remember how, when John Carew was a boy, he used sometimes to hide behind the arras in the parlour? You will laugh when I tell you this, but for an instant as it grew dusk I had the strangest fancy that I saw him there again, his eye peering out at me through the broken threads, but it turned out t'was only the wild imagining of a moment, as when we pulled the thing down, there was nothing there but a pile of dust and mouse droppings. Tiens, *Monsieur Pindar, says Mr Waterworks, perhaps your poacher is nothing but a phantom after all. . .*

S'truth, brother, I know not what to think. De Caus, Lord Nicholas and his lady have taken their leave, and bring this letter with them to Bishopsgate. I have made up my mind to stay here until it can be determined one way or the other – a mystery indeed. That, and to see the lawyer Wilkes when he comes from Marlborough.

Your dutiful brother,

Ralph Pindar

TWENTY-SIX

Annetta

Bishopsgate.

GENTLY, PAUL TOOK THE letter from her.
'What does it mean?' Annetta said when she had recovered herself a little. 'Please, I don't understand.'

'I don't know what to say to you, madam—' Paul began, but she would not be put off.

'I believe you must tell me something, *Signore*. I beg your pardon, but I have come a long way to be told nothing.'

'But of course it is him, it must be him.' Her hands were clasped in her lap in front of her, her fingers laced so tight that her knuckles were white. 'Who else could it be?'

When he did not reply immediately to this, she urged him, 'And you, *Signor* Pindar, what do you think? What does your heart tell you?'

What did his heart tell him? Paul kicked at a log in the fire with the tip of his boot. In the flames it was as though he saw a picture of the two of them again: he and Carew, at Constanza's *palazzo* in Venice. It must have been one of the last times they had spoken. He – Paul – had not slept for two days and two nights and had drunk his own weight in wine, and in his madness he had held a knife to Carew's ear. He could feel himself flex his fingers, then the flick of his wrist, saw the blood run down the side of Carew's face. For a moment, looking at Carew had been like looking into a mirror at himself.

You may hate me, Paul, but you can't hurt me. You can't change who I am.

Paul. He had called him by his Christian name. Not Mr Pindar, or even Mr Paul, but just Paul, the familiarity of it a reproach more speaking than any other.

You are wrong, I don't hate you. Not all the time, anyway.

But was not true, he had never hated Carew as his brother Ralph did. He had loved him, always had done. As was only natural.

But no good would come of thinking about that now. Paul contemplated the sour-faced little woman sitting before him, her hair stuffed untidily beneath an old-fashioned hood that looked as though it had been plucked at random from a box of players' props. He made a mental note to get her fitted up with something more becoming, something more suited to her new life among them.

It was the day after she had stumbled upon him with Frances Sydenham in the gallery, but he saw with relief that by not so much as a flicker of an eyelash did she indicate that she had seen anything untoward.

So this was Carew's paramour. She looked, if not exactly old, then, what? He searched for the word. Desiccated. Shrunken. She had the starved look of someone to whom life has not been kind. The skin of her face was brown and sun-roughened, and she had hands like a peasant. He had a vague memory that the convent from which she hailed was famous for its physic garden; perhaps they made her work the soil for the good of her soul, shriving her for the stain of her long sojourn in Muslim lands.

And yet this was a woman who not so long ago had been a *kislar* in the House of Felicity; a confidant and companion of the Ottoman queen herself. Paul found it hard to imagine anyone less likely than this small person. He had expected someone more. . . silken. Someone more like – Frances. With an effort he pushed the thought of Frances away. In the cold – and sober – light of day, he could think of the previous evening's encounter with nothing but disquiet.

Carew's paramour. A nun from the Convent of Santa Clara. Paul almost smiled. *God in heaven,* it was all so wildly improbable, there was a chance some of it might even be true.

But now, here she was, and come all the way from Venice, and there was no choice other than that he – they – should make the best of it.

'Come, madam, let us sit for a while. This is not the conversation of a moment. There are so many things for us to talk of and I want us to be quite comfortable together. I have asked the kitchen to prepare some refreshments for you.'

He went over to the sideboard. There was spiced wine set there in a silver-topped flask, warm and flavoured with cloves and cinnamon, and beside it the special sweetmeat he had asked the kitchen to prepare for her.

'I thought you might like some *khave*? And some honeyed pastries. *Baklava*? Do you remember them, from your time at Constantinople? Please, do not get up, I will pour for you.'

'*Khave*?' He saw her eyes light up as he poured the black liquid. 'Ah, it has been many years now since I drank that.'

He handed her a small handleless cup, of a porcelain so fine it was almost transparent. The fragrance of the coffee, dark and pungent, filled the room. He saw that her hand shook slightly as she put the cup to her lips, and looked away quickly, so that she would not see that he had seen.

'*Madonna!*'

'*Le piache?*'

'*Benissimo.*' She gave a sigh of pleasure.

And when they slipped into the Venetian tongue, it was as if some subtle thing had shifted between them. When she spoke in her own language she became something other, less well spoken, but more confiding, more herself.

'You and I, *Signore*, I have this curious feeling that we have met before.' She was looking at him intently.

'I would that were true.' Paul smiled, and offered her more coffee. 'I always thought the Ottomans excel at so many things,' he ventured, 'although we are not supposed to say it. *Khave* is one of them.'

'I often think I should have stayed there. I did not belong in the convent; I was put there by my mother when I was very young. Apart from the House of Felicity it was the only home I knew. I should have stayed in Constantinople and never gone back.'

'And why did you not?'

'When the Valide died, they offered me marriage. It was either that or be retired to the Old Palace with a lot of weeping women. The marriage was to some great man.' She shrugged as though it were of no importance to her, 'I cannot recollect whom. One of the Sultan's viziers, I believe.'

'A vizier – I am impressed.'

Annetta took another sip of the *khave*. 'I was worth something in those days.'

'I have no doubt of that.'

'We all were. All the women who had been trained in the House of Felicity were considered to be of high rank. It did not matter what our estate had been before, high or low. We had connections – ties of loyalty – to the palace, and that was what mattered. And mine were the most excellent of all. I had been the Valide's personal slave, one of her chosen handmaids. We were only four.'

She glanced up at him, and he could see that this was a source of immense pride to her, that her sense of herself was rooted in it, and that all this had now been taken away from her.

'I know you were held in the highest esteem. Celia told me.'

'Does she talk to you much. . .' Annetta hesitated, as if not quite sure how to phrase it, '. . .about those days?'

He turned away, not wanting to meet her gaze. The truth was he had talked more on these matters to Annetta, this stranger whom he had only just met, than he had in seven years with his own wife.

'Celia wished only to forget.' And then, conscious of the untruth behind his words, he added quickly, 'When I was living in Constantinople the intelligence among the merchants was that the Valide herself had been a peasant girl from the mountains. Is that true?'

'Yes. She talked about it sometimes, towards the end of her life. Her father had been a shepherd. She sold herself into slavery to save herself from that life. There was a slave dealer of great repute, Esther Narsi, in Dalmatia. All the best girls came from her; I knew some of them myself. There was no shame in it, quite the contrary.'

'The Ottoman queen was always. . . a most surprising person. I met her once – if you could call it that. But it was all a long time ago.'

In his mind's eye Paul saw again the garden shimmering on the Bosphorus, and the little pavilion where the Valide had waited for him behind the lattice: a mythic creature, more beautiful and dangerous than a basilisk. He remembered the way he had stood there, dashing out his eyes, her presence all the more powerful because he could not see her; only hear the sigh of damask and silk pulling against stone, the music of her bracelets as they rose and fell against her arms, and her miraculous voice; smell the scent of musk and ambergris; the heat of the sun on his bare head: all of it seeming to him now like something from a dream.

With an effort, he dragged his attention back to the autumn afternoon in Bishopsgate, and the sound of the rain rapping its tattoo against the window.

'We spoke together. She had a way, I can't describe it, of telling me, without so much as uttering a word, that she had Celia. That Celia was hers now, her possession, and that I should not try. . .' His voice trailed away. 'That I should never try to reach her.'

Annetta was looking at him, her eyes as quick and black and wary as a bird's, and he was amazed at the ease with which he found he could talk to her.

'I heard.'

'You heard?'

'That the Valide had taken a liking to a young man in one of the foreign embassies.'

'*Dio buono*, you heard that?'

'You have nothing to reproach yourself for, it was probably what saved her life.'

But he merely repeated, 'You heard that?'

'Why so surprised, *Signor* Pindar? Gossip was like meat and drink to us in the House of Felicity. And I made it my business; I had something of a knack for it.' When she smiled it was as though he were seeing an altogether different woman. 'After all, what else was there to do?'

'So you chose the dowry, but not the husband.'

'Do you think that was so wrong?'

'To the contrary; I can see that you would have been quite wasted on a vizier.'

Annetta took another sip of her *khave*. 'I did not think that marriage would suit me. I did not think that I liked men. The thought of – congress – with a man was... quite beyond me. Not to my taste at all. Or so I thought.'

'With some ill-humoured old vizier with three other wives, I quite take your point.'

'Why do you look at me like that?'

'Like what?'

'Like a man who is about to dance a tarantella.'

Paul laughed. 'It is a long time since I danced the tarantella. I admire your frankness, that's all. No, I delight in it. It is a rare thing.' He looked at her – small, brown, prickly as a hedgehog – and realised he was enjoying their conversation hugely. 'And I have never met a woman who spoke to a man so like a... another man.'

'Is there some other way?'

'Most of us dissemble at least some of the time, or think we must. Most people fear to say what they really mean.'

'So much the worse for them.'

'I am inclined to agree with you, but I fear it's the way of the world.'

'But I have been so little in the world – in the world of men, that is – I have yet to learn its tricks.'

'Yes.' There did not seem to be much point in disagreeing with her. 'Yes, I can see that.'

Annetta put her empty cup down, shifted a little in her seat.

'And since I have not learnt its tricks, I must ask you again, *Signore*, about John Carew. Is there any point...' Looking up at him, she gave a small shrug, '... to my continuing to hope? Celia said you had your – how are they called? – intelligencers working for you?'

'That's true. Over the years I have heard that he had died of plague in Chios. But I also heard that he had volunteered as a mercenary; that he had sailed to the New World on the *Discovery*, and to the Indies on the *Hector*. I even heard that he had returned to Constantinople and was working as a cook in the Sultan's palace. If you knew John Carew as I do – and who am I to say that you do not? – you'd know that some of these may be true, or all of them, or none. Who can say? Carew always did defy intelligence.'

'*Ha!*' A small sound came from her that may have been a laugh.

'But now I have a question for you. The last time you saw him, might I know what was said between you before left? Did he tell you where he would go?'

She looked down at her hands.

'He told me he had a passage on a merchantman, but I don't remember where it was bound. Perhaps he didn't tell me, or perhaps he did, and I don't remember. I think I had the sickness on me already. I told him to go, and he did.' She looked up, her eyes glittering, 'and that must be an end of it. All that journeying – all that time on a boat – and I've always hated boats.' She gave him a small smile, 'all of it, for nothing.'

'No, not for nothing. If he is the stranger that they have seen at Priors Leaze, as might very likely be the case, we will find him. It is entirely natural that he would hide from my brother Ralph, so put your mind at rest about that. Carew was always one to play tricks, and trust me that nothing would delight him more than to play tricks on Ralph. We are bidden to their Majesties' masque at Hampton Court. It is an honour that we cannot refuse, not even for Carew. After that I intend to travel down to the old place myself, the arrangements are already in place—'

'—and I will come with you.'

'Very well. But the letter is not the only reason I asked you to come and see me. I have a proposal to make to you, *Signora*, if you will accept it—' he began, but Annetta anticipated him.

'If you think I have come here to beg for favours, then you think wrong.'

'It is you who would be doing us the favour.'

'I will not take the diamond back, if that's what you mean to ask me.'

Paul was taken aback. 'The stone belongs to you; it always has done, for all that you used it to rescue Celia. We cannot keep it. Celia and I are absolutely agreed upon that.'

'Nonetheless, I won't take it. It was freely given and I cannot take it back. My mind is quite made up.'

To this Paul said nothing. Instead he took the pouch and carefully shook it, so that the diamond fell into the palm of his hand. The two of them looked it for a moment as it lay there, pulsing with its strange pale blue fire.

'I won't ask you how you came by it—' he said.

'I can tell you that for nothing. I took it from her, from the Valide.'

'You mean you stole it?'

'I said "took", not "stole",' she said gruffly. 'The Valide was dead at the time.'

Paul was silenced.

'She died with it in her hand, but I knew she wanted me to have it.' A ghost of a smile was on Annetta's lips. 'At least that's what I chose to tell myself.'

She was leaning back now so that her head rested against the chair, and had closed her eyes, as though the conversation had fatigued her.

'It was to make amends, for what she did to Celia.' She was muttering to herself now, like an old woman who has been on her own a great deal. 'For taking her away from me, shutting her up in the Old Palace all those years, and leaving me alone. That's why I took it. I thought that if I used it for someone else – used it only for good – then it would not have the power to harm me.'

'So you know the stories?'

'What do I want with stories?' She turned away, as though suddenly bored by their conversation. 'It's a magical stone, everyone knows that.'

'It has an inscription on one side. Here, won't you let me show you?'

He held it out to her, but she shrank away from it.

'I saw the stone once, *Signore*, I don't need to see it again.'

'But you know about the inscription?'

'Inscription? I know nothing about an inscription. When I took the diamond I put it in my pocket and I never looked at it again. You seem as though you don't believe me, but on my life I swear to you it's true.' Annetta was beginning to sound angry. 'A stone such as this one, it is not a toy or a trinket. I was too afraid, not because I had stolen it, but because these things can bring *mala sfortuna*, unless they're handled carefully.'

'So you gave it to Celia.'

'I sent it to her, hidden in a parcel of sweets.'

'The Sultan's Blue in a basket of sweetmeats? I have heard everything now.'

'There was a Jewess connected to the palace, Esperanza Malchi. The Valide used her all the time to send messages and gifts between the palaces, and I knew that no one would ever question her.'

'And you hoped the stone might help her?'

'You are forgetting something. When Celia tried to meet you at the Aviary Gate, it was considered a very great misdemeanour. I have known some of the *kislar* be drowned for far less. The only reason she was kept alive was because of a whim of the Valide's, but once she was gone, so was Celia's protection. Once the Valide died I knew what they would do to Celia. The diamond was the only thing I could think of that might keep her alive: she would have been able to use it to bribe one of the eunuchs, to help her escape before they tried to kill her.' Annetta glanced again uneasily at the stone that Paul was still holding out to her. 'I never dared look at it all that closely. I didn't know of any inscription—'

'Then let me show you.'

He held the stone out to her, positioning it so that the long side was turned towards her. He traced his finger along the writing.

'It is hard to see unless you know that it is there: it says *A'az ma yutlab.*'

She was looking at him as though he were holding something that might suddenly turn round and bite her.

'Do you know what it means?' he asked.

'I speak the Arabic tongue.' Impatiently she turned her face away. 'I know what it means.'

'It means "my heart's desire".'

'*My heart's desire.*' She glanced up at him quickly, and then away again. '*Il desiderio del mio cuore.*' He saw her mouth the words, under her breath.

Then she turned to him and put her hand out, and for a moment he thought that she was going to take it. The tips of her fingers trembled. And then, 'Why are you doing this?' she said, snatching her hand away again. 'Why do you tempt me? Only God can know what is in my heart.'

The simplicity of this remark disarmed him.

'Take it! It's yours – it was always yours. It has served its purpose for us.'

'Served its purpose?'

'It has given us our heart's desire.'

She was staring at him now, in that way of hers, with her unblinking black eyes.

'Has it?'

'It brought Celia back to me.'

'Did it?'

The baldness of her statement took him aback.

'*Signora*...' For the first time Paul was lost for words. 'Look around you. I have everything.'

'You have *nothing*!'

For a moment he did not think that he had understood her properly.

'*Cosa?*'

'I look around me and I see nothing. Celia is still dead. Or, should I say, you are dead to one another. I have never seen two people more heartily unhappy with one another.'

Silence roared in Paul's ears.

'My advice is to take it, *Signora* Annetta,' Paul said, beginning to lose patience now. 'Take it while you still can.' He held the diamond out on the palm of his hand. The woman was stubborn, almost as stubborn as Carew. Sweet Jesus, they deserved one another. 'The stone is worth a fortune.' And then with one last effort to lighten the mood, 'Are you not afraid I might change my mind?'

'You may be that changeable, sir,' she said coldly, 'but you will find that I am not.'

'Madam, I don't know if you quite realise what you doing. Do you know what they are calling the stone? They are calling it "Pindar's Great Diamond". The whole of London clamours to see it. Every gem dealer, every collector, wants to buy it. They tell me even the King is to make me an offer for it, that he wants it before his son, Prince Henry, can get his hands on it. And I have refused them all under the mistaken notion that it must be given back to you.'

You who are no one. You who are nothing in this world.

He did not actually say the words, but to Annetta his meaning was only too plain.

'And what is so very great about that?' she countered. 'No one knows what the magical properties of the stone might be, except that it has them. The diamond is just as likely to bring *mala sfortuna* to the person who has it in their possession as its opposite: prosperity or riches or love. Or perhaps it just mixes them all up together – and you wonder why I am not so very eager to take it back?' It was Annetta who was angry now. 'How very convenient – to think that you can use me to take it off your hands. Why should I? Don't you think I have had ill fortune enough in my life? I don't want it, I tell you—'

Just then – with the fizzing, sparkling, ear-splitting sound of a Chinese firecracker – the room was filled with a tremendous bang. Both Annetta and Paul cried out at the same time as a heavy object crashed down the chimneybreast behind them and fell into the fire. Then there was a burst of flying embers as the logs tumbled from the grate, and the room was filled with a terrible high-pitched shriek, a cry of pain the like of which neither of them had ever heard before.

'*Jesus*!' She heard Paul cry out as he jumped back from the fire. '*Jesus*!' She heard him shout out again. Annetta screamed and put her hands up to protect her face as something came dashing towards her out of the flames. 'The beast, the damned beast!' She heard him shout, as a strange creature – half-human, half-animal – flashed past her, and was swallowed up in the shadows at the other end of the room. In the silence that followed, her eyes met Paul's, and each saw the expression of horrified incomprehension on the other's face.

A wisp of smoke hung in the air between them, and a strong smell of singed fur.

And then, before Annetta could say anything or calm the terrified drumming of her heart, she realised that the creature, whatever it was, was flying towards them again from the other side of the room.

'Watch out!' Her voice was hoarse. 'Here it comes again!'

'Jesus!' She heard Paul shout out again, only in the next moment to realise that it was not 'Jesus' that he was saying but 'Quirkus'.

'*Christos*! It must have got stuck up the chimney! Or tried to come down it. Quirkus, you damned. . . Arrgh!'

Even as he said its name the monkey was upon him. Letting the Sultan's Blue drop from his hand, Paul put his arms up to protect his face as with one bound the creature leapt on to him, first on to his shoulder and then on to his head, before bounding off again. In a frenzy of fear and pain the animal was now running amok through the room, leaping up the tapestries and window drapes, knocking down pictures, dragging the Turkey carpet from the table, and upsetting the plates and the wine bottle. Papers flew; the pewter platters on the dresser came crashing to the floor. A blue and white Chinese porcelain vase toppled on to its side, the lid came off and rolled slowly on to the floor where it spiralled noisily on its side before rolling off beneath the chest.

Eventually the monkey came to rest on top of the chimneybreast. It looked down on them, turning its little black face from side to side, its ribcage rising and falling, making small clicking sounds of distress and fear.

Gradually the room came to a standstill again. Annetta's hair had come loose from her cap, and was falling in dishevelled locks over her face. Paul had a scratch down one of his cheeks. The room was in such disorder – broken glass and plates were everywhere – it looked as though a small tempest had blown through the room.

And then—

'What in heaven's name?' said a voice from behind them. Mild. Amused. 'What calamity have we here? And after all my hard work to get this room straight.' Frances Sydenham was standing in the doorway looking from one to the other of them as though they were two sorry children; as though for all the world she might burst out laughing at any moment. She glanced up and saw the monkey clinging to the chimneybreast.

'Ah, I see you have found Quirkus for me, the naughty creature,' she said without missing a beat. 'I've been looking for him everywhere.'

When she held out her hand the monkey came down from its ledge, and went to her immediately. It clung to her, nestling its face in her shoulder. She made small, inarticulate sounds to it, as though she were talking to a child, and the animal seemed comforted by this. 'Bad monkey, naughty Quirkus, look how you've scratched him.'

The monkey was now clinging to her hip; she swayed a little from side to side as though comforting an infant. 'Look how you've hurt his cheek, you naughty little child.'

'It's nothing, just a scratch.' Paul dabbed at his cheek with the corner of one of his sleeves. 'He must have been hiding up the chimney and the fire smoked him out, poor creature.'

Annetta half-expected that Paul would be angry, would blame her for the destruction caused by the marauding monkey, but Paul was like a man in a daze.

'But the diamond, where is it...?' Only now did he become aware that in the commotion he had dropped the stone. 'It must be on the floor somewhere...'

But Annetta's quick eyes had already seen it. '*Santissima Madonna*! The creature has it! He must have snatched it from you.'

And sure enough Quirkus was holding something between his paws. But even as she spoke the creature looked up and sensing that Annetta was moving towards him, he grew alarmed again and flew out of Frances Sydenham's arms, dropping the diamond as he did so. It fell, bounced, skittered beneath the dresser. When both women darted forwards to pick it up, there was almost a scuffle. When they stood up again it was Frances who held the stone.

For a moment there was silence.

'The Sultan's Blue.' Her hand trembled slightly as she held it out, glittering in the firelight. 'My poor Quirkus—' There was the slightest possible catch in her voice. 'He does so like shiny things.'

Her gaze turned towards Paul, and then back to the stone again, as though she could not take her eyes off it. Her mouth was parted slightly; on the bottom lip was a tiny droplet of moisture, which caught the light like a seed pearl. And then suddenly she seemed to make her mind up about something.

'Here, take it; take what's yours.' She held the diamond out to Paul. 'Take it quickly.'

But it was Annetta who stepped forward. She was quite calm.

'You are mistaken, madam,' she said before she could stop herself. 'If you would be so good—' She put out her hand, '—I believe the diamond belongs to me.'

TWENTY-SEVEN

Paul

Bishopsgate.

AT FIRST, IMMEDIATELY AFTER Annetta took possession of the diamond, it was as though a deep peace had fallen on the great house at Bishopsgate. Whether or not it was because the stone had now been returned to its rightful owner, it was impossible to say, but that something had shifted there could be no doubt. It was as though the very house itself could breathe again. They all felt it: Paul, Celia and even Annetta.

It was now December. Soon it would be Christmas, and still Paul was kept in London. The high council meeting had been delayed by the death of one of the Levant Company elders, and now there was the Queen's Masque to attend. Paul chaffed, but there was nothing he could do about it.

Winter had come suddenly. Almost overnight the weather had turned as bitter as he had ever known. Eddies of snow whipped and clattered violently against the windowpanes, piling up in drifts along the ledges. Inside the house, however, the Christmas festivities were in full swing. In the kitchens wine was spiced and fruits candied; there were sugared plums and figures made from almond paste; and for days the house was perfumed with the smell of cinnamon and burnt sugar.

Two more letters arrived from Priors Leaze. When Paul came home with them, it was to find the house invaded by scores of tiny sprites. They ran screaming up and down his stairs, pelting one another with oranges. He saw a beautiful woman on the stairs, and for a moment he did not know her. It was Celia, pretending to be a bear. She was running and chasing two of the smallest sprites up the stairs. He watched as they ran from her, howling with delight, into an arbour fashioned from winter greenery. There was an unaccustomed colour in her cheeks from the exertion, and her hair was escaping from beneath her cap in small damp tendrils.

When she saw Paul she came down the stairs to greet him.

'What have we here?' He looked up at her. 'The Forest of Arden?'

'Can't you see? I am a bear. There are no bears in the Forest of Arden, everybody knows that.' She pushed her hair back from her face. One of the smallest of the sprites had tripped up over its unaccustomed wings, and began to cry. She picked it up and lifted it on to her hip, straightened its crown of twisted ivy, wiped its nose on her handkerchief, and stopped its cries with a piece of sugared fruit peel that she pulled out of her pocket.

She looked down at the child. 'Shall we show him how to be a bear?'

The sprite stopped its howling, nodded up at her trustingly. He watched them together, strangely touched.

He had never seen Celia in the company of children before, and as he watched became aware of something, the merest whisper of a sensation, as if something tight was unfurling somewhere in the cavity of his chest.

Candlelight caught at the side of her face. 'Why the smile, husband?'

'Can a husband not smile at his wife?' Paul took her wrist, held it between his fingers, feeling the softness of her inner wrist beneath his fingers. 'Besides, I have never seen you as a bear before.'

Something of the playful, holiday mood caught at them both. 'I believe I make a remarkably fine bear.'

'You? You are not nearly fierce enough.'

'I believe I may surprise you.'

'Perhaps you may.'

'You had better take care, or I may gobble you up.' She had reached the last step on the staircase and now she paused, and stood looking down at him. 'Shall we show him, Dorrey?'

She glanced down at the child on her hip. The child stared at Paul mutely with large eyes, buried its head in Celia's arm. She put him down; pushed him gently on his way.

'To be gobbled up by you?' Paul caught at one of the tendrils of her hair, tucked it back gently under her cap. 'I can think of worse fates.'

She said nothing to this, but he could see that she was pleased. As he made to carry on up the stairs past her, she put her hand out, catching at his sleeve.

'Won't you join us?' Her hand resting on his arm, 'Stay, you are always so busy – stay and be merry with us for a while. Remember what we used to say to one another, before we left Aleppo?'

'Yes, of course, I remember.'

In England. In England it would be different.

And something, the fall of light against the bronze stuff of her dress, the cedar smell of evergreen and cut wood, dislodged a fragment in his mind, and for a moment he conjured a memory of the two of them in some long-ago Christmas hall – had it been with Parvish, perhaps, or with Celia's father, Thomas Lamprey? – standing just like this, on the stairs. He caught at it, but it flew away from him, and was gone before he could grasp it. All he was left with was a sudden impulse to circle her small waist with his hands, as he used to do when they were young and green and thought themselves in love.

But he did not. The hard thing inside him, the carapace that he had grown to protect himself, rose up to crush the tiny stirring bud.

He took a step back. 'Perhaps later.'

'Go then.' Celia dropped her gaze, 'as you wish.'

In the soft light he could see that faint lines had appeared at the corners of her eyes. It occurred to him that although Celia was not old, she was now no longer young either. Where had the years gone? For the first time he saw how much it cost her to stand back, to let him go, and that she was doing this for him. And he felt the stirring again, deep in the cavity of his chest.

'Was it your idea,' he said, 'to bring the children in, I mean?' And then, as four small boy sprites careened past them up the stairs, 'Great heaven, where did you get them all from?'

'Some are our servants' children; but mostly they are children from the parish,' she said. 'It is the feast day of St Nicholas after all.'

'You are the mistress here, you may do as you wish.' He looked around him. 'Besides, they are. . .' He searched for the right words, '. . .a most cheerful addition to this household.'

'If what you mean by cheerful is noisy, then I'm afraid it's true.'

Paul reached out, circled her small waist with both hands. 'Then perhaps I will stay a while, it will do us both good to be cheerful.'

But even as he said it, he became aware of Frances Sydenham standing in the shadows of the little anteroom on the other side of the hall. Celia did not look round, but he had the notion that she too was aware of being watched. It was a moment of strangeness: the three of them standing there, like three still points on a compass, while all around them the Christmas revelry continued.

Paul had not seen Frances to speak to privately since the night in the long gallery when Annetta has disturbed them. A woman's ailment, he was given to understand, had laid her low, and he had been glad not to see her. He could not think about what had nearly passed between them without shame. He had not encouraged her, but nor had he discouraged her. He could not lie to himself: he had been complicit in it all along. But when he thought about that night more carefully, what stayed with him was not so much what would have happened had they not been interrupted, but the expert – yes, expert was not too strong a word – way she had cajoled and flattered and flirted with him. And all this under the roof of a woman whose friend she professed to be. Moreover, she had persuaded him to give her information that he was sworn to keep private. In fact, the whole episode, in the sober light of day, reminded him of nothing so much as a night with one of several women of his acquaintance, women of the town, not one of which would he willingly allow under the same roof as his wife.

Perhaps Celia's suspicions were right? Whoever she was, Frances was clearly not the respectable widow she professed to be.

Knowing that at the slightest sign from him Frances would approach them, he turned his back slightly, so that she was blocked from his view.

The musicians – two men with viols – were tuning their instruments.

'I've never seen so many lords of misrule; usually there is but one, but I will forgive you the extravagance, just this once.'

'It is at times like this that you must feel his absence the most, isn't that so?' Celia said. 'John was always a most excellent Lord of Misrule.'

'But that was my thought exactly – how did you know?'

'Can a wife not guess at her husband's thoughts?'

And it was true. Celia had always been able to tell what he was thinking. Until he found he could not bear it; until he shut her out.

'Can someone else mind the lords of misrule for a little while? There is something I would like to speak to you about. I have had two more letters from my brother at Priors Leaze, and they are most strange – I would like Annetta to see them too, can you find her?'

And then Frances Sydenham was standing beside them. She had approached them so quietly they had not seen her coming, or perhaps they had been too absorbed. She looked harried, as though the noise from all the children were making her ill. Even in the warm light of the Christmas candles, her face was very pale.

When she saw the letters Paul was carrying, her eyes darted from one to the other of them.

'Not bad news, I hope?' And when neither of them replied to this, she added, with an attempt at levity, 'Why such dark looks? You look like a pair of conspirators.'

Paul took a step backwards. And for the first time the thought occurred to him, *What is all this to do with you, my lady? You presume too much.*

He and Celia exchanged glances.

Celia's said, *I will fetch her to you*, and she turned and made her way up the staircase. Paul watched her go. Halfway up, she turned back towards him and smiled, raising her hand, which had been trailing along the banister, in the smallest and most delicate gesture of farewell. And he thought: now I remember, that's what she always used to do. And he found himself smiling; gazing back up at her small, receding figure, a still point in the still turning room.

Frances Sydenham was not smiling.

Or rather she was smiling at him, but it was a smile that did not reach her eyes. A smile nonetheless, that demanded that he be complicit with her.

Dear God! What a noise these children make, what a smell, her expression seemed to say, *and I know that we two, you and I, think the same on this.* There was an assumption there, he realised, that she now held a primacy in this household, and with him; that she could turn his attention away from Celia, and towards herself, with one small pluck at his sleeve. How could he not have seen her working on him?

'You don't care for children then, I take it?' Paul said.

'No more than you do.' She screwed up her nose, waved the handkerchief she was holding in front of her face, with an expression of distaste.

'But they liven the place up though, wouldn't you say?'

'If I had known every last unwashed urchin in the parish had been invited here, then trust me, I would have prevented it,' she murmured, looking around the room.

Paul allowed himself a few seconds before he replied to this. 'But it was my wife who invited them, I believe.'

The reproach was clear. Normally Frances Sydenham was a woman alive to the slightest nuance – it was one of the things that he had always found to admire in her – but not today. Instead, she made an impatient gesture, a small shrug, as if to say, *Great heaven, well, of course it was, you can't possibly think any of this was* my *idea.* She looked at the children as though very the sight and sound of them was making her ill.

'You must thank heaven every day that Celia's monstrous child was taken from her.'

Now, as some small sprites came racing down the stairs towards them, she took a step closer to him to keep out of their way. Frances swayed, put her hand on his shoulder to steady herself, and then allowed it to linger there just a little longer than was strictly necessary. He noticed a strange odour coming from her person, either from her breath, or something spilled on her gown perhaps. And now, as he felt her fingers stroking, apparently abstractedly, at the velvet stuff of his sleeve, he felt a wave of revulsion for her. He had a feeling that he was meant to take her hand, or put his own over hers, and that by her proximity she was offering herself to him, again, as absolutely plainly as if she had spoken it out loud.

He took her hand away from his shoulder.

'Madam, I fear you are still not well. . .' he began, but at that moment he saw her glance up to where Celia was standing at the top of the stairs. And he knew at once that he had intercepted a look that was not meant for his eyes. And that Frances's gaze, when it rested on his wife, was very far from benign.

Priors Leaze

The Eve of St Nicholas, 5th day of December, 1611

Esteemed brother,

Our father is the same, convinced, beyond anything that we can say or do, that John Carew is here. He says he will not die until he sees the boy one last time.

He still calls him 'boy' – it is a marvel, is it not? At least, this is what I find myself thinking: that it is a marvellous thing, the love our father bears for him, after so long. Like a bewitchment. John Carew, the kitchen boy.

I tried to speak to the old poacher again, the one who calls himself Moocher. He is locked in one of the barns, until we can get him to the Assizes to be tried. He raves: talks about a herd of milk-white horses, and I can get no more sense out of him.

The nights are long here, and I have no company but a pack of dogs and an old man in his dotage. I believe that our father is half-crazed. When I sit with him sometimes in the hall, I see him move his lips as though he is speaking to someone.

I can hear you laughing at me. You should not laugh, but rather pity me. There is nothing to do in this infernal place but think. Last evening, I heard a noise like a tapping upon the windowpane and I was beset by a wild thought that it was John himself. John become weary of his own tricks and knocking to be let in. I ran to the casement, and for a moment I could almost imagine that I saw his face behind the glass, but when I got there it was only the branches of the old medlar, scratching across the window in the wind. And that was almost a. . . I was going to write 'a disappointment', but, i'faith, I hardly know what it was. I set myself to thinking about my young friend Lord Nicholas, and how his costume for the Queen's winter masque must become him – he is to be a fay in the court of Oberon – and I find myself instead lost in a reverie about how it might be to meet my old playfellow again after all this time.

I'faith, I hear you say, what kind of enchantment is this? A few weeks at the old place and my brother Ralph is grown womanish – he sees John Carew everywhere, now behind the old arras, and now at the window casement, and you would be right. My sojourn here has a purpose, and it is not to think upon the old times. And so: to business.

The lawyer Wilkes (who brought with him your letters) is come from Marlborough to draw up the papers. There is but one impediment, which is that our father will not now put his sign to them. Instead, when I was out, my man Chambers told me that he had sat long hours with the lawyer in his privy chamber. I know not of what they talked. I tried to persuade Wilkes that our father's mind is gone, and that it would do just as well if I made his sign for him, but the man is as prim as a vestal virgin on the subject, and gives me such black looks and scuttles away as though he thinks I might devour him, and I do not think even I can press him on the point.

Your dutiful brother,

Ralph Pindar

Postscript
So Carew's *inamorata* is come to these shores. Is there anyone who is not looking for him?

Priors Leaze

The Feast Day of St Nicholas, 6th day of December, 1611

My dear brother,

It will surprise you that I write again so soon. Last evening, after I thought I saw John Carew at the window, I made up my mind to ride out to the burnt-out house at Starling's Roost again. There are most certain signs that someone has been here: the embers of a fire, no longer warm, but fresh enough; the skins of a dead coney. A deer antler placed across the ruined doorway.

I had forgotten how strange and wild this place is. I had the strangest fancy that there was someone watching me, some-one watching me from the woods, as though the very trees had eyes. I walked a little way along the pathway, to where the old holloway begins: the Drover's Path, as the old folks call it. I even walked a little way up it, until I remembered the tales they used to tell, of how anyone who climbs it will meet their dead self coming the other way, and all manner of other strange tales, of ghosts and spirits and I know not what, which is why no one in our times has ever ventured there.

Winter is come, and the trees have lost their leaves. A lone-lier place it would be hard to find. The air is hard and cold as stone. They say we will soon have snow – and I found myself thinking, if Carew wanted to hide, there would be no better place. You are perfectly right in your surmise: our people will not come here, even when they swear they will. Even now, the place smells of witchery.

I dream about her every night, brother: the witch of Starling's Roost. In my dream I see the flames and hear her screams again——

I want to leave, but he won't let me.

You write that you will come here as soon as you may after the Queen's Masque at Richmond, that you cannot refuse a royal command; but I write to beg you not to delay. The snows may come any day now, and then the roads will become impassable. Come soon: nay, come now. (This last word scored under several times.) *It is most urgent that you do not delay.*

Your brother,

Ralph

Postscript
(added later in a different ink)
I do believe I shall go mad myself in this place if I do not soon see another Christian face.

TWENTY-EIGHT

Paul

Bishopsgate.

RALPH'S FIRST LETTERS HAD been, like the man himself, full of vanity and bombast. But these... these were almost deranged.

Was there something Paul had missed? Perhaps there was a clue in the letters. He took all seven of Ralph's letters out of the chest in which he kept them, and laid them out in order on the table. Then he looked them through again carefully.

When Celia arrived with Annetta in Paul's chamber, he read out the two latest missives from Priors Leaze to them at once.

'It is not your father but your brother who is half-crazed.' Celia looked at him in dismay.

'They are the ravings of a madman.'

Celia took the letter from him, reading one of the lines out loud,

'"*I dream about her every night, brother... I see the flames and hear her screams again*"... What does he mean?'

'He is talking about Carew's mother. She was burnt to death in a fire at a place called Starling's Roost,' Paul explained. 'It was widely believed she was a witch.'

'And was she?'

341

'No, just a simple-minded girl,' Paul said. He took the letter back. 'Nothing of what he says makes sense. But that's not all. He writes something else here that is most curious. "*Carew's* inamorata *is come to these shores. Is there anyone who is not looking for him?*"'

'Why is that so curious?' Celia frowned.

'Because I am quite certain that I have never written anything to him on that subject.'

'But how else would he know?'

'How indeed. . .'

'You must have written him—'

'—but I am quite certain that I did not.' Paul was adamant.

'Quite certain?'

'Beyond a doubt.'

'But you write so many letters, you must have forgot—'

'No, I have not forgot.'

'Then his intelligence comes from elsewhere.'

'From where?'

'Who else can write?'

'Your Sydenham woman can write.' Annetta, who had remained silent until now, spoke for the first time.

'But she hardly ever goes out; and she never receives or sends letters, that much we all know,' Celia said.

'She might not, but what about the maid?' Annetta asked. 'What's her name – Nan?'

'Nan?'

'Yes, I often see her together with the Sydenham woman. They whisper together in the corridors. The girl is supposed to sleep with me, on the truckle bed in my room, but she never has, not once since I've been here. She goes to the *milady*'s room instead and sleeps there.'

'How do you know?'

'I've seen the lights under the door, and heard them talking together. And I've seen the girl go out; almost every day she leaves the house on some commission or another, sent by the *milady*.'

'Do you remember that time you caught her listening outside my door?' Celia asked Paul. 'She said she'd dropped something, but you knew she hadn't—'

'—and you told me then that you thought she read your letters—'

'I know she did – she read all my letters, until I took care to hide them.'

'Then we must send for her—' Paul said.

'No, not just yet,' Celia said. 'There's nothing to say they are not perfectly innocent errands. Wouldn't it be better to find out where she goes, and what she does?'

'But how are we to do that?'

'I can do it,' Annetta said.

Paul and Celia turned to look at her.

'You?'

'*Ma certo*. I can follow her the next time she goes out. It won't be difficult.'

'No,' Paul said. 'You are a stranger here; how will you find your way?'

'I won't need to know my way, I'll be following her.'

'Supposing she recognises you?'

'Then I will wear a mask. If I don't manage it, nothing is lost by it. At least let me try?'

When Annetta got up to go, Paul motioned to Celia that she should stay behind.

He closed the door behind her, and for a moment they were silent together.

'Celia. . .' he began, but then stopped, as though uncertain how to proceed.

'Yes?'

'Celia. . .' he began again, and then, still not knowing how to go on, he put his arms out and drew her towards him.

'I don't know how. . .' he said, his chin resting now upon the crown of her head.

'Then don't,' she said. 'Don't say anything, not just now.'

'But I must—'

'No.' She reached up and put her finger against his lips. 'Not now. We will have time for all this later.'

He pulled her still closer until her she was obliged to lean against him, her cheek pressed against his chest.

He gave a sigh. 'Can you ever—'

'One day,' she said, 'when all this is over.' But all the same he felt a sigh go through her too, echoing his.

'But in the meantime there is something I want you to have.' Celia reached into the pocket at her waist, and took out a small brown stone. 'Remember this?' She held it out to him. 'You gave it to me on our last night in Aleppo.'

'Of course I remember, I gave it to you as a keepsake. A pebble in the shape of a heart. A poor exchange for the Sultan's Blue, I remember thinking.'

'No, a very good exchange. I keep it with me always. Here, I want you to have it now.'

'You have kept it all this time?' he said in wonder. 'But it's just a stone.'

'No,' Celia smiled, 'it's not just a stone.'

And when he took it from her, she leant towards him again and closed her eyes, and felt his kisses rain down upon her, as if he would never stop.

TWENTY-NINE

Annetta

Bishopsgate.

I T DID NOT PROVE difficult for Annetta to leave the house unobserved. Behind the kitchens and through a series of sculleries, she found a door that led out on to the street; not into Bishopsgate itself, but into Half Moon Alley, a narrow, muddy passageway that led down one side of the house and its grounds. Servants and tradesmen, the many purveyors of foodstuffs and other goods to the Pindar household, used this back entrance, which could not be seen from the main house. If she were careful, Annetta would be able to slip in and out with ease.

As she picked her way to the corner of the alleyway and peered round it into the street, she was just in time to catch sight of Nan's neat figure heading off in the direction of the city gates. If she were going to find out what the maid's frequent forays away from the house were about, this was her chance – but now that the moment had come, Annetta's nerve almost failed. *Dio buono*! What had possessed her to suggest she should walk through these unknown streets, in an unknown city? What if she should get lost? Or insulted? Or robbed?

Where are you when I need you, John Carew? her heart cried out. But it was no good: she was on her own. There was nothing for it, follow Nan she must. Annetta took a breath and stepped out into the street.

At first she thought that the thoroughfare of Bishopsgate Without, with its constant rattle of carriages and carts, was bad enough, but once she passed through the gates and into the city itself, the noise and confusion almost overwhelmed her.

People hurried by, too intent on their own business to notice her: a small, thin woman looking anxiously about her. At first she took pains to keep out of sight, but soon she realised that in her dark cloak and mask she was unlikely to be recognised by Nan, even if the girl had been vigilant. But Nan, suspecting nothing, never looked round.

To give herself courage, she tried to imagine John Carew walking beside her. This was his city; these were his people. There was no situation in which John would not know what to do. She found the thought of this comforting. Slowly, Annetta began to relax.

It was a fine December day. The sky was a pale blue and the air sharp. The water in a drinking trough for horses was frozen over, and a rind of sparkling frost clung to the wooden shingles of the roofs. Released from her household duties Nan took her time. She bought a pie at a shop, stopped to give a coin to a beggar sitting at the door of a church. A woman leaned out of a window and called to her familiarly; Nan answered back with some cheerful words that Annetta could not catch. A young man in blue and red livery whistled at her and called her by name. Nan had clearly walked this way many times before.

At first it was easy going. The girl walked straight, keeping to the same road which led directly south from the city gates towards the river, a fine wide thoroughfare lined with shops and the mansions of the rich. Behind their walls, Annetta could see the spindly branches of the winter trees, the last of their leaves glowing like golden doubloons in the watery sun. She never knew there could be so many gardens and orchards in the middle of a city. There were churches here, too, and the ruined remains of monastic buildings, the arches of their great windows sticking up among the rubble. A group of merchants rode by, the silver bits on their horses reins jangling in the cold air.

After a while they came to a fork in the road marked by a stone cross. Here Nan suddenly turned off the main thoroughfare, heading deep into a maze of dark passageways, so narrow and twisting that Annetta might have lost sight of her almost immediately if it had not been for a piece of scarlet cloth covering the top of her basket.

In these back alleys the press of people seemed greater still. Annetta found that she had to flatten herself against the walls to make way for other passers-by. The shops were smaller, many of them just wide enough for the shopkeeper to sit inside. Some had a sign painted with a picture denoting their trade, but most had not. They passed a row of cobblers, another of men working with leather. The air rang with the sound of their hammers. There were several inns along the way, and a public bakehouse from which the smell of rising bread and cooking meat steamed into the air. Through a servants' gateway in a wall she caught a glimpse of a fine building built around a courtyard like a Venetian *palazzo*; she also had a glimpse of silvery-green clipped lawns and raised flower beds laid out in geometrical shapes, and an improbable flash of a peacock tail, purple-blue and gold.

Then, as though suddenly conscious of her dilatory progress, Nan began to walk faster, and it became harder to keep up with her. Annetta, wearing her thin slippers, felt the cold seeping into her feet. Several times she caught her foot, and stumbled on the loose cobbles.

Once or twice she lost sight of Nan altogether, and it was only by the sheerest good fortune that she chose the right turning and caught the flash of red cloth on Nan's basket bobbing ahead of her.

Soon they had entered an area where the walkways were no more than the narrowest of lanes. There were no mansions with fine gardens here, only the cramped and noisome dwellings of the poor. Whereas before Annetta had felt herself swallowed up in the throng, now she became uneasily aware that her presence in these narrow lanes – a warmly dressed woman walking alone and ostentatiously masked – was attracting attention. The mask had given her the courage of anonymity when she had first left the house, but now she felt as if it were lighting her up like a beacon. She wished that she could take it off, but she did not dare. In a yard a group of women were sitting mending fishing nets. They watched her pass by with hostile eyes. A man standing in a doorway called out after her, an obscenity that she could not understand. The alley ran with evil-smelling effluent.

She pulled her cloak more closely to her, and her fingers closed around the pocket hanging from her belt.

What now, John Carew?

In her mind's eye she could see the glitter of his eyes. *What makes you think you're worth robbing?*

Ha! Che stronzo! She thought to this, but it cheered her all the same. Besides, there was no going back now.

And then suddenly the day turned. She had set off from the house in silvery winter sunlight, but now the sky was the colour of iron. The temperature dropped sharply. A few times Annetta thought she could see flakes of snow. And then, turning a corner, she found herself at a dead end.

She had smelt the river before she saw it – a mixture of pitch, tar, oakum and rotting fish – and now here it was, right before her. She had only taken the merest glance at the heaving brown-grey swell, at the dark shapes of the boats and galleons, the flotillas of little skiffs clustering at the wherries, and the looming mass of a great bridge to her right, but it was enough. When she looked round again, Nan was gone.

Cazzo! She spun around, first one way, and then the other. Still nothing. Filled with sudden panic, she began to run up and down the riverbank, first in one direction, towards a caulker's yard, then in the other, but to no avail. Nan had simply disappeared.

She turned her head from side to side, but the mask, with its two small slits for eyes, so impeded her view that she became maddened by it. *Cazzo*! She could not bear it any more; she must take it off.

'What you lost, sweetheart?'

As Annetta's fingers fumbled at the strings, she heard one of the wherrymen call up to her. His mate said something that she did not catch, and they all laughed.

'Won't do no good looking for it round 'ere.'

She was still fumbling with the strings, which had knotted themselves at the back of her head.

'Wrong end, sweetheart. You won't find it up there.'

'Go on, you show 'er, Will.' More mocking laughter. 'Will 'ere 'll show you where to find it.'

Annetta wrenched the mask of at last, breaking the strings. From the corner of her eye, she thought she saw one of the men coming towards her. *Run*! A voice that sounded very like John Carew's echoed in her head. *Run*! And with that she picked up her skirts and ran, the sound of their mockery echoing over the water behind her.

A little way along the path she came to a row of tall brick houses. In the middle of them was a small archway through which she could see a narrow lane. Thinking that it might lead her away from the river, she ran towards it; but when she passed through the archway she found herself not in a lane at all, but at the centre of a large, cobbled courtyard.

On the far side there was a doorway, above which a lighted torch flickered.

And beside it, on the cobbles, was Nan's basket.

No sooner had she spotted the basket than the door opened, and there was Nan herself standing in the doorway. She had her back towards Annetta, and was speaking to someone who remained just out of sight behind the door. Annetta was trapped. There was no time to run back, or even to withdraw from sight, not even time to tie the mask back on. No time to do anything...

Santa Madonna! Annetta's heart was fluttering so hard she thought she might faint.

But then, just as suddenly, and quite improbably, it was as though she could hear John Carew again:

Just brazen it out.

What? I can't!

Yes, you can, woman. Do it now! Be brazen! Just walk towards the door. Not too fast, not too slow, mind. Say to yourself: this was my purpose all along. It is the most natural thing in the world that I should be here. Just do it!

Fanculo! Annetta swore out loud. *If this goes wrong, you'll have me to answer for, John Carew.*

It won't, woman, you'll see. Don't think I haven't got myself out of worse scrapes than this.

And there was nothing else for it. Holding the mask to her face with one hand, and drawing her cloak around her with the other, Annetta did the only thing possible:

holding her head high, willing herself to be calm, she began to walk towards the open door.

Nan hardly glanced at her. Instead, she nodded to the servant holding the door for her and stepped respectfully to one side to let Annetta by. As they passed one another, Annetta saw her lean down to pick up her basket, and as she did so, tuck two things quickly inside, hiding them beneath the cloth. One was a small bottle, a vial made of dark brown glass; the other was twist of pale blue sugar paper, of the kind in which powders are dispensed in apothecaries' shops.

And then she was sweeping past the unsuspecting servant and into the house. And the great door swung shut behind her.

She found herself in a *loggia* or entrance hall, the wooden panelling painted black. Several doors led from it, all of them closed. At the far end, towards the back of the house, was a handsome staircase leading to the upstairs floors. Inside it was dark and very warm; there were many sconces on the walls and up the stairs, in which candles blazed as though it were night. Against the wall to her left was a small table, and on top of it a blue and white porcelain urn filled with lilies.

Lilies in the dead of winter! How was that possible? Annetta gazed at them in wonder. The air was perfumed with their sweet, thick scent, masking some other odour, something dark and bitter that she could not identify.

Santa Madonna! *What now, you scapegrace?* Annetta addressed John Carew furiously.

And what now, indeed? For she was truly trapped.

The manservant who had been standing at the door was a Moor with a gold earring in one ear. He was dressed like a Christian, but wore neither stockings nor shoes, so that his feet and legs, from the knee down, were bare.

'Wait here,' he instructed. 'Madam will see you shortly.'

Before Annetta could reply he had let himself out through one of the closed doors and disappeared from view.

Madam? Did they have such a thing as a she-apothecary in this country? Looking about her, Annetta thought she had never been in such a strange place in her life. Fear gripped her. She put her hand against the panelled wall to steady herself.

Now what? For the love of God and the Holy Saints, now what?

What are you afraid of, woman? It was almost as if she could hear him whispering into her ear. *You have nothing to fear, I am here with you, and besides, you are the bravest woman I know.* And the smallest breath of air, a feeling of warmth, like the tip of an angel's wing, seemed to brush down one side of her face.

Clearly the best thing to do would be to take her leave, before 'madam', whoever she might be, should arrive and start asking questions. If Annetta were questioned she would simply say that she had come here to buy something – but what? Seeing Nan tuck the paper and the glass vial into her basket, the thought that had immediately occurred to Annetta was that this was an apothecary's shop; but this was like no other apothecary of which she had ever heard tell. And besides, she was not at all sure that she could get out of the house on her own. She had seen the Moor lock the door with a key after he shut it, and now she realised that he must have taken the key with him, for it was no longer there.

Just then there came a loud knock on the door. The Moor appeared again, treading silently as before. Producing the key from his pocket, he unlocked the door again. A female figure, heavily cloaked and veiled but with the air of a gentlewoman, stood on the threshold. The Moor seemed to have been expecting her, for he stood to one side and the woman passed by him wordlessly. She did not address him, nor, by the slightest word or gesture did she acknowledge Annetta, but glided past them both, still in her veil and cloak, and made her way up the stairs to one of the upper floors.

The Moor relocked the door and disappeared as before, and the house fell silent again. For all the warmth in the room, Annetta was shivering. Her feet in her thin-soled slippers felt frozen and bruised. At first all the only sound in the *loggia* had been the faint ticking of a clock near the stairwell, but now as she listened more closely she became aware of other sounds. From somewhere in the distance – behind one of the closed doors, or on an upstairs floor – she could hear, very faintly, the sound of women's laughter, and sometimes the lower tones of a man, or men, and the tread of footsteps overhead, snatches of conversation, and sometimes song.

Many minutes went by, but still no one came. To pass the time she began to examine the pictures on the wall. Above the urn with the lilies was a painting of a naked woman bathing, watched by some old men; another showed a woman and a swan. The swan's body was thrust between the woman's legs, its neck wrapped sinuously around her neck. Annetta gazed at them with fascination.

'Leda and the swan,' said a voice behind her. 'Legend has it that when Zeus, the king of the gods, wanted to lie with Leda, he took the form of a swan.'

A strange-looking woman with pale skin and a bad complexion was standing behind her. If it had not been for the authority in her voice, Annetta might have mistaken her for a servant, for she wore a gown of plain brown worsted, a linen cap, none too clean, and a lace collar dyed a dirty yellow colour. She reminded Annetta, somewhat improbably, of the Dutch woman who came to the Pindars' Bishopsgate house each week to launder and starch their collars and ruffs.

'Forgive me, I didn't mean to startle you.'

'You have some pretty pictures,' Annetta said, playing for time.

'But you didn't come here to look at my pictures. How may I be of service?'

There was nothing for it.

'Lady Sydenham sent me.'

Annetta realised immediately that she had made a mistake. If Frances had sent her, then why had she not come together with Nan? But to this the woman said nothing.

'Lady Sydenham?'

'Frances Sydenham.'

Her eyes narrowed. 'Frances?'

'Yes.' The familiar name almost got stuck in Annetta's throat, but she managed it in the end. 'Frances.'

'I see.'

For a moment the two women stood looking at one another. Neither spoke.

'It is customary, if it would not be to much of an inconvenience, to remove your mask,' Madam ventured at last. 'A mark of confidence, shall we say.' She gave Annetta a chilly smile, 'Fear not, you are among friends here.'

'As you wish.'

When Annetta lowered her mask the woman took it from her, and looked it over carefully.

'Venetian.' A statement, not a question.

'Yes.'

'Silver thread. Most handsome.' She handed it back. 'You are most welcome, madam.'

'Your servant.' Annetta bent her knees into a swift courtesy.

'And you are?'

'I am... Mrs Pindar.'

'Indeed.' The woman's strange, lashless eyes were the colour of dirty ditchwater. 'I did not know that Frances's... sphere of influence...' She hesitated only slightly over her choice of words, '... extended all the way to Venice?'

She said this with such a decided air of someone eliciting information that this time Annetta had no choice but to reply.

'My lady's influence...' she said carefully, playing for time, 'has always been... extensive.'

'Indeed!' The woman's eyes took on a sudden gleam. 'And – tell me, madam – Lady Sydenham is... your good acquaintance?'

'Naturally.' By the Holy Virgin and all the saints! Annetta could only hope she sounded convincing. 'My Lady Sydenham is my *very dear* acquaintance.'

'Ah, the divine Lady Sydenham! She is in good health, I hope?' Something about the woman's tone suggested, very faintly, that she wished Lady Sydenham to the devil.

If Nan had been here buying powders for her, would she not know all about Frances's health? The interesting possibility now occurred to Annetta that madam had not the least idea that Nan had come here on Frances's behalf and that, like Annetta, she was herself playing for time.

'My lady is so good as never to speak of her health with me.'

'How curious when she is, as you say, such a dear acquaintance. In my experience, ladies of good acquaintance are never happier than when discussing their little ailments, even the most delicate ones. But no doubt,' she ventured, 'that is because you have perhaps been unwell yourself?'

She took a step closer to Annetta and without so much as a by-your-leave, took her suddenly by the chin.

'What was it?' she said, turning Annetta's face this way and that, inserting her finger between her teeth so as to look at her tongue, examining her for all the world as though she were a physician. 'An ague? The sweating sickness? Jaundice?' Close to, Annetta became aware of a strange odour clinging to the woman's person, something acrid, and behind it a faint whiff of rotten eggs. Although her hands seemed clean enough, dirt of some kind was lodged beneath her fingernails and the tips of her fingers were stained. On the forefinger of her right hand was a yellowing nail, at least an inch long. Annetta tried to draw away but the woman gripped her.

'What was it?'

'The plague.'

'Ach! Je, arme ding...' She made a guttural sound at the back of her throat. 'I could give you something to improve this complexion if you wish, but in my experience once a woman has lost her looks, there is never much to be done.'

Her gaze was not unsympathetic.

'I had the pox, and all my hair fell out. It's never grown back.' She pulled her cap a little to one side so that Annetta could see where a few grizzled tufts remained. 'Eyelashes. Eyebrows. Everything. But what's to be done? Sometimes it is best to let well alone. I took to painting my face for a while, to cover the scars, but look what it did to me; the lead eats your skin – like so.' She put her hand to her face, which was covered with lumps and carbuncles. 'Quite like the old English Queen, so I'm told.' Her lips narrowed into a thin smile. 'But then I was never much to look at in the first place. But you, you must have been a pretty girl once.'

She let Annetta go at last.

'But listen to me rattling on. I must not keep you standing here, you must be tired.' She seemed, inexplicably, to have taken a liking to Annetta. 'Come into my parlour, we can talk there in perfect confidence.'

Throwing open one of the doors which led off the *loggia*, she ushered Annetta inside. The room was empty except for a dresser containing a number of large glass bottles and vials, and on the top half, a number of drawers.

To Annetta's dismay, she closed the door firmly behind her.

'You seem a little anxious, if you don't mind my saying so.'

'I suppose, just a little.' This was true enough. To dissemble too much would be as bad as to dissemble too little.

'There is no cause, you are among friends here.'

'I thank you; I thank you warmly.'

The truth was, the thought of being in a confined space with this woman was making Annetta feel nauseous with fear.

'If... Lady Sydenham... sent you.' She seemed to hesitate over the name, 'then I am imagining that either you have an unwanted... obstruction,' she said slowly, choosing her words with care, 'or perhaps it is singing lessons that you require?'

Annetta was mystified. 'I believe... both.'

'Both?' The woman's painted eyebrows almost disappeared into her cap. 'Are you quite sure?'

'Why not?'

'Why not indeed, madam.' Her eyes gleamed as though at some private joke. 'You are most... industrious.'

'Indeed.'

'Well now, the obstruction I can help you with immediately,' she said, becoming brisk. 'I have some powders ready made. And as to the singing lessons, they can soon be arranged. May I know how often your singing master requires your attendance?'

'I am. . . not entirely sure at present.'

'But they will be regular lessons?'

'I believe so.'

'Well, that can wait.' Madam wiped her hands a little thoughtfully on her apron. 'Perhaps you would you care to see a room?'

Annetta heard these words with dismay. All she wanted to do was to get out of this place as soon as possible.

'I thank you, but no, that won't be necessary.'

The woman hesitated. 'That is most unusual, if I may say so.' Her efforts at courtesy were beginning to fray a little at the edges. She looked at Annetta with an attempt at patience. 'Usually the singing master requires it. Are you quite sure – if I may be quite blunt – you know how he likes to be accommodated?'

'Perfectly.' With an effort, Annetta held her gaze. The strain of keeping up a conversation she did not altogether understand was beginning to make her feel quite faint. She held her chin up a little higher. 'Your. . . singing rooms. . . come most highly recommended.'

The sound of a door opening and closing again on one of the upstairs floors, of a man's heavy footsteps on the landing, made the woman glance up.

'Would you be so kind as to wait in here? I shan't be a moment.'

She left the room, pushing the door behind her as though to shut it, but in her haste it did not quite close. Through the crack Annetta saw a man in merchant's attire come down the stairs. Silently he handed her a packet, which she secreted in the pocket beneath her apron. Then came the sound of the front door opening and then shutting behind him. A few moments later a second woman, as heavily veiled and cloaked as the one she had seen earlier, followed him down the stairs. She murmured a few words that Annetta could not catch and then she too was gone.

Madam came back in. She went over to the dresser and began to pull out the little compartments, muttering to herself. She spoke in English, as before, but her muttering was interspersed with snatches of another tongue, deeper and more guttural, that Annetta could not identify.

'Now, first things first. For the obstruction – *lieve hemel*, where did I put them – let me see now, here's sea holly and black hellebore.' She opened more compartments in the dresser. 'Juniper, yes. And rue. Some pennyroyal if I can find it – where did I put it now – *ah! ja hier is het, hier is het—*' She turned to Annetta. 'You must listen to me carefully, now. Here are two preparations. If I may ask you – how long since your last course?'

'My last course?'

'I mean – how long since you last bled?'

'I believe. . . several months.'

'And you are quite certain there is. . . an obstruction?'

'Yes.' Annetta heard her own voice, as though it belonged to someone else, sounded faint with alarm. '*Ma certo*. I am quite certain.'

It was now most suddenly and forcefully clear to her what kind of business this was, and the very thought filled her with horror.

'Forgive me, madam, but you do not look. . .' The woman seemed to search to find the right words, '. . . fit for purpose.' She sighed. 'Ah well, stranger things have happened. So long as you know that it would be dangerous to take these preparations if the obstruction were merely. . . a fancy on your part.'

'A fancy?' Annetta tried to feign outrage. 'It is no fancy, I assure you.'

'That may be so, but perhaps if you would allow me to examine you? To be quite certain. I have many years' experience, as I'm sure your friend. . . the lady you mentioned. . . can attest.'

'No. . . I. . . that won't be necessary.'

The thought of the woman's stained fingers, and that long, yellowing nail touching any part of her flesh, let alone feeling between her legs or prising open her woman's parts, made Annetta feel ill.

'You are turned pale, madam. Come, there was no modesty at the beginning of this adventure, so why now?' She drew near again, and Annetta could see quite clearly now how the skin of her face appeared to have been eaten away, rutted and furrowed as if worms had been burrowing just under the surface.

'Have no fear – you would not have to undress – I can palpate you through your chemise.'

The woman placed her hand on her belly, but Annetta shied away.

'*Madonna,* I thank you, but no!'

'Well.' She gave a small, indifferent shrug, 'if you are quite certain.'

She made herself busy again, measuring out herbs and powders from the jars on the dresser. She worked rapidly, sometimes using a pair of small brass scales, at other times her fingers: a pinch of this, a pinch of that, and then tying them into parcels with paper and twine.

'Here, I have prepared some powders for you.' She held up a packet done up with blue sugar paper similar to the one Annetta had seen Nan hide in her basket. 'And here.' She held up a second, smaller packet in the other hand, 'I give you a further preparation for internal use. Do you understand me?'

'I. . . believe so,' Annetta said. A feeling of revulsion like a tide of dirty water was beginning to seep over her.

'This one.' The woman held up the first package, 'you must boil in water, and then drink it. It has a bitter taste, and some find that equal parts of cinnamon will take some of its bitterness away. But this one.' She held up the second, smaller package, 'this is a very harsh medicine. I would caution you only to use it if the first one does not work. In this one you will find another powder, the ground root of the black hellebore. The alchemists say it is a herb of Saturn, and there are sullen conditions which attend it, but that can't be helped. In my experience for bringing on a woman's courses, it has no equal. You must boil the root in water, and then take a small piece of rag, which when folded up tight is about the same size as a walnut, then you soak the rag in the water, a day and a night – when it turns quite black, like the root itself, you will know that it is ready. Then you insert the rag inside your woman's parts, like so—' She held out her forefinger with its long yellow nail, and made a twisting probing gesture, '—and mind to push it up as high up as it will go.'

'I thank you for your kindness, Mrs. . .'

'I am Mrs. . . Miller.' She hesitated by only a breath over the name, but even that tiny hesitation should have been enough to alert Annetta. 'But your Lady Sydenham would have told you that, surely?'

'Yes, but of course she did. Mrs Miller. I remember now.' She gave a small bow. 'I thank you, Mrs Miller, I am indebted to you.'

Annetta put out her hand to take the packet, but the woman pulled it away.

'Not so fast.'

'Why. . . what?. . . is something amiss?'

'I think that should be my question.'

'I don't understand—'

'I think you do. I am no more Mrs Miller than you are. My name is Mrs Van de Velde. And that woman who you said sent you here is no more Lady Sydenham than I am the Queen of Spain.'

'But—' Annetta began to protest but she could see that it was useless.

'That woman – *Lady* Sydenham – *ach*, no, is that really what she calls herself?' Mrs Van de Velde made a sound of the deepest disgust in the back of her throat, as though she were about to spit. 'Even *she* would not have the nerve to send someone here so openly. And even if she had she would have warned you never to reveal her name to me.'

'I don't understand—'

'No, I don't believe you do.' Mrs Van de Velde was looking at Annetta with an expression that she could not read. 'What are you really doing here? Are you looking for her? Because if so, let me tell you, you won't find her, not under my roof. I would pull this house down, brick by brick – I would sleep in the street rather than give that woman shelter. Every last whore in London may come here to keep their assignations, but she, who is the biggest whore in all England, may not. For all I know she may not even be here in London any more. Last I heard she was in the Low Countries, in Antwerp, in keeping with some diamond merchant.'

'I know nothing of diamond merchants.'

'But you are looking for her, no? Isn't that why you came here?' Mrs Van de Velde leant forward and said in a low voice full of sudden malice, 'What did she do to you – did she cheat you? Steal from you? Bewitch your singing master and take him from you?'

'No!' Annetta could only whisper. *Not me. Not yet.* 'You are wrong, I am not looking for her. That is not why I came. I know where she stays – just outside the city walls, in the place they call Bishopsgate. She lives with a merchant of the Levant Company and his wife, who are recently returned to this country from Aleppo.'

'And they are people of some estate?'

'Of very great estate.'

'Of course they are.' She put a hand on her hip, 'and how long has she been there?'

'Not long, two months.'

'But long enough, *hnn*?'

'They stopped in Antwerp on their journey home, and a merchant there – an acquaintance of the English merchant – asked them to give her safe passage. Just after her husband died.'

And suddenly, from nowhere, there it was again: a faint feeling of warmth, as though a feather had stroked her cheek. And in the same moment it came to her: a memory of Frances Sydenham standing in the doorway on her first unhappy day at the house in Bishopsgate. The yellow quinces in a bowl; Frances's pallid face. The way she had stepped back from the threshold, holding her handker- chief to her lips as though the smell of the fruit had made her nauseous. One hand resting on her belly beneath her loose jacket.

'Her husband!' She heard the woman give a snort of derision. 'And she lies with them still?'

Annetta's met her gaze and held it there. 'She lies, Mrs Van de Velde, of that much I am quite certain.'

THIRTY

Paul

Bishopsgate.

THE HALL WAS IN darkness. Paul stood listening, but there came not a sound. The house was utterly still and silent. He walked up the stairs, and on the first-floor landing paused for a moment outside the great gallery. The door was just a little ajar. He listened again intently for any signs of someone within: a chair creaking, the pages of a book turning. But there was nothing – only a light, faint and flickering, beneath the door.

When he pushed the door open Paul could see immediately that someone had recently been there. The light he had seen was coming from the fire, which had been well banked up. A flask of wine and a plate of bread and cold meats had been laid out upon the sideboard. The cabinet to the right of the window, the one where he stored his correspondence, stood open, the display shelf pulled out.

He took a few steps into the room and looked around. The gallery was empty. The only sound came from the dull whispering of the flames, the sudden movement of a spent log falling from the fire-dogs.

Standing in the middle of the room, his shoes in his hands, the absurdity of what he was doing struck him suddenly. What in the name of God was he doing creeping around in his own house in the middle of the night? And in his stockinged feet, moreover?

After everything that he now knew about Frances Sydenham, there was no more need for pretence.

When Annetta had come home and told him her story, he had gone immediately himself to talk to the she-apothecary, Mrs Van de Velde; he had also been to the Exchange to make some enquiries of his own from various Muscovy Company merchants of his acquaintance. And now he knew everything, or thought he did.

He knew, at least, what he had to do. He went over to the chimney place and rested his brow against the cold stone mantel.

'Why, sir, whatever is the matter?'

Frances Sydenham was sitting in one of the high-backed chairs. It had been placed facing away from the door, which is why he had not seen her at first. She rubbed her eyes, looked up at him sleepily. 'Why, you look as though you have seen a ghost.'

For a few moments all he could do was stare at her.

'What in God's name are you doing here? And don't pretend to me this time that you are looking for that damned monkey of yours.'

She answered him quite calmly, 'Quirkus? No – I wasn't looking for Quirkus.'

'Then what—?'

'I was waiting for you.'

Frances was fully dressed, her feet were shod; only her head was bare, a single lock of hair falling over one shoulder.

'I can think of no business so urgent that you must come looking for me in the middle of the night,' he said coldly.

Frances Sydenham looked up at him, trying to conceal her surprise. The hostility in his voice was not something that she had encountered before. And now, although she made an effort to appear calm, her heart was beating fast. She had taken a big risk in coming here again, knew she was in grave danger of overplaying her hand.

When Frances stood up and went over to him, he moved over to the sideboard.

'Paul—'

A log fell in the grate, the sudden sound, unnaturally loud in the silence of the room, made them both start. With one quick movement Paul moved towards her, forcing her to twist to one side so that she was facing him.

When he pressed her back against the sideboard, she saw that he was holding a knife in his hand.

'Why, is something the matter, Lady Sydenham?' Slowly he moved the knife so that the tip of the blade was pointing towards her breastbone. 'Surely you have seen a knife before.'

All he could hear was a long, slow exhalation as though she had been holding her breath. In the dark room he saw her pupils were so dilated that her eyes were almost black, and for one moment she was utterly strange to him, a creature he did not recognise, and from whom he could almost recoil.

'Who are you?' He rested the blade of the knife against her breastbone, 'and what is your business here among us?'

For the first time she seemed to falter.

She licked her lips as though her mouth were dry. 'You know very well who I am.'

'I know who you say you are.'

She gave an uncertain laugh. 'Don't be absurd.'

'You remind me of someone.'

'And who might that be?'

'A lady I used to know in Venice. A curtezan. A *corte-giana honesta*, an honest curtezan.' Paul looked away from her briefly, and then back again. 'At least that's what she liked to call herself, but she was a prostitute really.'

He bent towards her, so that their faces were almost touching: 'Constanza Fabia, pros-ti-tute.' He watched her carefully, letting the words sunk in. 'She had a thousand faces, one for each man she entertained – and, oh, she was a most *excellent* player, I should know for I was one of them – and it seems to me,' he spoke slowly, 'that you are a lot like her.'

The insult was deliberate, so carefully calibrated, that for a moment she looked as though she were about to protest, but then she seemed to think better of it.

'Nice company you keep, Merchant Pindar.' She gave a small shrug. 'But your Venetian whores are of no interest to me.'

'Why, is that because you are one yourself?' When she said nothing to this, he added, 'Do I shock you?'

She held his gaze without blinking. 'You know that you do not.'

'What would shock you I wonder, Lady Sydenham?'

When again she did not reply, he went on, 'Does it shock you to know that I know that you have no more right to call yourself lady than I do?'

He saw immediately that he had struck home.

'Sir Ambrose was a Muscovy merchant, knighted by the King himself.' With an effort she continued to hold his gaze. 'Ask anyone—'

'Oh, I have,' he said, 'I have just had a most enlightening conversation with such a merchant, recently now returned to these shores, but that particular gentleman was not in fact married to you. The wife of Sir Ambrose

Sydenham, Muscovy merchant, was a woman of unimpeachable character, one Mary Simms, nearly as old as he, who predeceased him at the age of sixty-five by only a matter of months.'

He was aware that she had become very still.

'I see you have been busy, sir, most industrious. I congratulate you.'

'I have extremely good intelligencers – it's one of the things you should know about me – nearly as good as your own.' Paul's gaze left her for a moment, scanned the room again: he saw now what he had only half-seen before, and it struck him forcibly. That the cabinet had been opened, and that his inventories, receipts and piles of correspondence were lying in disarray on the desktop. He remembered Parvish's rule – the first rule of business, the golden rule – never leave your effects lying around where others may see them.

'You were not waiting for me at all, were you? You were going through my papers.' He put his hand into the inside of his quilted doublet and pulled out a letter. The seal of red wax was broken, hanging from it by a thread. 'Is this what you were looking for?'

Her gaze flickered towards the letter and then quickly away again. 'I don't understand you.'

'Oh, but I think you do. But we will come to the business of my letters in a moment. First let us discuss the intriguing matter of your several husbands. The merchant I have just now left, told me how you seduced an old man in his dotage when his wife was still warm in her grave. How you tried to make him marry you; how you spent all his money, even tried to get him to make you his heir.'

'What of it?'

'So you admit it, then, you were not Sir Ambrose's wife. You are not who you say you are at all.'

Frances seemed about to say something, but then she changed her mind and instead gave an indifferent shrug.

'What's this?' he said when she did not reply. 'Cat got your tongue?'

'I admit it freely.'

'He says that you were nothing but a common whore, and that Sir Ambrose found you in a brothel. And I suppose you are now going to try to persuade me that none of it is true.'

'That none of what is true? I was never Sir Ambrose's legal wife, that much is true, but in all other ways, yes. . .' She nodded slowly, '. . .I believe I have a perfect right to make that claim.'

'So you were not his whore?'

'You mean did I lie with him? Yes, I did. And from when I was very young.'

'Ah, now we have it – the truth at last—'

'The truth? You have no idea how much I have longed to tell you the truth.' She looked at him imploringly, 'how it has grieved me all this time. . .' She made a move towards him, to put her hand on his shoulder, but he flinched away.

'You lay with a man old enough to be your grandsire.'

'The truth is. . .' She hesitated, '. . . the truth is that when I was a girl I was Sir Ambrose's ward.'

'Oh monstrous—'

'Monstrous? Is that what you call it?'

'Well, don't tell me you lay with him for love?'

'For love? What does that mean?' Now it was Frances's turn to pull away. He watched as she walked over to the window, standing there silently for a moment or two.

'As a matter of fact, I *did* love him.'

'You expect me to believe that?' he said softly.

'No, I don't expect anyone to believe it – a maid of sixteen and a man of almost threescore... who would believe such a thing? It is true nonetheless.' Her shoulders sloped. 'He was all my world. I had no one – was all alone – and so was he—'

'Don't think to make me pity you, because I do not. And besides, he wasn't alone, as I understand it. He had a wife still then living.'

'Yes, he had a wife. Mary.' Frances said the name as though she had tasted something sour. 'Peevish, sickly Mary. Always scolding, always complaining, always in a great chafe about something or other. Poor man, how she did scold him! She gave him no peace. She was no companion to him. His children were all dead. His heirs – distant cousins of his wife – did machinate against him—'

'—so you thought you would console him?'

'We consoled each other.' She ignored his taunt, 'but not in the way you think, not at first anyway. He taught me things, Latin and arithmetic, even some Greek. He read me poetry – have you ever read the poems of Dr Donne?' She turned to him hopefully, but when Paul said nothing she went on, 'He didn't laugh at my desire to learn, or my love of beauty. You see I always loved books.' She turned to him again, 'Remember when we first met in Antwerp, remember how I noticed your books?' She put her hand out to him again, but as before he shrugged her away. 'You can have no idea what it was like, in that house in Norfolk, no one to talk to except an ill-tempered old woman who hated me heartily, and the sound of the sea pounding in your ears day and night, the chimneys smoking, and the lattices rattling. The loneliness of it. And the cold. Sweet Jesus, I was always cold. An ice wind blowing down all the way from Muscovy itself...' Her voice trailed away and she fell silent, lost in her own thoughts.

After a while Paul said, 'Did not this Sir Ambrose think to find you a husband of your own?'

'Oh yes, he was very correct, and besides,' she added bitterly, 'in those days I had a big enough dowry. I was married to a wool merchant from King's Lynn. John Staples was his name.' She gave a small laugh. 'John Staples, my husband – how strange – I have not said his name, nor even thought it, these last ten years, and yet that is what he was.'

'And what manner of man was he, this first husband of yours?'

'I was sixteen, what could I know possibly about men? All I knew is that he was not up to me.'

'Not up to you? An honest wool merchant not up to a sixteen-year-old maid, and already another man's whore, if I understand you correctly. You certainly have a good opinion of yourself, madam.'

'Don't waste your breath feeling sorry for *him*. He married me for my money. He was not young – although he was younger than Ambrose – but he was well-to-do, and my guardian was persuaded that he would at least be kind. But he wasn't kind. I was always quick, and I learnt how to be a good manager; I managed his affairs perfectly – not only his household, but his accounts too – and he liked that well enough – but my books? Oh no! The poetry and the plays? These were childish things, conceits that must now be put away. And why? Because he saw that they pleased me. I do believe it was the only reason.

'But of course I did not – *could* not – give them up. I was sixteen and married to a man I barely knew – my books were the only things of beauty, of solace, in my life. But my husband locked me in the house and burnt my books. And when I contrived a way to get more, to replace the ones he had taken, he told me I was cunning and that he must beat me for it. And he did – he beat me with a switch on my bare flesh until I bled. Said it was against nature for a woman to be learned – that my only duty was to obey my husband, that it was his right to beat me if he wished, that the reason he could not get a child on me – and oh! how he tried, although his embraces were loathsome to me – was punishment for my sins, of pride, of vanity. That he would beat them out of me too, so help him God. I was allowed the Bible, but that was all. But I never would give in to him, never! The truth was I was stronger than he and he hated me for it.'

'And what of his family?'

'Do you mean his sister and his mother? Those mealy-mouthed, homespun little women, with their plain clothes and their white kerchiefs, shivering over their prayer-books?' She gave a contemptuous laugh. 'Not they. *They* did not lift a finger to help me; they said I was wilful and unruly and I deserved to be beaten—'

'I can imagine it. A very peacock come to roost in their henhouse.'

'You may mock me, sir, but this is no mocking matter.'

'What did you do?'

'I ran away.'

'You ran away?'

'If I had stayed I truly believe he would have killed me – or I him. I hated him that much—' She spread her fingers, stared at them, palms upward, '—I hated him so much I sometimes used to think that I could have killed him with my own bare hands.'

'I don't believe a beating with a switch ever killed anyone.'

'Don't think that I am asking for your pity, Paul Pindar, and it was not my body that he would have killed; there are worse things than that, surely you of all people—' She broke off, drawing her fingers through her scalp as though she would pull the hair out by the roots. 'Sweet Jesus, have you understood *nothing* about me?'

How could she explain to him the slow shrivelling of the self? The death of the mind? The sound of a stranger's footfalls on cold tiled floors? Her soul slowly turning the colour of the grey Norfolk skies?

'I believe I understand less and less with every passing moment,' Paul said, 'but please, do enlighten me if you can – I am enthralled,' he added drily. 'Where did you run to?'

'I went to find my guardian in London to ask him to take me away.'

'To take you where?'

'I didn't rightly know – away – anywhere—'

'And he agreed?'

'At first I couldn't find him – London was so immense; I was overwhelmed. I had never been out of my own country before. I had no idea even how to begin. I knew one person, a cousin of my mother's, and she took me in. I lived with her while I looked, searching at the Company's house, even at the docks—'

'But you found him in the end?'

'Yes.' She looked down at her hands again. 'Eventually. At first he was angry and he tried to make me return to my husband's people. Told me it would be a sin for him to come between a man and his lawful wife. But I begged and I begged. . . and eventually he took pity on me.'

'A Christian gentleman indeed.'

'Ah, you mock me again, sir. Ambrose had always loved me. And I him. Besides. . .' She shrugged, '. . .I had no other currency. Nothing else to sell.'

She gave him a look of such sadness – that for one moment, he almost pitied her.

'He kept you in London?' he asked.

'No, he couldn't keep me in London in case my husband or his people came looking for me, so he took me with him on his voyages to Muscovy. And later, after we learnt that his wife had died, I took the name Lady Sydenham. He would have married me—'

'—except for the inconvenient fact that you already had one husband still alive.'

When she said nothing to this, he added, 'Not to mention the Dutch husband, poor fellow, who came after him.'

'Dutch husband?' She glanced up at him, wary suddenly. 'I don't understand you—'

'I think you do. The Dutch husband, who you somehow managed to fit in between the Norfolk wool trader and the Muscovy merchant.'

'I – I – don't know what you mean...' For once Frances seemed at a loss to know what to say.

'Mr Van de Velde, I believe that was his name.' He was watching her closely now. 'A merchant from Antwerp, and I say "husband" in the loosest sense of the word, of course.'

'But how—?'

'How do I know about Mr Van de Velde? Why, from a certain Mrs Van de Velde.'

Frances sat down suddenly. She had turned very pale. 'You have seen her, seen Marie?'

'Yes, I have seen her.'

'And what did she tell you? That I stole her husband away from her?'

'Something like that—'

'—the woman had the plague, what could he want with her any more?'

'The "much-married Lady Sydenham", it all begins to make sense now. I can't say I wasn't warned. What a fool you must take me for – that whole story, about Sir

Ambrose, all of it lies. They tell me he loved his wife dearly, until you took him from her and broke her heart, and to think, if I had not been to visit Mrs Van de Velde myself, I might even have believed you.' Paul still had the knife in his hand. 'Who are you really? What is your business here?'

When she did not answer him he positioned the tip of the blade against the thin border of lace at the top of her bodice. Now he pushed against it, inserting it so that it made a tiny tear in the fabric. Most women would have shrunk from him at this point, or cried out, or tried to pull themselves away, but Frances Sydenham did none of these things. The only sign of stress was the tiny pulse throbbing in her throat.

'Who are you?' he asked. 'What are you doing here among us?'

The knife was so sharp that the thin silk began to tear and fray, and as it did so Paul had the mad urge to dig it in still further. Imagined himself drawing the blade slowly down the entire length of her body, slicing the garment in two.

'And why not?' he said, almost to himself, and then, in a whisper, 'It's what you want, isn't it?'

And before he could stop himself he pressed a little harder: and there was a small sound as the silk began to tear. . .

'Do you suppose my hand is still shaking? Better pray not.' He was so close to her now that he could smell her hair, the skin of her neck. 'Tell me, was I to be next on the list? I rather think that was what you had planned, was it not?'

Something about the way she smelt – cloves and stale sweat – seemed to madden him and he drove the knife in still further, in and then, until there was a tear several inches long through the silk along her breastbone, and when she flinched, he felt a sudden surge of joy. . .

'Who are you? I can keep going, you know. . .'

Beneath the silk was a chemise of fine lawn cotton, and a stomacher of hard horsehair covered in quilted cotton. 'I can keep going,' he repeated, 'shall I? The knife is quite sharp enough. They say that carving is a noble art.'

But Frances had had enough. She took a sharp breath, sucking in the air through her teeth with a hissing sound, and tried to wrench herself away. But in a trice Paul had put his other arm round her back, and was pinning her to him now so she could not pull free. With his other hand he drew the knife steadily down the fabric of her bodice, the tear was now three inches long—

'Enough! You have gone mad, sir! I do believe you are gone quite mad. I heard that you do sometimes fall into a melancholy, but this is too much.' She pulled herself free at last.

Letting her go, Paul went over to the cabinet. Pressing a hidden catch, he opened one of the concealed drawers and took out a packet of letters. 'Were these what you were looking for, my letters?'

Frances shrugged.

'I see you will not answer me; no matter. Let's not play at parlour games any more. You've no need to answer my questions, Lady Sydenham. I know exactly who you are,' Paul said. 'You are my brother Ralph's intelligencer.'

Frances sat down suddenly. Turning her back to him, she took out her handkerchief and held it to her lips.

'I knew, when I read my brother's letters through again, that he must be receiving intelligence from someone, and it was you; you were sent here to spy on me. And I was fool enough to imagine that the reason you came here in the night was to look for me.' He gave a small laugh. 'But you weren't looking for me at all, were you? What was it you were really looking for: my accounting books?

My trading ledgers? Or was it perhaps – just perhaps – the diamond? Did my brother send you here to steal the stone, is that it?'

'No! I am no thief!' Frances was gripping the sides of her chair.

'But you don't deny it?'

'It is a magical stone, you said so yourself. Not even I would dare take it, not for anyone. He knew that—'

'Then what were you going to do? Use that thieving little monkey of yours to steal it? Send him down the chimney so that no one would see you go in or out?'

'No!'

'If it had not been for my brother's letters, I doubt that any of us would ever have known. It was Ralph who gave you away.'

'I don't understand. . .'

'It's all in here.' Paul held out the packet of Ralph's letters. 'When Celia and I looked at them again and read them all together, we learnt everything we needed to know – it's all in here. The letters, and a little help from Nan.'

Frances made an inarticulate sound under her breath.

'Celia complained to me once that she thought Nan might be reading her letters, but at the time I put it down to one of her imaginings. The only surprise to me was that Nan could read at all. Later I remembered she had told Celia that her last mistress had taught her. Of course Celia did not think to ask her who that mistress was.' Paul paused. 'It was you, wasn't it?' When she did not answer him he went on, 'And for a woman who almost never left this house, you seemed to know a great deal of the ways of the world. But that was because Nan carried your letters out, and brought you the replies in secret. Let alone all the other commissions she undertook for you at the house of the she-apothecary, Mrs Van de Velde – your mother's cousin – the one you took refuge with when you left your first husband, and whose kindness in taking you in you repaid by stealing her own husband away from her as she lay dying of the plague.'

'Forgive me,' Frances said in a low voice, pressing her handkerchief still harder to her lips. 'I find I am not well—'

'And we all know why that is, don't we?'

He made as if to approach her, but Frances flinched away from him as though she expected to be struck.

'Whose child is it that you bear? My brother Ralph's or the unfortunate merchant who came to me in Antwerp and begged me to take you home to England with us?' Paul remembered the way the man's eyes had slid away from his, not quite wanting to meet his gaze, asking him, in the name of Christian charity, to take the poor defence-less widow away with him. And how it had seemed to him, even then, that anyone less defenceless than Frances Sydenham would have been hard to find.

'Or perhaps you are not entirely sure yourself, which is why you sought out Mrs Van de Velde and her powders, or sent Nan to her on your behalf. I am told she does a most successful trade among certain ladies of the town in removing unwanted "obstructions".

'But tell me, for I am curious, why did you agree to do my brother's work for him? What kind of hold does he have over you? There must be something. Or are you deluded enough to think that you can make him marry you?'

'Marry that man?' There was no pretence left now between either of them. 'I would rather cut my own throat.'

'What then?'

'You know your own brother, clearly—'

'I am giving you a chance to speak, so I would advise you to do so quickly.'

'He took my child.'

'You have a child?'

'Yes, I have a child, does that surprise you? A little boy. He must be about two years old by now. Your brother took him away from me, sent him to his house in Wiltshire – he said he would be well looked after there, while I was. . .' Frances hesitated. 'While I otherwise engaged. But we both know that he holds him as surety in case I should have been tempted to change my mind.'

'That sounds like my brother. But you? A mother who doesn't even know the age of her own child—'

'How did you find out?' she interrupted him. 'Was it Nan? By the saints, I'll whip the girl so hard she'll wish she had not been born.'

'Nan confirmed what I already suspected, but it was not her. As I have just said, it was my brother's letters that betrayed you. In his second letter to me he informed me, very precisely, how much money Prince Henry has spent on gemstones in the last year, a figure you repeated to me exactly a few nights ago when you were here in this room. How else would you have known it?'

'It is common knowledge that the Prince collects jewels.'

'Perhaps. On its own this would not have been enough to alert me. It was the fact of Celia's friend Annetta coming here to Bishopsgate, and her claims to the diamond, that he could not, by any other means, have known. I have never breathed a word to anyone about it, not to any of my fellow merchants, not even to Parvish, and for good reason. And Celia would hardly have written to him. You were the only other person from whom he could possibly have learnt those things.'

'He wrote to you about the nun?' Frances stared at him. 'He would undo me so?' Then her look of surprise turned to suspicion. 'No, it cannot be, I don't believe you. This is a trick!'

'I assure you it is no trick.'

But Frances was not listening. 'The man has gone mad! Truly, I think he has lost his mind.' She seemed agitated now. 'But no, this is a trick, it must be. Show me where he writes such a thing!'

'This was waiting for me at the Exchange today.' Paul took out the latest letter from Priors Leaze and handed it to her. 'Read it.'

Priors Leaze Manor

The country of Wiltshire, 1611

My brother,

    He's here.

    No one has seen him, but I know that he is here.

    Day and night he torments me. He gives me no rest.

    In the night I hear footsteps around my bed. The sound of a man's breath, as though there were someone lying next to me on the bed. He always was a Trickster.

    The lawyer Wilkes, who has lain in the chamber next to mine these last few nights, looks at me strangely. He says that he has heard it also, but that it is nothing but mice at their nightly play; that they do scratch about behind the wainscot. And then he scuttles off as though he is a-feared to speak more with me. Faugh! The man makes my flesh creep. I swear he has not changed his linen in a sennight. His notary's cloak and tunic are so ingrained with grease and sweat I swear they could stand up on their own. He looks more and more like a beetle every day.

    Last evening I woke in the night. My chamber looks out across the old gardens, across the fields to the woods and the brow of the hill. Looking at them washed in moonlight I had a fancy that the trees in the orchard are like black men, marching. The grass in the old gardens is hard-carpeted with frost, as beautiful and terrible as fairyland. If you gaze out for long enough you can just see the lights, very faint like will-o'-the-wisps, at Starling's Roost.

    I must have stared at it for longer than I thought, was perhaps in some kind of dream, for when I came to, it was to find that my hands had fair frozen to the windowpanes.

But I've seen the lights. I know he's there.
I want to leave, but he won't let me.
Not until I go back there again. Back to Starling's Roost.
And when I do, I fear. . . I fear most terribly what he may do.
If you ever loved me, brother, come at once.
Bring his inamorata.
And let her bring the diamond.
There must be something that he wants.

THIRTY-ONE

Paul

Bishopsgate.

FRANCES LET THE LETTER drop from her hand. 'Tricksters, beetles, will-o'-the-wisps...' She seemed genuinely shaken. 'Sweet Jesus – the man is quite unhinged. What does it mean? What is it of which he is so afraid?'

'Never mind what it means, that is no concern of yours. He writes here: *Bring his* inamorata. *And let her bring the diamond.* How does he know that the *Signora* has taken possession of the stone, if not through you?'

Frances stood up again, and went over to the fireplace. She rested her forehead against the stone overmantel. For a long time she said nothing. Then, finally, she began to speak.

'I was to tell him everything, everything I could possibly find out about the diamond. Whether you kept it here at Bishopsgate, or in some other place; what was its value; its size and character; whether you were like to sell, and if so to whom. Whether there even *was* a diamond, or whether it was just a story put about to add to the lustre of your reputation.

'When he heard the rumours that you would not sell, he did not believe them. I was charged to see it with my own eyes – but not steal it – I swear—'

'And then?'

'His letters became strange, like the one you have just showed me. He no longer mentioned the diamond, but raved about I knew not what: about an old man and a herd of milk-white horses. He seemed afraid, afraid for his very life. And then the letters stopped, and I didn't know what to do.

'I knew that letters from him were still arriving here for you. I hoped that they might tell me, at the very least, when I could expect his return out of Wiltshire, whether he planned to come here to Bishopsgate, or go straight to Richmond, to the Queen's Masque—'

'The Queen's Masque! What has that to do with all this?'

'It has everything to do with it,' she replied. 'Can you not divine it?'

'Strange to tell, but no, I can't; I am sure you will enlighten me.'

'From our conversations I was soon persuaded that you would not by any ordinary means sell the diamond. I wrote him that in my opinion you would never part with it, unless. . .'

'Unless?'

'Unless your hand were to be forced by some great authority.'

'And how did he – did you – think to bring this about, this "great authority", whatever that may be?'

'There was only one person, or people, who might make you change your mind if you, or your wife, were to come to the attention of either of their Majesties, I knew you would not – could not – long refuse.'

'Oh rare!' He almost laughed. 'And, pray tell, how were you going to do that? You, a woman of no family, and of only the most uncertain reputation. And I – I am a plain merchant, for all my fortune. My wife is the daughter of a sea captain. No man in his right mind with connections at Court would countenance us getting the entrée.'

'That is as may be, but his wife might.'

'His wife?'

'There is much talk of the King's jewels, and of his son, Prince Henry's. But it might interest you to know that Her Majesty the Queen is also a great collector of gemstones. I knew that it could not be long before news of the diamond reached her.' She gave a faint smile. 'It's true that I am a woman with nothing, no family, no connections, but I know what human nature is. All this time I have had only one real weapon in my armoury—'

'And what was that?'

'Curiosity.'

'Curiosity?'

'Yes, curiosity; the boundless curiosity of women.' She smiled when she saw the look on his face. 'Ah, I see you do begin to catch on at last. Yes, all those great ladies who came to visit; all those great ladies, I might add, with connections at Court. It was only a matter of time before their doings reached the ears of the Queen. Your wife, sir, whether you like it or not, is become a great curiosity.'

'And it is you who have made her so. You have trespassed, in every way, on her kindness and trust—'

'Yes, I made her so,' she interrupted him fiercely, 'but it did not take much. Come, you have only to think on it: a young woman captured by corsairs and sold into slavery, who resided many years in the harem of the Great Turk, who even became his concubine, or so it is widely believed. And when she was at last ransomed comes home to England in possession of the biggest diamond the world has ever seen. And let us not forget the trifling matter of the mermaid baby she bore. And, oh, by the by,' she added, 'how your brother Ralph did laugh when he discovered that it had been none other than Parvish's agent chasing it for his collection.

'In short, sir, no traveller's tale, no chapbook fantasy, has ever been bettered, only this one has the very great merit of being true. It was but the thing of a moment to get those great ladies to come here to look at her. No elephant, no long-necked giraffe, no ivory-horned unicorn in the Great Turk's menagerie could have excited their attention more. There were some, it's true, who did scruple a little at first, whether they should be so condescending as to visit a mere merchant's wife, but I knew that once one came, the others would surely follow. Although I confess even I was somewhat surprised by their alacrity. Fashion, it seems, knows no scruples.

'Her Majesty would never come here to Bishopsgate, but it would be well within her power to issue you with an invitation to the masque, as it has so proved.'

'A most ingenious plan,' Paul conceded. 'But to what purport? To have us brought to Court, or to the Queen's Masque, as curiosities, and then what? To make me sell the stone to their Majesties—'

'Not sell, give.'

'And I thought my brother wanted it all for himself.'

'So ask yourself *why* he wanted it,' Frances said, impatient now. 'To gloat over it in solitude, like a dragon in his lair? To adorn the neck and breasts of some fair mistress? Not he. Your brother Ralph's only purpose is his own advancement in the world. His ends are not served by keeping his treasures out of view. His desire is for glory, for show, for the lustre of his good name, for honours, titles, who knows, even a position at court—'

Paul crowed. 'A position at court? I have heard everything now. My brother deludes himself if he thinks that would ever come about.'

'Stranger things have happened.'

'Very well, let us suppose for a moment that I had been persuaded to give the stone to their Majesties, then the honour would have been all mine; and that, in my dear brother's view, I know is something devoutly to be avoided.'

'But not if he were the one who was seen to bring it about,' she countered. 'Consider this: if, by his machinations, your brother could make it seem that he had been the one who persuaded you, for the great love and devotion he bears their Majesties, when it was well known that you would never part with it, his place in your story is assured. You know your own brother. You know very well how he can lie and twist and spin the facts to suit himself. And not all of it would be lies. He could, with perfect truth, claim that the stone was in his family. Whatever your fortunes, your reputation, they would, like the comet's tail, pull his behind you.'

'And you would use Celia so? Use her to serve your own ambitions, or his, knowing, as you surely did, that her mind was still so very delicate?'

'Oh, save me your sermons! You! You, didn't stop me; you encouraged me even. It was all done in plain view. You made it so very easy for me that I often wondered whether in fact you had not guessed at my purpose all along.'

The barb hit home.

'I thought you were helping her, helping her to find her way in her new life. . .' he began, but Frances was not listening.

'I even wrote to your brother about it,' she went on, 'but I soon realised that you did not. That you were in fact quite blind to everything that was going on under your very nose. Men are such very simple creatures. And you, sir, the great Merchant Pindar, who gives himself such airs, with his books and his pictures and his collections of porcelain, you are just the same as all men.' She had walked over to him as she was speaking, and now put her face up to his, so that he could feel her breath against his cheek, smell her sweat. 'Not thinking with your brain,' she whispered, trailing her hand up his thigh and between his legs, 'but with this thing.' Her hand closed around him, 'The worm that lies between your legs.'

He gripped her wrist and twisted it, and was pleased to see her flinch with pain as he pushed her away, but even as he did so Ralph's mocking words came back to him.

My friends tell me my good sister, your wife Celia, is much visited by ladies of the Court. Chapeau, *brother. I confess I did smile a little to hear that. Who cares if they do dine out upon her notoriety.*

'Your brother always thought your marriage to Celia was a *mésalliance*. I knew better, I knew how he could use it to his own advantage—'

'Quiet!'

'No, you asked me to speak and so I shall.'

Whatever power Frances may have had over Paul was now slowly draining away, and the loss of it made her reckless. She no longer cared what she said.

'Your wife is a most unhappy lady.'

'You know nothing about my wife—'

Frances held her ground. 'You are mistaken. I know a great deal. I know that you do not lie with her—'

'Shut your mouth, before I strike you.'

'How much of a fool are you, Merchant Pindar? Your wife is a most unhappy lady and your entire household knows it.' She watched the second barb go in, a look of satisfaction on her face. 'They hear her crying at night – oh yes, you look stricken now, and well you might. You keep her here like a little dog, a little dog on a silken cushion. I do believe that Quirkus has a better life than she.'

'My wife is not well.'

'There is nothing wrong with your wife!'

Frances was now holding her wrist with her other hand as if it pained her.

'Why I do believe you have broken my wrist,' she said with a small laugh. 'Ah, you look so coldly upon me, sir, you should not. Women such as I, who find ourselves all alone in the world, we must shift for ourselves, and in any way we can. We cannot be in the world as you men can; we must work in the dark. We do these things because we must, or poverty and destitution will surely follow.' She put her hand to her face. 'And I am no longer young. . . So what now, Paul?' She turned to him, her whole demeanour softened. 'What is to become of me?'

The fire crackled in the silent room. When he did not answer she seemed to collect herself again.

'But so it is: you have found me out, and I have nothing left to lose. There is a strange power in that, is there not?

'So let me tell you this. You and I, sir, you and I together could have been something, had we but world enough and time. You know I speak the truth. We still could.' And when her gaze met his, it seemed to Paul that in her eyes was an expression a thousand ages old, 'If you would still have me? I have never met a man before. . . who was quite like you.'

And for a moment he almost believed her.

Brother,

I go out every day now to Starling's Roost to look for him, but still the Trickster hides.

In a few weeks it will be Christmas. The frosts have come in earnest now. The first of the snows fell yesterday, no more than a powdering across the brow of the hills and over the tips of the trees, but the air smells of it, sharp and sweet. Inside the forest, when the sun shines, it is like a blue glade, so beautiful I can scarce tear myself away.

Both our steward Pitton and my man Chambers have tried to stay me from going back there, but I pay them no heed. Some days ago I fell from my horse (the creature took fright at something hidden in the trees, and when I tried to force it on, it reared up and bolted for home). I was not hurt, but I find that now I am obliged to walk here each day. It seems that it is not only the people who are infected with the fear of this place, but beasts too.

To them it must seem like a kind of madness that I return here. They say nothing – for I do believe that they are as fearful of me as they are of the place itself – but even I can see that they are thinking it. They have heard the old stories about the ancient burial grounds at the top of the hill, and sprit folk who live beneath it. Do you remember the old tales, brother? The tales our old nurse told us, about the spirit huntsmen on milk-white horses who on moonlit nights chased their phantom prey across the brow of the hill. The tales of how if you listen carefully you can hear the tiny hulloah of their phantom horns winding down the old holloway they call the Drover's Path; and the lonely cry of their hounds, and the beat of ghostly hooves.

Or the tales of Old Pitton, the blind man, the gransire of our present steward who they said was the last man known to have walked the length of the Drover's Path, and was bewitched there and his eyes turned to jelly. Christos, *brother*, how many tales were there! How many years since I thought of this? I swear had quite forgotten it all, until now.

But I was compelled to return. Just before I fell from my horse I thought I saw something hidden in a copse of trees just behind the burnt-out house. The fall winded me, and I hit my head, but I broke no bones, thank the Lord, and when I had recovered myself and could stand again, although somewhat weak and winded, I went to try to seek out what it was that had frightened the horse. And sure enough when I came to the place again, I found it.

Something black and white. The body of a dog. But not just any dog, brother, but old Robin, John Carew's dog.

I must have hit my head harder than I thought for I don't remember how I returned to the manor that night, and how I found my way the Lord only knows, for it was fully dark by the time I came back.

They were out looking for me with tapers. They tell me I was still carrying the dog; had carried it in my arms all that way.

Only a small dog, but heavy as a sack of stones.

I was in a daze, and hardly knew myself, but I could hear their voices.

'Look, it's Master Ralph come home.' – 'He's found old Robin.' – 'Look, he's found the dog.' The people clustered round me, but seemed afraid to come too close, even though it seemed to me then that their faces did glow as red as devils in the torchlight. And from their eyes I knew how I must have looked, with mud spattered across my face, and my beard matted, my clothes torn; I believe I must have been half-dead with cold. And it was as if I had never properly seen them before. And I remember thinking, faugh! I never knew there was so much ugliness in our people, their winter faces gaunt, with their bent backs and their crooked limbs and wall eyes, but at the same time they were as familiar to me as my own face in a glass, and there was a kind of comfort in that. I think I may even have made a move towards them; perhaps it was on my lips to ask for help, I don't remember. But not one them made a move to succour me.

Then there came another whisper through the crowd, and I heard the voices behind, the voices of the women whispering among themselves. 'See, it's the Master!' – 'It is the old man, God save us.' – 'Old man Pindar.'

And a hush fell upon them. And then slowly the crowd parted. And there, to all our amazements, was our father standing in the doorway, like Lazarus himself risen from the dead. And for a moment I stood there, the dead dog still in my arms, and all was silent around me. And then I took a step towards him, and for one wild moment I had it in my head that he had come to embrace me, but instead I saw him raise his right arm to me, in which he had his walking stick, and tremblingly strike me a blow – and even though his blow had no more force in it than a hollow reed from the riverbank, I found myself cast down, falling to my knees at his feet, bowing my head while he rained down blows upon my head, my neck, my shoulders.

'What have you done?' I heard his voice, gasping for breath. 'What have you done! What have you done to my boy!'

THIRTY-TWO

Carew

*The Eve of the Feast Day of St Thomas the Apostle, 21st day
of December, 1611. Events occurring at Priors Leaze Manor
in the country of Wiltshire.*

J OHN CAREW WAKES UP suddenly in the dead of
night, realising that he does not know how long he
had been asleep.

These days he seems to spend a great deal of his time
asleep; sometimes he thinks it might be whole days altogether, although he is never entirely sure.

Time is confused.

When he is not asleep he finds himself drifting through
the owl-dark house in a dreamlike hinterland, somewhere
between waking and sleeping. Sometimes he finds himself
looking down at the slumbering Ralph; at other times he
is with his mother again. Carew can see her quite clearly
now, lying in the old man's arms. She is singing to him,
her head crowned with bindweed like a forest queen.

Since the last time Ralph went to Starling's Roost,
and came back with the dead dog, he has barely ventured
from this room. His beard is unkempt now; his linen sour.
The suit of fair green velvet, that he wore when he first
arrived, lies trampled on the floor in a corner, splattered
with mud and torn by briars. There is no one left at the

manor now to help him. His man Chambers is long gone; the lawyer Wilkes, too. The two serving girls, Anne and Alice, have returned to their own homes, taking the child with them. They come each day to put food on the kitchen doorstep, but not for love nor money will they ever again venture inside the house.

The change in their master frightens, but does not surprise them. Master Ralph has been to the Drover's Path, so they know a bewitchment has taken place.

Left all alone, Ralph seems quite unable to help himself. He has locked himself in his room, and spends long hours in the damp and loveless chamber at the top of the house, scribbling letters that no one will now receive. His desk is a makeshift thing, a table that he found in the kitchens, one broken leg propped up with books; his ink is watery. When Carew creeps up behind him to look over his shoulder, he sees with satisfaction that Ralph's writing is almost illegible now, the letters are large and spidery, the lines slope crazily down the page. There is no fire. The room is cold as the grave.

On the coldest nights a sprinkling of frost forms on the rotted remains of the old Turkey carpet; the insides of the windowpanes are pewtered with ice. The only candles left in the storeroom are made from the meanest country tallow and the room stinks like an alehouse, of smoke and singeing fat.

Ralph mutters and moans in his sleep; his dreams are unquiet, as well they might be. Of what does he dream? Does he see himself dressed in fine velvets again, holding the priceless diamond that will never now be his? Or, as seems most likely, does he dream of the night all those years ago when he set fire to Starling's Roost, burning Carew's mother in her bed? Does he still hear her screams?

Ralph has wedged a chair up against the door, but these days none of these things are an impediment to Carew. Sometimes, to amuse himself, he runs his fingers through Ralph's hair, or blows out his candle, or breathes in his ear and pinches him beneath his nightshirt, and then he can make him start up with terror in the dark. But of late he has found that he is growing bored with this game, has lost his taste for it.

There are times when he thinks that Ralph can almost see him; but dimly, as through a glass darkly.

And so now, venturing out of the shadows at last, he stands there, in full view, one hand on his hip. After all these years, Carew finally gets what he has come for. The old score is settled. There is nothing Ralph can do to touch him now.

Now, when he sees him at last, the fat man gives a great cry, and runs to the corner of the room.

'What do you want? What do you want, boy?' His voice is hoarse. 'Get you away from me, Trickster!'

Ralph runs to the door, but he can't get out, so he crouches instead in a corner, his back against the wainscoting. His eyes are bloodshot and staring, the eyes of someone who cannot sleep. His hair, long and greasy, stands up like a lunatic's upon the crown of his head.

'It wasn't me,' Ralph pleads. 'It wasn't me, I swear it.' His eyes are glassy and staring. 'I broke the window, it's true. I threw the first stone, and shouted at them to throw their torches in. How was I to know they would follow me? I was only a boy.' He hides his head in his hands. 'I was only a boy like you.'

'And now they are going to say that it was me who killed you, too, but it wasn't me, I swear. I found your body when I found the dog, it's true.' His voice turns shrill. 'But it wasn't me who killed you. You must have been there some time – the starlings had pecked out your eyes – but I knew it was you, all the same. I'd know you anywhere.'

Ralph cannot leave Priors Leaze before Carew does, that much they both know. Perhaps he never will. Perhaps Ralph will die right here, at the old place, the house he planned to pull down around his father's ears to make way for a new one, the great modern mansion with waterworks and grottos and who knows what other kickshaws and folderols the French *ingenieur*, Salomon de Caus, could devise.

For what are any of these things without love? And who will love Ralph now? Who has ever loved him? He sits on the floor, shivering in his own filth, mouthing something that Carew cannot quite catch. He starts with terror at a dead beetle on the floor as though it were the devil himself. No lunatic in Bedlam could be more sorry. A younger, more heartless Carew would have laughed heartily and thought it a merry sight – but not now.

Ralph, his boyhood companion, and his tormentor. Seeing him like this, John Carew can almost pity him. And with this thought it is as though something breaks open inside him. And he knows that his work here is nearly done.

Perhaps, he thinks to himself, perhaps it's time to go?

But there is one thing that Carew is certain of: he – Carew – will not leave before Annetta comes. More than anything he wants to see his woman again. Every day, as the rest of the world grows dim and he more insubstantial, he sees her more clearly. He knows she is coming. He feels her very close. Sometimes he can feel her standing beside him. Each time he sees her she grows more beautiful: he sees the rose of her cheeks, the proud curve of her nose, the exquisite mole on her upper lip.

'Carew, *mi amore*, put it down now,' she says to him, and the very sound of her voice makes him want to weep. 'Come, my darling love, put your burden down.'

And he knows that she loves him, has always loved him, and is coming for him. And the thought is like balm to his sorry soul.

And now the dogs are barking. Their hulloahing, heralding the approach of strangers, carries far and sharp in the thin winter dusk.

In the barn where he is still locked, Moocher hears it. Half-starved and half-frozen, he raises his weary head, giving thanks to God that deliverance is on hand. In the parlour, old man Pindar, his life seeping slowly from him, harkens it too. Mumbling prayers for his own passing – he reaches with a trembling hand and what little strength is left in him for his dog's head to quiet it. Carew, gazing out from an upstairs window, can just make out the massy form of horses and a carriage approaching, its lanterns shining like two pinpricks of light in the distance. There is a sprinkling of snow on the ground, and although there is not so much as to have blocked the road, Carew knows very well what a perilous journey this was to have undertaken at this time of year, and what they have risked to come for him.

Paul, Celia and Annetta – they have arrived just in time. On the horizon only a crack of light remains in the violet dusk. Fat flakes have begun to fall, the first of the winter snows. Up the narrow valley behind the house a yellow moon is rising. The trees, stripped of all their leaves, raise their spectral fingers over the Drover's Path.

And then the carriage stops with a jolt, lists to one side. Carew can hear the shouts of the coachman as the wheels slide uselessly in the muddy slush. Three figures emerge wrapped in cloaks: a man and two women. The women are first, they run stumbling towards the house, the man shouts after them, but they pay him no heed.

Annetta has come for him, so he knows it is time to go. He looks around him. There is only one thing that remains for him to do.

The old man sits in his chair by the fire, just as he always did. He is awake, and perfectly alert. His gaze is directed towards the door. Something about his demeanour gives Carew the odd notion that he has been expecting him. He has his hand on his dog's head; the lurcher looks up at Carew as he comes in, his hackles bristling. The old man tightens his grip upon the dog's neck.

'Stay!' Carew can see his fingers working at the fur on the dog's neck, trying to reassure it. If he himself were afraid he gives no sign of. 'My good dog, stay.'

Carew opens his mouth to say something, but the words seemed to have become lodged in his throat. For a moment the two gaze at one another across the fire-lit room.

It is the old man who speaks first.

'Is it time?'

Carew stares back at him. For the moment he has no words. Standing there, on the threshold of the room, he feels, for a brief moment, as though no time has passed at all, and he is twelve years old again.

'Is it time?' Carew repeats foolishly. 'Time for what, sir?'

'Have you come for me?'

Does he think he is a servant, come to take him to his bed? When John Carew, still perplexed, does not reply immediately, the old man adds, 'I have made my peace with the Lord, and I am quite prepared.'

There is a rushing sensation in Carew's ears. He tries to speak, but it is a moment before he manages to get the words out. 'I have not come to take you anywhere.'

Carew tries to take a few more paces into the room, but his legs are turned to stone. Eventually he takes a step, stands awkwardly with his cap twisting in his hands.

'Do you. . . do you not know me, sir?'

'Yes, I know you,' The old man's eyes, cloudy with age, are looking up at him. 'I'd know you anywhere.'

If the old man is frightened he gives no sign.

'Can you not come closer? My eyes. . . not so good now. I'd like to see you, John, just one last time.'

Carew can see his fingers still working at the dog's collar, gentling him. But when Carew takes a pace forward, the dog curls its lip and lets out another low growl.

'Hush, Chase,' the old man says to the dog. 'Don't be a-feard; he doesn't know you as I do.'

Carew takes two paces more. For a moment he has the odd idea that he is seeing a young man, a man no older than himself, staring out at him from the carapace of someone now very old. His heart turns over in his chest.

'I wondered when you'd come.'

Carew walks slowly across the floor until he is standing at the old man's chair. His whole body feels light, as though he is floating across the room.

'Why did you run away? You were only a lad.' A tear runs down the old man's cheek. 'They told me you were dead.'

Is that what you thought? Is that what they told you?

'What's this, John? Come now, why do you kneel?' There is a tremor, very slight, in the old man's voice. 'Come, you are a big boy now – you must be twelve years old at least – why do hide your face?'

Carew opens his mouth to say something, but there are no words that can ever say what he feels. He feels as though his heart must break.

The old man goes on as though he is talking to himself.

'Paul wrote to tell me that he had found you – in London, running wild – brothels, playhouses and I don't know what, half-starved, he said, living on air. He took you with him, as his servant, which was only right.' He nods to himself. 'To Constantinople, then to Venice, with the Company. More trouble than you were worth, he said, always in a fight.' The old man gives a wan smile. 'You always did like to fight. Come now, look at me; let me look at your face.'

But Carew, kneeling at the old man's feet, can only shake his head. He is aware that the old man is reaching down, trying to stroke his head, but if he touches him, he feels nothing: his hand against Carew's head has no more substance than a frail autumn leaf.

'It was a sin. I knew it was a sin—'

What was a sin?

But the old man seems to be talking to himself now, rather than to him,

'—but I confessed it,' he went on. 'I am shrived, in the old way; I've made my peace.'

What was a sin?

'You mean you didn't know? But of course you did.' Shaking his head, the old man smiles down at him. 'You were my sin, John.' He rests his hand gently on Carew's head and his eyes close for the last time.

'I always loved you best, you know.

'My best beloved.

'My son John.'

THIRTY-THREE

Annetta

Events occurring at Priors Leaze Manor in the country of Wiltshire.

I T WAS AT THE White Horse Inn at Marlborough that they finally learnt the truth about John Carew.

His body had been found, half-buried beneath the leaves, in the ruins of an old house in some woods near the manor, one of his own knives between his shoulder blades. He had been dead for many weeks when they found him, as long ago as All Hallows, they thought, or perhaps even before. Despite the cold his body was already rotted away, like a piece of fallen fruit; his eyes pecked out by carrion birds. But the belt with his knives was still there, and a gold chain that he always wore round his neck. They had brought these things to Paul, who stared at them in silence for a long moment, before nodding in recognition.

In the end it had been the lawyer Wilkes who had raised the alarm; not only had he had his concerns about the neglect of the old man, but also he was wary of the fear and disquiet of the people, and their talk of some kind of bewitchment that had taken place, and all kinds of strange happenings at the manor.

Annetta, so exhausted by their journey from London, and nauseated by the swaying of the carriage, had not at first gathered the lawyer's name, only registering a small, sweating man who smelt so powerfully of unwashed linen that she thought she might faint from the stench. His information, or as much of it as she had been able to follow in her dazed state, was mostly dusty talk of wills and covenants and title deeds in which, even if she had been able to follow it properly, she would soon have lost interest. The *signor*'s other brother, she gathered vaguely, was still there, although it seemed that he had fallen from his wits and it was going to take two sheriffs, at the very least, to dislodge him from the upstairs room in which he had locked himself.

Annetta had sat throughout the conversation in mulish silence, not raising her gaze from the table for anyone, not even for *Signor* Pindar himself, and most especially not for this repulsive lawyer person droning on and on, whose robes were the colour of a cockroach, and whose sleeves were fretted with some glistening substance that looked, to her unforgiving gaze, a lot like slug trails.

Occasionally Celia or Paul asked her a question, to which she answered with gruff monosyllables, but mostly what she thought about during this disturbing conversation was of how the inn's lingering odour of mutton and old cabbage was turning her stomach and how right now, that moment, she might very well be willing to give away the Sultan's Blue itself, if only they could have brought her a good honest plate of *gnocchi* with a little meat *ragu* to set it off.

She had been thinking of Suora Angelica's *ragu* and *gnocchi* when they told her that John Carew was dead.

At first she could not seem to register what they were saying at all. She remembered Celia kneeling on the floor next to her, saying the words to her, but she – Annetta – had felt nothing at first. It was not shock, or horror, or even grief that assailed her, at least not at the beginning, but a feeling of something terrible gnawing at her entrails, and a sensation of nausea, such as she remembered having sometimes at the convent when fasting at Lent or as some penance after confession, as though it were her body alone that could register a pain that her mind, as yet, could not.

At least he will never see me like this, she thought. But neither would she ever now feel his arms around her, or hear his voice, or kneel at his feet like a Dorsoduro prostitute begging for love, and she trembled to think of the vast grief that lay ahead of her.

Now, inside the carriage that was taking them to Priors Leaze, her feet were like ice.

The ostlers at the White Horse Inn at Marlborough had laid down a layer of straw on the carriage floor, but already it was so sodden with mud and melted snow that it afforded none of them any protection from the cold. When the winter winds blew, icy draughts seeped through the cracks in the carriage walls.

The journey from Marlborough was so beset with difficulties – the wheels becoming stuck time and again in the icy ruts of the rural road that was hardly fit for a hay cart – that all three of them had lapsed into an exhausted silence. Celia and Paul dozed fitfully or sat staring from the window in a traveller's daze of cold and fatigue.

There was in any case not much to be said.

Paul had placed Carew's knife belt over his knees, and was holding the chain in the palm of his hand, looking at them from time to time as though they were more precious to him than his precious diamond, and she knew that, like hers, his mind was refusing to keep pace with his heart. Neither of them could yet believe that John Carew was dead.

He looked to her like a man sleepwalking.

'He was coming home – after all this time, he was coming home.' Paul stared down at Carew's belt. 'I never really believed. . .' he began, but the words trailed away from him, as though he felt himself suddenly quite unequal to the task of explaining what he had or had not believed. 'After all this time—'

And she had not known what to say to him. *After all this time.* All that hope, all that journeying – and in a boat, too! – and for what? If only she could weep, but she could not. All she felt was a sense of vast emptiness opening up before her.

'I had not known he was your brother,' she managed at last, her voice hoarse with the effort of speaking at all.

'He was my father's natural son, so it was not much talked about, although there must have been many who guessed at it.'

'Yes, I suppose they must. . .'

And she remembered then how when she had first seen Paul, on that morning in Bishopsgate, she had the strange idea that she had met him before; now she realised that it had been something about him that had always reminded her of Carew. How could she not have guessed?

'Did you always know?'

'No, not always. But I remember very well the time I first realised it. Carew ran away from home – he had been in a fight with my brother Ralph – and I hadn't seen him for several years. I looked for him everywhere, all over London, and when I finally found him, in a Southwark stew, at the sign of the Blind Bear if I remember rightly, when I looked at him, I knew immediately. As you will see, his resemblance to my father is quite uncanny.'

'And your brother Ralph?'

'I think Ralph must have guessed it sooner than I. They were much closer in age, and were brought up together. Carew was always my father's favourite, and he made no secret of it. He loved the son as he had loved the mother, for all that she was a simple-minded girl. The great tenderness he showed John was a terrible torment to Ralph, and the source of all the bad blood that came after. I think it seemed to him as though Carew had done nothing to earn my father's love, but always had it; while Ralph, who had tried everything to earn it, never could. All his ambition, all his striving, all the running after wealth and honours, all to make our father love him. But you cannot make love where none exists.

'There was always something... different... about my brother Ralph, as though the humours in him were malignly mixed. He was jealous of John to the point of madness — attacked him once with a knife. I think he would have killed him that day if my father hadn't been there to pull him off. I think he felt that John had stolen his father's love for him, and he could never forgive him for it.'

'Did he hate him then?'

Paul was silent for a long time while he considered this question.

'No, I think Ralph loved him,' he said at last, 'but sometimes, when love cannot find its right expression, it turns sour, and that is a far more terrible thing.'

It was almost nightfall when they reached the old place at last. They could hear the drums already.

Paul sat up. 'Listen, do you hear that?'

'Hear what?'

'Listen—' He leant forward, peered from the carriage window into the dusk. They could see the house now, its dark form looming towards them through the shadows.

'There it is again.'

'Yes, I hear it now.'

The sound – not only drums, but the banging of pots and pans, and the cracking of whips – was audible now to them all. As their carriage drew ever closer, tiny pinpricks of light could be seen, hovering like fireflies around the house.

'What is it?' Celia turned to Paul, 'What's happening? Have they come to greet us?'

Paul hesitated. 'It's a custom in these parts – they call them "rough days" – the people believe that the drumming will drive out evil spirits—'

Suddenly, their carriage listed to one side and came to a halt. Paul swore under his breath. He opened the door and got out, and the two women could hear him talking to the coachman. When he came back he said to Celia, 'You must go quickly now, go into the house and I will talk to them. They will listen to me.'

'I don't understand,' Celia began. 'Who are they? Talk to whom?'

But Paul was in too much of a hurry to explain.

'Just go inside the house and find my father, then take him to the barn. You will be safe there. Don't come out until I say.'

Annetta and Celia found themselves in a decaying hall that smelt of dogs and damp in equal measure. Ribbons of blackened cobwebs hung from the rafters. To one side of the hall was the entrance to a little parlour. Soft yellow light came under the door and a small sound, like a child whimpering softly. The two women approached the door slowly and pushed it open.

An old man was sitting in a chair beside the dying embers of a fire. The source of the whimpering was a dog at his side. The creature was thrusting its nose beneath the old man's arm, which hung down limply at his side.

'Father?' Not wanting to alarm him, Celia spoke to him softly. 'Father, it is I, your daughter Celia.'

When he did not respond, she turned to Annetta. 'He must be sleeping.'

'Then you must wake him,' Annetta replied. And then, anxious suddenly, 'Hurry! I'll watch here.'

She hung back in the doorway while Celia went in. She knelt down at the old man's side.

'Father. . .' She put her hand on his shoulder, but then drew back quickly. 'Dear God—'

'What?'

'I think – I think he – I think he might be. . .' Celia put her hand to the old man's face. 'And yet, he is still warm.'

'Then try him again,' Annetta urged her, 'but be quick, we must be quick. Here, I'll do it. *Signore!*' she called out hoarsely, her voice ringing out unnaturally loud in the deserted room. 'Wake up, *Signore*, we must take you out of here.'

But the old man sat motionless. His eyes and his mouth were open, but his head lolled against the back of the chair. When Celia shook him gently, he listed slowly over to one side.

'*Santissima Madonna*, I know a dead body when I see one.' Running into the room, Annetta pulled Celia to her feet. 'Come, we must go quickly. *Poverino*, it's too late for him now.'

The two women made their way back into the hall. There they paused, listening. Outside the sound of the drums was louder now.

'What does it mean?'

'I don't know.' Celia shivered.

They looked at one another.

'The *Signore* said to go to the barn; we'd best do what he says.'

'But we can't, not yet.'

'Why not?'

'We can't go yet, not without his brother. We must find him and take him with us.'

'Ralph?' Annetta looked at her in exasperation. 'Now you are the one who has fallen from her wits.'

Celia looked over Annetta's shoulder and up into the darkness at the top of the stairs. 'They told us he had locked himself into one of the upstairs chambers. He may still be up there—'

'And you are going to choose *this* moment to get your courage back? *Cazzo*! You sit around moping for weeks on end in that great house of yours, and now this? Oh, this is too much—'

'Don't you want to know what happened to John? He might be the only person who can tell us.'

'Your husband's witless brother? He is not going to tell us anything.' Annetta pulled her arm away. 'I know about mad people – mad people are dangerous people,' she hissed. 'Believe me, we'll all be much safer if he stays locked in his room.'

But Celia was quite decided. 'No, we must find him,' she said, 'here take my arm. If you help me, it won't take us long.'

At the top of the stairs they found themselves in a long dark passageway. A number of rooms led from it. They made their way along it as fast as they could, pushing open the doors one by one and peering inside. But there was nothing and no one to be found. Eventually they came to the very last door. When Celia tried the latch, it pushed up easily, but the door would not open.

They looked at one another.

'He's in here, he must be.'

Celia tried the door again, putting her whole weight behind it this time. It opened a small crack, but would go no further.

'There's something wedged behind here.' She put her eye to the gap and looked inside.

'What can you see?'

'Nothing.'

'Try knocking.'

Celia rapped on the door softly.

There was no reply.

She knocked again, harder this time, but still there was no answer.

'Come, we've done our best, we must go—' Annetta was pulling on her arm.

'Just wait, one more minute—'

'For the love of God, we don't *have* one more minute—'

The drumming, growing ever louder, was now very near. Annetta ran to the window.

'Look, come quickly. I can see lights – and people, many people – gathering outside—'

Celia joined her. Below them was a crowd of people, men and women, their faces glowing red in the torchlight.

'What do they want?' Annetta asked.

'I don't believe their business is with us.'

'You are too trusting, and I think your husband would agree with me. Why else would he have told us to take your father to the barn?' Annetta looked down at the gathered crowd. 'It's not just drums they have, but fire too—'

But Celia was not listening. She banged with her fist on the door again, more urgently this time.

'Sir, will you not come out from there?' she called. 'It is your sister Celia, your brother's wife. I am come to help you.'

She put her ear to the door, and this time she heard, very faintly, a creaking sound: a man's heavy tread upon the floorboards.

'I can hear someone there,' she said to Annetta, and then, through the crack in the door again, 'good sir, won't you come out?'

'Get you away from me, fiend.' Ralph's voice came faintly from behind the door. There was a shuffling sound, as though something heavy were being dragged across a bare floor. Then a fit of coughing. 'Away, away, I want nothing to do with your tricks.'

'Sir, I beg you, this is no trick. On my honour, we are come to help you.'

'I want no help from you,' the wheezing voice replied. 'Get you gone, fiend!'

Just then the drumming ceased abruptly. Through the silence came a sound more ominous still: the sound of a window breaking.

'Quick, we haven't much time. We must think of something to persuade him away from here.'

'But what? What does he want?'

'I don't know what he wants, but I know what he thought Carew wanted. Remember the letters?'

'Yes, but—'

But already Celia had put her mouth to the door again.

'We have brought what you asked for, sir. We have brought Carew's *inamorata*; we have brought the diamond. If you will come out, I will show them to you.'

There was a long silence. More coughing.

'Don't you want to see the diamond?' she repeated. 'I know you do.'

'Why should I believe you?' a voice came eventually. 'The fiend always lies.'

'I am not the fiend, I am your friend. Open the door and I will show it to you.' Celia turned to Annetta. 'What are you waiting for? Get it out. When he opens the door we must have something to show him if we are to bring him away with us.'

'Get what out?'

'The diamond, of course.'

'Have you lost your mind? You think I have brought the *diamond* with me—?'

'Oh, we don't have time for this! Of course you have it with you. You, Annetta, who stitched ever last *piastre* she ever had into her undergarments in case one of the *cariye* should try to get her hands on it. Paul said you refused to trust it either to his strongbox or the cabinet, so I know perfectly well you keep it on your person somewhere. Come, out with it now.' She began to pat Annetta all over her body. 'Where do you keep it?' She was almost shouting now. 'In your bodice, you chemise, your garter? Come on, where? And *rapido*—'

There was no use arguing.

'*Madonna!*' Annetta pulled up her skirts and took out a little bag, which had been tied beneath them, and tipped out the stone. She held it out to Celia, but Celia shook her head.

'No, it must be you who shows him. Go, put it up to the door so he can see.'

'Oh, very well.' Annetta went up to the crack in the door, and held out the diamond on her outstretched palm.

'See, sir, the Sultan's Blue. Open the door and you can hold it yourself.'

They waited for what seemed like a long time. And then, just when Annetta had given up hope, she heard the sound of something heavy being pushed back from the door, and a key turned in the lock.

It opened at last. And a man stood before them, breathing heavily from his exertions.

He was so like him it almost took her breath away. And for that split second all Annetta could think was, *My God, it's John Carew!* But no sooner had her heart begun its useless bound of joy than the diamond was knocked violently from her hand as Ralph seized her by the wrist, pulling her into the room with such wild strength that she seemed almost to fly from one end of it to the other, falling to her knees on the floor by the window.

He slammed the door shut behind her and turned the key, locking them both inside.

THIRTY-FOUR

Annetta

*Events occurring at Priors Leaze Manor in the country
of Wiltshire.*

S HE WOULD HAVE KNOWN Ralph as Carew's
brother anywhere, and yet in the next moment she
found herself thinking, there were no two people in the
world who could possibly have been less alike.

Ralph Pindar must have been a big man once. Now his
flesh hung from him. His clothes, such as they had once
been, had all but rotted away. He wore no stockings and
his skinny shanks stuck out from beneath a pair of filthy
breeches, giving him the air of some half-starved desert
saint. His beard, beneath his drooping jowls, was long
and ill kempt, his skin grey. No Bedlam beggar could
have presented a more sorry sight. She wanted to cry out,
Don't hurt me please, but fear choked her. Annetta shrank
away from him as far as she could, into a far corner of
the room.

The room was cold as the grave. Against the door was
the old truckle bed that he had used to wedge it shut;
next to it an earthenware crock half-filled with water. In
one corner were some stubs of candles arranged in a half
circle, and now, instead of rushing at her to beat or stran-
gle her, as she half feared he might, he scuttled back to

a spot inside the circle and sat there trembling, his back hard against the wall.

The room stank as powerfully of human ordure as any open latrine on the Giudecca.

'There you are,' he said in a hoarse voice, 'I've got you what you wanted.'

When Annetta said nothing to this, he repeated his words, 'I have got what you wanted: the girl and the diamond. Are you not content?'

'I don't understand—'

'Shut your mouth, I'm not talking to you!'

His words alone were like a violence to her.

It was a few moments before she had the courage to speak again.

'Then. . . to whom. . . do you speak?' She could feel a constriction in her chest; fear gripped her so tightly she could hardly get the words out.

'To him, of course,' Ralph growled, pointing a grimy finger into the empty shadows in another corner of the room.

Annetta looked where he was pointing, but all she could see was an old *po*. Piles of human faeces, where Ralph had relieved himself over many days, spilled over its sides on to the wooden floorboards. Beside it was the Sultan's Blue.

Annetta looked away quickly, to hide what she had seen.

'There's no one there.'

'*Ha*! He's there, a-right. He's always there; I try to shut him out but he gets in anyway. *Ho*, there, Trickster! Show yourself – I know you are there! It's your lady love come to find you, much good may it do her.'

'You are mistaken. . . there is no one there.'

'That's what you say,' Ralph gave another loud cackle. 'He's come to torment me – come to murder me in my bed,

416

just as it was done to him, but I'll get the better of him, you'll see. I won't sleep, I won't sleep, so I won't – then he can't – haven't slept for days. Can't sleep for lice anyway.' He began to scratch violently at his head with both hands.

When he had finished scratching he sucked at his fingernails like a starving man.

'I eat them, you know, the lice. I ate Wilkes too,' he added. 'He wouldn't sign the papers, so serve him right, I say.'

From somewhere in the house below them, Annetta could hear the sound of more glass shattering.

'Who killed John Carew? Was it you?'

'Me? No!' Ralph put his hand up and covered his eyes, and for a moment she thought that he was weeping. 'I found him, in the woods. I couldn't tell anyone, how could I? Everyone would have thought it was me, but it wasn't, I swear—'

'Then who?'

'The old man, of course, the poacher.'

'Poacher?'

'The old man in the barn.' Ralph wiped his eyes fiercely on one filthy sleeve. 'Moocher.'

'Moocher?'

'You heard me. The old vagabond murdered him weeks ago on the Drover's Path, for this.' He reached down on to the floor behind him and picked something up which he now flung at her.

A small soft object fell at her side. Annetta picked it up. It was her old embroidered pocket from the House of Felicity.

So he had kept it. All this time, he had treasured something of hers. So perhaps he really had loved her, after all this time. Her own words came back to her. *Live*, she had begged him, *live, so that I will have something to live for*. But now he was dead, what did she have to live for? And as her numbness began to fade, she realised that it was not grief she had begun to feel at his loss, but anger at her own.

What'll I do? What'll I do, now you've left me here, left me on my own?

But there was no time for weeping now. Instead, she heard the sound of more glass breaking. Still huddled against the wall, Annetta looked over at Ralph.

'How do I know? How do I know it was the vagabond who killed him and not you?'

'Because he told me so – I made him. He denied it at first, of course, but I beat it out of him, beat him till he confessed.'

On the other side of the locked door Annetta could hear renewed banging, and the sound of voices, Paul's now as well as Celia's, but they sounded muffled and far away, and she knew that she was now as far from their help as if she had been floating away from them on a bark down the Bosphorus.

And then the voices stopped. In their place there came a strong smell of smoke. She turned to Ralph with a new sense of urgency.

'We must go from here. Sir, I beg you, stop this nonsense now.'

'Go?' he whimpered, rocking himself from side to side. 'Go where?' A muffled sound was coming from him, she could not tell whether he was laughing or crying, perhaps both. 'You think to go from here, madam? Never! The fiend won't let you—'

The smell of burning was unmistakable now, stronger than before. 'But we must go,' she urged him. 'There is a fire, can you not smell it? If we delay any longer it will be too late.'

Ralph was still rocking himself from side to side. 'You think I don't know him by now? He won't let us go, not now.'

But Annetta had heard enough of his rantings. 'You mad old fool, then why don't you ask him?'

'Oh, I have, I have,' Ralph said. 'Look,' he shrieked, pointing to the corner, 'he shakes his head – the fiend shakes his head, can you not see him? The girl and the diamond. The girl and the diamond. He'll never let you go now.'

A wisp of smoke curled under the door and into the room. *John, John, what'll I do? What'll I do?* She was almost sobbing with fear.

Go now, just stand up and go – it was as though she could hear Carew's answering voice in her ear – *For the love of God, woman, just pick up the diamond and go!*

And so Annetta stood up. She went over to the filthy *po*, reached down, and picked up the diamond from the floor. Then she walked over to the door. But no sooner had she reached for the key in the lock than she heard the sound of Ralph staggering to his feet behind her, and she knew he was coming for her.

Quickly, quickly. . .

But the thought of Ralph behind her, the thought of him seizing her as before, filled her with panic, and her panic made her clumsy. She could not get the key to turn! It was an old key, and rusty, and all her strength had drained from her.

Quickly, quickly now! It was as if Carew himself was urging her on.

She was rattling the key in the lock with both hands, but still it would not turn. There came a great bellow as Ralph came lunging at her from behind, and just as she felt his hands on her, the key turned at last and together they fell out of the room, into the corridor, and into a broiling, choking wall of smoke and heat.

In their fall Ralph loosened his grip and Annetta pulled herself free. Thank God! Still holding the Sultan's Blue, she rolled away from him and began to scramble on her hands and knees down the corridor and away from the smoke. To no avail. Almost immediately she came to a dead end. There was nothing for it but to go back again; coughing and choking on the smoke, she flattened herself against the floor and crawled back in the direction from which she had come.

Smoke was now billowing towards her from the stairs. She could not see any flames, but she knew the fire must be somewhere very close because she could hear a roaring sound, like a tempest wind, coming from she knew not where. She was trapped. There was only one place to go. She went back to the room that she had just left and somehow dragged herself inside and slammed the door.

But even this room was now full of smoke. Her eyes were streaming so profusely she could hardly see. Somehow she managed to crawl to the window. When the rusty catch would not open, she put her arm up and smashed the glass with her elbow.

A blast of winter air almost blew her off her feet, but she gripped the window frame with both hands and managed to stay upright. Below her she could see a crowd of people looking up at the burning house.

And in among them were Paul and Celia. They were shouting something to her, but the sound of their voices was obliterated by the roar of the fire. They were waving their hands, making signs for her to jump. And she knew that it was her only chance. Already the heat was so intense that she could feel it burning into her skin; her face and her hands were scalding as though she herself were about to burst into flame.

Annetta looked down and saw that already sparks had caught at the hem of her dress. All this while she had been holding the diamond in her hand; now she raised her arm, and threw it out the window as hard as she could.

She must jump, she must: it was her only chance. Annetta put her head through the window and began to climb out. But someone was behind her pulling her back. There was a man standing behind her. She could feel his hands on her, drawing her back into the room. She kicked out at him as hard as she could. Struggling with all her might, she fought him away.

Then she was putting her leg over the window frame, but her skirts got in the way, and she fell back again. Not only her dress but her hair was now aflame. There was a stinking smell of singeing flesh and she knew it must be her own.

And as she fell back into the room there was a great noise, a blast greater than any anything she had ever heard before, and a flash of light as the door behind her caved in and a great ball of fire roared into the room.

And his hands were on her, wrapped around her, steadying her and holding her fast.

Put it down, my love, John Carew said, *my most darling love, you can put it down now.*

And after the noise there came silence.

And she was standing at the top of an old holloway, looking down. Overhead the branches of the trees grew thickly. Below her were shadows and an unseen land. She knew had been here before, in a dream perhaps, but she could not remember when.

She walked slowly down along its length and, after some time, came to a place like an orchard. It was spring and the apple trees were in bloom. Through the trees blue-bells spread out as far as the eye could see.

He came walking slowly towards her through the blue furze, and when she saw him she sank to her knees and wept.

'Why do you cover your face?' he asked when he reached her at last.

'I am old,' she said. 'What will you want with me now, John Carew, now that I am old and grey?'

'You are beautiful,' he said. 'Even more beautiful than I remember.'

'Well, you would say that, wouldn't you, John Carew,' she said.

'Why would I say that if it were not true?'

'You? What do you know about true?' she said. 'You, the *monachino*, the seducer of nuns. You'll say anything to get what you want – I know the likes of you—'

'Stand up,' he commanded.

'What, already?' she said. 'Don't think you can tell me what to do—'

'For the love of God, come here, woman,' he said, and she could hear the smile in his voice. 'Please?'

And so she did. And all around them the petals fell, softly on to the ground below.

THIRTY-FIVE

Paul and Celia

Christmas Eve, 1611. Bishopsgate.

SOMETIME BEFORE MIDNIGHT, TWO shadowy figures made their way into the gardens. Slowly they walked together across the lawns, past the grotto, to the orchard at the very far end of the grounds. One of them, helping herself along with the aid of a stick, held a stainless steel casket in one hand; the other, a torch and a garden spade.

In the orchard they stopped by one of the newly planted saplings.

'Here?'

'Yes, beneath this plum tree. There are seven in the row and this is the middle one. I counted them this morning. That way we won't forget where we have buried it.'

Paul handed the torch to Celia and began to dig. Although the ground was hard with frost it did not take him long to dig a hole wide enough and deep enough for the casket to fit inside. Celia leant down and placed it in the ground. Swiftly, he shovelled the earth back over the hole and stamped it down.

Together they stood for a few moments looking at the beaten ground beneath which the Sultan's Blue now lay buried.

'Will we leave it there for ever?'

'No, not for ever.'

'Until when then?'

'I suppose... until such a time as someone needs it. Until there is some just cause...We'll know when the time is right. Until then, that is where it stays. We are agreed?'

'Yes.'

Seeing her shiver in the cold night, Paul put his arm around her shoulders and drew her to him.

'Paul?'

'Yes, my sweet?'

'Do you think any of us have ever really understood?'

'Understood the diamond's powers? I think Annetta was the one who came closest to it. I remember her saying that no one would ever know what the diamond's properties are, except that it has them. She believed that is was just as likely to bring *mala sfortuna* to the person who has it as its opposite: prosperity, or riches, or love. Or perhaps it just mixes them all up together. What about you, what do you think?'

Celia thought for a moment. 'You don't think...' She hesitated, '...it could be just a stone?'

Paul laughed. 'Like this one, you mean?' He took the heart-shaped pebble from his pocket.

'Yes, exactly like that one,' she said, laughing with him. 'Only bigger.'

'Who can say?' Paul pressed the earth down again with the toe of his boot. 'And now that it's buried, I hope it won't matter now.'

'What I mean is,' she added, 'that our fate is in our own hands. Or in the hands of God. Not with any stone.'

For a moment they stood together looking up at the stars.

'Look, there is the North Star.'

'And there Aldebaran—'

'And there, look, the belt of Orion—'

In the distance, somewhere far away towards Finsbury Fields, a dog barked. Closer to them, a church bell struck midnight.

'Listen,' Celia said. 'The bell of St Botolph's. It's Christmas Day.'

'So it is.' He kissed her tenderly. 'You are getting cold, wife. Come, let's go in.'

Celia turned towards the house. In the windows, the lights were blazing.

'Yes,' she said, putting her hand in his. 'Let us go in. Let us go home.'

1643. Bishopsgate.

A N OLD MAN STANDS alone in a darkening room. In these uncertain times, it has been a more than usually irksome journey from Oxford back to Bishopsgate, but he is now home. In his chamber, he leans down stiffly to unbuckle his shoes, more of an effort with each passing day. When he lies down briefly to rest upon the bed, his gaze alights on the same old water mark staining the canopy. After all these years he still wonders how it got there. The drapes of Celia's once magnificent bed are faded; dusty and fly-spotted with age. There are even some tears in the fragile silk, but Paul will not have them changed. Everyone in the household knows that: nothing that once belonged to the mistress can ever be moved or changed.

The repose will do him good, for he is sorely fatigued from the journey; his bones ache from the Oxford damp. But his abiding feeling is one of relief: the Sultan's Blue has been passed on at last. His instructions to Lord Rivers were very precise: he would give the great diamond to the King's cause on one condition, that it should as soon as possible be destroyed. They must agree to take it to Antwerp, where it must be broken down into several stones by a diamond dealer – he has given them the name – after that, they could do with the gems as they wish: pawn or sell them, or even keep them if they so wish, until such a time as their King should return to the throne.

Now, lying on his bed in Bishopsgate, Paul imagines that it is as if some spell has been lifted from him. He feels it in his body mainly: a sensation of release, a lightness of spirit, a giddiness almost. Even though he is lying down he puts his hand to the bedpost to steady himself.

He lives mainly in this room now, the bedchamber he shared with Celia until her death, for more than thirty years. In a while his servants will bring him his supper: a little fricassee of pigeon breast, and some thin soup, easy to digest; a bread trencher, such as they had in the old days, will be his plate. In his old age, Paul's tastes, like his dress, are simple to the point of asceticism. Although there is no one left with whom to share the irony, it is one that he enjoys. The great house at Bishopsgate, on which he once spent so much energy and money, is like a second skin to him, but it no longer takes up his time. His treasures – the Cathay porcelain and the *pietra dura* work, the silver, the gemstones, and the gold – are all sold. He has no use for any of them now.

Now, since Celia's death, he has only his dog to keep him company, a lurcher called Troubadour, the great-great-grandson of Chase, one of the Priors Leaze dogs from long ago. His dog and his books, Paul finds, are all he requires. Occasionally Troubadour sleeps on the bed with him, never mind the fleas or the hair. Now that Celia is no longer with him, the creature is a warm presence at his side at night, and he is comforted by it. If there is a resemblance at these moments between him and his father, old man Pindar of Priors Leaze, he is not in the least perturbed.

Paul was never quite able to decide the exact moment when he fell in love with his wife.

Sometimes he thinks it had been that same Christmas tide when the parish children had come to play, and Celia had pretended to be a bear; at others that it had been on the voyage home, when they had stood for hours on deck watching the dolphins sport against the bow waves; or perhaps even before that, on that faraway Aleppo rooftop, when they had lain side by side watching the stars. Or that long-ago Christmas, more than thirty years ago now, when they went together to bury the stone. He does not think he will ever know, and besides, it does not matter now.

Sometimes he wonders about Frances Sydenham. By the time they returned home after the great fire at Priors Leaze, it was to find that she had long gone. Over the years they heard rumours: that she had returned to Norfolk or to Antwerp; or had sailed to the Indies with a merchant from the Dutch East India Company. Neither of them ever saw her again.

As to his creation, the great house at Bishopsgate, Paul will not be there to see its demise. In later years, when he is long gone, the orchard and the gardens will be the first to go. Flynn's Livery Stables will come to occupy space where the fashionable grotto once stood; and a dairy, selling fresh cream and butter to the gentry, will find its way into the old gatehouse. Cows and goats will graze the old knot gardens. Half Moon Alley, along which Annetta had followed Nan, will become the entrance to the Sir Paul Pindar Stout House. Two grocery stores, Allsopps and Vickers & Co., will arrange their wares in the double-fronted bow windows of the once magnificent entrance hall. A notary's office, Barclay & Perkins, will lease the attics where Annetta once slept. Gradually, as the years pass, other households will encroach, one by one, until the once proud mansion will become nothing more than an oak-fronted curiosity in a row of shabby tenements.

And then, much later still, after more than two centuries have ticked by, the house will have outlived its purpose altogether. When they come to pull it down to make way for the new railways, all that will be left to bear witness to that long-ago story, is the mansion's carved oak front, which will survive in a dusty London museum.

John Carew. Celia. Annetta. Paul.

All gone.

Who would believe it, if it were not true?

ACKNOWLEDGEMENTS

My thanks are due to everyone at Bloomsbury who made this book possible, most especially to Angelique Tran Van Sang, to David Mann who designed the cover, and, of course, to Alexandra Pringle, whose vision and patience were with me, as always, every step of the way.

Thanks also to my agent Gill Coleridge, and to Cara Jones at Rogers, Coleridge and White; and most especially to Gillian Stern who made the editing of many drafts a joy.

I would also like to thank my mother, Jenny Hickman, whose house in Wiltshire, and its numinous surroundings, were the inspiration for Priors Leaze.

Katie Hickman
London, 2016

A NOTE ON THE TYPE

The text of this book is set in Adobe Caslon, named after the English punch-cutter and type-founder William Caslon I (1692–1766). Caslon's rather old-fashioned types were modelled on seventeenth-century Dutch designs, but found wide acceptance throughout the English-speaking world for much of the eighteenth century until replaced by newer types towards the end of the century. Used in 1776 to print the Declaration of Independence, they were revived in the nineteenth century and have been popular ever since, particularly amongst fine printers. There are several digital versions, of which Carol Twombly's Adobe Caslon is one.

ALSO AVAILABLE BY KATIE HICKMAN

THE AVIARY GATE

A stunning tale of intrigue in the Sultan's harem from the bestselling author of *Daughters of Britannia*

Elizabeth Stavely sits in the Bodleian Library, her hands trembling as she holds a fragment of parchment, the key to a story untold for four hundred years...

Constantinople 1599: the English merchant Paul Pindar must deliver an extraordinary gift to the Sultan. Grieving for his lost love, drowned in a shipwreck, he hears rumours of a new golden-haired slave in the Sultan's harem. Could this be his Celia?

'A hugely enjoyable novel, multi-layered, vividly depicted and a fascinating story, filled with the colours, sights and scents of Constantinople in the sixteenth century'
JOANNE HARRIS

'Lie back on your ottoman and relax. Katie Hickman will take you to a magical land, the Topkapi harem in Istanbul in Istanbul in 1599 ... This is a box of Turkish delight'
INDEPENDENT

"A magical, engrossing read ... An absorbing novel of intrigue and forbidden love'
GLAMOUR

ORDER YOUR COPY:

BY PHONE: +44 (0) 1256 302 699; BY EMAIL: DIRECT@MACMILLAN.CO.UK

DELIVERY IS USUALLY 3–5 WORKING DAYS. FREE POSTAGE AND PACKAGING FOR ORDERS OVER £20.

ONLINE: WWW.BLOOMSBURY.COM/BOOKSHOP

PRICES AND AVAILABILITY SUBJECT TO CHANGE WITHOUT NOTICE.

WWW.BLOOMSBURY.COM/AUTHOR/KATIE-HICKMAN

BLOOMSBURY

ALSO AVAILABLE BY KATIE HICKMAN

THE PINDAR DIAMOND

A tale of lust, greed, and danger set in seventeenth-century Venice, *The Pindar Diamond* is a gripping and superbly told historical novel

Venice, 1604. When rumours of a rare and priceless diamond begin to circulate amongst the gamblers and courtesans of the Venetian demi-monde, the Levant Company merchant Paul Pindar becomes convinced that the jewel is linked to the fate of his former love, Celia Lamprey. As his obsession with the mysterious stone grows it becomes clear that there are other, more sinister forces at play. Is the diamond real, or is it just a trick to lure him to his ruin?

'Beautifully written, glamorous, disturbing and very dark'
WENDY HOLDEN,
DAILY MAIL

'A vividly sensuous tale'
DAILY TELEGRAPH

'Nuns, precious gems, swashbucklers and courtesans, plus a plot to keep you on your toes, are stirred and shaken into pure escapism'
SUNDAY TIMES

ORDER YOUR COPY:

BY PHONE: +44 (0) 1256 302 699; BY EMAIL: DIRECT@MACMILLAN.CO.UK

DELIVERY IS USUALLY 3–5 WORKING DAYS. FREE POSTAGE AND PACKAGING FOR ORDERS OVER £20.

ONLINE: WWW.BLOOMSBURY.COM/BOOKSHOP

PRICES AND AVAILABILITY SUBJECT TO CHANGE WITHOUT NOTICE.

WWW.BLOOMSBURY.COM/AUTHOR/KATIE-HICKMAN

BLOOMSBURY

ALSO AVAILABLE BY KATIE HICKMAN

TRAVELS WITH A MEXICAN CIRCUS

**The delightfully beguiling account of novelist Katie Hickman's
adventures with a Mexican circus**

Katie Hickman went to Mexico looking for magic. She found
it in the circus – Big Top, clowns, elephants and all – where
cheap, torn materials and tarnished sequins are transformed
into nights of glittering illusion. Gradually adjusting to the
harsh ways of the circus's nomadic lifestyle, she soon became
absorbed into this hypnotic new world, at first as a foreigner
but later as 'La Gringa Estrella', a performer in her own right.

'A wonderful writer … An adventure hard to beat in terms of
sheer exotic allure'
GUARDIAN

'Mexico will not have been portrayed more vividly since
Graham Greene's *The Lawless Roads* … Enchanting'
DAILY TELEGRAPH

'Magic is at the heart of Hickman's narrative, not just
in the fabulous illusions of the acts themselves or the
superstitions of the circus people, but in the fantastic
stories of the characters she presents'
SUNDAY TIMES